2 50

THE HALL IN THE GROVE

THE HALL
IN THE GROVE

ISABELLA ALDEN

LIVING BOOKS®
Tyndale House Publishers, Inc.
Wheaton, Illinois

Library of Congress Catalog Card Number 94-62155
ISBN 0-8423-3177-8

Printed in the United States of America

99 98 97 96 95
6   5   4   3   2   1

CONTENTS

WELCOME

——◆━❧━◆——

by Grace Livingston Hill

As long ago as I can remember, there was always a radiant being who was next to my mother and father in my heart and who seemed to me to be a combination of fairy godmother, heroine, and saint. I thought her the most beautiful, wise, and wonderful person in my world, outside of my home. I treasured her smiles, copied her ways, and listened breathlessly to all she had to say, sitting at her feet worshipfully whenever she was near, ready to run any errand for her, no matter how far.

I measured other people by her principles and opinions and always felt that her word was final. I am afraid I even corrected my beloved parents sometimes when they failed to state some principle or opinion as she had done.

When she came on a visit the house seemed glorified because of her presence; while she remained, life was one long holiday; when she went away, it seemed as if a blight had fallen.

She was young, gracious, and very good to be with.

This radiant creature was known to me by the name of "Auntie Belle," though my mother and my grandmother called her "Isabella!" Just like that! Even sharply sometimes when they disagreed with her: *"Isabella!"* I wondered that they dared.

Later I found that others had still other names for her. To the congregation of which her husband was pastor she was known as "Mrs. Alden." And there was another world in which she moved and had her being when she went away from us from time to time; or when at certain hours in the day she shut herself within a room that was sacredly known as a "study" and wrote for a long time while we all tried to keep still; and in this other world of hers she was known as "Pansy." It was a world that loved and honored her, a world that gave her homage and wrote her letters by the hundreds each week.

As I grew older and learned to read, I devoured her stories chapter by chapter. Even sometimes page by page as they came hot from the typewriter, occasionally stealing in for an instant when she left the study to snatch the latest page and see what had happened next; or to accost her as her morning's work was done, with: "Oh, have you finished another chapter?"

Often the whole family would crowd around when the word went around that the last chapter of something was finished and going to be read aloud. And how we listened, breathless, as she read and made her characters live before us.

The letters that poured in at every mail were overwhelming: Asking for her autograph and her photograph; begging for pieces of her best dress to sew into patchwork; begging for advice how to become a great author; begging for advice on every possible subject. And she answered them all!

Sometimes I look back upon her long and busy life and marvel at what she has accomplished. She was a marvelous housekeeper, knowing every dainty detail of her home to perfection. And a marvelous pastor's wife! The real old-fashioned kind, who made calls with her husband, knew every member intimately, cared for the sick, gathered the young people into her home, and loved them all as if they had been her brothers and sisters. She was beloved, almost adored by all the members. And she was a tender, vigilant, wonderful mother, such a mother as few are privileged to have, giving without stint of her time, her strength, her love, and her companionship. She was a speaker and teacher, too.

All these things she did and *yet wrote books!* Stories out of real life that struck home and showed us to ourselves as God saw us and sent us to our knees to talk with him.

And so, in her name, I greet you all and commend this story to you.

Grace Livingston Hill

(This is a condensed version of the foreword Mrs. Hill wrote for her aunt's final book, *An Interrupted Night*.)

FOREWORD

by Robert Munce,
grandson of Grace Livingston Hill and author of
The Grace Livingston Hill Story

TALES OF ISABELLA ALDEN:
THE HOBBY OF A LIFETIME

For Isabella, writing was just a hobby—yet it continued to progress throughout the years. In addition to her magazine and newspaper articles, she even wrote some books, though she didn't send them to any publishers. When she was in college, one of her friends told her about a contest for unpublished writers. This friend knew Isabella had finished a book and pressed her to send in the manuscript. Isabella, modest to a fault, only said she might get around to doing it sometime.

When the end of the school year came, Isabella was packing to leave college for summer vacation. This same friend was helping her sort through a trunk of papers and books, when, lo and behold, there was the manuscript!

"You didn't send it in, did you?" her friend exclaimed. "It's your best story ever."

"Throw it in the trash," came the less than encouraging reply.

Several weeks later a letter arrived at the Alden home. Imagine Isabella's bewilderment and then delight when she realized her friend had not thrown her manuscript away. Indeed, she had sent it in to the contest—and Isabella had won!

Isabella's life became a busy one. She married a Presbyterian minister, had children, and was in demand as a lecturer, an author, and a temperance worker. Her son, a professor at Stanford University and the University of Illinois, became the leading authority in the United States on the writings of Shakespeare and followed in his mother's shoes when he took up a pen to write several scholarly books.

One of the drugs that plagued society then and now is alcohol. Isabella, along with others, campaigned against tobacco and alcohol. Whether society accepted them or not was irrelevant. These things were destructive to the body and spirit, and ruined health and family, and Isabella spoke out against them whenever she could.

But the overriding and underlying power of Isabella Alden and her family was a strong and true devotion to God and family. They took time for each other while pursuing careers. Family, friends, and even strangers were more important than selfish pursuits. Isabella, her husband, their children—and Isabella's beloved niece, Grace Livingston Hill—all knew they could reach thousands through their writings, but they stopped without hesitation to work with individuals. For above all, they sought to glorify the God who had so richly blessed them.

May you find blessing and enjoyment as you read this story!

Robert L. Munce
June 1994

1

LITTLE BYPATHS

MRS. Robert Fenton sat down in the little red-covered chair in the dining room, broom in hand, and wiped from her usually bright eyes two large tears.

That dining room was a fair and pretty creation. A poem, or a picture, done into real life. Mrs. Fenton had never written a poem, never painted a picture; but she had woven a touch of the genius that has to do with these into the furnishing of this home room. A sitting room it was, as well as dining room.

In fact, the proper name for it might have been the tea room; for the prosaic meals of breakfast and dinner were taken in a commoner spot, and the dainty teas, set out on fair damask and garnished with china and silver, were all that she permitted here.

There was nothing very remarkable about the furnishings. I am not sure that the Fentons had money enough to be remarkable. There was just that delicate blending of shades and tints, just that disposal of a few yards of muslin and lace, just that arrangement of a pot of ferns and a jar of fuchsias and a box of violets that, united, form a fair whole, resting the eyes—yes, and the very hearts—of look-ers-on.

As a housekeeper, as a wife, as a mother, Mrs. Fenton excelled. Her own small hands performed all the lighter duties in the home and performed them well. Her bread was of the lightest and sweetest. Her chambers were kept in that delicate purity which rests weary heads, and sometimes hearts. Her windows were as clear as hands could make them; her snowy curtains were looped in graceful folds, and with just the right tint of ribbon to blend well with surround-ings. Her vines and plants climbed and budded and blossomed in luxurious fashion. Her husband's but-tons were always in place, held by firm threads of her placing; his collars and cuffs shone brilliantly, for her own hands clear-starched and ironed them. Indeed, in whatever department of home life you looked, you would be likely after thorough investigation to pro-nounce Mrs. Fenton a model.

And yet, in the warm summer morning of which I write, she left her berries scorching on the vines and her pretty tea room in disarray while she sat, with sleeves up-rolled, and leaned her brown head against the broom and let the teardrops fall unheeded on her white work apron. Not many of them: She was not a woman given to weeping. She arose presently and brushed back the tears in impatience at her weakness, and swept vigorously, and reduced the room to its accustomed beauty, omitting no item of usual routine, all the while with certain sad-looking wrinkles in her forehead and a sore spot in her heart.

What was the trouble? Well, you remember that I said she was a model mother. Young Robert Fenton, her only boy—indeed, her only child—was the dar-ling of her royal mother heart.

For fourteen years she might also have been said to live and breathe for him. She had sacrificed time and strength and quiet for him, in that royal way which is a characteristic of motherhood, with that grand wholeheartedness about it that never uses the word *sacrifice,* nor dreams that it has anything to do with her experience. She had rejoiced over the perfect limbs and dimpled arms and broad white forehead of her beautiful boy. With delight had she fashioned cunning garments for him.

What a pleasure it had been to brush his rings of yellow hair. How careful she had been about his bath, and his milk, and his walks. How she had guarded his beautiful eyes from glaring lights. She had watched over the first doubtful steppings; she had watched over the first marvelous pearl that appeared in the rosebud mouth; she had rejoiced over the pearls of words as they began to drop from the baby tongue—"mamma," "papa," "baby." Will the English language ever beam for her again with the fullness of beauty that it had that day when Robby Fenton first said "papa"?

On through the years had the work and worship gone. Days of agony, nights of sleepless watching, when the small idol was fever parched; days of perfect thanksgiving, when the glow of health came again.

How she had studied, this mother, to teach Robby the most careful forms of speech. How she had watched to keep his heart and mouth pure. How she had entered into his childish plays and plans. She had been an engine, or an engineer, a passenger on the train, or a brakeman on duty, according to the changing mood of the boy for whom she played. She had learned the terms which the boys used at ball, marbles, and, indeed, all boyish games, on purpose to be able to talk sympathetically with Robby. She had hovered over the bookshelves and counters where juvenile periodicals were stored and studied the merits of this and that pictorial, lingered over pages filled with accounts of boyish exploits, and bought lavishly at last from a somewhat slender purse. She had talked over with Robby the stories in his books and treasured up sentences which indicated his preferences to bring them forth in aid of her next buying.

Never had a boy had a more tender, thoughtful, appreciative mother. And he had well repaid her care. Through fourteen perilous years of life had he come in safety. Straight as an arrow, morally as well as physically—a grand, truthful, earnest-hearted boy.

Was there need for tears in connection with such a boy as that?

Let me tell you: There had come to that mother, on the very morning of which I write, a sudden, rude awakening.

It chanced that her boy Robert was rapidly approaching the crisis of the disease known in these days as examination fever, and, in his intense desire to "pass," heart and brain were being strained to their utmost tension. He had been tempted to late hours over his books the night before and had overslept that morning; yet, between the hasty mouthfuls of breakfast which he took, he made dashes into certain studies in which he was to be examined that day.

"Do you really suppose I'll *pass,* Mother?" he asked the question for perhaps the thirteenth time as she came through the room, bearing an armful of fresh table linen. Be it recorded that, hurried and preoccupied though he was, he sprang forward and opened the door for his mother.

"Of course you will pass," she answered, regarding him with smiling face and fond, proud eyes.

"I don't know about it; the examination is awful hard this time: The fellows who went through it last year say this is about the toughest one we'll have. History is the worst. Dates, you know; they go and mix themselves up so horridly. I'm *awful* on dates. I wish I had my book here; I don't see how I came to forget it."

So the boy talked on, more to himself than his mother, who passed in and out, intent on household cares, yet wearing always a sympathetic face and having an answer ready for whatever could be answered.

Presently he appealed to her again, his handsome face clouded with anxiety.

"Mother, if you'll believe it, I can't remember when that old Severus rebuilt his stone wall! I don't suppose you can help me?"

It was hardly a question, though it closed with the upward inflection. It would have been plain to a listener that the boy did not expect help from his mother; yet there was a note of wistfulness in the words—an eager reaching out for sympathy and help from the mother who had sympathized with and helped him every day of his life.

"No, dear, I don't remember anything about it, I am sure."

The mother spoke gently, almost humbly, and turned at once that her boy might not catch a glimpse of tears.

He did not dream of tears. He was a quick-witted boy, but he was only a *boy*, and an eager, anxious one.

"Oh dear!" he said, a world of pent-up impatience in his voice: "How I do wish I had somebody to help me! All the other fellows have folks that they can ask when they get in a tight place."

He did not speak *to* his mother; he did not mean any reflection on his mother. He was a boy who would have flushed to his temples in indignation had anyone hinted that she was not the wisest and best mother that a boy ever had. She had passed on into the next room, and he was simply talking aloud. He did not know—how should he?—that every single word he spoke felt like a stab in that mother's heart.

I said it came to her as a revelation—this bitter truth that her boy was growing beyond her—in fact, *had* grown beyond her. Only fourteen years old, and he talked about "Severus" and "St. Alban" and "Ethelbert" and "Athelstane" and "the Saxon line" and "the Danish line" and she knew not what else. Half the time she could not tell whether they were the names of persons or places. How *much* he knew, this boy of hers! She was proud of him? Oh yes; indeed she was.

And yet—and yet—he was growing away from her.

What was this stone wall about which he talked so glibly?

It felt to her like a veritable wall—yes, and of stone, reaching up and up to the very sky; aye, even beyond! Who could assure her that the intellectual wall now being reared might not put ages between them in the life to come?

She had read a poem once—somewhere—about two lives that clasped hands together across a tiny stream scarcely more than a thread; the two had walked and whispered together. But the stream had widened and widened, and the hands had dropped apart, and the whisperings together ceased. By and by they could only *shout* to each other; and at last even the shoutings were lost in the roar of ocean, and the divided lives went their separate ways.

The poem had saddened her when she read it; it came back to haunt her this summer morning, and it seemed to her that she could lean forward and distinctly hear the roar of that separating ocean. The little stream had begun; what was to hinder it from growing and growing until it divided her life from her boy's? And yet, she would not have it otherwise; would not, at least, have that boy's rapid mental strides interfered with. Oh no, indeed! Yet the tears fell over the thoughts of his onward march. While she sat in her little sewing chair, she went rapidly over her own past. How did it happen that her boy was already ahead of her? Oh, easily enough; the same story has been often lived, and often told: Her early life had been one of toil and poverty; three months at third-rate country schools in winter, and the eldest daughter of a large family struggling to live: Such had been her story. She had done well, better than many; she had been judged "a smart girl." She had been the best parser and the best speller in the district school; but district schools were not then what they are now, and the ambitions and plans and the actual *knowledge* of her fourteen-year-old son were as Greek to her. "If I could go back now," she told herself mournfully, "and be a girl again—a scholar in the school where Robert is—I could keep step with him; but it is too late; he is ahead of me, and will go farther from me every day!" Do you wonder that the tears fell?

You have watched plants grow? You know how the tiny bud appears and grows and grows, opening a little every day? You dimly perceive it, you hardly realize that it is growing, but suddenly there comes a morning in which it has blossomed. Apparently, it did it all in the night. It is so with poisonous plants, I suppose. Mrs. Fenton had dimly felt from time to time, for months that her boy Robert was getting into a world of his own.

When he came to her with questions born of pondering over his lessons, questions about things of which she had not even *heard,* she had felt it; and yet, it was as if the full blossom of this bitter truth had flashed before her but this morning.

Still, she did not continue to sit in that little sewing chair and weep; as I told you, such was not her nature. She brushed aside the tears with impatient hand.

"Well," she said, "if I *don't* know who Severus was, nor when he built a stone wall, nor why he built it, nor anything about it, I know how to make a pudding for dinner; and I don't see but Robert enjoys puddings quite as well as though he had never heard of Severus and his stone wall. I most wish he hadn't!"

So she put her pretty home in order and made her pudding with special skill and care; and Robert and Robert's father ate and enjoyed and praised it. Yet the mother's heart was sore. She could not forget Severus; he represented to her a long line of worthies—past and to come—in her son's life, about whom she knew nothing.

2

"C.L.S.C."

WHEN afternoon quiet rested on the pretty house, Mrs. Fenton dressed herself with careful hand and set forth to find rest for the weariness of her heart.

She could not settle down to sewing; there was no housework to do; she did not feel like reading—she would make some calls.

Not that she did not read, occasionally, other than juvenile literature: She had read Mrs. Henry Wood and Mrs. Mary J. Holmes quite extensively. It had been a mere matter of chance that she had fallen in with those authors: She did not know what to read, and Mrs. Wood's *East Lynne* had fallen in her way, and therefore she had read it. In her youth, no one had directed her reading; she had read what she happened to. She continued to do that still.

But Mrs. Wood and Mrs. Holmes failed to satisfy her on this June day. She wanted to get away from herself and her surroundings; she determined to call on her friends.

She had many friends—pleasant, chatty ladies who talked with her cheerily about their homes, their furniture, the trials of hired help, the discomforts of housekeeping, the faults of even the favorite dressmaker, and the queerness of the latest fashions in bonnets—all the little narrow circle of interests around which they danced. For excitement, there were bits of gossip to discuss. Somebody was always doing what he or she ought not and affording food for thought and comment to the more circumspect. It was among such friends and such interests as these that Mrs. Fenton hoped to forget Severus.

I do not know that it made her heart less sore to remember that the boy's father had an interest in common with his son, from which she was shut out. Robert Fenton, Sr., without being what scholars would call a mathematician, was quick brained where figures were concerned, and his business life had developed skill in the use of certain commonsense rules by which he arrived at mathematical results in a way that surprised and won the respect of his son. So, many an evening, the two bent over columns of figures with interested faces, and the mother, looking on, was glad and sorry—if you can imagine both these states of mind possessing her at once.

Behold her presently ushered into the pleasant parlor of Mrs. Chester, a calling acquaintance a trifle higher in the social scale than was Mrs. Fenton. That is, her parlor was larger; was carpeted in body brussels, and the tables were marble topped, and the upholstery was done in satin damask, and about it all there was a certain air of "style" which told the looker-on that money was plenty. Into the fashionable darkness and coolness of this room went Mrs. Fenton and dropped into one of the great easy chairs with a sigh. She was just in the mood to wish that the money so lavishly displayed about her had been hers.

If it had, in her youth, she would have known all about Severus and everything else by this time! While she waited, she took up first one book and then another with a listless air and laid them down again. *Library of Poetry and Song.* She was fond of certain kinds of poetry—or had been—but she couldn't imagine what would tempt her to read a poem today. She thought fiercely of that one which she read long ago about those "divided lives"; she wished she had never heard of it. She reached after a ponderous book—it had such a handsome binding—and laid it down quickly, her sigh heavier than before. *History of All Nations.* What an *immense* book! How could people ever read it through, much less *study* it! All about "Severus" was in that, she supposed; all about everybody—people with whom her Robert would make acquaintance and grow familiar, and whom she would never know! Mrs. Fenton was astonished at and ashamed of herself. She felt a strange lump in her throat and resisted with great difficulty the temptation to break down just then and there and have a good cry.

She dived after more books; she must in some way get her mind away from this one subject, or she would disgrace herself. There was a little, pink paper-covered volume, hardly six inches long, lying at one side. "A child's book," she thought, and she reached after it, telling herself a little bitterly that "children's books were just suited to her capacity," and mechanically turned the pages. Suddenly a pink flush spread over her face, and with bright eyes and eagerly parted lips, she stopped over this sentence: "Severus the Emperor, eighty-nine years later, A.D. 210 rebuilt this wall of stone." Lo, here was Severus himself! Or, at least, definite knowledge concerning him. Emperor of *what,* was he? What stone wall did he rebuild? Who built it first, and for what? Every one of these questions she found answered for her in the space of six lines in that wonderful pink book! Here were the magic figures that had troubled her Robert in the morning. Two hundred and ten years after Christ! She had never known that date before; be sure she will never forget it. She searched eagerly through the book for more information concerning Severus. Her enemy he had been all day; she didn't like him; it would relieve her to know that there was nothing about him which ought to demand admiration.

While she was searching the small record, the door opened, and Mrs. Chester, fresh from an afternoon toilet, rustled in.

"It is very warm," she said after the first greetings; "I hope you will excuse my keeping you waiting; the truth is, I was in the hands of my dressmaker, and she was particularly trying this afternoon. She twisted and turned me around as though I had been a lay figure, and ripped out, and pinned up, and I believe, after all, she has the darts too low; and that, you know, is a most exasperating fault. I am just worn out!"

Now Mrs. Fenton had been "exasperated" and "worn out" scores of times by the very same dressmaker, and Mrs. Chester naturally looked to find in her a sympathetic spirit and fairly launched on the subject of dressmaking—the trials to undergo in darts too low, and darts too high, and short waists, and narrow chests, and awkward loopings, and ill-hung skirts—every lady knows there is no end to the subject. Instead of sympathy and commiseration, Mrs. Fenton with a very animated face and voice asked abruptly:

"Mrs. Chester, whose book is this?"

"That!" said Mrs. Chester in a surprised tone, bending forward and looking at the little book as though she thought she might need a magnifying glass in order to view it properly. "Oh that is a little thing belonging to Miss Katie Wells of Brooklyn. She is visiting my girls; she is quite a little student—leaves her books around everywhere."

"A schoolgirl?"

"Well, no; she graduated from school two years ago. One would think she might have done with school-books, but she seems not to be. She belongs to some society—literary, you know—and she studies a little every day. I tell her she might as well be in school yet; but she seems to enjoy it."

At this moment there was an influx of young ladies: bright, sparkling girls in airy summer lawns, with delicate laces at throat and wrists, and a general air of bewitchingness about them. The dining-room door that opened to admit them from outdoor life somewhere showed a glimpse of a trim figure in neutral-tinted calico moving deftly through the room—closing blinds, folding newspapers, setting back stray chairs, restoring the room to after-dinner propriety. She looked with appreciative eyes after the billows of muslin that floated past her; those creatures belonged to another world than hers. *She* lived in the workaday world: Mrs. Chester's dining room and kitchen and cellar bounded her horizon.

"Caroline is a good, faithful girl," Mrs. Chester said from the depths of her easy chair, in answer to the question that her caller could not help making; for she was a friend of Caroline's. The mistress watched the deft fingers with a complacent face, feeling a certain comfortable sense of ownership therein. The door between the two rooms, having been carelessly closed, swung open again, and Caroline, moving to and fro, was occasionally visible. So, the working and the talking went on together, with only a half-open door between them.

Mrs. Fenton watched Caroline with almost a look of envy on her face. The probability was that she cared nothing about Severus. She was contented with the place which she filled. *She* had no boy to grow away from her and grow ashamed of her! These thoughts recalled the existence of the little pink-covered book, and she addressed Miss Katie Wells with eagerness.

"Why, that," said Miss Katie, responding in a tone equally eager, "is a Chautauqua textbook. I belong to the C.L.S.C."

I am afraid you would have laughed, could you have seen Mrs. Fenton's puzzled face. She lived nearly a thousand miles from Chautauqua, in a town not specially noted for literary attainments, and her reading, you will remember, was on a somewhat limited scale. She had actually never heard of Chautauqua. The word sounded to her like the jargon of an unknown tongue. She knew less about "C.L.S.C." than even about Severus.

Miss Katie, seeing the wonder, hastened to explain: "You know about Chautauqua? No! Well, it's—why, dear me, it is everything! I don't know how to describe it—where to begin, you know. It is a lovely city in the woods, on a lake; we go there every summer; we have a cottage there, and we attend the meetings. Wonderful meetings! Grand speaking, and grand singing, and—well, *everything* to enjoy! I like it better than the seaside, ten thousand times."

Miss Katie was young; was, in fact, in the very zenith of the adjective-abounding age, and—and *loved* Chautauqua.

Mrs. Fenton, however, retained her bewildered look. What had a fashionable summer resort, with an occasional lecture or concert for the benefit of the pleasure seekers toying away the summer there, to do with this small book full of hard names—Severus and the like?

"Do they have a literary society there?" She asked the question timidly, feeling that she was stepping beyond the bounds of her knowledge.

"Oh yes; there, and everywhere, almost; the C.L.S.C.'s are springing up all over the land. We meet once a month—our Circle does—and we have most *delightful* evenings. Some of the studies that I used to hate at school—and that I managed to learn very little about, I must say—as we take them up in the Circle are really delightful."

Mrs. Fenton could not suppress a little sigh. "It must be very pleasant to have wealth and leisure, and go to such places and improve oneself," she said earnestly.

Did Miss Katie detect a quiver in the tones, or, being a born Chautauquan, couldn't she refrain from breaking into a glow of explanation?

"But you don't need to have wealth and leisure: That is one delightful feature of the scheme; it reaches those who have neither. Why, in our Circle some of those who have done the best are hardworking men and women who must have very little opportunity indeed for study. There is a Miss Harris—a sewing girl; she told me herself that she had never been to school but nine months in her life, and she actually stood first in our examination! She studies evenings and mornings and when she is walking to and from her work, and—well, she says she hardly knows how she *has* found time to do it; but she will get her diploma, without any doubt."

"I should be afraid she would neglect her sewing, if she were working for me." Mrs. Chester said this with a languid smile of indulgence, both for the enthusiast and the offender, since the latter was *not* working for her.

Miss Katie turned toward her with flashing eyes:

"No, ma'am, she doesn't. Because she is trying to improve her mind is no reason why her hands should be less skillful in the work that they have learned; and she is an honorable girl, so of course she doesn't use time that doesn't honestly belong to her."

"No," Mrs. Chester said, "but a preoccupied mind is so apt to make mistakes. Suppose, for instance that my Caroline out there should be seized with a whim for improving her mind—which I earnestly hope she won't—do you really believe she would be as useful and happy in her present position as she is now?"

"I'm sure I don't see why; if she happened to become interested in history and biography and literature generally, why should you expect it to affect her skill in bread making or table setting?"

Mrs. Chester gracefully shrugged her graceful shoulders.

"I don't know about it," she said; "I am afraid I am not in sympathy with these new ideas. I fancy that people would do much better to stay in their proper spheres, instead of trying to creep up into higher ones."

Whereat the flash in Miss Katie's eyes became very apparent; it was evident that with this sort of talk she had no sympathy. However, she controlled her voice to answer quietly:

"As to 'proper spheres,' ma'am, I supposed that in

this country one's sphere was what he made it. I am sure neither you nor I can tell what Miss Harris may be called upon to do in life. Even if it should be always to make dresses, I shouldn't expect mine to fit any less perfectly because she will know how to talk intelligently with me—or with her children, for that matter, if she should ever have any."

Mrs. Fenton's cheeks glowed. For fourteen years she had been able to talk intelligently with her boy Robert. Oh, to do something to make sure of being able to be his intelligent companion in the fourteen years to come! She almost turned her back upon Mrs. Chester in her luxurious indolence; she questioned and cross-questioned Miss Katie; she made a most unfashionably lengthy call; but when she left she went directly home, bubbling over with new schemes, as thoroughly posted in regard to the plans and aims and directions of the Chautauqua Literary and Scientific Circle as a half hour of contact with a young enthusiast like Katie Wells could make her.

"I didn't know that Mrs. Fenton was literary in her tastes."

This was what Mrs. Chester's daughter said, as she looked after the departing steps of their caller. The mother smiled, with that superior air which such women know how to assume, as she said: "I am afraid, dear, she is one of those persons who like to appear literary without understanding much about it."

And Miss Katie, who had taken a fancy to the trim little woman whose cheeks had glowed so sympathetically for her dear Chautauqua, answered with spirit:

"It is a real relief to find a woman occasionally who even wants to *appear* literary. So many of them seem to want to appear like nothing but lay figures dressed up to set off the latest fashions to the best advantage!"

One little additional feature of this day stands out pleasantly in Mrs. Fenton's memory: At the supper table she said to young Robert as she served him to berries:

"Well, my son, did you 'pass' in history, do you think?"

"Oh, Mother, there is no telling yet awhile. We had a tough time; still, I'm pretty certain about most of it. Don't you think the old fellow that I was worrying over this morning was among the first questions on our list?"

"Who? Severus?" And the silly mother's hand actually trembled as she passed him a glass of milk.

"Yes'm; and I'd give fifty cents, this minute, to know whether I got the dates right! I knew it was either two hundred and ten or one hundred and two after Christ, but I couldn't, to save my life, tell which. I said the figures over twenty times, and each time I was less sure which to take."

"And which *did* you take, finally?"

"Well, at last I said: 'Here goes for two hundred and ten, right or wrong; I won't change again'; and I didn't."

"I am glad of it, for two hundred and ten is correct."

The mother's face was smiling, but her foolish heart beat so loud that it almost seemed to her, her husband and son must hear it. Young Robert dropped his fork and gazed at his mother.

"Are you sure, Mother?" he asked her eagerly.

"Quite sure, my son. I was reading about him only this afternoon and took particular notice of the date."

Then young Robert, without further ceremony, dashed back his chair and came around to his mother and placed a hearty kiss on her flushed cheek.

"Hurrah!" he said; "then I don't believe there is a *single* miss in my history paper. That was the only question I felt real doubtful over. Wouldn't it be *just splendid,* Mother, if I were perfect in history?"

This little scene confirmed in the mother's heart— if it needed any confirmation—the determination to belong forthwith to a Chautauqua Literary and Scientific Circle, if she could find one to which to belong.

3

• ━ ✦ ━ •

THE OUTLOOK

IT often happens that what we cannot find in this world ready-made to our needs, we proceed to manufacture.

Mrs. Fenton, after a diligent search, discovered that the little town of Centerville had neither part nor lot with this new and fascinating Literary Association.

So, though it was new business to her, as soon as ever the midsummer canning and preserving were attended to, she set about bringing a Circle into being.

Casting about in her mind which way to venture first, shrinking from Mrs. Chester as one who would think she was trying to creep up out of her sphere and heartily wishing that Miss Katie Wells were a resident instead of a visitor, she determined to call first on her pastor, the Reverend Mr. Williams. He was a literary man; he wrote very learned sermons that she did not understand and read them carefully to his congregations: Surely, he was the proper person to be interested in a literary society. Perhaps, if they could start one, and study diligently, after the lapse of years she might acquire learning enough to understand some of his sermons! Who knew?

So behold her in his study, eagerly recounting what she knew and wished, after which, listen to him:

"My dear Mrs. Fenton, I'm afraid you will be disappointed. This is not a literary community; you would find it hard to interest them in anything of the sort."

"Oh, I don't know," she answered, laughing. "I am not in the least literary, and I am very much interested; it seems to me we have a good many young people who might be so much benefitted. I was thinking of the Ward boys as I came by; they seem to have so few friends and so few interests. No mother, you know; what if a society of that kind could get hold of them and help them, wouldn't it be doing a good thing? Don't you think, Mr. Williams, they are in danger of being led into very great temptations?"

Mr. Williams smiled on her benevolently. "My dear madam, I am afraid you do not realize that the list of lessons which you have read over to me would be like actual Greek to the Ward boys. The course is really for scholars, and the Ward boys belong to a class who have neglected what few advantages they had earlier in life and must suffer the consequences."

"Then is there no help either for people who neglected their advantages, or for those who had none to neglect? Must they be content to be dunces?"

"Well, not so bad as that, my friend"—in tones exceedingly benevolent—"not so bad as that; there *are* comforts in life, even for those who do not understand Greek and Latin and the like. The truth is, there are two sides to this question: There is a mischievous side to it. I really think that to set young people at work over studies about which they know nothing and about which they are destined to know nothing, will have a tendency to unfit them for the places which they are to occupy—arouse false ambitions and encourage false hopes."

That this was the baldest nonsense, little Mrs. Fenton felt in every nerve; but she did not know how to set about refuting it. She was no logician. However, after a moment's silence she rallied sufficiently to say:

"Well, Mr. Williams, if James Ward were my son, I would run the risk of rousing false ambitions and encourage any sort of hopes that would keep him from hanging around the street corners, smoking third-rate cigars."

Mr. Williams smiled good-naturedly.

"I appreciate your motives," he said in his most patronizing tones, "but, my good lady, I am really afraid that the Ward boys are beyond the reach of any 'Circle' save that in which they now move. The Sabbath school has failed to reach them, and I confess I have very little hope that any literary effort will accomplish it."

Now Mrs. Fenton, who knew exactly how the Ward boys had been managed in the Sabbath school, was by no means so hopeless of reaching them; but she did not know how to talk to Mr. Williams.

"Then you really are not in favor of having a Chautauqua Circle here?" she asked him, after a pause, in a disappointed tone.

"Why, my dear friend, I see no material out of which to construct one. You are an energetic lady, I am aware, but I hardly see how you can, of yourself, compose an entire Circle, scientific or otherwise. Whom could you possibly secure to start the matter for you?"

"I did not know but you would head our list with your own name, sir."

And now Mr. Williams's surprise can be better imagined than described.

"Well, really!" he said, his whole corpulent little body shaking with laughter: "At the risk of appearing very conceited, I shall have to remind you that I completed the circle of studies which you were so kind as to read over to me when I was about the age of your boy Robert, or a trifle older."

Mrs. Fenton's entire face was covered with a mortified glow. She was a courteous lady, having great respect for her pastor, and had meant no offense. The gentleman's manner had obliged her to think that his dignity had been offended. Besides, what was to be done with a man who believed the Chautauqua Literary and Scientific Circle to have chosen a course of studies so scholarly that it could reach none but scholars, and at the same time so juvenile that he was through with it at fourteen.

Had Mr. Williams been other than her pastor, certain bright little sarcasms that fluttered through her brain would surely have found voice. As it was, she made haste to answer with blushes: "I beg your pardon; I did not mean to intimate that you needed the study for your own benefit; I have heard that clergymen and professors and many eminent scholars take up this course for the sake of encouraging the young people."

"That is very laudable, certainly," Mr. Williams said, resuming his benevolent manner; "that is, if they have time for such things. The truth is, my time is so fully occupied now with my own studies and my large congregation that I have no leisure left to devote to school teaching, even if scholars could be found."

From this interview Mrs. Fenton went home in haste and ordered her house vigorously. She canned peaches and grapes, and made jelly and cleaned her china closet; made a very black fruitcake, and began a new set of shirts for her husband.

Three long bright days did she give to intense physical labor, trying thus to shut out other aims. She worked laboriously, but while her hands were busy, so was her brain: She could not get away from her recent awakening. The circular of the Chautauqua Literary and Scientific Circle and the private letter of instruction which had accompanied it appeared to her as if by magic whenever she opened her drawer. Once she thrust them in desperation under a pile of infrequently used clothing—at the very bottom of the drawer—but young Robert in a spasm of frantic haste sought a clean handkerchief, and tossed and tumbled everything into royal confusion, and behold! there was the C.L.S.C. circular the topmost article in the mass. Besides, the said Robert, busy with his vacation pursuits, appealed to her constantly for sympathy as heretofore, keeping ever before her heart the possible desolation of years to come, when his pursuits should be entirely among the world of books—away from her: for young Robert was a born student.

One sunny afternoon she pushed an unfinished shirt from her with the energy born of decision and made known to the sewing machine her determination.

"I just believe I'll try the Butler girls; they have nothing of any consequence to do, and they are young and energetic about some things. They were good scholars at school, I have heard."

Now I am really sorry that my usually quick-witted little woman made the blunder of going to people who had arrived at a grown-up age without finding "anything of consequence" to do, expecting to enlist their immediate interest in anything worth doing. But she did it. She mistook their position also. In their own estimation, they had work well worth doing. Miss Effie believed that to have a "perfectly exquisite dress" and ten-button kids and slippers of just the right size, and to go to Saratoga or Newport, or Long Branch or Niagara, or *anywhere* that there were hotels and hops, and dance nearly every set nearly every evening, and appear on the following mornings in bewitching costumes of white lawn and yellow lace, and take walks with unexceptionable partners down to the Congress or the Columbia for a glass of water or down to the beach for a view of the tide, or down to the falls for a dash of the spray, *anywhere*—these minor accessories were of the very smallest importance, so that the white lawns and the sun hat and the partners were unexceptionable—was sphere enough for any person. Between the dancing and the dressing, and the walking and the sleeping, to lounge on the bed with a copy of the latest novel and read the sensation portions—this was Miss Effie's idea of existence. Between these periods of life, to shop, and consult the dressmaker and the milliner, and fashion new lace sets was employment enough. Imagine Miss Effie getting through with forty minutes a day of *Merivale's History of Rome*.

Miss Irene, the elder sister, was of a different stamp. To put it in simple language, and small compass, she was a dauber. She sat for hours and hours and *hours* daubing away at a square of canvas, making square-looking cows, and preposterous-looking people, and bluish green foliage such as never grew, and hills in danger of toppling over and upsetting the cows. From

Miss Irene's window, where she sat and daubed with her mussy palette and her many-colored fingers, there waved and glowed a picture of hill and vale, and gleaming water, and shimmering sunshine, such as would have filled the heart of a real artist with great throbs of joy. I do not think Miss Irene ever spent fifteen minutes in studying the living picture. In truth, she thought it exceedingly commonplace and would have judged a person "queer" who admired it; and she presumed to sit there, so near to that wondrous painting, and daub her miserable caricatures of lake and sky. She puttered in pottery, also, spending large sums on old grotesque-shaped jugs; spending hours on designs that made them more grotesque still. It was on such a couple that Mrs. Fenton called for sympathy and cooperation.

Miss Irene was daubing: creating a stormy sky looking down on a peaceful, sunny landscape. Why should not thunder and lightning and broad, still sunlight appear on canvas together, if artists of Miss Irene's stamp chose to have it so?

Miss Effie was lounging, novel in hand.

"I have heard of Chautauqua," she affirmed; "Katie Wells goes there every summer. She just raves over it; but I should think it would be decidedly slow. She says she never heard of a hop while she was there. They don't even have lawn dances, or anything! Just go to meetings from morning until night! I'm sure I don't know what would tempt me to go to such a place."

"If they would have an artists' reunion there, I might be tempted," said Miss Irene, daubing away complacently, "but I don't believe I care much for the other things. I should really enjoy meeting those who could sympathize with me in my profession."

"But I'm not talking about *going* to Chautauqua,"

explained Mrs. Fenton. "I'm sure I haven't the faintest hope of ever going there; it is about the Literary Society that I want to talk to you girls. Come now, Effie, close your book entirely and sit up straight, and let us talk about it. I want you to get the others interested; we can have a real large society here if we set about it."

"I think literary societies are just horrid!" exclaimed Miss Effie, rising on one elbow. "We belonged to the Brouté Club once; we read Shakespeare and Milton and all those—the dullest evenings I ever spent in my life; perfectly dreadful! I used to say then that I'd never be such an idiot as to get caught in another literary society."

"Oh, well," explained Mrs. Fenton, "these Circles are different; it isn't just listening to one person reading something that you don't more than half understand; you have an opportunity to study the subject and find out all you can about it, and then get together and talk it up. Why, the members pledge themselves to give forty minutes a day to study."

"Oh, horrible!" said Miss Effie, sinking back on her couch. "You needn't talk anymore to me, Mrs. Fenton; the idea of studying *anything* for forty minutes a day is not to be endured for one moment. If you had spent as many years in school as we have, you would know how perfectly insufferable any such notion must be. We really are not equal to it; you see, we have been through the mill."

"I haven't time for it," said Miss Irene serenely, as she daubed into existence a wicked-looking dog, with ears and tail such as were never seen on created dog since the world was. "If I were not so absorbed with my painting, I might give it some attention; but this passion that I have for art consumes all the time I have."

"I'm sure I don't see why you want to paint any more pictures," Miss Effie said discontentedly. Her sister's "passion for art" was as great a bore to her as was a literary society. "The house is just overrun with pictures. I was telling Mamma only yesterday that the parlors looked like an auctioneer's rooms, and she said she knew it; besides, paints and frames and all that cost ruinously. I should think you could use your money to better advantage. I'll tell you what it is, Mrs. Fenton," her eyes brightening as she saw a chance to vindicate the literary tastes of the family, "you ought to talk to Jack. He is at home; did you know it? Yes; he came last week. Jack is literary, you know; he'll appreciate your scheme. I mean to call him."

Now "Jack" was twenty-three, and wore immaculate linen and gold eyeglasses, and carefully nurtured a moustache, and carried a cane, and had just graduated. Little Mrs. Fenton knew him well as a boy, but as a man and a graduate he quenched her.

"Oh, Chautauqua!" he said, crossing one shining boot over the other and looking down upon her from under his shining glasses with an immensely superior air. "I know all about that; it was a chimerical idea in the first place. You can't take people who have grown to be men and women, and make them over into scholars by a few hours of study. And as for people rushing off there in the woods to spend their time, anybody who understands human nature might have known how that would end. American people rush into *anything* with enthusiasm and rush out of it equally fast. It would do very well for once—something new, you know—but who, except a visionary person, would expect it to last?"

It happened that the bright-eyed woman who listened to this outburst of superior wisdom had not met Miss Katie Wells several times for nothing; she was thoroughly posted.

"But when are they going to begin to weary of this place?" she asked the oracle. "The meetings have been held there for several years, and every year the crowds increase, and the same persons keep coming. I should think it was time for a little reaction if the idea is simply an excitement. Why, I am told that the numbers who gathered there last year were far in advance of any season yet."

"Oh, well!" said young Jack, shifting his position uneasily and putting the left shining boot over the right one—it was not so easy as he supposed to talk about a matter of which he knew almost nothing, provided the person addressed knew whereof she spoke—"I suppose people enjoy the fun of going there; it is much cheaper than watering places generally, and a certain class like the *sound* of going to a literary gathering, even though they haven't two ideas in regard to literature or anything else. What I object to is this false idea that ignorant boors can buy a dozen books and read at them less than an hour a day and then go through an examination farce and *graduate* and receive a *diploma* and all that nonsense. It lowers the standard, Mrs. Fenton; it really does."

On the whole, it was a good thing for Mrs. Fenton that she had come in contact with this young man. The insignificant absorption of the young ladies had disheartened her, but this moustached, spectacled, embryo man, so wise, so vain in his diploma, so determined that no one else should secure one, inspired her with a determination to earn a diploma of some sort at the earliest opportunity.

She was good-humored; he did not irritate her; he seemed too young and too pedantic to waste ill humor on. She laughed at his sneer, as she said: "I don't see why I shouldn't know as much as I can, even if I have no chance to reach the heights of wisdom that you college boys attain. As for the diploma, I suppose it is given only for the work that is actually done. I should like one. I mean to earn it, if possible. What is the harm in learning all one can?"

"Oh, there is no special harm, I suppose, if you really enjoy that sort of thing; but I can't quite understand the taste. Why, dear madam, it isn't *learning,* it is simply *skimming*—superficial work, you know. The whole Chautauqua scheme about which people talk so much is just as superficial as possible; and really, we scholars shrink from that sort of thing."

Whereupon Mrs. Fenton laughed again—she couldn't help it; not at his idea, for the frank truth is, she did not understand it; she was not sufficiently skilled in the use of language to be absolutely sure what that word *superficial,* that rolled so glibly and so frequently from this scholar's tongue, meant. Of course she had a general idea of the use of the word, but who knew whether this wise man could not trip her up on some of its finer shades of meaning? She would not venture on doubtful ground; but she could laugh. She knew enough of books and of study to recognize the folly of the words *we scholars* from the lips of this fair-faced youth.

"I don't know," she said pleasantly. "*I* am not a scholar at all; but I *can't* see any reason why I shouldn't try to know as much as I can."

Then there came a new element into their conversation, even a pale-faced, quiet-voiced mother—a mother of many cares and anxieties; a woman who had come up from grinding poverty into comparative wealth without being able to lay aside the sense of care and perplexity that had been a constant accompaniment of her earlier life. Worried about her children she was too. Not that she was not proud of Irene's paintings and Jack's wisdom and Effie's beauty; but she was a mother who had wanted more for her children. For herself, the life she had led, the burdens she had borne, the perplexities that had swarmed around her would have been unendurable but for that other life hid with Christ in God. She had longed to see her children feel this power and yield to the spell of this inner life. For years she had prayed daily for their conversion; and as yet, none of them had seemed to give the vital question a serious thought.

This mother, who had slipped quietly in during the conversation, listened to Mrs. Fenton and the girls and Jack, getting thus, bit by bit, the history of Chautauqua—the story of the sewing girl, who, out of her limited time and meager opportunities, was getting so much, and the habitual look of perplexity deepened on her face. Then, as one suddenly resolved upon breaking the silence of years, she dashed into the very heart of the subject:

"But Mrs. Fenton, wouldn't you be afraid that anybody so eagerly interested as that sewing woman is would be tempted to neglect—"

"Oh! to neglect her sewing, you mean," interrupted Mrs. Fenton, a touch of impatience in her voice. "That is what Mrs. Chester says; but I'm sure I don't see why, because a woman is interested in study and willing to give her bits of leisure time to it, she should at once be suspected of growing unprincipled and robbing her employer."

"I wasn't thinking of that," Mrs. Butler said, speaking meekly, "but I was wondering whether she wouldn't be tempted to neglect her Bible, and—well, yes, I will say it—and her *praying?* It seems to me, sometimes, as though folks who got all buried up in an idea, like Irene here with her painting, forget all about the next world, and about studying their Bibles, and praying a good deal, and getting ready for the end of it all. I was wondering whether this kind of study that uses up the little bits of time wouldn't be likely to be another thing in the way of their Bibles and their prayers."

Now to Mrs. Fenton this argument was as a bombshell; it vanquished her. Why? Because she had no personal knowledge, no experience in the matter. She could not explain: "Oh, no, Mrs. Butler! The tendency of these earnest studies is not to draw the mind away from God, but rather to strengthen faith by enlarging the circle of thought; and, absorbing though they may become, they bear no comparison with that other, higher absorption, the union of the soul with Christ. If you allow them to press in between you and your best friend, Jesus, and separate you, it is your own foolish turning of a genuine help into a hindrance, and not a necessity of the plan."

None of these things could Mrs. Fenton say because, with all her unselfish love for her son, she had never given him that best earthly treasure, a mother's prayers. Wishing the best that even Christ could do for her boy and heartily believing in Christ as the Savior of the world, with strange inconsistency she had never asked him to be the Savior, the Friend, aye, the Elder Brother of her boy. So she had no argument with which to meet Mrs. Butler's question, other than to say: "Why! I'm sure I don't see what the two things have to do with each other. I mean, I see no reason why a person couldn't be a member of a literary society and a Christian at the same time."

And Irene, as she sat back to get a better view of the last splash of paint that she had transferred to canvas, said: "Why, Ma! what a strange idea. People can't read their Bibles *all* the time."

"No, of course not," the mother answered hastily; "I didn't mean anything." Then she heaved a disappointed sigh; the silence of years had been broken, and nothing accomplished. She had meant her oldest daughter's devotion to art, and her son's devotion to himself, and Effie's devotion to dress and dancing, as much and more than she meant the Chautauqua Literary and Scientific Circle, and none of these had understood her.

As for the son, he pushed his impertinent glasses higher on his nose and tapped his boots with his tiny cane and smiled down in conscious superiority on both these small, silly women, and believed as little in his mother's Bible as he did in Mrs. Fenton's literary aspirations. He had risen above both these follies.

Oh, for a Katie Wells, with her warm heart's love anchored on the Rock and, at the same time, her enthusiastic love for study to have enlightened them all!

As it was, Mrs. Fenton went slowly homeward, having food for thought.

4

PICK 'EM UP, CAR'LINE!

SHE poured tea that evening with a somewhat pre-occupied air and presently said: "Robert, what is the precise meaning of *superficial?*"

"Shallow," answered her husband, laughing. "Who have you found this afternoon that is described by that definition?"

"Jack Butler, I believe," she said, joining in the laugh; "only he hasn't an idea of it. He thinks he is as deep as the Atlantic, at least. Is that the exact meaning?"

"Shall I see what the old fellow himself says about it?"

This was young Robert's way of alluding to *Webster's Unabridged,* and he dragged the great book from its shelf and gave himself up to the study of *superficial.* "Reaching or comprehending only what is obvious or apparent; not deep, or profound," he presently read. "Is that what you're after, Mother?"

"Yes," she said. "Then it is actual knowledge as far as it goes, isn't it?" This to her husband.

"Why, yes, only it is shallow, as I told you."

"Oh, well, I should like to know if even a *little* knowledge isn't better than ignorance! Suppose a stream isn't very deep; if it is water that we need, it is much better than no stream at all, isn't it?"

"What *are* you driving at?" was Mr. Fenton's wondering query. Whereupon she gave him the history of the C.L.S.C. as it had grown in her mind, omitting all particulars concerning Severus and making no reference to Mrs. Butler's bombshell, which had troubled her all the way home. What if *she* ought to give herself up to the study of the Bible and win young Robert's attention to that? But he was not interested in the Bible, and—lamentable truth!—neither was she; and he *was* interested in study, and would continue to be; she must be able to sympathize with him.

It is a pity to have to record it, but the sad fact is, she had never come in contact with a mind that had impressed her with enthusiastic love for the Christian life as a half hour's talk with Katie Wells had impressed her with Chautauqua.

Doubtful as to how her husband would look upon this new enthusiasm—whether he would laugh at it as simply amusing or frown on it as folly—she watched his face and discovered a swift, keen look bestowed upon his son, which telegraphed to her as plainly as though he had spoken the fact that the father had his hours of foreboding lest the present advantages he was able to give his boy should put leagues between them by and by.

Beyond this sudden look, however, he offered no opinion; but young Robert was eager with his interest and voluble in expressions of delight.

"Let's you and I have a Circle, Mother. And next summer we'll go to Chautauqua. I know all about that: Sam Wheeler's uncle Will goes, and he says it's just grand! Wouldn't that be a splendid plan, Mother?"

All this time—and although it has taken but a short space to tell about it, the actual living stretched over several weeks—there was one person eagerly interested in Mrs. Fenton's efforts to establish a branch C.L.S.C. This was none other than Mrs. Chester's deft-handed Caroline.

A few words are needed, in order that you should understand this handmaiden's character. Among her earliest recollections was the one of being carried across the fields, through the dew of the early mornings, in her mother's arms, and established on the kitchen floor in the home on the hill, there to amuse herself with clothes basket and clothespins, with an occasional treat in the shape of a bar of soap and a row of shining *real* pins.

By and by there came to her a delightful opportunity: The fair baby from the nursery on the hill came out in white garments and was established on a bright rug spread over the clean kitchen floor, and she brought—oh joy!—gaily painted blocks: red and yellow and green, with wonderful pictures and wonderful letters gleaming on them.

"Pick 'em out, Car'line!" the mother had said, her strong bared arms akimbo, as she watched the small hands finger the blocks. "Pick 'em out, if you can; maybe you can learn 'em all; who knows?"

And in course of time Car'line did pick 'em out—every one. And the little incident serves to give the keynote to her life. "Pick it up, Car'line, maybe you'll have use for it; who knows?"

Whether it was a chance to learn the gaily painted letters, or to learn to write, or to learn to make bread, or sweep a room, or cut a garment, this one idea, with variations, was held before her by a wise and ambitious mother—a mother who had nothing but strong, good sense and unwavering faith in God to leave as a heritage to her daughter on that day when (just after the daughter was fifteen) she was suddenly called upon to leave her laborious life and enter upon her inheritance.

Since which time, Caroline, accepting the dowry, had gone steadily on her way, "picking out" and "picking up," saying often to herself in tender, reverent tone, "I may have use for it; who knows?" This principle carried out had made her clear of brain and quick of hand; thoughtful, watchful, invaluable in the kitchen, in the sewing room, in the sick room, and had brought her face-to-face at last with the Chautauqua Literary and Scientific Circle, eager to "pick up" from it. She may have use for it; who knows?

One evening just as the delicate china teacups were being washed at Mrs. Fenton's, Caroline presented herself, arrayed in one of her favorite gray-and-white calicoes as carefully made as though it had been a silk, and, quite as a matter of course, so unused were her hands to idleness, reached for the tea towel and dried the pretty china while she talked. She was somewhat acquainted with Mrs. Fenton; they had washed dishes together before. Mrs. Fenton was an invaluable aid at church fairs and festivals and sewing societies, and as Mrs. Chester's share in church work of this sort was always performed by proxy, namely, by Caroline, it had followed as a matter of course that the two efficient women had worked together and grown to understand each other.

"Mrs. Fenton," she began with characteristic directness, "may I join your C.L.S.C.?"

"Why!" answered Mrs. Fenton, astonished, yet

laughing, "if we only had one for you to join, I would be glad. I don't seem to find any people who are willing to be made into a Circle."

Then the whole subject was carefully discussed, both women entering into the details of their experience; Caroline last.

"I never had any regular opportunities," she explained; "Mother did her best, and did wonderful things for us, too; but Father was sick, and times were hard—they always *are* hard, you know, Mrs. Fenton, to people who have nothing—and I just *had* to work, even when I was a baby. Why, I never went to a regular school but one afternoon in my life! I have just 'picked up things.' Now it has come to be second nature; I almost have to keep picking up whether I want to or not. This time I *want* to. I know about that C.L.S.C. I happened, perhaps a year ago, to hear some people talking about it: They had been to Chautauqua, and they sat before me in the cars—that time I went to Chicago, you know, to take care of Renie Chester and bring her home—and they talked nearly all the time about the meetings at Chautauqua and the new literary society. I learned a great deal that afternoon; I made up my mind then and there that I would be a 'Circle' myself as soon as I could bring it to pass." This last with a modest little laugh. "I wrote to the superintendent about it; fortunately for me, a young girl in front of these ladies grew interested and asked a dozen questions; so I learned just how to proceed. He answered me; a good letter. I think I shall always keep that letter, for more reasons than one. Do you know, Mrs. Fenton—" speaking slowly, and with a hesitating sense of her own great poverty— "it is the only letter I ever received. I bought one of the books when I could—I have to do things slowly, you see. I've commenced, and I like it; but there are a great many things that I don't understand, and I long so to ask questions of somebody. Miss Katie Wells was very kind to me; she told me a great deal about the Circle. I didn't tell her I was trying to do anything in that way; I thought Mrs. Chester might not like it; but when I heard a few days ago that you were going to start a society. I decided to do a very bold thing and ask to be allowed to join."

Now, at the risk of lowering my friend Mrs. Fenton in your estimation, I shall have to admit that a struggle had been going on in her mind during this interview. She was not a proud woman in the unlovely sense of the word; at least, she did not know that she was; but she had looked forward to the thought of gathering around her scholars: men and women of cultured minds, to whom she could look up, of whom her son Robert stood in admiring awe, of whom she could learn. It *did* seem a downfall to have, instead of the minister and the professor and perhaps a lawyer or two, only Mrs. Chester's second girl. She meditated telling Caroline that she was discouraged; that there was no use in trying to form a Circle in that town, and she meant to give it up. But as she listened to Caroline's quaint yet quiet story, her mood changed.

"Then you actually have a Circle already established!" she exclaimed in great astonishment, "and here you are asking if you can join mine, when I haven't been able to secure one member yet! I'll tell you what I'll do: I'll join yours right away, and we'll have a C.L.S.C. in spite of them."

You should have seen the pretty pink flush that stole into Caroline's cheeks at the sound of these cheery words of fellowship. She had lived a lonely life hitherto: serving others, yet never coming into the magic Circle which meant friendship; for years she had felt herself hovering on the outside of things which she was capable of enjoying. In Mrs. Fenton's hearty words she saw a "chance." Surely, here was something for her hungry heart to "pick up." The C.L.S.C. had already widened the boundaries of her life.

One doubtful backward glance did Mrs. Fenton give as she turned away from the china closet, all the pretty dishes safely housed within. She knew well what a busy life Mrs. Chester's second girl must live: how few the spare minutes for study must be; where was she to find even forty of them in a day unless she stole them from needed sleep or from something else?

Caroline was a Christian. What if Mrs. Butler were correct and all these new plans should tempt her to neglect her Bible? Mrs. Fenton neglected her own Bible: had she not been such a careful housekeeper, the dust of disuse would have accumulated upon it; but then, Mrs. Fenton was not a Christian, and by some curious process of reasoning she made herself think that that was a good excuse for neglect of her duty. She had no desire to lead Caroline astray, and she determined to sound a note of warning.

"Do you never feel afraid that books and study and matters of that sort may tempt you to neglect more important things? I don't mean your work," she hastened to add, as she saw the pink flush deepen on Caroline's cheek and guessed that she might have been called to bear hard hints of this sort from her mistress. "I know you are strictly conscientious, but—well, I mean more important things, you know. I have heard people say that there was a danger of neglecting the most important book for others."

Then did Caroline's eyes brighten, albeit there was a wondering look on her face.

"Dear Mrs. Fenton," she said earnestly, "do you know, one great reason why I want to study all these things is to know more about this wonderful world that my Father has made? I want to study the works of his hands. Don't you see, this *could* not make me less interested in the book that he had written for *me?*

"And surely learning more and more of the things which he has done will not make me less eager to talk with him! You never become so much interested in Robert's clothes that you forget all about Robert's real self, do you? And yet I know there are people whom study tempts to neglect the Bible and the closet. I have watched young ladies and gentlemen whom I thought were doing that very thing; but it seemed to me all the time that their motives for study were a good deal at fault; and also that they really knew very little about real communion with Christ at any time. I don't think it was the fault of the studies. You know people can make a temptation out of anything. At least, I suppose they can. I have never had any temptation to neglect Christ. Dear Mrs. Fenton, since Mother went away he has been my *only* friend; until now he has grown so dear I *could not* get along without his constant presence."

And Mrs. Fenton, watching the earnest face from which the clear eyes looked out, felt an immense respect rising within her for Mrs. Chester's hired girl; also, she decided that there was evidently a type of religion about which Mrs. Butler knew nothing. Also, she made one resolve: that come what would of it, *she* would from this time forth be Caroline's friend.

It happened that the evening which followed this

inauguration of the Centerville C.L.S.C. was a somewhat eventful one in Mrs. Fenton's quiet world.

She and Caroline having planned what they would do and how they would do it, Caroline went home happy-hearted. Young Robert closed his books, kissed his mother good-night, and went away to his room. The father, after carefully turning the keys on the outside world, came and stood in front of his wife's chair and looked thoughtfully down on her.

"So you can't start your Circle, eh?"

"Oh, yes indeed! Or rather, I found one already started. Mrs. Chester's Caroline began several months ago. She is the first sensible girl I have found in six weeks."

Over this information her husband whistled. He had always liked Caroline, but he had felt a suspicion that his wife remembered that she was Mrs. Chester's second girl.

"Two to a Circle, eh?" he presently said. "Suppose I come in and we make it a triangle?"

"Will you, Robert? Oh, *will* you?" And in her eagerness she rose up and stood beside him.

"Why, I don't see anything to hinder. You and I have started out together in enterprises before now and made a comfortable thing of it. I must say I approve of this idea as far as I understand it. I fancy it will be a good thing for the boy to see us interested in what just now interests him most. Besides, it will help to keep him in sight. We've got a smart boy, Martha, a talented boy, and we are proud of him, as we should be; we don't want to hold him back, and we don't want to lose his company. The only way I see is to trot on after him, and I'm ready."

Now, only those who have had a dreary sort of unspoken feeling that the absorptions of business and the wider range of thought offered by the outside world are possibly drawing away their husband's interests from the home and the wife can understand the throbbings of Mrs. Fenton's heart.

Was it possible for this "Circle" to draw the family into a closer Circle?

As a usual thing, every town of considerable size has its intellectual giant; its man of mark, looked up to, quoted, admired, and reverenced.

Centerville had such. The Reverend Gilbert Monteith, a very eminent professor in a very renowned college, a linguist of unusual powers, a pulpit orator, a scientific man in a special sense, a traveled man who spoke of the Old World with the freedom and familiarity that others used in speaking of their native village; a cultured man, in the largest and best sense of that sometimes abused word. What of excellence or strength, mental or moral, could not be applied to Dr. Monteith?

And Centerville was his native town, and he had come home to it for a year of rest. Within a few days after the forming of the triangular Circle, as Mrs. Fenton was passing out of her front gate, Dr. Monteith came down the elm-lined walk, lifted his hat courteously, and paused with a genial, "Mrs. Fenton, I believe."

Mrs. Fenton, much fluttered, for she had not even a bowing acquaintance with the great man, admitted that such was her name.

Whereupon he proceeded to state that he had heard she was about forming a Chautauqua Literary and Scientific Circle, that he was much interested in those societies, had looked into their method of work with a great deal of care, watched their growth and success with pleasure, and that, if it would be agreeable, he would like to be considered a member of their branch and attend the meetings when he was in town.

Imagine Mrs. Fenton's sensations! She, blushing and stammering, tried to explain: it was only the weakest of weak little efforts—not worthy of being numbered among the C.L.S.C.'s of the land; it had almost no members.

The great man smiled on her genially; was glad that she had not been disheartened by trifles; hoped and believed that she would succeed. He would like to review the studies of his early days; perhaps at the same time he was refreshing his own memory he might be helping along some of the younger ones.

Of course, others would come in. There was no reason why the enterprise shouldn't succeed in that town as it had elsewhere. He would himself invite certain of his young friends to join them, if she was willing.

In short, when Mrs. Fenton finally took leave of him and walked away, it was with the feeling that the success of their poor little C.L.S.C. was assured.

5

THE WARD BOYS
DISCUSS THE SITUATION

THEY were respectively "Jim" and "Joe." It is doubtful if they realized how the full Christian names would sound as applied to themselves. Seventeen years, in fact, nearly eighteen years, had they lounged through the world being familiarly known by these shortened names. Twins they were. And their mother had delighted in them for only eight years when she had suddenly left them. They vividly remembered standing together, shivering in the gloom of a rainy autumn day drawing near to its close, and watching with terrific curiosity the ugly-looking box lowered into an uglier-looking hole in the ground, feeling sure that within that box was their mother. Hadn't they seen her lying there? They vividly remembered how the wind groaned among the leafless branches of the great old tree which stood just at the foot of that awful hole. They vividly remembered just how the feet of the bearers sounded as they shuffled through the dulled yellow and brown leaves that bestrewed their path. I don't think that either of them in all the intervening years had ever listened to the toll of the church bell without being carried instantly back to that day and that box and that hole and thinking just how the earth sounded on the box as the sexton rattled it in and the minister said: "Earth to earth, ashes to ashes, dust to dust."

There were certain other things about those early days that they vividly remembered: for instance, their mother's kisses; for she had been a mother who had kissed them often and tenderly—stealing sweet little chances to do it when she washed their faces and brushed their brown curls; for in those days they had brown curls. *She* had not said "Jim" and "Joe," but "Jamie dear" and "Little Josie." Sometimes, in specially gloomy weather—nights when the lights were out—they almost fancied they could hear her voice. But they never spoke of these things to each other.

They never heard the diminutive names anymore; and they had never, since she went away, received any of those little tendernesses which boys as they grow older are half ashamed of and always love. Their father was a good sort of dull man. Silent by nature; repressive—loving his wife and mourning her truly, yet never speaking to her of his love, nor showing it in a hundred nameless ways dear to a wife's heart—rarely speaking *of* her after she was gone. Loving his children truly, yet showing it as little. Silent at home and dreary. Apt to speak sternly when he spoke at all. Absorbed in business, disliking noise, whether it were made by shouting in loud laughter or by quarreling. Equally stern in hushing both. I do not know that it is much wonder that his boys grew up unacquainted with him, shrinking away from him, seeking to find their pleasures elsewhere than in the dreary house; nor do I much wonder that they were a sore disappointment to their father. Perhaps it was in the inevitable nature of things that these two results should be. I know they would have been surprised and incredulous had anyone hinted to them that their father loved them.

He was invariably severe nowadays. Not that they wondered much at that: they knew as well as any persons could that they had grown up to be street loungers, with nothing in or about them to admire. There were times in the darkness of those nights of which I spoke that they were sorry for this result; but this they never said to each other.

On the particular evening in which I introduce them to you, they were sitting in their own room. A dingy room it was; in fact, it was that dreariest sort of a room: one where there was furniture and material enough out of which to make a pleasant place, had only skillful and also loving hands had to do with it. As it was, the carpet was dingy, not only with long use, but with careless sweeping; the chairs were broken or maimed; the bedstead had lost part of its lower posts; the bed was spread up with a dark blue-and-brown comforter, while clothing and toilet articles and old boots and old hats lay about in wild, and at the same time desolate, confusion. A mother would have known that no *mother* ever entered that room. For that matter, there are some fathers who would have been sure that no father came either: and they would have been correct. Mr. Ward long ago ceased to look for his children in their room.

Something of interest was being discussed, or at least considered. Jim, his feet lifted to a comfortable position on the table before him in dangerous proximity to the smoky lamp, thoughtfully chewed an unusually large quid of tobacco while he gazed at a sheet of notepaper whereon certain lines were written in a delicate feminine hand.

"What *is* this C.L.S.C. anyhow?" It was the smaller and, though they were twins, what appeared to be the younger brother, Joe, who asked the question. He sat just across the table, meditatively nursing his knee, his eyes fixed on an envelope which had evidently covered the letter and which was addressed "Messrs. James and Joseph Ward."

"Well," said James, withdrawing his limbs from the table and spitting vigorously before he answered, "it's a sort of a literary society, just as she says: you read the letter."

"But what do you s'pose it's all about?"

"Why, it's for fun as much as anything, most likely; there are different ways of having that article, you know. I think likely it is made up of a kind of people that get most of their fun out of books. They discuss things, I presume—like a debating society, or something of that sort. This Chautauqua is a kind of camp-meeting place. I heard Bob Fenton telling the boys in the store something about it last week. Crowds go there every summer and have a kind of a genteel spree. I don't know what they do; it isn't exactly a camp meeting, for he was telling of some very funny times they had there; comic lectures and the like. There's a fellow who makes pictures with chalk, quicker than lightning—real good likenesses, too, so that the folks recognize them. I couldn't make out quite what it all was; but I know this thing, this C.L.Q.P.X., whatever it is, is mixed up with it. Bob seemed to think it would be jolly; but then he is all for books. That's a cute youngster—that Bob Fenton. He is better company now than lots of the older fellows."

How would young Robert's mother's heart have throbbed in foreboding could she have heard that admiring sentence about her cherished boy. It was good that Mrs. Fenton had designs, real *motherly* designs, on the Ward boys and had already spread her net to try to catch them. She may do more toward a shield for her own boy Robert by this movement than she will ever know of this side of heaven. Not that the Ward boys mean to do him harm, but they have been street loungers—not to use a harsher term than that—for several years; and they have already discovered that "Bob is a cute fellow."

The boys had company this evening. He sat now in his favorite lounging attitude, his elbow leaning on the dusty table, his frowzy head leaning on his hand, while with the fingers of the other hand he beat a tattoo on the table, leaving marks of his fingers in the dust. This was Paul Adams. How he chanced to be given a name which was so utterly at variance with his character would be a mystery if sensible people had the naming of children and were in the habit of waiting to see in what direction they would develop before settling that important question.

However, I do not know that people who were acquainted with Paul Adams's mother ever wondered at her choice of name. He was her one treasure in what had been to her a world of trial and disappointment. He was but a cooing baby when his father died suddenly and violently, leaving Mrs. Adams to take up life's burdens alone and support herself and baby as best she might.

This is such a commonplace statement that it will at once commend itself to you as true. I suppose there is hardly a person in the world who cannot recall a history similar to this. In spite of which fact, each person's sorrow remains distinct and individual. Such things refuse to be lumped; and still the old heart cry goes on: "There is no sorrow like unto my sorrow!"

Mrs. Adams had a little bit of a neat house and a tiny garden to help her along; but there had been times when she had mournfully said: "If it were not for my house I would go away and try to get work somewhere else; but it seems as though I must stick by my place to live in, though I can't eat it nor burn it."

From such a home, as you can imagine that to be, had Paul Adams come up until he was in his eighteenth year.

A queer boy was Paul. His mother was the only one who wouldn't own, and yet certainly she was the only one who was keenly alive, to the fact that he was a disappointment. In her way, she was as careful a mother as Mrs. Fenton. She had spent hours over the darning and patching that she patiently did for him, forming plans for his future: plans to give him an education; to start him in the world; to make life brighter for him than it had ever been for her. This was when he was a little boy. She had struggled and sacrificed in order to keep him neatly clothed and to give him tastes now and then of what other happier boys with fathers had to brighten their lives. Secretly, she had earnestly desired that he should grow up to be a great man; yet she was a true mother in that she put first of all the desire that he should be a *good* man. For this she worked the hardest in her weak, timid way. Often and often she read over the story of his namesake—Paul the apostle—glorying in the power and moral grandeur of that character. It was a dim memory of this great man that had caused her to name her two-days-old baby Paul. Perhaps the very absence of courage in her own nature made her long the more ardently to see it develop in her boy.

But it gradually became apparent, even to her, that there were certain things that Paul would not do. In the first place, he would not take kindly to the idea of an education. To be sure, his opportunities had been confined to the commonest of country schools, with one of these poor drudges for a teacher who taught because she knew nothing else to do to keep soul and body together, and who concentrated all the powers of her being in a grand hatred of her work. But the fact remained that others had come out, even from such teaching, with a passably fair start on the road to learning and had acquitted themselves with credit afterwards in the academy ten miles distant, which was the center of Mrs. Adam's educational aspirations.

Paul was not a credit to himself during the days which he spent in the stuffy schoolroom full of vile smells and flies in summer, and slippery with mud and snow in winter.

He whittled much; he made and threw many paper balls; he ate many apples; he tripped the feet of any careless boy who passed that way; but as to *studying* he did just as little of that as possible and made so uncreditable an appearance on examination days that when he was fourteen, his discouraged mother took him out of school altogether and set him to hoeing in the garden.

This was less trying to his nerves than the school-room; still, it was anything but a desirable life, and young Paul soon learned how to manage so as to get along with very little exercise of that kind. Not that he ever refused to work: when his mother hinted that the garden ought to be hoed, he went at it; the main trouble lay in the fact that he did not *stay* at it. Long before noon his hoe would be found sticking in a hill of potatoes, and Paul himself would be down at the corner lounging on the steps of the largest grocery in the town. In short, from any standpoint that you were pleased to look at him, Paul was a bitter disappointment to his mother.

Perhaps, if it were not a strange thing to say, I might also hint that his mother was in a sense a disappointment to Paul. She never scolded him outright, but she made endless whining talks at him that sometimes drove him as near to distraction as a good-natured boy can come. By means of these weak talks she led him gradually to feel that the ugly little kitchen in which she sat and sewed was the most dismal and hopeless spot in all the wide world, and every opportunity was to be seized for escaping from its atmosphere. Yet his mother would have promptly and unquestioningly have given up her life at any time to save his—she *loved* him so! And certainly he, in his lazy fashion, loved his mother.

If the mother had known the truth concerning him, the reason for his utter lack of application at school was not because he had not fair mental powers, but because he had failed to see any occasion for using them in that direction. The teachers into whose hands he had fallen had an utterly unfascinating way of presenting truths. To Paul's mental vision, there was simply a confused drawl of words to spell, and words to read, and figures to count, without a suggestion as to how they were to be applied outside of the spelling book or arithmetic. Paul could not see any way in which they would be likely to help him either to hoe the garden or get rid of hoeing it. He had no occasion to spell words; why should he care to know how they were spelled? He had no letters to write; why should he desire to write well? He had no calculations to make, nothing to buy, or, what was equally to the point, nothing to buy with. What earthly difference could it make to him how much six percent interest on a certain sum of money would be in a year? Where *was* the money? Not in his hands, certainly, nor in his mother's; and those who had it seemed entirely capable of reckoning its market value without his help.

This was the way that young Paul had reasoned; not aloud, mind you; he knew various platitudes that might be urged against this sort of talk had he ventured to produce it; they did not strike him as having any direct bearing on himself, and he didn't want to hear them. All he wanted of life was a good time; and, let alone, he fancied that he might be able to make one.

The fact is, Paul Adams's faculties were all asleep, and nobody with whom he came in contact had brains enough to awaken them or interest enough in him to try. Which was it?

His religious education was not one whit in advance of the intellectual. Not that in this his mother could not have been his teacher, at least in a degree. For through all the trials of her life she had kept an abiding faith in her Lord and was absolutely certain, at times, of this one thing: that a "crown of life was laid up for her," for sure she was that she should "love his appearing." Yet she was like many another Christian in that the cares of this world and the deceitfulness of poverty had made her look upon the crown and the glory as sure indeed, but *so far* away that their light was obscured by mountains of daily frets and cares that rose between. Also, she was one of those strange mothers who, though she had an eager, and at times I might almost say a consuming, desire to see her son a Christian, yet never mentioned the subject to him in a direct way, but contented herself with feeble hints which exasperated him.

So far as he had been able to discover, religion was a wishy-washy affair, amounting to very little, and that little he neither understood nor cared for.

Since the feeble restraint of school days had been withdrawn, and the garden had proved too dull and dreary to endure, and the woodpile, by reason of its smallness, really required very little time, Paul had degenerated into a street loafer.

His vices were not strongly marked. As yet, he drank nothing stronger than cider and an occasional glass of beer: the reasons being that he had no money to spend in that direction or any other and no hereditary tastes in that line to indulge. However, as the force of example was strong about him, his mother lived in constant terror; for she was only too well aware that money seemed always to be forthcoming for the indulgence of such tastes. Every night she went early to bed in winter to save lights and fuel, and in summer for very weariness of herself. But she lay awake listening for the sound of her boy's footsteps, afraid that she would not hear them; that he would be tempted to late hours and the vices which accompany them: afraid to hear them lest they might be staggering; rising on one elbow at last to listen for their nearer approach in an agony of fear and apprehension and lying down at last with a tremulous "Thank God for one more night!" when they sounded firmly on the walk. Strange to say, young Paul was rarely out later than ten o'clock, the sole reason being that he had a good-natured desire not to "scare" his mother. He smoked cigars when he could get them. Not that he began by being particularly fond of them—in fact, he found it unusually hard work to learn. He had to devote to this accomplishment the courage and perseverance that would have told well for him in other directions; but it is a taste that once acquired a boy will gratify if he can.

So, to put it in brief: at the time our story opens, Paul Adams was an ignorant, good-natured, tobacco-chewing, cigar-smoking street loafer.

He had one friend; in fact, I ought to say that he had two friends—namely, the Ward boys. It was so rarely that the names of the twins were separated that it seems unnatural to use the singular number in connection with either of them; yet it was Jim who contrived to be the leading spirit both of his brother and of Paul Adams. Not that they were in the least alike. If I must admit the fact, Jim Ward was a quick-witted, energetic young scamp. Much farther along on the downhill road than was Paul. Perhaps their intimacy might be explained in part by the fact that it was Ward's nature to lead, and Paul was sufficiently good-natured, as a rule, to allow himself to be led. Occasionally, it is true, he resisted the other with a steady, offhand determination that surprised and vexed him. For instance, there had plans developed several times that involved staying out nearly if not quite all night. These plans Paul had steadily refused to carry out: all coaxings and all ridicule fell on him unheeded; he good-naturedly replied to the one and laughed off the other. He simply *would not* stay out all night, nor half the night, and "scare" his mother.

"She has botheration enough, the land knows!" he was wont to explain, "and I'm bound she shan't have that." By degrees the Ward boys learned that when Paul spoke in that quiet tone which hinted at a sort of reserve strength, they might as well coax a stone. The trouble was, he very rarely used that tone, but good-humoredly allowed himself to be led along the down-hill road as fast as the Ward boys cared to travel, without putting forth a hand to hold himself back.

On the evening in question Paul Adams, as I have said, sat in a listless attitude seemingly uninterested in the conversation between the brothers. Social distinctions are very queer things. It was an unspoken but at the same time clearly recognized fact to the Ward boys that they were several degrees above Paul Adams. Why, perhaps would have been somewhat difficult for them to explain. It is true that they lived in a brick house of large size and respectable appearance, at least below stairs; it is also true that Mr. Ward, Sr., had a respectable bank account and was adding to it steadily; yet why these things should have actually added to the importance or social standing of his sons is perhaps a problem. The affirmative answer to it seems, however, to have been accepted by the world. Certainly the Ward boys never doubted it; therefore, the conversation concerning the C.L.S.C. had been carried on entirely between themselves. Presently their guest raised himself to a sitting posture, took deliberate aim, and snapped a peanut shell so skillfully that it hit Joe on the nose as he said:

"I s'pose you would be kind of astonished if you knew that I had had a bid to that meeting."

"You!" The tone sufficiently indicated the astonishment.

"Yes, sir, I: just as sure as you live and breathe the breath of life. It's my opinion that it is a nicer-looking one than yours—the writing is nicer, anyhow; hand-some enough to be print. Signed with a flourish, too, such as they say would be about the hardest to coun-terfeit of any that are made. I showed it to that new bank clerk this very day, and he said he was pretty good at copying, but he shouldn't like to have to undertake that."

"Who wrote it?"

"Well, to the best of my knowledge, the man wrote it who signed his name to it. The writing is the same; it's a private letter, you see; none of your circulars." And with visible signs of pride on his face young Paul unfolded and spread before the two pairs of eyes that immediately bent forward to examine it, a sheet of heavy, cream laid paper which contained in a few cordial sentences a hearty invitation to be present at the next meeting of the C.L.S.C., to be held at Mrs. Fenton's, signed Gilbert L. Monteith! The Ward boys stared at the name, then at each other, with astonished and significant glances. They hardly knew what they thought. Still, whatever they might come to think of it, the present fact was that, for some reason unknown to them, Paul Adams had been very highly honored. They could not help having a feeling of respect for a fellow who held in his possession an autographed letter from Dr. Gilbert Monteith.

James Ward arose abruptly, strolled to the one window, and looked out into the darkness while Joe carefully refolded the valuable letter and returned it to the owner.

Presently he at the window spoke his mind: "I tell you what it is, boys, I for one am going to that meeting. I mean to see what there is of it. I've got a chance to see, and I mean to. You can do as you like, but I intend to go." Up to that moment, Paul Adams had been extremely doubtful about *his* ever putting in an appearance at the C.L.S.C.—whatever that was— but on being appealed to by Joe as to what he was going to do, he replied with alacrity: "I've no kind of a notion of not going. Suppose a fellow would slight such an invitation as that!"

"Well then," said Joe somewhat ruefully, "I don't see but I've *got* to go; there's no fun in staying away alone, but I'm blessed if I can see any fun in going."

Thus was the momentous question decided.

6

LAUNCHED

PAUL ADAMS had an item of news to communicate to his mother the next morning at the breakfast table. He commenced it in the form of a question: "Mother, have I got a clean shirt?"

Mother opened her eyes in surprise at the question. Paul was not given to caring whether his garments were clean or soiled and was apt not to don the carefully ironed and carefully mended garment that she regularly laid out on the bed for him every Sunday morning, until after earnest explanations on her part that she must have the other one to wash. Behold, now it was only Thursday, and he was inquiring for a clean shirt!

"Why, yes," she said hesitatingly; she had a habit of speaking hesitatingly, as though she were never sure but that what she was about to say would not be better left unsaid; "your Sunday shirt is all washed and mended and looks nice, though the bosom is giving out a little; you ought to have two new shirts, but I don't know how to manage it, I really don't."

"Never mind," in utmost good nature. "I don't

want two shirts; one will do. But I want it *tonight;* I'm going out this evening. Likely as not I won't be in quite as early as usual; can't tell."

The widow Adams sat down her cup of weak tea untasted and gazed in dismay at her son. It was coming now—that nameless, dreary something which she had been dreading all these years. Paul was going to fix himself up and go off to some disreputable place and do some disreputable thing.

"Going out!" she repeated, dismay in voice and manner. "Why, where are you going?"

"Oh, going to spend the evening with some of the fellows. I'm not going far away, but I may be later than common."

"Well, but Paul, you always spend the evening with some of the fellows or somewhere else; I'm sure I can't tell when you've spent one with me. There's something more than that; because if there isn't, why should you need a clean shirt? Your *Sunday* shirt! Remember, if you put it on tonight, why, then you won't have one for Sunday, as far as I can see. I *can't* wash and iron and mend the other between this and Sunday, I don't believe, on account of that sewing for Mrs. West that I promised this week. Don't go off with any of them disgraceful fellows, Paul! Don't do it!"

Paul chuckled. He had a vision of himself sitting in Mrs. Fenton's parlor—he had passed the house and glanced up at it often enough to feel sure that there was a pretty nice parlor within—himself sitting there in company with Dr. Gilbert Monteith, for instance, and his mother calling him a disgraceful fellow. For some reason not understood by himself, he was not disposed to tell his mother anything about the invitation out.

"The shirt will do well enough for Sunday, too; don't bother!" This was all the explanation he offered.

"But why should you want a clean shirt in the middle of the week?" she persisted. "There's some goings-on that you don't tell me about."

Whereupon the graceless boy chuckled again: "I'm going to the C.L.S.C.," he giggled. "Going to join it." The look of horror on his mother's face satisfied his ideas of fun. He knew very little about those mystic letters himself, but still he was certain that he was better posted than his mother. He was dimly conscious that he had been honored; his mother would be sure to think that it was something disgraceful, and the idea was irresistibly funny.

"What's that?" She fairly gasped the words.

"Blessed if I know," said Paul, laughing so hard that his cup of tea nearly choked him. "I'm going tonight to find out."

"Don't do it, Paul, I beg of you; don't! It's one of them disgraceful secret things; I've heard of them. Oh, you needn't laugh. I'm older than you, and I've heard of a sight of things that you don't know nothing about. As long ago as when your father was a young man, they tried to get him to join, and he never would. 'I won't do nothing that I can't tell my mother about if I'm a mind to,' he said; and he stuck to it. How many times I've thought of that and hoped that my boy would never do anything that he couldn't tell his mother. And here you are going into it, and you'll go right straight down to ruin: I'm sure of that."

Paul was in no way dismayed at this prospect; in truth, he had heard enough about it to become hardened. His mother had been sure, ever since he could remember that he was going to ruin, and had told him so with tears. He was inexorable: he would make no explanation, and he would insist on putting on his clean shirt that very evening and going to that disgraceful C.L.S.C.

I hardly know how to explain to you how it was that a boy who had always been so regardful of his mother's "scares" as to refuse to stay out late at night should yet have allowed her to work her poor nervous heart into spasms of fear over this new departure, when a few words of explanation would have filled that same heart with motherly hope and pride. "I don't know how to explain it to her," he told himself as he shut the door with a little bang, vexed at her tearful face when there was no cause for tears. "I know it's nothing that she need cry about this time, and that's enough. S'posing I should tell her, she'd go and talk about it: tell all the old women on this street, like enough, and be pleased and all that, and I dare say it won't come to anything, it isn't no ways likely I'll ever go more than once, and then she would just be disappointed, and what's the use?" And I really believe that the strongest motive he had for silence was that vague fear of another disappointment for his mother. Yet he disappointed her in one way or another every day of his life. He was certainly a queer boy.

Poor Mrs. Adams! She had a miserable day. I offer no excuse for Paul; I am ashamed of him. As for his mother, shall excuse be offered for her? She was an adept in borrowing trouble; she had practiced for years; true, her life had been one of real practical troubles, yet it is also true that some of her most severe trials had been borrowed: wrought out in the darkness of the night, lived over in anticipation, wept over, struggled with, in a measure endured, and they never came. Yet, so far from learning wisdom by this long experience, she still expected them, or others worse than they, and wrought at her sad problem all the same. She looked again at her boy's shirt, making sure that every button was in its place; she sought out a clean handkerchief and laid it beside the shirt; she brushed his best coat with careful hands and mended a tiny rip in the sleeve; and she had an hour's labor with the shining shirt front, dampening, rubbing, ironing, because there had plashed on it two or three hot tears. Had Paul known that the tears really fell, he would have made some effort to relieve his mother. As it was, he came home from his business of lounging earlier than usual, dressed himself with marked care, taking most unusual pains with his hair and looking altogether so neat and respectable that his mother felt a little thrill of pride rise up among her fears as he passed through the kitchen. She had not ventured further opposition. The only question she asked was the tearfully put one: "How late do you expect to be, Paul?"

"I've no kind of an idea," he said cheerily. "I don't know where I'm going, you see; nor what will be done with me"; and the mother groaned.

Ah, but had you been able to peep into Mrs. Fenton's pretty parlor that evening! Paul was right in his surmise that it was a particularly pleasant room at all times; but on this occasion, the first regular meeting of the newly organized C.L.S.C., its mistress had done what she could to make it more than usually attractive. She had labored half the afternoon to make her ivies and ferns trail and droop in just the right direction, and at dusk came Caroline, fresh from Mrs. Chester's greenhouse, bearing a choice collection of cut flowers. It was late enough in the season for these to bring special joy to Mrs. Fenton's heart.

"See!" said Caroline, "they are all going out this

evening, and Mrs. Chester said the beauty of these would be gone by tomorrow, so if I had any friends who would like them I was to take them; wasn't she nice?"

"Very," said Mrs. Fenton in glee; and while she arranged them in her pretty vases with skillful hand, she wondered whether Mrs. Chester would have given her flowers had she known they were destined that very evening to help people up out of their spheres!

All four of the burners in the pretty little chandelier had been lighted, Mrs. Fenton remarking apologetically when her husband laughed that she *did* like light! The delicate bell-shaped shades drooping over the gas jets added their beauty to the general effect. I have before told you that Mrs. Fenton was an artist, so far as regarded the adorning of her home, and she had exerted herself to the utmost to make it an attractive spot on this first evening of their venture into the world of literature.

I ought not to use the word *venture*. It had already passed beyond the limits which surround that word. The preliminary business meeting had been a success, both as regarded numbers and enthusiasm. There were found to be those in Centerville not too much absorbed in painting or self-esteem to appreciate and join hands with the new scheme. Whether the imposing name of Dr. Gilbert Monteith announced as president of the organization had much to do with rapidly swelling the list of members, who shall say? Certain it is that Mrs. Fenton had on her list a comfortable sprinkling of names from high sources. In fact, she had one or two that Mrs. Chester had tried in vain to secure at her fashionable evening gatherings. Yet she had been true to her first motherly ambition to "get hold of the Ward boys." This desire she had mentioned, not without some anxiety, to Dr. Monteith when he called one evening in an entirely informal way to talk over their plans—for the bright little woman had been unanimously chosen secretary. Would Dr. Monteith think she was lowering the standard of the C.L.S.C. by trying to introduce to its membership such doubtful young men as these? Also, what would he think of Caroline? These questions made Mrs. Fenton's heart beat fast; but I rejoice to tell you that she set her pleasant mouth in firm lines and told herself that whatever Dr. Monteith or anybody else thought of Caroline, *she* was to belong, provided *she* (Mrs. Fenton) had anything to do with it. If any person objected to Caroline, it should be the same as though they had objected to *her*. The Ward boys might be doubtful, perhaps they were; perhaps it was foolish to try to do anything with them—in that line, at least; but Mrs. Chester's Caroline was another person. She was not left long in doubt as to Dr. Monteith's opinion. His handsome eyes flashed instant sympathy, and his cordial voice said: "My dear Mrs. Fenton, that is one of the best of the good thoughts that you have had concerning this movement. If we could get hold of these two young men, we might save them, and through them I am half frightened to think how many others"; and then he, in his turn, astonished Mrs. Fenton.

Did she know anything of a boy, or a young man rather, by the name of Adams? His mother was a poor struggling widow, and the boy was no comfort to her; was always hanging around the street corners; was constantly with the Ward boys and others of their stamp; was going to ruin, he feared; and yet he fancied the boy had capabilities. His father was a man of unusual strength of mind. Dr. Monteith had known *him* when a boy, and although he had had almost no advantages he had picked up a good deal of various sorts of knowledge and was a man of sterling worth and much promise at the time of his sudden death. Dr. Monteith, by reason of his busy life, had lost track of the boy until quite recently, a fact which he regretted. Did Mrs. Fenton think it possible to reach just such a boy as he was through such a channel?

Mrs. Fenton felt that her fair face was showing crimson blushes. She was so *astonished*. Yes, she did know Paul Adams—by sight at least—and she knew his mother very well. Mrs. Adams occasionally did fine starching and ironing for her when she was pressed for time, and many a nice bit of comfort from her cellar and pantry had found its way to Mrs. Adams's home. She did not tell Dr. Monteith all these things, but her voice, at least, must have expressed her surprise, for he smiled as he said:

"I am not at all sure that we could reach him. I don't know that he has an idea of ever trying to be other than what he is, but for the sake of his father I should like to get hold of him. Would you have any objection to my inviting him to join us?"

Oh, no indeed! Fancy her making objections to anyone whom Dr. Monteith might choose to invite to her house! But after that she had not deemed it necessary to commend Mrs. Chester's Caroline to his special forbearance. That same Caroline looked very pretty on the evening in question. She had not in any sense stepped aside from her usual dress; it was a dark, plain dress, costing so little by the yard that it would have surprised even Mrs. Fenton, who was a practical economist; but it was made with exceeding care, was perfect in fit, and the soft cheap lace at throat and wrists set it off as much as "real" lace at an unmentionable price would have done; better, indeed, because of one's instinctive sense of the fitness of things. While at work among the flowers, Caroline had, from force of habit also, pushed into the braids of her hair a cluster of scarlet fuchsias, and, whether she knew it or not, they fitted her perfectly. As the peal of the bell announced the first arrival, she turned away from the flowers with heightened color and a little laugh as she said:

"It seems to me as though I ought to retire to the kitchen or the nursery. Where shall I sit, Mrs. Fenton?"

"Just where you please," said Mrs. Fenton promptly. "Don't you go to being foolish, Caroline; there will be no one here who will not respect you in proportion to the respect which they have for themselves. That is our president, I think. Isn't it grand that we have such a president?"

The parlor filled rapidly. Mrs. Fenton was jubilant and yet not quite satisfied. She had not before realized how eager she had been to secure the Ward boys; but as often as the bell would peal, a flush of expectancy would rise on her face, to fade again as only others of their immediate Circle were admitted. A close observer would also have discovered that the genial president was on the alert, watching for what had not as yet appeared. They came, however. The three came together; somewhat late, for at the last moment, Jim's courage had failed him, and he had announced his intention of "giving it up."

Not so Paul. He was astonished with himself for having entered into any such engagement, but once having donned a clean shirt and blacked his boots and spent unusual thought and care on his personal appearance, he was resolved that it should not be for naught. In this Joe agreed with him, and by dint of much coaxing, they finally prevailed upon the one who was usually their leading spirit to reconsider. I don't think I shall be able to set before you a description of the effect of that brightly lighted, flower-perfumed room on those three young men. The Ward boys were almost as unused to such scenes as was Paul. It is true they had a parlor at home, but it was always closed and dark, the dust having gathered about even their mother's old-fashioned portrait. As for Paul, the neat, clean kitchen, lighted only by one small lamp, so old that it was always out of order, was, you will remember, his daily lesson in the refinements of life. Of course he immediately adopted extravagant views as to the beauty of Mrs. Fenton's parlor. But while taste and elegance undoubtedly had their effect on these young men, they were as nothing compared with the courteous and cordial greeting which was given them. Dr. Monteith arose from his chair of honor near the study table, and, coming forward, gave a hand to each, while in few words of pleasant greeting he assured them of their welcome; and every member of the Circle chose to follow their leader's example, albeit some were amazed at their own action. Certainly, whatever the C.L.S.C. might develop for these three, their first impressions were exceedingly pleasing.

I will admit to you that all three understood little of the subjects that were discussed during the evening. "Merivale," said each to himself at intervals; "what *is* Merivale, or *who* is he? Does it mean a man or a woman or a place?" Now each had that degree of self-respect—if indeed that is the proper name for the feeling—which made him resolve to discover as soon as possible all about Merivale, without admitting for a moment to the others that he was not thoroughly posted. "Rome? What about it? Did they mean that little village on the railroad forty miles or so north of here? It wasn't likely, for who ever heard of anything happening in Rome worth talking about?" Yes, they knew, everyone of them that there was such a city, country, or town across some ocean, renowned for something. The momentous questions were, which ocean, town, city, or what?

Presently James Ward, the more daring spirit of the three, leaned forward and possessed himself of a book that lay on the table exactly like one in Mrs. Fenton's hand to which he could see she occasionally referred. *Merivale's General History of Rome.* Merivale was, then, doubtless a man and had written a book about Rome. So much for knowledge! You need not smile if I admit to you that James Ward felt in a certain sense triumphant. He had one fact which an hour before he had never heard of.

Young Paul, whose keen eyes were in all portions of the room at once, quietly held out his hand for the book as James was about to return it to the table and in a twinkling placed himself on a level with his friend. He went farther. He opened to the title page and read: "A History of Rome from the Foundation of the City to the Fall of Augustulus." He opened curiously to the first chapter and read the heading slowly and with great care, "The Site of Rome." "My!" said young Paul to himself, "that is a queer spelling!" his only knowledge of the word being derived from s-i-g-h-t. He read on. "Its configuration and geological formation. A glance at the Italian peninsula, at the basin of the Mediterranean, at the empire beyond it."

All Greek to Paul Adams. He laid down the book

with a hardly suppressed sigh, and there flitted before him the memory of sundry wasted days in the old dingy schoolhouse. He wondered curiously whether had he studied more and tripped boys less he should understand this sentence this evening. What of it? Why should he *care* to understand it? What difference did it make to him where Rome was or where Augustulus fell? Why had he come here this evening? Why, indeed, but that—as he raised his eyes at that moment he met the genial ones of Professor Monteith, and something, he was not metaphysician enough to know what, made him immediately wish for a second time that evening that he knew a little something.

Although Professor Gilbert Monteith was heartily interested in the Literary and Scientific Circle and meant to give it his utmost strength and the benefit of his thorough education, it gives me great joy to tell you that he was more interested in human lives and human souls than in any phase of scientific truth that could possibly be presented. He meant to aid the few earnest students gathered about him, and he meant also to save these three boys if he could. He gave his mind to so shaping the questions, so commenting on the answers that the whole was well calculated to awaken the curiosity of those who knew nothing concerning that ancient city. In short, he so skillfully introduced our novices to the seven renowned hills and the flowing Tiber and the curious legend of Romulus and Remus that not only was Mrs. Fenton heartily interested and Caroline's eyes glowed and young Mr. Bennett, the law student, declared to himself that this was something worth having, but, what was infinitely more to the point, three young men on the high road to ruin roused themselves from their lethargy of ignorance and indifference, and positively resolved to keep the vantage ground that they had gained, and put themselves in a way to hear these people talk.

Moreover, in the course of the evening, young Robert Fenton, without the least intention of adding to the spell, without the slightest knowledge that he did any such thing, pushed his chair closer to Dr. Monteith and began to question.

The Palatine, and the Aventine, and the winding Tiber, and the Vatican were names that rolled so easily from his young lips, and the questions he asked were so promptly recognized as of importance and so carefully answered that, while Mrs. Fenton's cheeks glowed with motherly pride, the cheeks of the Ward boys glowed with shame. "Just to think," murmured James to himself, "that fellow is only fourteen!" and young Paul said within himself: *That youngster knows enough to ask about what he don't know, and I vow I mean to learn so much anyhow!*

The first regular meeting of the C.L.S.C., viewed from human standpoints, was certainly a success. The pleased Circle detached itself into little groups when the formal meeting was over and discussed their hopes and plans.

"We shall have to be very busy, some of us, to get forty minutes a day in which to read." This Mr. Bennett remarked in a general way. "Merivale is interesting, but he doesn't say much about law, and I have to keep Blackstone ever before my mental vision." Whereupon Caroline thought, but did not say: *Merivale may be interesting, but I fancy he doesn't say much about setting tables and clearing them off, and making desserts, and dusting parlors; I shall certainly have to be very busy.*

7

"Isn't It Nice?"

"ISN'T it nice?" This is what she said to James Ward—a little "pink and white" girl who could hardly reach to his elbow. Not an intellectual girl at all; one who knew almost as little about Rome as did the young man before whom she stood, save that she had a fashionable seminary education and knew the *names* of things tolerably well. A girl who frizzed her hair when frizzes were the height of the fashion and banged it when that style was in vogue; a girl who wore trains one day, or round dresses reaching just to the tops of her boots the next—according to the dictates of the most fashionable dressmaker whose advice she could ask. If you had been going to select a woman to give an impetus to a dawning intellectual sense, the last person you would probably have chosen would have been this small, pretty Aimie Allison, with features like the latest Parisian doll, expression and all. Yet those three words, spoken in the softest of feminine voices, were destined by fate—or no; let us be reasonable beings, and say by Providence—to work as complete a transformation in the plans and purposes and final destination of James Ward as can possibly be imagined.

How could they do it? Well, who can account for these things, or explain the subtle law by which they work? It was not that James Ward "fell in love" with this small bit of flesh and blood beside him, whatever that coarse expression may mean to those initiated; it was not that he realized any special personality in the matter: It was, simply that he had watched young men and young women heretofore from a distance: they up a story or two, at least; he below, looking up; never, by any chance, *beside* them. He had seen this very girl at church, seated in her father's pew, shielded by her father's presence, surrounded by an atmosphere of respectability and choiceness; he had seen young men, her friends and companions, greet her familiarly, on passing in or out; he had from his seat in the gallery or his position in the upper hall looked down on all this and still felt himself looking *up,* not down: it had all been *above* him. This he had never reasoned over, but simply in a dulled sort of way felt; accepted as a kind of necessity of circumstance. Now he stood beside her in a carefully adorned parlor, she surrounded as usual by that atmosphere of safe, pure respectability: Professor Monteith on one side, Mrs. Dayton Allen on the other, and Mr. Bennett, whom everyone spoke of as destined to be a brilliant young lawyer, just in front of them, and she had looked up to him—James Ward—and said: "Isn't it nice?"

Do you see, what I mean? There came at that moment to the young man a sudden revelation of the fact that there need be no precipice between him and all this safe nicety—he forever below and they above. This small, pretty girl stood on a level with him now, nay, looked up to him literally and addressed him as one of them. What was there to hinder his trying for a place that would make it a matter of course for her and for all such to at least greet him on a level? I declare to you that, so insensibly had this motherless young man slipped downhill, he had never realized that there was a time when he was not necessarily down there; and there had never occurred to him before a possibility of climbing back. He had accepted his worthlessness as an inevitable birthright. Aimie Allison would simply have laughed had she known how her good-natured little question set his pulses to throbbing; yet Aimie Allison never had so great reason to be proud of her brainless little frizzes as on that night when they helped to awaken the energies of an immortal soul. He looked down at her—this boy on this girl, who had been miles above him always heretofore—with a curious feeling that he was older by years than he had ever been before and that she was younger.

"*What* is nice?" he said. He hadn't the least idea how to talk with a young lady. He had no sister, and the few girls whom he knew well enough to shout a greeting to in the streets as he passed them, he felt now that he wished he did not know at all.

"Why this idea, all of it. The meeting together and studying and talking it over, and having such grand men as Professor Monteith and Mr. Bennett and all those to help us."

Us! Whom did she mean by that word so glibly used? Actually herself and him—James Ward? It sounded like it. *Did* he think it was nice? He had told himself not three minutes ago that he was a fool for being there and that he would never be caught in that trap again. It was one of the many revulsions of feeling that he had endured.

He suddenly resolved to be sincere and see what answer he would get. "I suppose it is nice for you people who know all about these things, but I am nothing but an ignoramus. I never took kindly to my books," the sentence closing with a half-bitter laugh.

"Oh, I don't know much about these things!" Her sentence closed with a little laugh too, not a bitter one, though; fresh, and girlish.

"Don't you?" He looked down at her now, smiling partly at the pretty features and partly at himself in wonder that he felt so much at ease talking with a well-dressed young lady who belonged to the upper circles.

"No, I don't, really. I used to study history in school, of course, but I always rather hated it; it seemed so dull, you see. My little sister was asking me only this afternoon what was the principal river in Rome, and do you believe I could tell her? I'm glad I have discovered this evening. I know so much now, anyway. I think it would be nice to know one new thing every day; don't you?"

He hadn't a clear idea what he thought, except that for some reason utterly unknown to himself it gave him intense pleasure to hear her confess her ignorance of Rome. Someway, it reduced the precipice that was between him and people. Why did this fair bit of flesh stand talking with him when Mr. Bennett stood almost at her elbow and was entirely willing to talk with her? Oh, the reason was simple enough. Little Miss Aimie had been a good deal astonished, possibly a trifle scandalized, when she saw the Ward boys march into the room. Why, everybody knew they were just street loungers! As for Paul, he was not enough on a level with her social horizon for her to know him at all. She had been in a puzzle for some seconds over the others, but when Dr. Monteith actually laid aside his books, and arose and shook hands with them, and gave them a general introduction to the company, little Aimie settled it behind her frizzes that they must be rather "nice" after all. Anyway, people whom Dr. Monteith introduced were to be talked to, for the time being, at least. So she talked to James Ward because she happened to be standing nearest to him when the Circle broke up. It was all a "happen," then? Yes, just as much of a happen as anything is in this carefully planned world. Well, it helped to send James Ward home looking thoughtful. Joe put his hands in his pockets and whistled; what he thought about anything he kept to himself until they reached their favorite corner, then he halted, waited for the two who were coming along in silence behind him, and said:

"Let's go in and have a smoke and talk it over."

Whether it was Miss Aimie's influence or the combined influences of the entire evening that made his brother James so unusually gruff, I cannot tell; certain it is he answered with most unnecessary bearishness: "I won't do it. I'm going home."

Joe, though generally good-natured, was not proof against such uncalled-for growls as this and answered promptly: "Bow wow! Go right along! Come in, Paul, and have a soothing puff. I'll stand treat."

"Can't," said Paul laconically.

"Why not?"

"Oh, because I can't. It's late; I'm going home."

"It isn't late, either; just a few minutes after ten."

"Well that's a few minutes later than I generally am. I don't mean to stop *nowhere* tonight, so you needn't coax." It was the quiet tone of decision that meant just what it said.

"Oh bother," Joe said. "You're both cracked to-night." And he too made a virtue of necessity and went home.

It was unusually early for the Ward boys, and as their father, lying awake, heard them stumbling upstairs in the darkness, he wondered with a gloomy sigh what mischief those fellows had been about now to get in so early. As for the widow Adams, her pillow was wet, and her nose was red, and her eyes were sore, all because of tears that had dropped; dropped in a slow, desolate way ever since half past eight, when she had turned her lamp down until it gave one dim wink, and went to bed to wait and watch for the coming of her idol. The *worst* had come at last; she felt it in every nerve: the ruin that had been menacing her so long was about to burst upon her. In what form she had been fruitful in conjecturing. Certainly there was no danger of her being taken by surprise; for she had had her boy brought home shot, drowned in the creek, thrown from a disreputable carriage with all his ribs broken, carried helplessly intoxicated in the arms of two boon companions—all this since half past eight! And it was only ten. How late would her nerves hold out? What else *was* there for her to imagine? Oh, don't laugh at poor sad-hearted widow Adams. Send your only boy out to walk at night over streets spread with snares and pitfalls at every step, as our large towns are, and see how you will feel. Her poor elbow was sore with its duties of lifting her up and letting her down again, as she listened while step after step crunched on the gravel outside, and none of them were his. "He won't come till midnight at the very shortest," she murmured. "He said he would be late. I knew what that meant. I've been expecting and expecting it." Then the weak tears dropped. The widow Adams was too enfeebled in body, too utterly worn out with hard work, even to cry *hard*. It was fifteen minutes after ten by the old-fashioned clock in the corner when she raised herself for the fifteenth time on that much-enduring elbow to say, "Oh, dear that's his step!" and then, "No, it isn't; Oh, dear me!" But this time she added, "Yes, it is! I'd know his step anywhere, even if it was unsteady. Oh dear!" Then the door was carefully opened.

"Mother,"—a steady, low-toned voice—"are you asleep? Don't get up; I see the lamp. All right; good night!" And he clambered up the steep staircase. Then the tears came faster, in very astonishment and satisfaction. Yes, his step was steady once more, and his voice was steady. There was no smell of liquor came in at the door with him. She hated liquor, did this long-suffering widow Adams. She could detect its scent—it seemed to her—almost miles away. But then, "He has been somewhere that he oughtn't to have went," she said drearily, "or else he would have told me about it. Oh, dear me!"

I can reecho it from my soul. "Oh dear me!" that in our Christian country mothers' hearts have to be wrung by so many terrors that are so liable to be! As for Paul Adams, he was unusually quiet. He whistled not a note as he made steady preparations for bed. His mind was full of grave thoughts; there was no room for whistling. The problem looming up before him that he intended in his heart to meet and conquer was: "How shall I go to work to get a *Merivale's History of Rome?*"

It was an actual fact, though a lamentable one that Paul, almost young man as he was, with a widowed mother whom, by all rules of Christianity or civilization, he should have supported, had no settled business in life, nothing definite to do, save to split the kindlings when there were any to split, work in the garden when his mother could coax him to do it, shovel paths when he had to, and pick up odd jobs as they chanced to fall in his way.

His mother, poor thing, comforted her heart by saying with her lips that it was a "dreadful bad town for poor folks. There was her Paul couldn't find any work from one month's end to another." Down deep in her heart she knew there was nothing that Paul tried for so little as something to do; also, she knew that Farmer Judkins, who had known her in her girlhood and who occasionally brought her a bushel of apples or a sparerib, said as soon as he got out of the house, "Sho! What a worthless coot he is! I'd risk but he'd find something to do if he wanted it." All the same the mother respected Farmer Judkins for keeping his lips closed before her. Even she did not know what spasmodic efforts had been made in her favor by the carpenter around the corner: offering Paul steady wages—small, indeed, but steady—for steady work. Paul had shrugged his shoulders and said: "I don't believe you better try me, Mr. Tucker; I ain't steady at anything but eating and sleeping." But this episode his mother didn't know.

On the evening in question, one of the boy's employments seemed to be deserting him: He could not get to sleep. Through the moonlight he could count every knot in the wood of the unfinished room, and for a time he could not fix his mind on anything but the act of counting them. "What the mischief do I care *how* many there are!" he said aloud and angrily at last, and then he set himself to work in earnest to find what it was that was keeping him awake. And strange as the experience was to him, he discovered that he still wanted very much indeed a *Merivale on Rome.*

Why? Ah that was what he could not have explained to you. He had had a glimpse into another world and he liked it; but he had by no means as yet decided that it could be other than glimpses which would fall to his share. Nevertheless, the determination grew to secure a *Merivale* in some way. "I wonder how much the thing costs?" he asked himself, and asked in vain, having less knowledge of the market value of books than of almost any other thing. A few moments of silent thought induced the next explosive sentence: "Folks that are at work making money, getting regular wages, can buy books when they want 'em." It seems a strange thing to say, but really Paul Adams was getting his first touch of respect for labor, by reason of forcing himself to think of its remarkable results. What else he thought as he lay there staring at the posts of the old-fashioned bedstead he kept to himself, only announcing the result in the tone which the Ward boys called his stubborn one, and from which they knew there was no appeal: "I vum I'll do it tomorrow morning." Then he turned on his side and went to sleep.

Meantime, pretty little Miss Aimie Allison simpered home in the moonlight with young Bennett, the law student, and tried to be wise and talk about Rome with its seven hills, and was duly flattered by the attention which the brilliant young man bestowed on her, but acknowledged in her secret soul that she felt more comfortable while talking with James Ward. It was a little difficult to keep the seven hills located where they ought to be and not to confuse the Vatican and the Apennines, not being entirely sure as yet which either word represented; now, with James Ward it had not mattered. "By the by," said her companion, suddenly leaving Rome and coming down to Centerville, "how did those Ward boys and that Adams youngster happen to stray into our gathering, do you suppose?"

"I'm sure I don't know; wasn't it funny?" with an amused little laugh.

"Rather; I presume they felt somewhat like the historical fishes we occasionally hear about. I saw you trying to make talk with one of the Wards; how did you succeed?"

"Why, he talked quite well," Miss Aimie said hesitatingly, not sure of her ground. Perhaps this was an absurd thing to say to the brilliant young man.

"Did he indeed? I am surprised to hear it; I didn't suppose he had two ideas in common with people having brains."

How many brains had Miss Aimie, had he been able to measure them? Young Bennett didn't know; but he knew she was a pleasant little thing to walk home with. As for Caroline, young Robert Fenton got out his cap and walked home with her, his mother remarking as she stood in the door and looked after them that she wished young men had common sense. "Why didn't Mr. Bennett see her safely home? It was right on his way, and that simpering little Aimie might have thought of and proposed it to him if she had any brains." And her husband had laughed and replied:

"You are good at planning, Martha, but when you get young Bennett to come down from his height long enough to walk home with Mrs. Chester's Caroline, let me know."

8

"I Know I Shall Stick"

YOUNG Paul opened his eyes intent on the same subject on which they had closed the night before. Neither did it seem less important to him by prosaic daylight, as things are apt to do. More difficult to accomplish perhaps it looked, but he *meant to accomplish it*. Therefore he made a hasty and even more silent breakfast than usual, ignoring his mother's wistful hints that he would tell her how he passed the evening, and went out uptown with a quick step utterly unlike his usual lounging gait. His object was regular employment—such as would bring money. Where to look for it he did not know. It was an unpropitious time of year in which to find work that he was capable of doing, whatever work that would be. He fully realized that his qualifications were limited. But behold as he turned the corner, a placard hung in the window of one of his favorite lounging places: "Boy wanted." This looked encouraging; it might be merely an errand boy—well, certainly *he* could run errands; and it tells well for the downright earnestness of Paul that he did not shrink from this form of work—so much younger than his years. On the other hand, if they wanted one to stand behind the counter and sell tobacco and cigars, why, certainly he was capable of doing that. "Can't need much brains for *such* work!" said Paul, with a contemptuous sniff and a dawning sense of the intellectual inferiority of "such work." Then he boldly turned the knob and went forward. The proprietor was well known to him. He vouchsafed him at first no answer beyond an astonished stare and then a hearty laugh.

"Honor bright, Paul, do you really want something to do?"

"Honor bright; I mean business, and you'll find I can stick to it!"

"What do you want me to hire you to do, now honestly? Smoke cigars?"

"No, only wheedle others into buying them, and make 'em think a miserable little two-cent one is a prime lot, best brand, and worth five cents at the very lowest. I know how, and I can do it."

The proprietor laughed and flushed. "You know too much," he said; "altogether too much. You have smoked too many cigars to be able to do much at selling."

"Then you won't hire me?"

"Not if I know myself, my boy. I mean to have a clerk who hasn't learned how to smoke."

"You want the pleasure of teaching him yourself, do you? All right"; and Paul shut the door and walked on. A curious sense of having had his good intentions ill treated came over him; it was a new feeling to have to bear. Heretofore his life had been on too low a plane to have been troubled with sensitiveness.

He stood at the corner perhaps five minutes trying to resolve not to go down to Tucker's. It was not the time of year to expect work of a carpenter, he argued. Stores and groceries were more likely places now that the holiday season was coming on. To be sure, there weren't many stores to try and help had always seemed wonderfully plenty; but then perhaps he better try them. So he did: walked up the main street on one side and down it on the other, stopping at every probable and finally every improbable place; and it was not until toward noon that he came back to that corner and strode resolutely down the street toward Tucker's carpenter shop. The truth was, he thought he didn't want to be a carpenter. And though he did not put it into words, he had a half-defined feeling of energy about him which he expressed afterwards by the sentence: "You see, I knew I should stick to it that time, and I wanted to be rather careful. I always know by my feelin's when I am going to stick."

Mr. Tucker, though for the sake of the boy's father had several times offered and urged work, was not in so accommodating a mood now; truth to tell, he had announced some time before that he "washed his hands of Paul Adams and should never try to do anything more with him: He was a shiftless fellow, and always would be; and he was going to the bad as fast as he could, and he—Jonas Tucker—couldn't help it." But then, all this was said under the firm belief that Paul Adams would never come his way asking for work. He wasn't ready to give it. He was suspicious of this sudden outburst of industry; he half believed there was some trick hidden away under the apparent honesty of purpose; but for all that, Jonas Tucker, being a good man in his way, found it not so easy to wash his hands of a responsibility after all. He argued the case with Paul, however; assured him that this was not the time of year when carpenter work was flush and that he would have no idlers about him, nor slippery fellows; everything had to be up to the mark, and if he *should* ever hire a boy to work for him again—which was doubtful—he should certainly discharge him for the first mean trick he did. And every word of objection he uttered developed in Paul Adams a curious determination to carry his point and get to work in the carpenter's shop. What he had started out upon reluctantly, as a last resort, he found himself doggedly bent on accomplishing. "I know I shall stick," he said to himself. "I feel it all over me; and I ain't sure but I shall kind of like to stick just here."

"What's started you up all of a sudden?" questioned Jonas Tucker, breaking in on his argument to ask this point-blank question. The answer was unhesitating:

"I want some money."

"Oh, you do! I should think it was about time. You've been acting all along as though you didn't know there was any such stuff as money in the world. What do you want money for? To help your mother?"

"No," said Paul Adams as promptly as before; but a streak of dark red blood began to creep up into his cheek. The question had roused a hundred others. What if he *should* earn money for his mother; support her as he had heard of sons doing? What if he *should* buy a carpet someday for the horrid little kitchen, and a lamp that didn't smoke, and a stove that would bake? It is an actual fact that the boy had slept so effectually through his seventeen or eighteen years of life as never to have considered before that such marvelous results were possible.

But he had no idea of telling Mr. Tucker about the new ideas, so he added to his no only this explanation: "I want it for myself."

"For yourself!" said Mr. Tucker in scorn. "A great

boy like you! What have you done yet for your mother but give her plenty of sleepless nights and red eyes, I'll be bound." And feeling by this time that he had no more "washed his hands" of the young man than he had gotten rid of his own heart, he determined to improve this opportunity, and then and there, standing in the shop door, the north wind blowing advance flakes of a coming snowstorm all about them, he read the boy a solemn lecture on the sins and follies of his youth and the probable evil disposition which he was about to make of his first earnings, provided he should ever earn anything, which was extremely doubtful. Little of which did young Paul hear. He was occupied in thinking if he should ever be able to buy a new lamp for his mother, what sort of a lamp it should be; and should the shade be pure white or have pink flowers on it?

But he "stuck" and was hired. No less to Mr. Tucker's astonishment than his own.

Not many days thereafter young Bennett stepped into the one large bookstore which Centerville possessed and, while stating his order, stopped in the midst of a sentence to say to the clerk who was a friend of his:

"What is the matter? You look as though you had seen an apparition."

"I have, and it has stunned me. The millennium is coming, or the world is coming to an end, or else there is going to be an earthquake."

"Why?" laughing at his dazed air; "what has happened?"

"Do you know the Ward boys?"

"Oh yes, I know them when I stumble over them at the corners or some other lounging place; what of them?"

"What would you say," asked the clerk, leaning over the counter and speaking in a confidential tone, "if you should see one of them buying a book?"

"Why, it might suggest the millennium, I admit," Bennett answered, laughing. "I didn't know they ever purchased any sort of book: a dime novel, I suppose?"

"No, sir, it wasn't; it was a history; the toughest of its kind, too. We don't sell a copy of it in a hundred years. In fact, I believe we never sold a copy, nor kept it to sell, until Dr. Monteith ordered a couple and we sent for a dozen. But I'd like to know what had got into people all of a sudden; come to think, they're all gone but one, and we've got an order for two more. What do you suppose is up?"

Light began to dawn on young Bennett's brain.

"Oh, you are talking about *Merivale's Rome,* I suppose." Still, he was astonished, as was evidenced by his next question: "Did the Wards really buy a copy?"

"They did so. Jim came in here as lofty as though he bought a book a week, and said he: 'Parker, I want a history of Rome, by a man named Merivale.' If he had asked me for a photograph of the man in the moon I couldn't have been more astonished; but I got it for him, and he paid for it and walked off. That was yesterday. But after all, it was nothing to the sensation that we had this afternoon; that was what cut me up so completely. I've sold next to the last copy of that very book, and you couldn't guess in a month of Sundays to whom. Do you happen to know that good-for-nothing youngster who hasn't a whole shirt to his name, I'll venture—unless his mother has earned it for him by going out washing? His name is Adams; Paul Adams."

"Yes, I know him; you don't say he has bought a book too?"

"He has bought a book too," repeated the clerk solemnly; "came and looked it over with the wisdom of a sage; demurred a little because the cover was black instead of brown; said he always had a hankering for brown things, and hated black; demurred still more at the price; said it was 'most an awful price' he should think for one book; but he took it and paid for it and went away peering into it as though it had a spell about it in some way. Now what does it all mean?"

"I really am not sure, but it means that those fellows are in earnest," said young Bennett musingly. "I declare, it looks as though they had ventured in; but I confess that I am astonished."

"Ventured into what?"

"Literature," replied young Bennett, laughing immoderately now. "Don't you know we have a literary society? I am sure I asked you to join it. *Merivale* is one of the books on our course."

"And the Ward boys and this young scamp of an Adams have joined!"

"Why, so it seems. I didn't know they contemplated it; they strayed into the meeting a week or so ago. I don't know how they happened to. I thought it was some good nature, or fun, of Robert Fenton's—we met at his father's; but really, this looks like an attempt at joining us."

"Pooh!" said Parker the clerk in intensest scorn.

"Oh, now that won't do, you know," was the lawyer's answer. "It isn't impossible that they may have determined on the sudden to make an effort after respectability; other young fellows have done the same and made men of themselves."

"And begun with *Merivale!*" answered Parker. "What egregious nonsense! Why, I know a little of history, and I give you my word of honor that I never saw a stupider edition than this same *Merivale;* I don't believe even a scholar could get interested in it; and the idea of Paul Adams! Why, he doesn't know three lines of the multiplication table! Stuff and nonsense."

It did look funny to them, and the two young men burst simultaneously into laughter. Bennett was the first to recover his gravity.

"I confess," he said, "if I had been going to mark out a course of study for them I should not have commenced with *Merivale,* and I doubt if any of the trio will look into it far enough to know whether it is dry or fresh; but I can't help being sort of glad to hear that they have actually bought one book. It adds to one's self-respect to see the gleams of manhood even in these worthless fellows. I say, Parker, come and join us and watch the joke."

"And study *Merivale!*" said Parker with a shrug of his shoulders. Nevertheless, when left alone he took down the only remaining copy of *Merivale* and looked it over curiously. If the Ward boys and Paul Adams had brains enough to read any of it, certainly he ought to have!

Doubtless the two young men would have been more amused still could they have seen Paul Adams that evening in his bit of a room by the light of a tallow candle. For some reason unexplainable to himself, he was averse to sitting by the smoky lamp in his mother's kitchen and studying his new book. He preferred the tallow candle which he had bought with his own money and set in a wooden block which he had hewn out at the carpenter's shop that day. The plan in the Adams's household had heretofore been for Paul to take the smoky lamp after his mother was through with it and retire by its vile light. So the tallow candle was an innovation.

If I were an artist and could draw a picture of poor Paul as he bent over *Merivale* on that first evening, you might laugh; doubtless you would; and yet, unless I am mistaken in you, your heart would have gone out in sympathy. How utterly hopeless it looked to him! He read over the first sentences six times without having an idea as to their meaning. He read through the entire page, and then closing the book found that he had not the remotest idea concerning it. The language was such as he was utterly unused to hearing. The subject was one about which he knew absolutely nothing. Of what earthly use was it for him to pore over that array of words? A dismal feeling of the impossibility of accomplishing anything tugged at his heart. Here had he spent a large part of his first earnings on a big book which was written in an unknown tongue! He would take it back tomorrow morning. He would tell that simpering clerk that he had made a mistake; it was not the book that he wanted—in fact, there was no book such as he wanted upon the earth. He would get back his money, and buy a gallon of oysters and ask the boys, and have a jolly evening, and let old Rome sink if it wanted to—provided it were now in existence, of which he was not perfectly sure. Then he would—and then he stopped. Why did there, just at that moment, come a vision to him of the fine form and finer features of Dr. Monteith? Why did it seem to him that he could feel the clasp of his hand and hear his genial voice saying: "Good evening, my friend, we are glad to see you. Mr. Harvey, this is my young friend, Paul Adams." *My* young friend! When had Paul Adams ever supposed he would hear such a sentence as that from such lips as those? He shaded his eyes from the blinking tallow candle and thought it all over. Was Paul Adams ambitious? He had never dreamed of such a thing. In truth he had never dreamed of any opportunity for being ambitious. He did not know the meaning of the word. He gave no thought to it this evening, but he knew he liked the sound of Dr. Monteith's voice and the clasp of his hand. I wonder if it is possible that some of those unseen beings who, after all, seem so near to earth and who may know some of the ends from the beginnings, all but held their breaths as they waited while Paul Adams hid his eyes from the blinking light?

He raised his head at last, and into the face there had come the stubborn look again, and he gave his decision aloud: "No, I won't. I've begun and I'll *stick!* Now then, old fellow, if you know anything at all about Rome and I know *myself*—and I think I do— I'll find out what you say. If there were nine hundred and seventy-nine thousand pages and each page was a yard long and took a week to read over, I'd go through it *now,* so there's no use talking." Then he spread the book on the rickety stand before him, fastened it open with two bits of board brought from the shop, spread out his feet under the table, leaned his hands on his knees, and said in a firm tone: "Now, then!" and set to work.

Eight o'clock, nine o'clock struck slowly and solemnly from the bell in the church tower not far distant. The kitchen door opened, and the tremulous voice of widow Adams called: "Paul, are you upstairs? Whatever are you about up there in the dark?"

"I've got a light."

"A light! Dear me! Where did you get it?"

"Bought it."

"What for? Are you sick?"

"No."

"Don't you mean to go down street tonight?"

"No."

"Dear me, Paul, I'm dreadful afraid you feel sick."

"No, I don't; I've got something I want to do."

"Can't you come down here with me and do it?"

"No, I've got to be up here."

"Paul, ain't it something that I can do for you?"

"No," said Paul again, in a loud tone, and then to himself: "It's nothing that I can do for myself in seventy-five years, as I see." Whereupon he chuckled a little; something of the ludicrousness of his mother's trying to read *Merivale's Rome* for him suggested itself.

The kitchen door shut slowly, irresolutely. His mother snuffed suspiciously and winked her eyes over her long, dark seam. "Something's going wrong," she murmured. Poor woman! As though something had not gone wrong with her most of the time since she was born! "He's been different ever since he went out that evening. There's some dark doings going on, and something will come of it. Oh dear me!"

The bell in the church tower tolled ten, and still Paul Adams sat over his book. A few leaves had been turned and turned back again; in fact, the first chapter had been carefully gone over I do not know how many times. Certain words scrawled in an unformed hand on a bit of paper indicated that a resolve had come to Paul to secure a dictionary somewhere, soon, and discover their meaning. A map that had been discovered had been turned to and carefully studied, and certain heavy dots made with the aforesaid pencil indicated that Paul had a suspicion that the places of which he had been reading were pictured here. The kitchen door opened softly again, and the quavering voice called:

"Paul, I've got some real hot water here. If you feel the least bit sick I can bring you some and soak your feet, and I can make you a cup of ginger tea in a twinkling." Then Paul laughed loud and long.

"I don't need soaking inside or out, Mother, just as true as you live. You go to bed; I'm going in a minute." Then the door closed again; but the long-suffering mother said:

"Something's to pay. Oh, dear me!" And two or three tears fell on the long seam she had finished.

The candle burned winkingly now, and needed snuffing sadly. Paul arose at last with something between a whistle and a sigh, unceremoniously blew out the blinking eye, regardless of the horrible odor therefrom, and prepared for rest, his thoughts busy with the evening's work. Not a question as to whether he should "stick" or not. He had one rare and helpful quality. He never took up settled questions and unsettled them again. But he had new thoughts tonight. He moved about slowly.

There's about a hundred and fifty questions that I'd like to ask somebody. I wonder who I'll ask? None of my friends know that's certain. I wonder how Joe and Jim get on? If I spend my evenings in "this confined and secluded eminence" I shan't know much about them. I vum, I believe I knew that first chapter pretty near by heart. Well, there's only eighty chapters. That isn't quite three months, after all. Oh, I'll stick, I know I shall! I'm as tired as though I had been weeding turnips a week without stopping. But, after all, it kind of seems to me as though I liked it.

9

SPHERES

MRS. CHESTER was in her element. It gave her almost more pleasure to gather her friends about her at a select entertainment than to do anything else in life. She was so comfortably conscious that her house was the largest and pleasantest and best furnished of any in town. It was so agreeable to think that her appointments were of the nicest, her servants almost the only really well-trained ones in the neighborhood, and that her guests would be certain to go home commenting on the perfection of all the details. Why should she not enjoy giving pleasure to people? It was not a large gathering. In the first place she did not believe in "crushes," and in the second place, if she had, there were not choice people enough in Centerville to fill her large parlors. She had none but choice people, so-called.

To be sure, the Van Martins were always invited, although Mr. Van Martin was not given, at any time, to using very choice language and, when he was angry enough, was liable to use oaths and was only too apt to come home frequently the worse for liquor. But then, as Mrs. Chester sweetly remarked, his wife was a most estimable woman, a perfect lady in dress and manners, and for her part she thought it uncharitable to let people suffer for the sins of their husbands. I really suppose Mrs. Chester is correct, though why, since she believed in and adopted that principle, she never invited Mrs. Barber, who lived at the foot of Van Martin's lane and whose husband always used good language when sober and bought his liquor of a man who always bought it at Van Martin's wholesale house in the city, I shall not undertake to explain.

On the evening of which I write, a very select company was gathered in the handsome parlors, and sociability was at its height. The Ward boys were not there, certainly; neither was Paul Adams: in fact, at that moment he was poring over *Merivale* in a way that would have gratified that author. But Mrs. Fenton, in her becoming dark-green silk-and-velvet suit, sat in a cozy corner of the room talking socially with Dr. Monteith, while over at the piano young Bennett turned the leaves of the long and intricate piece of instrumental music which Miss Aimie Allison was faithfully banging for the benefit, apparently, of aiding the conversationalists to be more confidential about their chosen themes—for it was most noticeable that none of the company, if I except young Bennett himself, was listening to the banging. Caroline was there, of course. Mrs. Chester would have felt it impossible to give a social entertainment without Caroline's presence. She appeared from time to time during the evening, now with a salver bearing cut-glass goblets of water, again with ices and coffee and fruits, moving quietly, skillfully among the different groups with such a practiced eye for details that no one of the company was allowed to realize a moment's neglect, with such quiet swiftness that the business of waiting on the guests to the numerous dishes that fashion decrees necessary to an evening entertainment seemed to be gotten over with much less delay than is usual. Mrs. Fenton, watching Caroline in her dark, plain dress and linen collar and cuffs, her hair destitute of flower or ribbon now—for she was one who never added those little touches save among her friends—could not help thinking how entirely capable the girl was of sitting down beside her and enjoying Dr. Monteith's conversation. She detained her just a moment while she helped herself to fruit: "Dr. Monteith is telling me about his visit to Rome, Caroline, and it is more interesting than *Merivale.*"

"Is it?" said Caroline, smiling and flushing; she would not be guilty of saying she wished she could hear it, but Dr. Monteith glanced up quickly at the name of *Merivale* and said in a somewhat wondering tone: "Why, good evening!" It was evident that he had not recognized her before, though she had served him to coffee. "I am sure you must like *Merivale,* notwithstanding Mrs. Fenton's insinuation: it is beautifully written, I think."

"I did not say that it wasn't," Mrs. Fenton replied promptly; "still, I like best to talk face-to-face with one who has seen for himself. Don't you think that is an improvement, Caroline?"

"I should think it would be." And then she moved quickly away. What would Mrs. Chester think if she should see her second girl apparently carrying on a familiar conversation with Mrs. Fenton and Dr. Monteith!

"How is that?" the doctor asked, and he looked after Caroline with a puzzled air. "Who is Miss—Caroline? I can't at this moment recall having heard her other name. Is she a good friend of this family who makes herself useful?"

"Her name is Caroline Raynor; she gets it from a great grandfather of German extraction, I believe, and she has been Mrs. Chester's second girl for several years and is a good friend of mine. I believe I think rather more of her than of any other young lady of my acquaintance."

There was a little flush on Mrs. Fenton's cheeks that had not been there a moment before and a bright light in her eyes. She was by no means a strong-minded woman; perhaps I mean, rather, a strong-*hearted* woman; it cost her an effort to make this avowal. It was such a long stride away from conventionality, and Centerville, like most little towns, having a vein of aristocracy in them, with little to build aristocracy out of, was very particular about the conventionalities.

Dr. Monteith regarded her for a moment with a thoughtful air and a keen glance that looked quickly and satisfactorily beneath the surface of things, and then, screened from general view as they were by the overshadowing of a large and high ornamented fire screen, he suddenly held out his hand.

"Let us shake hands over the advance step which you have evidently taken, Mrs. Fenton, in putting real merit before the accident of position. I like that, and if I can at any time serve you in your plans, I shall be gladly at your service."

"I wish," said Mrs. Fenton to herself, "that that was something I could tell Caroline. What a grand man he is!"

Dr. Monteith was not ready to let the subject drop. He cross-questioned a little concerning Caroline. Wasn't she an unusual person for her years? What had been her advantages? How had she been reduced to her present position? How had Mrs. Fenton fallen in with her? By what means had she been induced to join the C.L.S.C.?

"Yes, she was an unusual girl," Mrs. Fenton answered emphatically. "She has never had any advantages save that of a good mother. She was not 'reduced' in position; on the contrary, she has advanced, her present place bringing her better wages and more quiet than she had ever enjoyed before. As to joining the Circle," the lady said, warming with her subject, "to tell you the truth, the Circle joined her; at least, our branch of it. She was actually struggling along alone; had commenced the course—last year's—and was making a brave fight. I had to go to her for much of my information after I became interested."

"But where did she get the idea, or learn of the existence, of such an institution? You say she has had no advantages above her present position?"

"She 'picked it up,'" Mrs. Fenton said, laughing, and then, moved by that subtle sense of being in company with a sympathetic nature, which we sometimes feel even in talking with strangers, she told him the story of the faithful, struggling mother and her homely watchword, "Pick 'em up, Car'line," which had held itself as a banner over the girl from her babyhood, urging her forward. When the brief story was concluded, Dr. Monteith sat in silence; that sort of silence which can be felt. Mrs. Fenton glanced once at the clear-cut, intellectual features, then dropped her eyes. Was it possible that there were tears in his?

"This story moves me strangely," he said at last, and his voice was certainly husky. "I had a good mother, and I came up through all the younger portion of my life in a hand-to-hand struggle with poverty."

It was about that time that young Bennett first noticed the existence of Caroline. He studied her face doubtfully for a moment, then bent his tall self to Aimie, who had finished pounding the piano and was standing at his side.

"Where have I seen that girl who is serving those tardy people in the back parlor to fruit? Her face looks curiously familiar."

"Why, Mr. Bennett, I am surprised at your disloyalty to our Circle! She is one of the prominent members."

"Ah, it is in that capacity that I have seen her. I remember now. Well, what is she doing here, in this position?"

"This is her legitimate position: she is Mrs. Chester's second girl."

Mr. Bennett elevated his eyebrows. He was a young man of fine family, with high notions as regarded birth and blood, and I am afraid money also. He did not mean to be a simpleton, but despite his usual good sense, he could not help saying to the bit of silk and lace beside him: "Upon my word, things are getting somewhat mixed."

"Yes," said the fair little parrot, "I think they are." And by so much did he make Caroline's road harder for her. All unintentionally, too, for young Bennett was a gentleman, and having been introduced to Caroline by no less responsible a person than Mrs. Fenton, had he met her on the street the next day, he would have acknowledged the acquaintance by a courteous bow without reference to her position as Mrs. Chester's servant.

The most dangerous people in society are the aforesaid parrots, who copy without thought what they see and hear, and who, like the genuine parrots, generally exaggerate the original. Miss Aimie Allison determined then and there that she really must avoid noticing Caroline again, as she almost had to do the other day.

Later in the evening Mrs. Fenton found herself seated by her old acquaintance Jack Butler, and it chanced that she had not held any conversation with him since the day he undertook to quench her literary aspirations under a deluge of words about the superficiality of the entire scheme. He had in no sense lost his patronizing manner.

"Well, Mrs. Fenton," he said, turning suddenly from a younger face to give her her crumb of attention, "how are your hopes? Do you still have a longing to see a Literary and Scientific Circle flourishing around you?"

"Why, Jack," said Mrs. Fenton, who had lost all sense of awe for the wise young man, "you are quite behind the times! Our Circle is formed and flourishing."

"Is it, indeed! I am surprised and congratulate you. Who is your presiding officer, may I ask? Upon my word, they ought to have elected you."

"Oh no, we have one much better suited to the position. We honored Dr. Gilbert Monteith with that office."

"Dr. Gilbert Monteith!" And Mrs. Fenton will always laugh when she thinks of the unbounded astonishment in Jack's voice and the sudden way in which he came out of his graceful lounging attitude into an erect posture and the instant dropping of his unnecessary eyeglasses, to give her a genuine stare from his own honest eyes as he said: "Why, how on earth—"

Just then occurred a diversion. It chanced that Jack's

little sister Laura was a special friend of Elinore Chester, aged six, and therefore had been permitted to come and help her small friend get in the way of her elders, and enjoy the unwonted lateness of the hour and unlimited cake and fruit. The said Laura, having wandered away from her companion for a few minutes and found the conversation of her elders uninteresting, had drawn a large book from the table near her and given herself up to its fascinations until suddenly, with the utter indifference of childhood to the interests of other people, she dashed into the midst of the conversation with a question:

"Jack, what is the Palatine?"

"Laura," said the sage gravely, "you should not interrupt conversation." And Miss Laura, who had probably been told that same truth about five hundred times, patiently leaned against her brother's chair and patiently waited while he constructed an unusually elaborate sentence, making it as long as he conveniently could, trying, meanwhile, to puzzle out for himself a reason why the eminent scholar in their midst should have seen fit to toy with this Chautauqua scheme. At the first semblance of a pause Laura repeated her question, her eyes riveted on the outline picture which had called it forth.

"Please tell me what the Palatine is, and where it is, and all about it, Jack."

"Really, Laura, I think I shall have to petition mother to send you into retirement if you cannot observe better manners!" The young oracle had flushed hotly, and his tone was that which in common parlance we call cross. He was so young and had made so little progress in the career of a scholar that he really felt it an overwhelming disgrace to be obliged to admit to his little sister that his present ideas of the

Palatine were too foggy to present to her with any degree of clearness. Indeed, so great was his present confusion that, for the moment, he hardly knew whether the word *Palatine* applied to anything with which he had ever been acquainted.

Part of his discomfiture was certainly caused by the knowledge of the fact that Mrs. Fenton's eyes had a mischievous smile in them, as though she were triumphing over him in some way, and he had a horror of being triumphed over.

"Oh, dear!" said the young seeker after facts. "I wish I knew." Then Mrs. Fenton bent forward and addressed her:

"I'll tell you, dear; it was—and is—one of the seven hills of Rome—the central one; very beautifully situated and interesting because of a great many things which you will learn when you are old enough to study history."

"Laura is much obliged to you, I am sure." It was Jack's voice, but the crossness had by no means gone out of it, and Mrs. Fenton wondered in an amused way which he would like to shake, Laura or herself; or whether he did not think both deserved it.

He went on with his attempt to show himself at ease.

"She is a terror to all her acquaintances, a perfect walking interrogation point; it is sometimes necessary to resort to sternness in order to be relieved of the nuisance of turning oneself into an encyclopedia. You are quite a historian, Mrs. Fenton."

"I don't pretend to be well posted," Mrs. Fenton said with dancing eyes, and a mouth that laughed despite her quiet answer: "My knowledge of history is quite superficial, but I believe it is correct as far as it goes."

10

ACCICENTS(?)

THE Ward family were at the breakfast table. A break-fast table where no mother presides seems at all times a dreary sight. And if, in addition to that, no feminine hand save a hireling's ministers to the comfort of the family, the desolation is increased. Still, there is certainly a difference in hirelings. The one who presided over the Ward household was the poorest of her kind. Therefore, the tablecloth was drearily spotted with yolk of eggs, coffee stains, gravy stains, and the like. Also, it was put on in a drearily crooked manner and had a dreary hole at one end. Mr. Ward, Sr., looked older by several years than he ought and stirred his muddy coffee in a desolate way, and looked with a discouraged air at the slices of stale bread and the untidy butter plate, and felt as though he wanted no breakfast for some reason, and yet must get through the form of eating it. His two sons were seated on opposite sides of the table and were the only other occupants of the room. Nancy, the housekeeper and maid-of-all-work, who usually occupied the seat at the foot of the table, was absent this morning intent on some kitchen work, and father and sons were alone. James was rather gratified over this state of things, for he had a matter of importance to bring before his father. Since the evening that we first made this young man's acquaintance, he had had some strange experiences. It would have been impossible for him to have explained to any person the reasons for the numerous revulsions of feeling which he had endured.

A hundred times—so it seemed to him—had he gone over the story of his past life and the possibilities of the future and pronounced himself a fool, and a dolt, and a hulking scoundrel, and sundry other hard names with which his street life had made him familiar. There were times when he told himself that it was too late to make any changes now; he was nothing but an ignoramus and would never be anything else. He was unlike Paul Adams, in that he could not settle a question at once and leave it settled; instead, he went back to it again and again, going over the same ground and coming to different conclusions according to the mood in which he started. There were days when he was not so much disgusted with anything in life as with his copy of *Merivale*. There had as yet been no time in which he had settled himself with a determination to master it: Such a determination as Paul brought to his first chapter. Yet by degrees had James Ward been drawn steadily toward the decision for which his friends were watching. Such a succession of curious and apparently trivial incidents as had contributed toward this decision!

One afternoon when he was coming slowly down the street with his head bent on the ground, going over the problem and wondering how he could decently reply in the negative to a note that Dr. Mon-

teith had sent him, giving him a special invitation to
the next Circle, he came in direct contact with that
gentleman. He had studied out an answer by that time,
and it was in the negative, and he felt cross and defiant;
in the precise mood not to care what Dr. Monteith
thought of him. "Now for it"; he said, as he saw the
gentleman approaching rapidly: "I'll tell him no, I
won't come; that I wasn't cut out for a scholar, and
there is no use in trying to spoil the pattern. I'll tell
him there are too many literary stuck-ups now, and I
don't want to swell the number, and that I think my
kind of life is the gayer of the two, and I mean to stick
to it, and he can just let me alone."

Did Mr. Monteith, careful student of human nature
as he was, see the defiant glitter in the young man's
eyes? If he did he made no sign; neither did he ask for
any momentous decision. Instead he said heartily:

"Ha! Ward, perhaps you are just the man I want.
Don't you pass Mr. Allison's on your way home? I
thought so. Could you accommodate me by calling at
the door and leaving this package for Miss Aimie? It
is some C.L.S.C. circulars that I promised she should
have this evening. She wished them for special reference, I think, and I am unusually busy tonight."

How was a reasonable person to refuse so simple a
request as that, even though he were cross? Young
Ward did not see his way clear to saying no, albeit he
took the package somewhat reluctantly.

"Thank you," said the doctor still heartily, ignoring
the ungraciousness, if he saw it. "If you chance to see
Miss Aimie, perhaps you will be kind enough to
explain to her that the full course is not announced in
this circular; there are certain studies not yet arranged
that will be duly announced later."

If he should chance to see Miss Aimie! The suggestion was a startling one. He had never rung Mr. Allison's doorbell: he had never expected to as a caller. It seemed to him a very near approach to that condition to be sent on an errand to Miss Aimie with a verbal message for her. The suggestion was not entirely unpleasant; still, it was not in the least likely he should see the young lady. "I know one thing, I shan't ask for her," he told himself as he transferred the package to his pocket.

But behold, Miss Aimie was in the hall, on her way to the door, when the bell rang. She was in her new walking suit, and the cunningest of fur caps was perched jauntily on one side of her head; a great green bird, looking as though it had just alighted there to peer at her a minute, adorned its front, and altogether Miss Aimie was pretty to behold. She advanced and opened the door herself. Now, although her good resolution not to be acquainted with Caroline was taken so recently, young Ward was a different person. He certainly was no second help in anyone's house, and he was a young man. Miss Aimie was of the type of silly girlhood to whom a young man is a continued and irresistible source of pleasure. To be sure, young Ward bore a most unenviable reputation; she had more than once heard her father say that he was a hard case and would bring up in state prison yet if he continued to do nothing but lounge around the streets and smoke cigars; but still, she could no more help being chatty and agreeable to him than she could help looking like a butterfly that was going to float away into the air.

"Oh, good evening," she said. "Are those the circulars that Dr. Monteith promised me? I'm going to send one to my cousin Harvey. I want him to get up a Circle, but I don't believe he will. Harvey is a real dunce about books; he doesn't like to read; he *hates* history, he says; but I tell him this is very different from sitting down alone and reading. Don't you think so?"

Young Ward admitted that he did, and then he bethought himself of Dr. Monteith's directions and gave them as lucidly as he could; and Miss Aimie thanked him and chatted on, and finally it transpired that she was just going downtown and would walk with him as far as the corner; so they went down Main Street together; and it is a singular fact that it was the first time in his life that young Ward ever found himself walking in the pleasant light of a winter sunset side by side with a well-dressed, ladylike girl! I am not sure that he was conscious of any connection between the two when he reconsidered the question of the Circle after leaving Miss Aimie at the corner and concluded that perhaps he would do well to try a little while, anyway. He could drop off at any time he chose. If he could have gone home with Aimie and been invisible while the Allison family gathered at the supper table and listened to the conversation, I cannot undertake to say what effect it might have had on his resolution. Something like this occurred: "Aimie, did my eyes deceive me, or did I see you walking out this afternoon with that scapegrace of a Ward? I put on my glasses and came to the office door to look after you, and even then I felt as though I must be mistaken." It was her father's voice, and her mother exclaimed: "Why Aimie Allison! It isn't possible that you were out walking with *him!*"

In the same breath her sixteen-year-old brother said: "Upon my word, Aimie, you aimed high this afternoon! Didn't you?"

"Oh, now," said Miss Aimie, "what a commotion you are making about nothing. He stopped at the door with some papers that Dr. Monteith sent around to me just as I was going out, and I couldn't well avoid walking to the corner with him."

"Dr. Monteith! Is Jim Ward his errand boy?" This from the brother.

Then Miss Aimie: "No, he *isn't.*"

Then the father: "No, I'll be bound he isn't. He hasn't that amount of respectability about him. He is too lazy ever to be anyone's errand boy."

"My dear," said the mother, "I am afraid you are too careless about your appearance on the street. I hope you will take care that you are not his companion again, even as far as the corner. I shouldn't like to have your name mentioned in connection with him."

Before Aimie could pucker her pretty lips for an answer, her father saved her the trouble.

"No, indeed, Daughter; I suppose your good nature is equal to doing almost anything to save a person's feelings, but James Ward is not the sort of fellow whose feelings need to be carefully considered. I won't have you walking with him even to the corner. Don't forget it!"

"I haven't the least desire to, Papa."

And here the conversation drifted into other channels, father and mother Allison feeling comfortable over the thought that they had thus warned their lamb of the danger of evil associates and helped to guard her against future indiscretions. One cannot help wishing that Aimie had been the sort of girl to whom her father could have said: "Well, Daughter, I saw you taking a few steps with young Ward today; I suppose you remember whose banner you fight under while you walked with him and tried to prevail on him to enlist, didn't you?" But then, in order to make that remark, Mr. Allison would have had to be a different father from the one he was.

Meantime James began to grow very weary of his indecision and to wish that something would happen to settle it for him one way or the other. Something did happen. Curiously enough, Paul Adams had a hand in the matter. His devotion to *Merivale,* which continued at white heat, so absorbed his evenings that although Joe, especially, missed him sadly and tried heartily to beguile him into his old haunts, it had been in vain.

Joe, by the way, about whom I find I have said nothing, was insufferably bored by this entire matter. It took none of his time to reach a decision: he would have none of it. Books were not to his mind, never had been, never would be; he cared not a fig for Mrs. Fenton's parlor or for Dr. Monteith's notice. Miss Aimie might bow and smile upon him for a month at a time, and it would have made no more difference to him than her ignoring of his existence would have done. Save so far as it had ruined Paul and made his brother a silent nuisance, Joe bore the Circle no ill will, but he wanted nothing of it. It in no sense appealed to his sympathies. What was there that would?

"What is Paul about evenings, anyway?" asked James Ward, suddenly awaking to the fact that his brother had been grumbling for half an hour over some failure of plans owing to Paul's desertion.

"About! Why, he's swallowing that outrageous book that you were such a stupid as to buy. He pores over it all day in the shop and all night at home and is going stark crazy, I verily believe, over the blamed old Romans. I wish they had been drowned in their famous Tiber before ever I heard of them."

Here was food for thought. James Ward turned the puzzle over in his mind during the day, trying to solve it. When at school he had been judged a passable scholar, quick to learn when he chose to apply himself; and more than once his teacher had told him confidentially that there was the stuff in him to make a student of, if he would work. Down deep in his heart, James had always carried a sort of fancy that if his mother had lived and had wanted him to, very much indeed, he would have worked at his books and been a scholar to please her. But the father did not care for books, and there seemed nobody to please and no motive sufficiently strong to keep him out of mischief. But here was Paul Adams, who had never done anything in school, never been to any but the very ordinary common school, while James had spent nearly two years at the academy; and Paul Adams was poring over *Merivale's Rome*, while he had not been able to get through three chapters of it.

It chanced that that very evening Paul took a holiday and came down to see his old friends. They sat up until after ten o'clock in that same disorderly room, and James questioned and cross-questioned the boy thus suddenly transformed into the student. There was no denying the fact that he was desperately in earnest about Rome, and also wonderfully interested. More than that, he was able to impart information.

"See here," he said, and he had drawn from his pocket a thick, smooth board covered all over with dots and lines: "Here are the seven hills as large as life—that is, if you put imagination enough into it. And here's the Tiber winding along—goes this way and then that. Up here are the Apennines, and over there are the Alps; tall fellows those, I tell you; but the seven hills aren't so very high. This old Palatine is my favorite; nicest location that for a house that I know of! When I build mine I think of putting it there."

Then did James pour the puzzled questions at him, while Joe sat with his hands in his pocket, a look of unutterable disgust on his face, whistling *Hail Columbia*. There was certainly no doubt about it: Paul Adams was becoming acquainted with Rome.

If he can understand the book and get interested in it like this, there is no reason on earth why I shouldn't. This was James Ward's decision; and just then he leaned very far toward a definite settlement in favor of the C.L.S.C.

One more gentle wave would carry him over the bar, and it came to him the very next afternoon; came, too, through Aimie Allison's unthinking aid. He was passing up the one main street, and the afternoon being pleasant, it was unusually filled with promenaders, among them pretty Miss Aimie in a more becoming street suit than before, and by her side Jack Butler. He bowed, and Miss Aimie, albeit she would hardly have had the courage to have walked with him again to the corner, had no disposition in her gay little heart to ignore so admiring a bow as he bestowed upon her, especially as she insisted to herself that he had real handsome eyes!

"What on earth is that fellow bowing to you for?" said Jack.

"What fellow?" And the bright eyes were raised to the speaker.

"Why that Ward youngster. How does he happen to be sufficiently acquainted with you to bow?"

"Oh, we are acquainted. I met him at Mrs. Fenton's—at our Circle, you know."

"Upon my word! I did not know. Your Circle is no respecter of persons, it seems. Really that is too rich!" And Jack Butler laughed in a tone that so finished a gentleman ought to have known was too loud for the street.

Then he added: "Why, my dear Miss Aimie, your charity is unbounded; but that boy is simply a street lounger. He hasn't brains enough to be anything very bad. Still, I would just as soon you wouldn't recognize his bow."

Young Ward passed on, but his face was white and his eyes burned. He had not learned delicacy of speech in his street life, so perhaps it is not strange that he expressed himself after this wise: "You insufferable puppy! If I hadn't more brains than you have, I'd knock them out on the nearest tree. We'll see if I can't provoke some other emotion besides ridicule by belonging to a literary society."

And the momentous decision, having passed through as many windings as the Tiber itself, was finally made.

11

◄═╬═►

TO THE RESCUE

BETWEEN the succession of apparent accidents that
had at last brought James Ward to a decision and the
time that he sat with his father and brother at the
breakfast table, several weeks had intervened.

There had been four meetings of the C.L.S.C., and
both Paul Adams and James Ward were emphatically
identified with it. As for Joe, he might be called a
hanger-on; he attended the meetings because it was so
much a part of his nature to go where James did that
he would not have known himself had he done
otherwise. But it was always under protest: he growled
continually, and yet between times unwittingly
strengthened his brother's resolution by prophesying
that this sort of thing wouldn't last, that he and Paul
would soon get tired of pretending to be what they
were not and would drop back into the old life. Now
a certain type of character is always strengthened by
being assured of prospective failure. James Ward grew
more determined with every passing day to succeed.
Meantime, his father was watching him with a bewildered feeling that he did not know his own son. That

something had changed him was evident. Of his own will he had asked for a place in the store from which his indolence had shut him out more than a year before and was holding steadily to business hours and habits; but the father lived in daily expectation, like Joe, of seeing him "get tired of this sort of thing." The literary society he had heard of and dismissed with a half sneer. Not that he despised learning; he would have been not only willing, but proud, had one of his sons chosen the life of a student; but that they were no students, and could by no process of their own become such, or, indeed, *anything* else that was desirable, was a belief so firmly fixed that nothing as yet had shaken it. His manner toward either of the sons had not materially changed, and yet occasionally James imagined that there was a shade less gruffness than usual and that he listened with some degree of interest when business questions were being discussed. If James could have known how often he said to himself with a sigh: "If his mother had lived, she would have made a businessman of him, I believe," he would have understood his father better. On this particular morning James had a request to make, so strange in itself that his face was flushed with embarrassment, and he turned over and over in his mind various ways of presenting it. His father would be severely unbelieving as to the sense of the suggestion, and Joe would laugh. Both laughter and severity James Ward hated. Still, he proposed to brave them.

"Father, the literary society to which we belong has voted to meet at the houses of the different members. Could we invite them to come here, do you think?"

He was mistaken about Joe.

That young man was too much astonished to laugh: instead, he stared.

"Literary society!" and the father sneered. "Since when did you become literary?" This question brought Joe's laugh.

"I am not over and above literary yet," said James, striving to retain his temper, "but I belong to a literary society and would like to have them meet at our house if you have no objection."

"That is just another name for nonsense or, what is worse, I suppose, card playing and the mischief knows what, going on under cover of literature. I have heard of such things before."

James Ward felt very angry, especially as Joe laughed; to be sure, Joe was only laughing at his father's mistake in setting the company who gathered at the C.L.S.C. meetings to card playing or anything else that was disreputable; but how could his brother know that? Still, James, having a point to carry, struggled with his insulted feelings.

"We have nothing going on at these meetings that you could object to, sir; the names of the members are a sufficient guarantee for that."

"Your name, for instance"; this time with an undoubted sneer.

"No, sir, not my name. No one can understand better than I how worthless that would be in your eyes."

The moment the words were spoken he was sorry for them. With all his faults James Ward had never been guilty of actual face-to-face impudence toward his father; it had always seemed to him that a certain dim memory of his mother came between him and the words he might have said. Silence fell between them for a little, during which time James Ward told himself that this was the last favor he would ever ask of his father; that he had been trying for weeks to do his best and had been treated as sternly as though he were making rapid strides toward ruin all the time, which only served to show how little his father really cared for him. Just as soon as it was possible to get away from home he would go. He had been treated like a baby long enough. Just at this point the grim-voiced father spoke again:

"What names do you propose to offer as a guarantee of respectability?"

"Young Bennett, the law student, is a member, and the Fentons, and Mrs. Dayton Allen, and Judge Allison's daughter, and the Burtons; and Dr. Monteith is our president."

How James Ward enjoyed pouring out this list of eminently respectable names to the utter astonishment of his father!

"Who?" said the amazed man, apparently not daring to trust his ears over the last-mentioned name.

"Professor Monteith, sir: he is spending the year here, you know." There was no reply to this; whether the father was stunned or whether he was doubtful did not appear. Joe chuckled a little; he was capable of seeing the ludicrous side of most anything, and he rejoiced over his father's astonishment. In fact, much as he hated the Circle, he decided to volunteer some information: "You might keep on, Jim; we have a good many names more stunning than the ones you have given. We've got the top of the heap, sir, in our set this time."

Still no answer from the father. James drank another cup of coffee, helping himself, since the slovenly Nancy chose not to appear, and concluded that his plans were a failure. Then Mr. Ward said slowly, doubtfully: "Our house is hardly in condition to entertain company. We used to keep things in shape years ago, but we are far from having things like other people now."

Then James, speaking eagerly: "Oh, it is not like company. They don't need entertaining: All we want is a room with lamps and a fire in it. The parlor would do very well if Nancy were to sweep and dust it."

"I don't believe that chimney will draw. It is almost a dozen years, seems to me, since we had a fire in that stove; still, the chimney might be cleaned—ought to be, I suppose."

"It will be a good thing to get the room dusted. I went in there the other day, and I raised such a cloud of dust that it set me to coughing." This from Joe.

His father turned toward him, a puzzled look on his face. "Do you belong to this wonderful literary set, too?" he asked.

"Yes and no," said Joe, laughing. "I go because Jim does and because Dr. Monteith invites me every time he meets me, and because Bob Fenton, for some reason, likes to have me come; and he's a plucky little chap, and I like to please him; but I don't plunge into the books as though my life depended on knowing just how many times the old Romans turned around, as Jim and the rest do. I don't think literature is my forte, sir; but I give them my encouragement all the same. I'm a kind of honorary member, I guess."

"I hope they feel honored," was his father's sharp reply; but there was a little drawing at the corners of his mouth, as though if he had only been used to it enough to know how, he would have liked to laugh. Then he finished in silence his coffee, which James poured for him. At last he said: "There ought to be two or three new lamps before anything of that kind is done; Nancy has about ruined the old ones; they were bought a good while ago, I suppose"; and another sigh testified to his sense of the dreariness of the time since his home had fallen into decay. "Well, tell Nancy what you want, and I'll see that she does it; as long as you bring respectable people to the house, it can't hurt. But mind, I'll have no nonsense: none of the things that I forbade years ago must be done under this roof." A moment of hesitation, then a tremulous clearing of his throat, and the silence of years was broken: "Your mother didn't believe in any of those things, and if I did myself—which I don't—I wouldn't have her memory dishonored."

"It never shall be, sir," James Ward said in a low, moved tone, and Joe looked gravely down at his plate; and if the father had but known it, he had done more to draw his sons into the right road by that one sentence than by any words that he had spoken before in years.

So the formal invitation for the Circle to hold its next meeting at Mr. Ward's was given, to the amazement of some and the intense satisfaction of others. Indeed, Mrs. Fenton and Dr. Monteith shook hands over it, as a token that a long stride had been taken on the upward road. "We must do everything that we can to make that meeting a success," Dr. Monteith said heartily.

But it was very near being a failure. James Ward did his best. He mended the broken hinge of the stove door, and glued the broken ends of two wall brackets, and put new cord on his mother's portrait, and finally pulled off his coat one morning and gave the old stove such a coat of black and then such a polish as it had not known for years. The father on his part was mindful of the new order of things, and selected and sent up from the store four of the finest lamps in stock, and himself gave most careful directions to Nancy regarding their management.

As for Nancy, she was much dazed. She had lived in the Ward household for several years, and an innovation like this had never been seen. She grumbled not a little to herself over her extra work and declared that these new doings were not at all to her mind. Whether it was punishment or whether she hailed it as a relief, I will not attempt to say, but on the very day before the important evening, what did Nancy do but let her two cheeks puff out like pillows and her neck on either side swell even with her cheeks! An unmistakable case of mumps; and poor Nancy, unused to pain of any kind, rebelled at this, and believed that she was sick unto death, and insisted on being bundled into a sleigh and carried home. And the parlor was still unswept, to say nothing of hall and stairs; neither were the hundred little things done that crowd together calling for attention so sure as company is expected. What was to be done? James and Joe discussed the question with dismayed faces. Joe was sympathetic. He did not believe in the Circle, still he desired that it should receive all honor in his father's house. There was a free-hearted hospitality naturally about Joe that would have made him a good host, given the chance.

"We shall just have to give it up," James said at last, intense disappointment on his face. Just then came Paul on his way to afternoon work.

"What's up?" he asked, halting, seeing the look of dismay on the faces of both brothers.

How could Paul Adams help them? Still feeling the need of sympathy from some quarter, they gave him a detailed account of Nancy's unfeeling behavior and the disaster that had followed.

Paul stood first on one foot and then on the other,

to keep himself warm, and whistled. Presently he spoke: "There's Mother." So confident did he seem of this fact that the Wards looked around, expecting to see the small lean form of Mrs. Adams appearing in sight from around the corner; but Paul's eyes were cast meditatively on the ground, and after a brief silence from all parties, he continued: "She knows how to sweep and dust and all that kind of thing, you know; and she isn't going to be very busy tomorrow, because she was wishing this morning that she had some more shirts to make; and she is always ready to do things for folks, so that if you wanted her, you know—"

Here Paul paused, in doubt as to how to proceed. It was entirely new business for him—this offering to accommodate people with the loan of his mother. Light began to dawn on James Ward's troubled face; he felt a sudden sense of respect for Paul, nay, almost of envy: for had not Paul a *mother*? But he spoke eagerly:

"I begin to see daylight. You are pretty sure she would come, Paul, for a little while and help us through?"

Paul nodded emphatically. "She would if I wanted her to," he said with a certain confident air in her willingness to gratify him, which made the hearts of the Wards twinge again with a little touch of envy: they felt sure that their mother would have done things to gratify them.

So it was agreed that this new idea should be presented to the elder Ward forthwith. He received the intelligence with that sort of ejaculation which may mean almost anything according as you are in the mood to interpret; but at the tea table, after a more silent meal than usual, he said precisely in the tone that he would have used had the subject been up for discussion between them: "Very well; one of you go around to the widow Adams's this evening and see if she will come tomorrow morning and spend the day and do what is to be done; I'll give her a dollar." And the Ward boys knew enough of the widow Adams's condition and of their father's habits to be aware that this was a good offer for her, and benevolence in him.

Directly that dismal supper was concluded—and the family were each secretly astonished to discover how much more dismal it could be without Nancy than with her—James proceeded on his way. The widow Adams was not exactly averse to the proceeding, but she was bewildered. She had by no means recovered from her bewilderment over Paul; every added day that saw him go steadily to his work was an astonishment to her. For weeks she had believed that he was working to raise money to carry out some dark scheme, the details of which had been planned on that first memorable weekday evening when he had insisted on having a clean shirt. For she was still in lamentable ignorance of the proceedings of that evening; she had no friends who could enlighten her; she had heard nothing further of the C.L.S.C., so she brooded in silence. Do Paul the justice to understand that he had forgotten all about the mystery and had no idea that he was daily wringing his mother's heart. Within a few days a wonderful thing had occurred: Paul had brought home and placed on the kitchen table a brand-new lamp, filled and trimmed, which, when lighted, shed a halo of brightness over the dismal room such as it had not seen for years. Over this present, the widow Adams had both laughed and wept; since which time she had gone around in an utterly dazed way: She did not know what she thought. Still she looked upon this new departure with grave suspicion. What could the Ward boys want of her? Likely they wanted her to come to their house and sweep and clear up! Why, they lived in that great square brick house on the corner! The boys were just playing a trick on her. They were hard boys, up to all sorts of pranks; it had troubled her all her life that Paul would have anything to do with them. "I don't care if their father is a rich man," she would say with great earnestness—for to the widow Adams's vision Mr. Ward was a rich man—"I'd rather you would grow up poor as Job was after he lost everything, and be respectable." Then would Paul good-naturedly assure her that he was poor enough, and as to the respectability, he would think about it.

He gave over trying to enlist her sympathies in favor of the Wards, since he could not make her understand what was wanted; and trusted to their own efforts to bring matters right.

It proved not to be a very difficult thing to do. Dollar bills were not so plenty in the widow Adams's experience that she could afford to lose this opportunity of earning one by spending a day at the Wards, "with nothing in life to do," as she expressed it in a bewildered way to Paul when he ate his early breakfast the next morning. "Nothing in life to do but sweep and dust and get them poor creatures some dinner and supper."

"Get 'em good ones," said Paul, taking huge bites of his johnnycake. "I don't believe they have good things very often; that Nancy looks as though she didn't know how to comb her hair nor get dinner."

What connection there was between the two occupations, Paul did not explain. He looked his mother over from head to foot in her neat, straight, dark dress, without ruffle or pucker, her gray hair combed plainly back under the meekest of widow caps. Paul wouldn't have undertaken to have explained the difference, but in his estimation, there were miles of distance between his mother and "that Nancy"!

12

ENLARGING THE CIRCLE

"GOOD land!" This was the strongest form of emphasis of which the widow Adams was known to be guilty. Even this she used only on extreme occasions. That the present was a very extreme occasion, and that the exclamation was intended to show her dismay—not to say disgust—was apparent from her face. The occasion was when she first looked into Nancy's kitchen. It really was a sight to drive a neat housekeeper wild. Greasy floor; greasy tables; sooty walls; gray, ash-bestrewn, grease-streaked stove; greasy tins and sticky tins; and dishes roughened by long months of mussy washing setting in a sort of dreary confusion on sticky shelves. Plates of moldy bread and a jar of fat, moldy cucumber pickles, a plate of wilted baked potatoes, another of ends of meat, a bowl of very sour milk, another of moldy gravy: This was the furniture of the pantry. No wonder that Mrs. Adams, as she surveyed the scene with neat skirts gathered in a gingerly way about her spare form and intense disgust on her face, said again: "Good land! How anybody can be so *nasty* beats me!"

Mrs. Adams was not a member of any literary society—had never been; and she did not know that the adjective she used was an inelegant word. As for the dishcloth which she found lying in an ill-smelling little heap where the dismal Nancy had left it when the mumps got possession of her, with the aid of the tongs she unceremoniously landed it in the stove. Then she tucked up her skirts, put on a large apron that covered her clean dress, pushed her sleeves above her elbows, and went to work.

The hardworking little woman had spent many busy days, but perhaps none were ever busier than that in which she reorganized the Ward homestead. She felt herself honor bound to begin in the parlor because of the mysterious performances, which she did not yet understand that were to take place there in the evening. She still believed that the doings were to be more or less disreputable; but even in that case, there was no reason why they should be carried on in such a musty, dusty, ill-conditioned room as she found that parlor to be. So, though she sighed, she worked vigorously. The first move was to carry every article of movable furniture into the hall; then the systematic worker, with damp cloth and dustpan, carefully removed the dust that had accumulated on mantle and window seats, then spread the floor half an inch thick with cornmeal and used her broom vigorously; even the carpet must have been astonished over the treatment it received. When every washable article in that room had been washed and polished and arranged with a careful eye toward hiding faded spots and soiled spots and defects generally, even the widow Adams herself was astonished at the result of her handiwork.

"I'll be bound if it isn't a nice, pleasant room as ever was," she said admiringly. "When the fire gets made and the shades drawn and them lamps get lighted, it will look as cheery as need be. I'm free to confess that my heart felt as heavy as lead at the idea of making it fit to sit down in. That Nancy must have been a lazy creature before she took the mumps. But then maybe the poor thing don't know how to do."

With which charitable conclusion of her soliloquy she closed the renovated room and trotted back to the kitchen, for it was time to vary her duties now and get the Wards some dinner. Rapidly as she had worked, the short winter morning was going fast.

"Get us a bit of something," the head of the house had said to her. "Joe will bring up a piece of steak, but I don't suppose you will have time to cook it; and it doesn't matter much."

All this he had said with a sigh and a dreary face, as though life were in every sense a burden, and the widow Adams, without doing much logical reasoning over causes and effects, still told herself that Mr. Ward was growing gray most dreadfully fast for a man of his age, and she would cook the nicest bit of steak for his dinner that he had had in many a day, poor man! Had she known Nancy better, she would have been even more sure of that.

There was very little time for the dining room. Mrs. Adams sighed over it and shook her head at it and assured it that it should have the hardest scrubbing that was ever heard of that afternoon, if she could but get around to it; then she swept and dusted and foraged for a clean tablecloth and took brisk little runs from the panty to the kitchen, and from the kitchen to the dining room, and accomplished wonders in a short space, considering the fact that she stopped to wash every dish she touched. It was just a small, common table, with a coarse, clean tablecloth put on very evenly and with dishes set squarely, every one of them shining with cleanliness. It was just the simplest of dinners: a dish of baked potatoes, a platter of beefsteak, a plate of butter, a plate of steaming johnnycake, and a pot of tea. No pickles or fruits or relishes of any sort. Very little attention had Nancy paid to these unnecessary additions; but I find myself pausing in doubt over my ability to give you even a hint of the effect that it—the sum total—had on the Wards. They did not take in a single detail; they only knew that the whole was something that they seemed to have lost away back in the past and found again that day: It was just a little bit of home. The potatoes came out of the oven at just the right moment, and their clean, shining coats had been scientifically "cracked"—although Mrs. Adams had never even dreamed that any science was connected with the act—and the steak was broiled briskly over a bed of coals, turned and returned, and slashed, and patted with skillful hand, seasoned just right, and came to the table smoking hot. The johnnycake had been dashed together in almost breathless haste, Mrs. Adams having put her skilled nose to the sole remaining loaf of bread and uttered an emphatic "Bah!" She regarded her effort with sour milk and egg and meal a little doubtfully. "It was done in such an awful hurry!" she said excusingly. "I couldn't blame it for not being good."

But no one in his senses could have blamed the brown, flaky, dainty-looking loaf which sent out such a delicate aroma. Certainly the Wards did not. Mr. Ward, Sr., took his second potato, and his second bit of steak, and his third bit of cornbread, and finally remarked, in a grave way that for some reason he was uncommon hungry; he guessed he ate less breakfast than usual.

Well, the widow Adams certainly performed wonders in that house that day: hall and stairs testified to it, as well as parlor and dining room. These all in fine order, she had intended giving the whole force of her being to that dreadful kitchen pantry; but it chanced that in her search for something needed, she penetrated to the boys' own room. Mr. Ward's she had seen before, and made up the bed—not without sighs and regrets that she must not take time to sweep and dust and otherwise purify; but the dismal Nancy had done better for that room than anywhere else, and although her best was far below Mrs. Adams's worst, still, after all, there was a decided difference between this and the boys' room. This Mrs. Adams instantly recognized. She stood still in the middle of the floor, placed both hands on her hips, said "Good land!" in her most expressive tone, turned her eyes in each dreary direction for a relieving glimpse, and finally her dismay having reached its climax, she said, "Why, dear me! Good land!" then she set to work. Broom, dustpan, duster, hot soapsuds, clean bed linen, clean spread; there were clean things enough piled away on the closet shelves; but more than anything else did Nancy hate to make use of them, because then the soiled ones had to be washed; but, oh, the transformation in that room! What wonders a little sweeping, and dusting, and putting away can accomplish! Add to this a carefully kept bed, with every sheet and cover straight and smooth, the whole tucked scientifically in at the sides after being scientifically rolled down at the top, and you have changed a dreary waste into a homey room. It would be a curious study to trace the laws of influence and see in what remote quarters they touch and how strangely unlike the starting point is the message which it brings to some.

Here were certain people apparently as far removed from the Chautauqua Literary and Scientific Circle as though they lived in a world where it had not reached, and yet its influence was reaching out and touching them through unexpected and unintended processes. The small round table set carefully for supper, with its small white puffs of cream biscuit, its hard, shining pat of butter, its hot applesauce, its plate of soft gingercake and its fragrant tea, each one of them so simple in itself, having apparently nothing whatever to do with science or literature; and yet it spoke to that weary father and those motherless sons of the literature of home as nothing for years had spoken. Mr. Ward went swiftly through the cheery room to his own private bedroom to hide tears that started in his fading eyes. He did not know why they started. It was all such a surprise to him! He had not known before that he had no home. As for Joe, when he first entered his own room that evening to make ready for the unwonted scenes below, he stopped midway in the room, even as Mrs. Adams had done and, surveying the transformation with an air of utter astonishment for a moment, suddenly made known his opinion: "Upon my word! If the C.L.P.X.Y.Z. is to be thanked for this whole performance—from the johnnycake and biscuit and gingerbread up to this sort of looking bed—why, I bow down to it, and from this time am its most devoted admirer. I say, Jim, Paul's mother is an institution, isn't she?"

So the four new lamps were lighted, and the shining stove glowed, and the fire snapped and sparkled, and the long unused doorbell rang, and Mrs. Adams, her big apron laid aside, her dress unpinned and smoothed down, her face red and her manner a trifle flurried, received the guests: Mr. and Mrs. Fenton—

the latter shaking hands with her cordially; the Butlers—even Jack, who had condescended to come as the guest of young Bennett; Professor Monteith, whom she knew by sight, and who astonished her so by his appearance there that she had nearly dropped the lamp! What strange hallucination was this that her boy Paul actually supposed himself to belong to this gathering!

Her heart began to tremble over him. What a dreadful mistake he must have made! And he actually intended to come here this evening! Could she prevail upon him to stay in the kitchen with her? It was all some mean trick of those dreadful boys, and there she had made cream biscuit for their supper! For about one minute she regretted this act of motherliness. The next came Paul himself; came while she was putting a shade on the lamp, and Joe had opened the door to him, and behold, he walked into that parlor, his clean shirt in perfect order, his clothes brushed neatly, his hair carefully combed, and behold, Professor Monteith said: "Ah, Adams, good evening!" And then— could the widow Adams believe her eyes! She shaded them with her hand and reached for her apron to rub away the mist before she remembered that on this strange evening she wore no apron—Professor Monteith deliberately arose and gave his hand to her Paul and shook it cordially; and Paul, in no wise discomposed thereby, bowed right and left, and said: "Good evening, Mr. Bennett. How are you, Ward?" and dropped into his seat as one who was at home and at ease. The porcelain shade slipped from the poor widow Adams's trembling hand, and it was only her own Paul's quick spring and deft-handedness that saved it from crashing on the floor.

Then she made a hasty retreat, and perhaps, could

that C.L.S.C. have peeped through the keyhole at her, and have seen the way in which she dropped on her knees and have heard the tearful outpouring of thanksgiving that her Paul, her darling, her one treasure, was actually sitting in that parlor which her own hands had made neat, joining in conversation with those whom she had not hoped he would ever know, they would surely have discovered that they were building better than they had known; that the Circle of science was reaching farther than their most daring ambitions had dared to think: actually reaching to widow Adams herself and warming her heart as it had not warmed in all the seventeen years of her widowhood.

Speaking of keyholes, I shall have to admit that widow Adams spent a good deal of her evening that she had meant to be a busy one, peeping through one. She could not hear a word that was said in the parlor; indeed, she had no desire to. It was enough for her to see. It was such a sight as she had not expected to see in this world—her boy Paul sitting among the aristocracy of Centerville, with Dr. Monteith's arm actually resting familiarly on his shoulder, actually bending over him to point out a certain something in a book! She knew not what the something was; she cared not. *She* would never wade through *Merivale;* she might never hear his name; but such joy as he had given her mother heart he might well rejoice over in heaven.

13

◦━━◈━━◦

The Circle and Its Center

QUIETER and yet perhaps a busier winter was never passed by certain of the dwellers in Centerville than that one which had ushered in the Chautauqua Literary and Scientific Circle.

It was surprising even to the leaders thereof to see how the Circle widened. As the winter advanced and *Merivale* was conquered by some, endured by others, and laid on the shelf by all—another and less ponderous volume taking its place—many of the townspeople who had been least expected roused to interest and looked in on the monthly gatherings. The organization, having no cast-iron rules to hold it in check, smiled approvingly on what were known as honorary members, meaning a class of people, many of them young, and some older, who, not having leisure or inclination for the full course of actual *study,* yet liked to come when they could, or would—you might use both words on occasion and be correct—and listen to the questions and answers, or essays or lectures or informal conversation, as the case might be, putting in a word of suggestion or inquiry or actual help, sometimes, and who yet were not bound by any rules to come when there was any other place which they preferred, or any other method of spending the evening which chanced to suit them better.

Of this latter class were Jack Butler and his sisters Irene and Effie. Jack had been led to come at first from curiosity. He found it too much for even his cultured brain to solve the problem how such representations of the antipodes as Professor Monteith and James Ward were held together by a common interest; so he came to see. And, being a really well-read youth, who had done at least a *little* hard studying while in college, he became in a degree interested and so came often. His sister Irene came because Mrs. Fenton constantly urged her to do so, being moved by a benevolent desire to set that lady's enthusiasm off in another channel and so save the world, or at least her father's house, from a flood of paintings. As for Effie, she complained that it was a wretchedly dull winter, and half the time there really wasn't anyplace to go to, unless one looked in on that stupid Circle over which so many were going wild; for her part she could not see what its attraction was.

Meantime the winter and early spring sped rapidly. Matters outside the Circle had also prospered. Paul Adams, for instance, and the carpenter's shop in which he worked. He had assured himself that he would "stick," you will remember, and had been true to his word. Never had Mr. Tucker known a more faithful workman. Prompt as the sun, every morning and afternoon quiet, busy, persistent in his efforts to learn just what and how: This was the character that the boy had earned. So unlike that which was confidently expected of him that his employer watched him at first with suspicious and then with puzzled eyes.

"What in all nature can have come over the boy I don't don!" he would say in confidence to his wife as they sat together in the pause between the day and the night which the hardworking carpenter allotted to his own hearthstone. "He was the laziest, loafingist fellow that ever lived and breathed in this town; and that's saying a good deal, for whether we get our member elected to time or not, we've got our share of folks who have nothing else to do but loaf and talk it over. And I used to think when Paul got old enough to vote he'd join that set if he didn't do a good deal worse, and go on talking and loafing to the end of the chapter. But he's got to be the steadiest kind of a fellow; don't go nowhere of nights. I asked the widow particularly, and she says he is next to never out of nights at all, and then to some kind of a society that he belongs; I don't like that. Societies for boys of that sort are apt to mean mischief; but his meets only once a month, and he gets back inside of ten o'clock every time, and I'm beat if I know what has come over him."

Mrs. Tucker sewed away steadily on a pair of pants she was mending, fitted the patch neatly, gave a skillful twitch to it at the corner, and then rounded the corner like an engineer before she suggested a meek solution: "Maybe he's got religion."

Mr. Tucker poked the coals decisively and shook his head: "No, I thought of that, and watched him, and hoped with all my might that was the thing, and he had got turned around for good and all; but it ain't nothing of that kind. He don't go to church more than he ever did: his mother sits there alone, you see, every Sunday, and he never comes inside the prayer meeting. No, it ain't anything of that kind, and I don't know what it is. He doesn't waste his earnings that's sure; spends them as fast as he gets them on the house and his mother. He's bought her a new lamp and a new chair, and made her a wash bench, and got her a new dress, and I don't know what all: a dozen little things that don't take much money, but show which way his thoughts is going. The widow, she cries about every time I see her over some new thing he has got her. She cries for joy about half the time nowadays. It all looks well in the boy, but I'm puzzled to make it out. I watch him as close as a cat could watch a mouse. The other day I caught him working away, planing a board, and muttering to himself as if there was a dozen folks around him. Says I to myself: 'My fine fellow, you're mad at something, at last'—He's as good-natured, you know, as the day is long—Says I to myself: 'If I could catch what you was muttering about, I'd maybe be able to make out what wind is blowing you along, and where the harbor will be likely to be.' I listened for quite a spell, and he kept on like mad; and every time he got to the end of one lingo he'd look back behind him a second and then turn around and go to planing and muttering again. I couldn't make anything of it, and I didn't know but the fellow was going crazy. At last I see that he had some kind of a book blocked open with two bits of board, and he kept looking at it and muttering, and planing and looking and muttering."

"Why don't you have a talk with him?" suggested the wife, who had by this time conquered her patch and was hemming it down with neat stitches.

"About what? I don't know what to say to the boy. He does everything on the square and is by all odds the best boy I have had around for years, though to be sure that isn't saying much. I haven't got any fault to find. I'm just puzzled to know what has turned him around. I did ask him what he was muttering about, and he said: 'Oh, he was running over the dates for the next Circle,' whatever that meant, and then he got off a lot of stuff—figures and names—regular jaw-breaking fellows. I couldn't make anything of it, and there's nothing in it that would turn a boy like Paul Adams around, and I'm beat!"

Equally felt, but more silent, was the astonishment of Mr. Ward over his son James. He was not quite so bewildered, it is true, for he plainly saw that the C.L.S.C. was the talisman which had apparently charmed his son; and being a man who had a sincere respect for learning, he was gravely glad over not only the result as shown in James's steady attention to business and quiet evenings, but the producing cause thereof. His chief bewilderment arose from the fact that, having listened carefully to the essays and reviews that were read on a certain evening when the C.L.S.C. gave a general invitation to its friends to attend, he confessed to himself that what James saw in all those names and dates to interest him was more than he could imagine. From that time forth he was more bewildered and had more respect for learning than ever. He believed in his honest, sad heart that James was becoming learned, and there were whole evenings when he sat in silence behind the dining-room stove toasting his slippered feet, and pondering, not over the day's accounts, but as to whether it was possible that the boy's mother knew of the turn which he had taken, and was glad.

What about Joe? Well that in some form was the question which this father often asked himself anxiously. Joe was not a member of the literary society; was not interested in their books, nor their plans. He grumbled constantly over their infatuation and apparently believed with all firmness that both his brother and Paul had been ruined. At the same time, apparently from the force of circumstances, he changed his course of life; with neither James nor Paul to help him go astray, it proved not to be so pleasant a path as he had trodden before. Casting about him for something with which to while away the hours, he found that his father was entirely willing to furnish him with employment; so in a fitful and rather exasperating fashion he also became a clerk in the store. True, he absented himself on the slightest provocation and, when present, oftener lounged on the counters and whistled than he did anything else; yet even this was better than the life of entire lounging which he had heretofore followed, and his father, recognizing it, was really trying very hard to be patient with him: harder than Joe dreamed, and the other interested lookers-on trembled lest after all Joe should suddenly slip away from this slight hold and go hopelessly astray.

"We have caught the leader," Mrs. Fenton said anxiously one evening; "but the other seems bent on being his own leader and going to destruction in spite of us"; and she counseled young Robert to be more earnest in his efforts to win a hold on the young man who still thought him "cuter" than any of the older ones.

Dr. Monteith made almost no reply to Mrs. Fenton's anxious remark, but carried a grave, thoughtful face, and spent a longer time on his knees that evening than usual. Dr. Monteith had by no means given up Joseph Ward. Because the literary society had failed to reach him, it by no means followed that nothing would. What he earnestly wished was that he could have asked every member of that C.L.S.C. to make a special subject of prayer of young Joseph Ward, but some of them would hardly have understood what he meant. So he bided his time and said a few thoughtful words to Caroline and Mrs. Watson Bates and young Marshall.

During the sunny days that ushered in the spring that season, there was a sensation among the members of the Circle. Its next meeting was to be held at Dr. Monteith's, and, behold, a day or two before the appointed evening, each member received a little note from their president, stating that after the general exercises he proposed a social reunion, during which time certain friends who were specially interested in the C.L.S.C. would be introduced and talk with them; and it would give him great pleasure if every member of the Circle would take special pains to be present. No further intimation was given in the note, but it got out, as such things will, and fluttered through the membership that they were actually to meet the inspirer and instigator of the Chautauqua Literary and Scientific Circle. For that matter, the instigator of Chautauqua itself! Moreover, it was by degrees discovered that the invitations had not been confined to the members of the Circle, but were scattered quite generally through the community.

"It is nothing more nor less than a large party," explained Mrs. Fenton to her husband, her eyes dancing with delight; "a gathering of all the literary and most of the fashionable people in town to meet the members of our Circle, among whom none are more prominent than Paul Adams and Mrs. Chester's Caroline. I believe those two know more about *Merivale* than Dr. Monteith himself does. I do think that man is the sharpest, and at the same time wisest, planner I ever knew!"

"Why?" questioned her graver but equally satisfied

husband; "because he doesn't know so much about *Merivale* as they do?"

Among the invited guests was Mrs. Chester herself; and thereby occurred one of those curious incidents which are liable to happen in a town where distinctly marked grades of society exist and somebody succeeds in mixing them.

Mrs. Chester, by the way, was all unaware of the hold that the Circle had gotten upon her second girl. She knew indeed that Caroline belonged to some sort of a society and was dabbling with books that were much beyond her comprehension, and Mrs. Chester in her own world, among her chosen friends, did not fail to speak of and deplore this as a thing that was likely to unsettle Caroline's wits and give her false ambitions and vain aims. But she had no idea—how should she?—who the persons were that were engaged in helping to unsettle her. She had heard, indeed that Mrs. Fenton was interesting herself and that the Ward boys had reformed, or were, at least, much improved, but neither Mrs. Fenton nor the Ward boys came into her world very frequently. With the former, you will remember, she had only that sort of calling acquaintance which resulted in an exchange of calls once in six months, perhaps, sometimes even more rarely than that; as for the Ward boys, they occasionally brought home her purchases from their father's store. So when Mrs. Chester heard of the efforts toward literature as associated with such as these young men and her Caroline, she smiled pityingly and said: "Mrs. Fenton was a well-meaning little woman, but it was a pity she tried in such wild ways to do good"; and then she dismissed the whole subject from her mind. An invitation to an evening's entertainment at Dr. Monteith's was, however, a matter that she could appreciate, and she made preparation with evident satisfaction. The professor's house was rarely opened for large gatherings.

"Caroline," she said to that maiden, "you may leave the parlors until afternoon and finish that wrapper. Let the china closet go this week—I shall want your help elsewhere tomorrow—and I want Miss Celia's dress pressed out and the ribbon run into the puffs again; you may do that this afternoon. I shall need a great many little things done tomorrow and shall want these other matters out of the way. Oh! by the by, tomorrow is your regular evening out, isn't it? You will have to make some different arrangement for this week. I am going out and shall want you to remain at home with the children. I don't like to trust them with Hannah, she is growing so careless."

Then did Caroline stand transfixed with a feeling very like dismay. "Stay with the children!" Was she not the one appointed to read the main paper of the evening? Yet, at the same time, was she not Mrs. Chester's hired help? Had not that lady engaged and paid for her time, evenings included? Had she not a right to command even *this* evening of evenings if she would? Swift thinking did Caroline, and the conclusion was that she answered simply: "Yes, ma'am," in almost her usual composure of tone and turned away without giving her mistress so much as a hint of the heavy cross that she had laid upon her. Yet the engagement upon which she had so heartily entered must not be left thus. It involved a brief, carefully worded note which Caroline contrived during the morning to send to Dr. Monteith's.

"What an idea!" exclaimed that gentleman after a hasty reading. "Look here!"—to his guest with whom conversation had been suspended long enough to read the note—"this is the young woman of whom I told you; she thinks she cannot come to the Circle tomorrow evening because her mistress has an engagement. Preposterous! Half of my idea is to get her here to read her essay before certain ones who need to hear it. This thing must be arranged: What is the way to do it?"

One result of this talk was a morning call. Mrs. Chester heard the bell from her dressing room and opened the door to say to Caroline as she passed through the hall:

"You may say that I am engaged this morning: I cannot see anyone."

So Caroline, flushing over Dr. Monteith's cordial greeting, made haste to say that Mrs. Chester was specially engaged that morning, and—

"But we haven't called to see Mrs. Chester," interrupted the doctor; "our call was, I may say, almost entirely on you." Whereupon he introduced to Caroline the name which was so associated with one of the dearest pleasures and the highest hopes of her life: that to see him, and hear him speak, and shake hands with him was a greater honor than she had actually even dreamed of.

That she was intensely, almost painfully, embarrassed for a moment was evident; that she was quick-witted was equally so, for in an instant, though her cheeks were the color of the carnation pinks on the window, she said, with a quick deprecating look at her trim kitchen apron, throwing back the door of the parlor as she spoke: "Well, if you have really called to see *me,* I will go and get on a clean apron!" And she actually did slip away to don a trim white apron with pockets, and possibly to put a touch of cooling water on her glowing cheeks. Then she returned her quiet self and sustained her share of the bright conversation which followed.

"Why, I don't know," she said thoughtfully in answer to their inquiry. "I can hardly tell how I get time to do the regular amount of reading. I have to economize. There have been days when I was hard pressed and thought I was going to fail, but some fortunate lull in the round of work was almost sure to come in an unexpected way, and I would push through. Then there are certain duties which fall to my share that I find can be attended to while I am actually engaged on something else. I've proved the falsity of the idea that the mind cannot be occupied by two opposite trains of thought at the same time," she added, laughingly. "For instance, I committed long pages of events condensed from *Merivale* while I was setting the table for dinner; I suppose I must have thought where the plates and the castor and the napkins were, for they came into line all right, and I know I thought about Coriolanus and Cincinnatus and Claudius and all those: memorized those lists, you know. Sometimes, too, when I was drying the china or rubbing the silver, I would pin my little pink book open with a fork and make my brains keep my hands company. In that way I got through with Augustus Caesar and Tiberias and Caligula." Thinking of it afterwards, Caroline was amazed to recall how many items she had given the callers concerning herself; how fully she had been betrayed into explaining her plans and hopes—yes, and fears. It was not her nature to be communicative with people in general. She could only attribute it to the delicate way in which the two gentlemen evidenced their interest in her progress. As Dr. Monteith arose to go, he asked if Mrs. Chester would see him later in the day as a matter of convenience to himself.

He wished to consult her on an important subject. When Caroline gave this message and awaited her answer, Mrs. Chester arose from her chair in astonishment.

"Dr. Monteith! Is he in the house now? I will see him, of course! Why should I not? Why, Caroline, I heard no bell; who admitted him?"

"I did, ma'am; you will remember that as I passed through the hall, you directed me to say to whoever it was that you were engaged."

"But that was nearly, if not quite, half an hour ago. That ring of the bell surely could not have brought Dr. Monteith!"

"Yes'm; it was Dr. Monteith and his friend."

"And pray where have they been all this time?"

"In the parlor, ma'am. I gave your message, and the doctor said he would like to see me a few moments; and just now he directed me to inquire if you would see him later."

"Well," declared Mrs. Chester, perplexity and annoyance struggling together on her face, "this is certainly most extraordinary!" But she went downstairs immediately to confront Dr. Monteith.

If you had been in her parlor that afternoon you might have heard her talking in a somewhat excited tone to her intimate and somewhat confidential friend Mrs. Bacon.

"I never heard of anything more absurd in my life. Fancy me standing before Dr. Monteith—he declining to take a seat on the plea that he had already overstayed his time and petitioning that my hired girl might be allowed to attend the social gathering at his house tomorrow evening! I was so amazed that really I did not know what to say. I believe I blushed and stammered and acted like a girl in her teens. My dear

Mrs. Bacon, what are we coming to? What are those ridiculous people trying to do? And what am I to do? I couldn't, of course, refuse Dr. Monteith's request, but I wondered at his impudence in repeating his invitation to me. Does he suppose that I wish to mingle socially with my hired help?"

"Oh, well, my dear friend"—and Mrs. Bacon's voice was one of those soft, soothing ones which remind you of the purring of a favorite kitten—"it is a benevolent scheme of some sort which these good people have on hand; they really think they are helping the poor girls and boys who have had no other chances, and possibly they are, though it may be a mistaken way; still, I think the intention is good. I am told that they propose to greatly encourage the members of their little society by letting them read some extracts or something of that sort; exhibiting their acquirements, you know, after the fashion of the school exhibitions of the olden time. Dr. Monteith is peculiar, we are all aware; but then, he can afford to be, for, with all his peculiarities, he is so grand a man! I don't think I would mind, if I were you. Caroline is uncommonly bright, I think, for a girl in her sphere; and really, I don't wonder that a man like Dr. Monteith is tempted to interest himself in her a little."

In her way, Mrs. Bacon, who was about as clear brained as the aforesaid kitten, did a certain amount of good. She rarely stroked fur, either her own or others, the wrong way; and her claws—if she had any—were so effectually hidden in velvet as never to do any active damage. What damage she did to society was of a passive nature. She succeeded in so quieting Mrs. Chester's nerves that her voice was almost pleasant as she said to Caroline the next morning, turning back as she was leaving the breakfast room as though it were an afterthought:

"By the way, Caroline, Dr. Monteith tells me he is interested in your literary aspirations and proposes to give your reading class, or whatever it is, a lift this evening. I wasn't aware of anything of the kind; of course I would not deprive you of the pleasure of being present. I will make some other arrangement for the children." And Caroline, although her face flushed deeply, was able to express her thanks, and felt them, too. She sang over her work that morning.

14

The Tables Turned

IN some respects that was a unique gathering in Dr. Monteith's handsome parlors. I am inclined to think it was the first attempt Centerville had ever made to unite the actually intellectual with what had hitherto been purely social. A carefully prepared program was presented, which interested many and astonished all. Moreover, these persons who, like Mrs. Chester, came with a vague idea of seeing certain young people gathered, perhaps, on benches in the dining room, and put through the process of examination to the end that others might see what commendable progress they had made and pat them on the cheek—metaphorically, at least—saying: "Good children! You shall have a cake and an apple to take home"—a little after the industrial-school style, you understand—were greatly mistaken. There seemed to be no social lines drawn between the guests; nothing to distinguish the Circle from the friends invited to mingle with them, unless, indeed, I except a certain flash of intelligence passing between them as they met during the evening; a sort of indescribable look and tone indicating oneness of feeling and cordial sympathy in regard to some subjects, at least. But these things were only noticed by the initiated. Outwardly, it was merely a gathering of well-dressed, well-behaved people met to enjoy themselves.

Caroline's appearance astonished no one but her mistress. She had indulged herself in a new dress this spring, of some silvery gray material that fitted the light in her eyes and the color in her cheeks perfectly. It was made in so simple a style as to be almost striking and yet was wonderfully becoming. She wore no ornament whatever, unless the mass of soft white lace about her throat could be called an ornament. Yes, I forget; there was a single white rose in her hair and another at her throat, whose cool green leaves lay nestled among the folds of lace and fitted the rest of the toilet well. As I said, Mrs. Chester was the only person whom this young woman in her holiday attire astonished. It was too simple and plain, after all, beside most of the others to invite special attention, and the members of the Circle were used to seeing her in something that was always neat and becoming; but Mrs. Chester had not known before how she would look outside of the plain, dark calicoes and carefully made house aprons in which she daily went her round of work. She actually gazed after Caroline as she crossed the room, even wondering, for a bewildered second, who that graceful girl was; and the next she said: "Well, really!" and tossed her head and hardly knew what she thought.

It must be confessed that James Ward astonished more people than Mrs. Chester. The fact is no one had ever seen him dressed as he appeared that evening; nor had had an idea what a difference dress would make in him. His father, without seeming to be specially interested in what was going on, awoke one morning at the breakfast table to ask some questions. What was this party at Dr. Monteith's that he had heard talk about? Who were to be there, and what was to be done? James was posted; Dr. Monteith took care that he should be most thoroughly posted as to all that was planned and much that was hoped. He explained somewhat in detail and with an eagerness that could not escape notice.

"And are you invited?" was the next somewhat abrupt question. Whereupon Joe laughed good-naturedly:

"He invited! Why, Father, he is Dr. Monteith's right-hand man. Nothing can be done without him at the Circle, or anywhere. He and Paul will be running the whole thing before you know it."

"What nonsense!" said James, not without a flush on his cheek. To his father he only gave a brief answer in the affirmative.

"Are *you* invited, too?" This to Joe.

"Well, sir, I have that honor; but I've made up my mind to have a pressing engagement somewhere else that evening. The quality are all to be out in full force, and I don't stand high enough in the literary world just yet to be quite ready to show off; so I mean to *make* off."

The father smiled grimly; a smile that closed with a sigh. He was much more troubled over Joe than that good-hearted, foolish young man had any idea of. Nothing more had been said about the entertainment, but in the course of the day Mr. Ward handed James an order on the best tailor in the town to make his son as good a suit of clothes as could be made, out of the best material in stock, and send the bill to him. What tailor would not have done his best to make the clothes good, and the bill large, after that? The final result exceeded even the father's expectations, both as to the amount of the bill and the changed appearance of his son. The one balanced the other, according to his view of it. Had he known what a tender feeling there was in James's heart over the thoughtfulness of that note, they would have more than balanced. As it was, not even young Bennett himself came to the gathering in better attire, nor indeed carried himself better in it than did James Ward.

Of course Paul Adams had no father to balance tailors' bills; so he came in the clothes that he had worn for best until they were a trifle small in every way. Well for Paul that he had not yet reached the point where he cared greatly about this or, indeed, gave it much thought. Besides, he was of that happy temper to whom a word of ridicule, such as would have flushed James Ward's face with rage, would only provoke laughter. It was his mother who shed the tears for that family. If he had but known it, she wept copiously over his coat the evening before while she darned a small break because she could not replace it with a new one; wept the next day as she starched and ironed his best shirt because it was so old and so coarse; but the linen shone beautifully, and Paul whistled while he dressed and whistled when he went away to the party.

He presented a striking contrast to most of the guests, but of this he did not think at all. He had an important part to sustain in the evening's exercises, and this absorbed his attention.

A word about the literary portion of that entertainment: Dr. Monteith's aim had been twofold: to explain in a detailed and interesting manner what had been accomplished by the Circle and to increase its prospective size.

To Caroline had been assigned the task of preparing and reading a paper which should give her views of the lessons to be learned and the errors to be avoided by studying the greatness and weakness, the splendor and meanness, the rise and downfall of the seven-hilled city. It had been discovered that this young woman possessed an accomplishment as rare as it was pleasant. She was a natural reader—clear-voiced, round-toned, sympathetic. Dr. Monteith had declared in confidence to his friend that it was a perfect rest to listen to her.

As for Paul, the same watchful scholar had discovered that he had a peculiar talent for repeating striking and important events. He was able to forget the lapse of time and change of scene since those events had occurred and give them as though it had been yesterday. He was able to forget something less easily forgotten—himself—and give the story as though he had been present, and seen and heard. Therefore, certain vivid scenes in the history of Rome had been selected for him to tell the audience.

"Tell them exactly as though you were the only person who saw the act or heard the words, and it was not possible that any of us had as yet heard of the event." This was Dr. Monteith's direction, and he expected to have an entertainment worth listening to. All the more delightful, possibly, because Paul was not in the least aware that his talent in that direction was unusual. Besides these two central appointments, another that caused much more heartthrobbing was in contemplation. A careful list of questions had been papyrographed, and a card containing them was to be given to each guest, with the understanding that any question in the list could be asked of any member of the Circle, said member being expected to answer such questions as would bring out striking events and interesting details. The list was long; not that it was supposed that one-half or even one-third of the questions would be asked, but for the purpose of allowing the guests to select that which most interested them and also to prove that this was no prepared list of twenty or thirty questions, answers to which had been memorized in a few hours. Perhaps you can imagine what a Herculean task it had been to prepare this list of questions not only, but to prepare to answer them. It was long before the Circle would give its united vote to any such plan.

"It will be just horrid!" one quite young member had declared. "They will be absolutely certain to pick out the questions that we don't know: people always do. I might study up a few, but none of them would come to me; and I really think I am well enough known as a dunce now without proclaiming my fame in that line abroad." Others less outspoken were yet inclined to be of like opinion, but after eager discussion, during which their president reminded them that the very fact of the list of questions being so long would make it the most probable thing in the world for all to fail on many of them, consent was at last obtained.

Precisely at the hour named on the notes of invitation the guests were called to order, and the exercises of the evening commenced. Another opportunity for Mrs. Chester's astonishment! *Who would have supposed that she could read like that!* This was the lady's bewildered thought as she listened to the clear, full voice. That the paper read was really one of marked strength, Mrs. Chester was not sufficiently well read to know;

but there were those in the audience who did and who thanked God with full hearts that the Chautauqua Literary and Scientific Circle had given this earnest soul a chance.

I will not stop to tell you in detail how well Paul Adams fulfilled his trust; suffice it to say that there were those listening to him who, knowing absolutely nothing about the early story of Rome, were moved to indignation, and then almost to tears, over his simple yet graphic way of giving the details of certain startling events.

But the crowning act in the evening's exercises was yet to come. It so happened that the list of questions suggested to young Butler the idea of having what he was pleased to term a little fun. He had not forgotten his own great, though foolish, embarrassment at being asked a question concerning the renowned old city, which, at the time, he was not ready to answer. Why should he not have the pleasure of witnessing the embarrassment of another? He determined to level all his forces on James Ward, being—if the humiliating truth must be told—moved thereto by a certain feeling of annoyance over the fact that Miss Aimie Allison still bestowed bewitching bows upon him whenever they chanced to meet.

No sooner was the general exercise fairly opened than Jack commenced his fire, leveled constantly at the head of James Ward. In vain did others, not in the Circle, being able to see through his small design, try to avert the stream of questions into other channels. From every diversion he came back to James. There was little chance for any of the other members to distinguish themselves, save as some of Mrs. Chester's friends in great curiosity made several attempts on Caroline; attempts to which she promptly responded.

It gradually became apparent, even to the dullest perception that young Butler was resolved to give James Ward a thorough examination.

Now it so happened that James, having occupied a very quiet background at most of the Circles, was supposed to be only in a very limited sense acquainted with *Merivale;* while the actual truth was that, next to Paul Adams, no one had worked harder or mastered more of the facts in that volume than James. He was aware that he had not the actual *genius* of Paul Adams, but he knew he had a better literal memory, and he battled with and conquered dates and names in a way which presently gave him pride. Since the list of questions had been made out, he had found it a very satisfactory way of testing his own knowledge, and he found, to his surprise and delight that the answers were as familiar to him as though he had actually been present at Rome's triumphs and defeats.

From sitting erect with a bright red spot burning on each indignant cheek as the storm of questions and answers went on, Dr. Monteith gradually settled back in his chair, a look of composed amusement on his face. Jack Butler's small scheme had already failed. Why had not the young man sense enough to know it? If James Ward missed every question that was asked him after this, he had already shown sufficient knowledge of the history of Rome to stamp him as a student. Apparently, however, he had no idea of missing a question. His voice was steady, his face controlled, his whole manner assured and quiet; and Jack Butler, nettled exceedingly, was beginning to wish that he had let this whole business alone and not brought himself into such conspicuous relations with this hero of history.

"I beg pardon," he said. "I seem to be monopolizing the entertainment; don't let my interest in the subject keep you all quiet."

Dr. Monteith's answer was prompt and decisive: "By no means, my dear young friend," with possibly a slightly marked emphasis on the word *young*. "It is true we had in no sense designed this for an evening of special examination, and our friend Ward has not been working for a diploma; still, since it has progressed thus far, I beg that the examiner will kindly continue, at least until the student makes a break. What say our friends? Shall the few remaining questions be asked until there is a failure?"

Long before this, the greater number of the guests had entered into the spirit of the exercise, and the vote to continue was unanimous. Thus invited, there was nothing for the now exasperated examiner but to proceed, rushing at railroad speed over the remainder of the list, not one of which failed to receive an assured answer by the young man whom he had set out to mortify. It was a schoolboy scheme and deserved to meet with a real schoolboy defeat; therefore was Dr. Monteith rejoiced over the whole. Especially when, with the last question and answer, the entire audience, Circle included, broke into an involuntary burst of applause.

"Victory!" exclaimed Dr. Monteith, rising to his feet and holding out his hand to James Ward. "My dear friend, I congratulate you on knowing more about the history of Rome than I ever expect to."

This frank statement produced bursts of laughter. Formality and literature were alike at an end. Everybody was laughing and talking and shaking hands with young Ward, thus suddenly and most unexpectedly transformed into the hero of the evening.

The dining-room doors were thrown open. Coffee

and cakes and ices became the matters of special interest just then, and the pleased company broke into little groups, to laugh and exclaim over the peculiarities of the entertainment; and it chanced that, entirely by his own planning, the only discomfited person in the company was our immaculate and *"un*superficial" friend Jack Butler.

I shall have to confess that his discomforts were not yet at an end. Dr. Monteith, feeling confident that his greatest fault was an overpowering self-esteem, sought an early opportunity to congratulate him on his tact in having given them an unexpected entertainment, and then proposed that the company be invited to select from the same list questions that they would like Jack himself to answer in his own way, thus giving them a chance to compare the different shades of thought which would be presented by different minds. In the painfully eager negative that poor Butler felt constrained to press in answer to this flattering invitation, every vestige of self-esteem vanished.

15

A THEOLOGICAL REVIEW

THERE was one other person at that unique gathering who was an object of special interest. This was Kent Monteith, the doctor's son. None of the residents of Centerville were acquainted with him except by reputation, which was that of a scholar and traveler like his father; added to which he was a not-unknown artist. Indeed, for one so young he had achieved an enviable reputation, even in Europe. This fact was well known to the Centerville public through the industrious tongue of Miss Irene Butler, who was never tired of quoting what was said of him in the art reviews. Proud was she to be even so remotely connected with an artist destined to be famous as to have a speaking acquaintance with the father and be able to ask of him the latest news in art as reported by his son.

For days together had she looked forward to this eventful evening when she was actually to have the pleasure of meeting him face-to-face. Indeed, he was one whom almost any person might have been glad to meet.

"He looks very like his father," declared Mrs. Fenton after an earnest searching of the frank face. "A younger edition of his handsome father; and I am sure that flattery can go no farther, for his father is really the handsomest man I ever saw."

"I hope he will be half as good a man as his father," was Mr. Fenton's addition to this verdict. And when I tell you that even his own mother was satisfied in this respect, you will readily see that Kent Monteith was a man to admire. More than Irene had looked forward to meeting him on this occasion.

Now it happened that among them all only one young woman had been suggested to Kent as a person of interest. His father, after giving him a detailed account of the C.L.S.C. as it had branched at Centerville and a running commentary on most of the prominent characters belonging to it, had finished after this fashion: "There is one person who will be here tomorrow evening, and who is a member of the Circle that if you can find it in your heart to pay even quite special attention to, you will succeed in pleasing me."

"Upon my word, Father!" Kent had answered, laughing. "That is really a somewhat startling, and rather foreign than American, way of managing things."

"Oh, well," the father answered, joining in the laugh, "I am only planning for one evening, you understand, with a purpose in view; one with which you will sympathize when you hear her story. Her name is Caroline Raynor." Whereupon he began at the beginning of Caroline's story as it had been detailed to him by Mrs. Fenton and brought it down to the last meeting of the C.L.S.C., when Jack Butler had distinguished himself by giving her a cool stare and no other recognition, though Mrs. Fenton herself had undertaken to introduce them.

"Now you understand," explained Dr. Monteith, "that I don't expect to revolutionize society, neither do I have any particular desire to do so. Society, in one sense, will take care of itself; at least in this country; by which I mean that people reach their level in due time, fill the places that they are fitted by nature and taste to fill, and make a channel for their own lives which is satisfying. But where a person occupies for a time a niche in the world to which she manifestly doesn't belong and out of which she will assuredly move, to recognize the accident of position and ignore the mental and moral worth is despicable, is—I beg your pardon, Kent—intensely *un*American."

"Which is one of your synonyms for wickedness," the son said, laughing heartily. Nevertheless he asked many questions concerning Caroline, evinced as deep an interest in her welfare as his father could desire, and promised, without any further clue, to try to single her out from the large number of ladies who now, nominally at least, belonged to the Circle.

It was soon after Caroline's paper had been read that Kent bent forward to the chair in which his father was sitting and said in a low voice: "If I am not greatly mistaken, your protégé adds to her other accomplishments that of being a very good reader?" And Dr. Monteith, with pleased eyes, bowed assent.

It was therefore with a deference that had a purpose, and that certainly was very marked that Kent Monteith crossed the long parlor when the dining-room doors were thrown open and refreshments announced and offered his arm to Caroline. I really think it was about *that* time that Mrs. Chester's eyes became opened to what was going on. Before that she had been dazed; had hardly gotten away from her industrial-school idea and kept vaguely expecting the apple and piece-of-cake era to commence. But to see her second girl walk out to supper with Kent Monteith, the rising young artist but recently home from Florence, was too much for ordinary flesh and blood. Mrs. Chester promptly expressed her mind to her next neighbor.

"I really think, Mrs. Howard, that these quixotic people have taken leave of their common sense."

"Do you?" in utmost good humor. "Well, it cannot be said that your second girl has taken leave of hers; what a remarkable paper that was which she presented! I always thought there was something quite uncommon about her, but I did not suppose she had so cultured a mind. What an excellent thing this new society is for giving people a chance." After that outburst, Mrs. Chester turned away in dumb disgust.

But the acquaintance begun in the refreshment room in utmost good nature and, in order to further his father's wishes, was carried on by Kent Monteith because he became interested. She could converse that was evident; for he began at once to talk with her about the Rome which had been the topic of absorbing interest thus far to controvert some of the ideas which she had advanced in her paper; and while she steadily and intelligently held her own, she yet questioned him as to his different views in so keen a way that he speedily saw he must be clear and logical in his reasons if he expected them to have weight. She was not to be talked with like the average young lady whom he met in society. She knew almost nothing about society; but, without ever having seen it as he had, she clearly knew a great deal about Rome. The question was, how much did she know about other things?

"Do you think the same ideas which you have just been advancing apply to France?" he asked her suddenly, fixing a keen glance on her intelligent face the while. If she could have seen his thoughts they would have been somewhat after this fashion:

Now, if her knowledge is all confined to one book, she will try to generalize; to say yes and no, and flounder hopelessly over that question. He was mistaken. Her knowledge of literature was chiefly confined to one book, it is true, which she had very thoroughly studied; but she did not flounder. Instead, she fixed her calm, steady eyes upon him and answered promptly:

"Oh, I don't know: I am not in a position to know, or even to have an intelligent opinion. I don't know *anything* to speak of about France or, indeed, about any other part of the world except Centerville and Rome." This was a little laugh. "You must know that we have been working very hard over Rome half the winter, and of course I know a little and think a little about that country; but I know nothing else."

She is honest, he said to himself. Then aloud: "Were you fascinated with Rome that you held so closely to it and excluded every other country?"

"Not at all. I had one book that told me a great deal about Rome and almost nothing about any other place, and I wanted to learn all I could from that book, because books are scarce with me, as well as opportunities. This Chautauqua Society is the largest chance I ever had."

"*Merivale's Rome* could not have taught you to *read*," he could not help saying, with a marked emphasis on the last word. Her reading had pleased him because of its extreme naturalness.

"No," she said, the ready color flushing into her cheeks. "I never was taught to read; I read aloud a great deal to an invalid lady with whom I lived when I was a young girl, and she used to correct my pronunciation, but I never have had any lessons in reading."

"May you *never* have!" he said, speaking with more energy than the subject seemed to her to demand. He had been the victim of many professional readers.

"Tell me about this Circle," he said, as he helped her to an ice. "I was at Chautauqua for a few days last summer, but I don't know about the actual practical working of this scheme. Did you give the winter entirely to *Merivale?*"

"Oh no; we left him in the distance some time ago. Indeed, we are thoroughly interested in another book now."

"What author is being honored now? If you bring the same oneness of thought to bear on him that you must have done to *Merivale,* he should be a happy author."

"We are studying the *Philosophy of the Plan of Salvation.*"

"Theology?" a little startled.

"I don't know; is it theology? It is very interesting, but I don't know whether it would be called by that name."

"Do you like it as well as Rome?"

"Why, there is no comparison and no chance for one. Of course, it treats topics away in advance of Roman history. I don't suppose I am a judge as to whether it is as well written as the other, but of course it is more interesting."

"Why 'of course'?"

Caroline tried to steal a look at her questioner, a

little in doubt what all this catechizing might mean, but he was giving careful attention to the pickled oysters before him, and his grave, quiet face told her nothing.

"Why 'of course,'" she said hesitatingly. "Whatever tells us of God and of our relations to him is of infinitely more importance than the books that tell us only of other people like ourselves: how they sinned and suffered and died."

"Would you mind giving me the steps by which you reached such a conclusion?"

"They are almost self-evident, I think," she said quietly, though with flushing cheeks. "What has to do with my life in a world that will never end would seem to me to be of greater importance than what simply concerns the few days that I am to live on earth."

"Ah, but I don't accept your proposition. I believe that the knowledge we acquire here is not to be thrown away in a future existence. If I am to live at all in another world, I expect to keep growing wiser there, and not to begin at the alphabet either, but where I stopped when the soul was called upon to change homes."

"I suppose that is true," she said, looking frankly at him after a moment of thoughtful silence. "It is a somewhat new thought to me and a very pleasant one; but I think it increases the importance of the one subject, because I want to be very particular about the place where I continue my studies."

"I see," he said, smiling. "Now you are ready, I hope, to enlighten me as to this particular book."

"Well," she said, trying to be carefully literal in her reply, "I cannot do justice to the book, but I think I can introduce you to it." Her intense earnestness had a strange fascination for him. "I'm all attention," he said at last; "why don't you proceed?"

Then she looked at him again, puzzled to know how much he meant.

"You don't expect me to give you the entire book this evening?"

"I don't know. You seem to be doing well. I'm guessing at the filling in, you see: You are only supplying outlines. What next?"

They had left the refreshment room and joined the promenaders who were refreshing themselves in strolls through the long parlors. They were entirely engrossed in their subject, Caroline, at least, being utterly unconscious of the fact that Mrs. Chester was surveying her with astonished eyes; and Miss Irene Butler was almost overpowered with her impatience to talk with a real artist who had studied in Florence. She interrupted them at last ruthlessly.

"I beg your pardon, Mr. Monteith, but it does seem to me you have been unselfish long enough; you ought to be rewarded with a little pleasure on your own account now. Besides, some of us are longing to know about your experiences in Italy, and I, at least, have been looking forward to a feast when I might have opportunity to converse with you about our beloved profession."

"You have entirely mistaken my character. I never felt more selfish in my life. I am hearing about a book which interests me intensely from one who has evidently made its contents her own; and if there is any one subject more than another for which I have an unconquerable horror this evening, it is my profession. I've been working hard and have come home to rest. Miss Butler, are you a member of this literary society which seems to be creating such a sensation in your midst?"

Miss Irene gave a very positive shake to her head, with uplifted eyebrows. "Oh dear, no! My pursuits and aims in life are so entirely removed from this line of study that I have felt very little interest in the enterprise. Besides, I suppose the design of the Circle is to give an idea of what is going on in the world of books to those who have had no other opportunities. Isn't that the special aim, Caroline?"

It was the first time she had hinted that she even saw Caroline. Before that young woman could collect her startled thoughts to answer, Mr. Monteith saved her the trouble.

"Oh, I think the aim of the Circle is far wider than that. I happen to know that it is considered a very valuable review of work, even for thorough students. My father, for instance, expresses himself as richly repaid in personal advantage for the amount of time which he has given to the scheme. Scholars gifted with very keen brains planned the course of study with a view to benefiting a great variety of people. I'm inclined to think I shall find a Circle somewhere to join next year, if for nothing else but the comfort of belonging to the 'Round Table.' Do you know about the Round Table, Miss Raynor? No? Then you have never been to Chautauqua? There is a special delight in store for you."

"I have never been anywhere," said Caroline simply; "and I have almost as much hope of going to Europe as to Chautauqua."

She positively will not *pretend to any advantages that she has not had* was the mental comment of the young man who had set out to study her. Miss Irene held her ground firmly, resolved upon pressing the celebrated artist into communicativeness regarding his profession; but it was all to no purpose. Whether he detected the ring of affectation in her questions or the utter meagerness of her knowledge, or whether he was really too weary of the subject to want to talk about it, Caroline could not tell; in any case, he gaily resisted her efforts and *would* try to make her talk about the Chautauqua Circle, which subject she could not even *pretend* to understand, having kept herself until recently far above it. "How do you do again?" said a fourth voice at their elbow. It was the special guest whom all the others had been invited to meet. It was to Caroline that he offered his hand, as he said in hearty tones: "You gave us as fine a condensation of history tonight as is often put into a few pages. Monteith, how many people do you think study *Merivale* as this Circle evidently has this winter?"

"Very few," said young Monteith, and added: "I have been telling Miss Raynor that there is a delight in store for her such as she can hardly imagine. She tells me that she has never been to Chautauqua."

"And that she has no idea of being there, at least for years to come," Caroline said, much confused over her position in this central doorway, held a prisoner by Kent Monteith and talking with the most prominent personage in the company. "I think I must go," she said in undertone to Mr. Monteith; "Mrs. Fenton is waiting to speak to me."

"Is she? Which is Mrs. Fenton? I used to know her when I was a very small boy and came with my father and mother to the old homestead; as long ago as that, Miss Raynor, this house was the old homestead. Just introduce me again to Mrs. Fenton, will you?" And with a parting bow to the lady and gentleman, he passed on with Caroline, she more embarrassed than before. She had meant to slip quietly away to Mrs. Fenton's side.

"That was the truth, and nothing but the truth," her companion said gaily when they were alone, "but about its being the *whole* truth, I am more doubtful. I think I wanted to get away from the indefatigable lady who wanted to talk 'awt' to me. Did you ever chance to hear the way the imitation article pronounces that word, Miss Raynor?" Then, as seemed to be his custom, without waiting for a reply to the question he dashed into another subject. "I can't tell you how sorry I am that our review of that book was interrupted! I wanted to hear the logical progression of the argument. I'll tell you what, Miss Raynor, let me see you safely home this evening; then you can finish the review for me; will you?"

Then was Caroline's embarrassment intense. She had supposed it to be a sort of accident that had given her the company of this distinguished gentleman at the refreshment table, and the gratifying of a scholarly whim to see how well one book had been studied that had prompted his persistent questioning since; but to receive still more attention from him without acquainting him with her place in society seemed to this painfully honest girl an impropriety. What if Professor Monteith's son should take the long walk from his father's house to Mrs. Chester's door in company with Mrs. Chester's hired help? Caroline was sufficiently versed in the style of gossip rampant in the little town to know that it would be a painful experiment to the young man, if he were sensitive. At the same time, she appreciated his kindness and his conversation and disliked to decline his courtesy with apparent rudeness. As often before in her life, she resolved on the alternative of entire honesty.

The parlor was long and their progress slow, surrounded as they were by other promenaders; besides, Mrs. Fenton—eager little woman that she was—flitted twice from the station where they expected to meet her; so there was time for explanation. Caroline's voice was as quiet and self-sustained as it had been when she was reviewing Walker for his benefit. "I thank you, Mr. Monteith, but it is not right that I should accept your kindness. You mistake my position; I am not in society."

"No?" repeated Mr. Monteith with a purposely puzzled tone. "I supposed you were. I have been absent from my native land for a number of years. What has that term come to mean in this region? I thought you were my father's guest!"

"I beg your pardon." Caroline did not want to laugh, but she could not help it. "I mean that I was never in society before and do not expect to be again. It was your father's great kindness. I am not in the same circle with his other guests. You have met Mrs. Chester here this evening? I am her hired help: have been for two years and expect to be as long as I succeed in suiting her."

"I know Mrs. Chester. She belonged to one of the 'old families' that my grandfather used to tell about when I was a towheaded boy. I remember I used to think she did not look so very *old,* and I could not understand why that term was always applied to her. They live in the old homestead, my father told me, or in the grand mansion that they have built in its place; not half so fascinating a place, I'll venture, as the rambling old house was, but nearly a mile from here, is it not? Unless your author was a decidedly prosy old fellow, you will just have time to finish the review. May I walk home with you, Miss Raynor?"

She did not want to laugh. Her cheeks were the color of the scarlet fuchsias they were just passing; but there was such a sparkle of mischief in his eyes and such suppressed fun in his voice that she could not help it.

16

QUESTIONS AND ANSWERS

THERE was one pair of ears that evening eagerly listening for every crumb which fell from anyone's lips concerning Chautauqua. This was none other than young Robert Fenton. You will remember that he was the inspirer of this special branch and certainly was as much interested in its success as any human being could be. Were not his father and mother both members, and had he not had nicer evenings with them since this Circle came into existence, talking up Roman history, than he ever remembered before in his life? I will even admit that it added spice to his enjoyment to discover that he was an authority when controverted points were being discussed, and that his mother had once said to Caroline and young Charlie Mathers in his hearing: "I think you must be mistaken in your date, for my Robert says thus and so, and he is generally very correct." Oh yes, Robert Fenton was an intense believer in the C.L.S.C. and had an intense longing to visit Chautauqua. He drew near when he heard the name and presently made a bold petition:

"Won't you tell us all about Chautauqua? I mean to go there this summer if I can, and I think I can."

Now anybody who knows the man that has made Chautauqua what it is knows that the keen, questioning eyes and eager smiles of a wide-awake boy fascinate him instantly. He turned quickly at the sound of the fresh young voice: "All about Chautauqua? Yes, sir; with pleasure. Where shall I begin?"

So it transpired that there was another catechetical exercise that evening. One by one the promenaders halted in his vicinity, little by little the Circle widened until fully one-third of the guests had arranged themselves within hearing, to listen and question, while the one best posted told them about the place which had such a charmed life to some of them. "You ought to go, this season, everyone of you," Dr. Monteith said suddenly, breaking away from the listening group and joining a company who were trying to listen and yet were too far away to hear much.

"I hope for a very large delegation from our Circle. Mr. Fenton, have you decided to take your family?"

"Yes, sir," was that gentleman's prompt answer. "If nothing prevents, I hope to spend about six weeks there this summer."

"If Robert were within hearing he would applaud," Mrs. Fenton said, laughing. "He has never been able to bring his father to so outspoken a decision as that."

The group around Dr. Monteith were eager to question, and finding him well posted they poured out their queries. Several of them had already arrived at definite decisions. Even pretty little Aimie Allison declared she could go if she wanted to, and she believed she wanted to. She had intended to go to Long Branch, but someway it seemed to her that this would be "nicer." There were those who were gravely silent about the matter. James Ward had canvassed the subject somewhat thoroughly in his own mind and decided that it would be foolish to expect his father to expend so much money for what would look to him like a mere entertainment. Caroline, as she had said, had as much expectation of going to Europe as to Chautauqua; and as for Paul, he had not even given the matter a thought beyond the one involved in a very positive statement made not long before to Robert Fenton: "One of these days I mean to go there, but it won't be for several years yet." So these three, while they listened interestedly, did not give such listening as those who said: *"I'm* going!" But many were listening and questioning, evidently with a view to future plans. "What about the Teachers' Retreat," questioned Mr. Fenton. "Any benefit in that to people who never expect to be teachers?"

"Decidedly, yes. The very best educators in the country are to be there to exhibit what they consider the best ways of presenting thought to young minds. Aside from the personal benefit to be obtained through these lectures, conversations, and the like, no parent can afford to do without the knowledge and the stimulus which they present."

"What is the expense of living at Chautauqua?" came from another side of the room.

"Now that question is almost as difficult to answer as it would be for you to tell me what is the expense of living in Centerville," their victim said, smiling. "The truth is, it depends on the sort of living which you are pleased to want. If you keep house, it will depend on the number of rooms in your house, the size of your party, the brains of your clerk, and the economy of your cook, as well as on several other things. If you board, it will depend on the size and style of room you require and the number and variety of the delicacies which you are willing to pay for. There is a hotel with good accommodations; there are any number of private boardinghouses, with prices varying according to location and accommodations; there are cottages to rent, where you can, as I said, set up an establishment of your own; there are restaurants, where you can buy almost any necessary that can be thought of; there are tents, which you can rent for a trifle and roll yourself in a blanket at night and buy a pitcher of milk and some rolls at the baker's in the morning and live as cheaply as you can anywhere on earth."

"Somebody told my Fred that there was a School of Languages, or something of that sort," said Mr. Morris. "Is there any special advantage in that line?"

"Six weeks of thorough drill in whatever language you choose, or as many of them as you choose, the teachers among the best; some go so far as to say *the* best that can be found in this country or any other. Such work as that is worth a great deal to any scholar."

Thus the questions and answers continued, Dr. Monteith's clique seeming as deeply interested as the Circle in the front parlor, and all attempt to introduce any other topic having been suspended, it is safe to say that certain ones, at least, were wiser when they went home that evening than they had been when they came.

This matter of going home deserves a little attention. It marked an important era in the lives of some. James Ward, by the merest chance, had been standing near to pretty little Aimie when supper was announced, or it is probable his courage would not have been equal to waiting on her at the table; but the bright little efforts at conversation in which they two had indulged had had all the charm and novelty to him; and besides, was not Jack Butler exactly opposite, bestowing an occasional supercilious glance in their direction? What if he should ask to see Miss Aimie home, and what if Jack Butler proposed to do the same thing, and he should be in advance of Jack, and Miss Aimie should not refuse him? Would not that be a delightful triumph! It was a bold undertaking; how bold it appeared to him you will hardly be able to imagine, unless you are a young man who has been entirely isolated from the society of young misses until the very thought of attempting any of the most ordinary courtesies toward them flushes your face and sets your heart to throbbing.

It was a miserable motive. I regret that he had not a better one. But truth compels me to state that every time James Ward thought of his enemy, Jack Butler, and of his possible intentions toward the pretty Aimie, the desire grew upon him to attempt, at least, to discomfort him. Now it happened, strangely enough that the head of the pretty Aimie was somewhat troubled with a like thought. Since young Ward had been under the ban of her father's command, she had not even talked with him at the Circle. Not that she had avoided this entertainment, but he had been so absorbed in his work there as to have given her no opportunity; but on this evening, when he, having canvassed the subject, boldly invited her to the dining room, she had been standing beside her mother, and, receiving that mother's smiling nod of assent, little Aimie had accompanied with a light heart the one who was certainly the hero of the evening.

Half an hour afterwards, she twitched her mother's sleeve with an important question.

"Say, Mamma, suppose Mr. Ward *should* ask to walk home with me, what am I to say?"

"Well," said the mother, looking with admiring, and yet half-troubled, eyes on her pretty daughter, "I don't know; he appears like a very nice young man," and her eyes wandered over to where he stood and bestowed a swift glance of appreciation on his new and finely fitting suit. "He has made a most creditable appearance this evening in every way; and Dr. Monteith tells me he thinks very well of him indeed. I don't think Papa would object, Aimie, for this one evening."

"I don't believe he will ask me," Aimie said with a foolish little laugh. She referred to young Ward, not to her father. But he did ask her, and had the intense satisfaction of hearing her soft, pretty voice say to Jack Butler, "I am engaged, thank you," when he asked the same question soon afterwards.

Much ado was made in one way and another about that matter of getting home. "I suppose," Mrs. Chester said to her husband as she met him in the hall, herself wrapped for the walk, "I suppose we ought to have Caroline go along with us. It seems a very singular idea, but I really don't see how she is to get home unless we see to it. Would you send a servant down to tell her to get ready?"

"I don't believe it will be necessary for you to take that trouble," Mr. Chester said with twinkling eyes. "I saw her disappearing through the front door in company with young Monteith just before we came upstairs."

"Well, really!" declared Mrs. Chester. "I never heard anything to equal that in all my life!"

There had never been anything in Caroline's experience quite like that pleasant walk home in the moonlight. You will remember that she had no girlish memories to look back upon of walks with companions of her own age, who talked with her about things in which she was interested or cared particularly to hear her talk about anything. As for Kent Monteith, his real or pretended interest in the book that she had been studying hard had not subsided.

"Tell me the rest," he had said almost as soon as they were fairly on their way. "I think your author is clear-brained, at least. Let me hear more of him."

"The rest!" Caroline said, laughing. "I cannot think that you expect me to give you a history of our last month's work in one short evening!"

"Well, not each word in detail, I presume. I will be contented if you give me an idea of its effect on you. What new ideas beyond those which you mentioned has it given you? Or, in other words, what good has it done you?"

"What good?" repeated Caroline thoughtfully. "I think that is a question not easily answered. I cannot tell what *great* good it may do me in the future. I feel as if a great many weapons had been put into my hands that I had not before. How I am to use them, or with whom, my Father in heaven knows, and I thank him for giving me this opportunity to arm my mind."

"Then you accept all the ideas and suggestions found in the book?"

"Oh, I long ago accepted the facts about which the book treats. I found them in the Bible and took them for my own; but what is very pleasant to me is being helped to show others—some others who have had even less opportunity than I—the reasonableness of it all."

"That is just what I want. Show it to me, please."

"You do not come in my list," she said gently.

"And why not?"

"Because you have had abundant opportunities, and I cannot but think that you have availed yourself of some of them: it would be so exceedingly foolish to suppose that you had not."

"Well, suppose I have: and suppose that I find myself not helped as you have been. Suppose I feel utterly unable to see the reasonableness of it all. Suppose, for instance, I were to confess to a belief that the evangelical idea of prayer was entirely inconsistent with the idea that God knows everything, has planned everything, has settled everything, and, therefore, it cannot be changed, not even if the whole created universe were to pray that it might be. What have you learned from your book that can help me?"

"Nothing," said Caroline promptly. "I suppose there may be arguments for that class of persons, although this writer did not take up that phase of the subject; but I should think there was only one that would be perfectly satisfactory and unanswerable."

"Well now, if there is one which answers such a description, it is clearly your duty to give it to me, for I tell you frankly that I have never found it."

"I know it," was her quiet and, to him, surprising answer.

"May I be permitted to ask just what that quiet little sentence means? You know that I have never met this one unanswerable argument, do you mean?"

"I know you have never given it a fair and careful study, or you would not now be questioning the fact."

"You are very positive," he said, laughing a little. "All minds do not work alike, you remember; possibly it would not be so perfectly convincing to me as it has been to you." In his heart he said: *What an opinionated little thing it is, after all. I fancied I had found a curiosity—a young woman who did not suppose that she had scaled the heights of all wisdom because she knew a little about two or three things. The absurdity of her supposing that she has alighted upon an argument which I have not studied and could not answer if I chose!*

Then, carefully hiding all this undertone of thought, he added: "I am all attention and really almost overwhelmed with curiosity as to this unanswerable argument which has been hidden from me for so many years."

"I should think it would be an unanswerable argument as to the power of prayer, for a person to pray daily, sometimes hourly, and receive unmistakable answers to prayer. All the combined wisdom of the world, though it was poured into my ears in the form of arguments to which I could make no answer in words, could not convince *me* that God does not hear my prayer and answer, because I have daily proof from himself that he does just that thing. As to how he can do it or why he chose to do it; or how the seeming contradiction between that and his foreknowledge is reconciled, while it would be very pleasant for me to know, as it is pleasant for me to know so many of the things which I have learned in this book, after all, is not essential to my belief in the *fact;* and I really should think, as I said that the personal knowledge of the fact would be the only unanswerable argument to some minds. What is perfectly unaccountable to me is the fact that honest questioners do not apply this simple test to themselves and settle all doubts."

Now was the scholarly young artist astounded! He had studied carefully, he was gifted in argument for one so young, he believed himself to be thoroughly posted, yet there was undeniable truth in the fact that he had never personally tested the power of prayer.

"It is a test which is impossible to apply," he said at last, speaking shortly, all his gay courtesy apparently gone. "An honest man could not kneel down and pray when he did not believe that there was any such thing as answer to prayer."

"An honest man could kneel down and ask God to give him a belief in the doctrine of answered prayer; and if I were an honest unbeliever, I would ask God for that, on my knees, day after day, until I was convinced that I had come to him with all the sincerity I possessed, and laid the fact of my unbelief before him, and asked for help and had not received it. I have often thought that if all honest unbelievers would but stop their reasoning, trying to plan out God's work for him, and go to him with the whole story, how quickly it would silence all doubt, for faith is the gift of God. What proportion of them do you suppose really put that test, Mr. Monteith?"

"I don't know," he answered briefly; then, after a moment, "You say Walker does not discuss this phase of the subject?"

"Not at any length; indeed, I should hardly say that he touched upon it. He takes certain truths for granted; among them the power of prayer."

"Where do you find the unanswerable argument which you have been presenting so skillfully?"

"In the Bible: 'If any man will do his will, he *shall know* of the doctrine.' Have you studied that book carefully, Mr. Monteith?"

"Cross-examined, I declare!" exclaimed that gentleman; but the sentence was mental. To the questioner he gave a somewhat evasive answer and then most skillfully changed the subject. He had had enough of both Walker and theology for one evening.

17

"Yes, I Like It"

HE went home in a somewhat thoughtful mood. The quiet, clear-eyed girl who was "not in society," and whom he had thought to honor by his attention for one evening, partly to humor his father's whim, partly from mischief because of the undoubted sensation that he knew he could create in thus transgressing all the society people's sense of propriety, and partly out of pure good nature because he judged that it would be a new world to her, which he, knowing no one and caring to know no one in this region, could afford her as well as not. This same unimportant being had given him food for thought. It was a curious fact that the argument which she had presented had been, in a sense, unanswerable. What *was* a man to say to a person who calmly asserted that she had received not one, but many direct and emphatic answers to prayer? That she was mistaken? True, but then no *argument* lay therein, and you had by no means succeeded in convincing the person that such was the case. In fact, when one reduced the matter to actual logic, was not the weight of testimony against his side of the question? Here stood arrayed an army of scholars, among whom was to be found his honored father, calmly declaring: "All other proofs aside, we know this to be true: that God *has heard and answered us.*" Could he in reply say: "I know this to be true: that God has *not* answered me?" No, he couldn't, because the first part of the statement was lacking. God had not *heard* him, therefore how could he be expected to answer him? He actually was not a petitioner at all; had never tried to obtain audience with the King, and yet was presuming to declare in the face of those who had tried and been admitted that he *knew* no such thing was possible.

In this clearly unanswerable light did the folly present itself, having been called to mind by Caroline's few quiet words. And yet, I grieve to tell you that, *gentleman though he was*—a reasoning being, with more than usual brain power—he yet dismissed the whole subject with a careless "Nonsense! The idea of my plunging into theology, when I came home on purpose to rest! I wonder why that tiresome Chautauqua Circle, which is aiming to circle the world, I verily believe, had to put that into its list? Why couldn't it have been content with Rome and other tangible matters? She is a sharp girl, rather, for one in her position. Well, I've done my duty and given the sleepy old aristocratic town a nine-days' sensation; and she has done hers and given me a lecture on what is evidently her favorite topic; so we can both sleep with easy consciences tonight." But they didn't. The cultured young artist tossed for hours on a restless pillow. It is plain language, a word not often used in polite society—a word that he by no means allowed himself to use to himself, and yet he knew as well as though he had said it aloud that he was a *fool!*

Mr. Fenton went home chuckling. He was very

much amused with his wife. "I don't care," said that little woman, setting her lips firmly, "I don't like it."

"Don't like what?"

"This, any of it; I won't have Caroline made sport of."

"I don't believe he has the least idea of making sport of her; he is a good-natured young fellow, and his father has given him a hint, quite likely, of the way that Jack Butler and a few other apes of his stamp have treated her; and he thinks he will teach them all a lesson and give her a pleasant time in the bargain. I don't see why it wasn't a nice thing to do; a great deal better than letting her walk home alone, or trot on after the Chesters."

"Oh, well now, Robert, I know young men, and so do you; if Kent Monteith were a grand Christian man, like his father, and did such things with a purpose, it would be different; but he is just the sort of man to make the whole thing into a burlesque to entertain his artist friends with when he goes back to the city. They will shout over his caricature of Caroline, and he will think he is witty, and they will think he is jolly; and a nice time they will have of it, tossing her name about among them. I thought Caroline had more sense. I wonder she didn't decline his attentions on the spot."

All this set Mr. Fenton off into another laugh. "You women are queer," he said when he could speak; "it isn't two hours since you were admiring young Monteith because he was so fine a copy of his father, and now you are in a rage with him because he has treated your particular pet like a gentleman, instead of making a monkey of himself and pretending to be above her. How is a man to go to work to please you?"

"I don't quite know *what* I mean," confessed Mrs.

Fenton presently: "Only I know I am very much attached to Caroline, and I can't like to think of anybody laughing or talking about her, as so many will now. He has made her conspicuous; don't you see? And no woman ought to be made conspicuous. Still, if I thought he showed her attention from real kindness of heart, and not for the fun that was to be gotten out of it, I should feel differently. In fact, if I was sure it wouldn't injure Caroline herself, I wouldn't mind the rest."

"Injure Caroline! How? What do you mean?"

"Oh, it isn't easy to tell what I mean; give her ideas, you know. Kent Monteith is in the very first society in the city, rich and talented, and admired, and all that; and he has sort of singled her out from all our young people and given her special attention. It would be no more than natural if she should, on the strength of that, get some foolish ideas and go to fancying that he was struck with her appearance, you know, and all that nonsense, and get dissatisfied with her position, and—oh, well, I tell you I *don't know how* to express it. In fact, I hardly know what I think myself, this whole question is such a muddle to me. But I know I think a great deal of Caroline, and I don't want her spoiled, nor hurt; and I am afraid of such things as we have had tonight."

"I should think it *was* a muddle!" declared Mr. Fenton, still in utmost good humor. "You are mad at people who slight Caroline, and you are twice as mad at people who show her attention; so I don't know how you are to be pleased."

Mrs. Fenton laughed over this picture of her own inconsistency, yet was troubled and perplexed. It was true, as she said that she didn't know what she thought, only that she wanted to shield Caroline from gossip and from every possible harm.

Mr. Fenton essayed to help her, or to think aloud. "Women are queer; *they* do it."

"Do what?"

"Why, make the distinctions in society of which men would never dream, and when they get them made, they don't know what they mean by them. Did you see young Bennett walking away with Miss Harper tonight?"

This question seemed an entirely irrelevant one to Mrs. Fenton, so she answered wonderingly:

"Why, yes, what of that?"

"She is nothing but a music teacher, why don't you exclaim over that as mischievous?"

"Robert Fenton, what do you mean?"

"I mean," he said, laughing at her astonished, not to say indignant, face, "that she affords a good illustration of the distinctions about which I was talking. It is all right to receive *her* into good society, though I do hire her to give my boy music lessons. That is, we receive her into our society. We must remember that there is a society, here in America too that would look down on her with contempt because she earned her living. We have none of that nonsense. But because Mrs. Chester pays Caroline for sweeping her rooms, she mustn't be introduced to our friends. Now isn't that queer?"

"Oh, well, Robert, you know as well as I do that it isn't the mere difference in the kinds of work; whether it is our fault or not, it is a fact that, as a rule, the girls who work in our kitchens are not fitted, either by education or taste, to associate with us. They wouldn't enjoy it any better than we."

"But you don't think Caroline one of the ordinary

sort. Isn't she as well fitted by education and taste as most of us?"

"Of course she is. I think she is better fitted than half the girls in town."

"Then why not accept that fact, and not worry about her or act as though the accident of her position as a hired helper to Mrs. Chester had anything to do with it?"

"People won't," said Mrs. Fenton, laughing yet vexed.

As for Mrs. Chester, she grumbled a little the next morning before she left her dressing room. "I suppose my lady will be too lofty to wait on the table this morning. I am really afraid I shall feel embarrassed at the idea of soliciting her help," and she set the hair-brush down with a bang and looked annoyed. She believed her comfort with her rare help was gone.

Yet nothing about Caroline contributed toward this conclusion. Her dress was as neat and as severely plain as ever, her manner as quietly respectful, and her forethought for the comfort of the household as strongly marked as heretofore. Watching her with wide-open, jealous eyes during the day, seeing her go about her many duties with quiet care and usual success, Mrs. Chester gradually changed her mind. "She really *is* an unusual girl!" she told herself. "I don't think I ever even *read* of one like her before; and yet in English novels one is always reading about those rare maids who are more like friends of the family than hired help. I declare, I believe Caroline is superior to any of them."

Thenceforward Mrs. Chester adorned herself with a new character. She became the patron of her second girl; talked with her as to her hopes and plans for the future; aided and abetted them as well as she could;

arranged that the hours when she was off duty should be absolutely her own and not interrupted as heretofore by her mistress's whim; and in many ways showed herself a friend. Well for Caroline that she had the rare sense to take this help for just what it was worth and appreciate it. She did not resent the evident air of patronage that hovered about it all. She ignored the constant reminder that her sphere in life was low and, realizing that special kindness was meant, showed her gratitude in a hundred nameless ways. In short, mistress and maid grew nearer to each other with each passing day; nearer than Caroline, at least, had ever supposed it possible for her to come. As for Mrs. Chester, she grew daily so satisfied with herself and her experiment that she was in danger of becoming a reformer along the very line in which she had hitherto especially failed.

But all this is looking ahead. I am glad for Caroline's sake that she could not hear the conversation which passed between Mr. and Mrs. Fenton on that evening, especially Mrs. Fenton's share in it. She would have known then that, staunch as that little woman was in her friendship, she underrated the girl she was befriending. Not a thought of silliness connected with Kent Monteith entered our Caroline's mind. There was just this outgrowth from the evening's experience: "He was very kind," she said musingly; "very kind indeed. It is his father's kindness, of course, handed down to me through him; but it was thoughtful. It made the evening what it could not have been to me but for his forethought." Then, after a moment of serious thought, "Poor young man! With all his advantages, his superior education and high culture, not to have even tasted of the true wisdom!" and she added his name to the list of those whom she daily brought before God in prayer. And, really, if they had all but known it, this was precisely what Professor Monteith had hoped that the "rare girl" would do for his son.

Before the next day's sun had set, one member of the Centerville Circle had what was to him a marvelous experience.

Paul Adams, the next afternoon between three and four o'clock, was driving his plane vigorously over a rough board, when he was interrupted by a question from his employer, suddenly put, yet having that indescribable air about it which lets one see that it introduces an idea that has been industriously turned over in the mind for some time.

"What are you going to do all summer, Paul?"

"Work!" said Paul, sending the plane skillfully on its way, yet bestowing a shrewd glance on Mr. Tucker. What did the man mean? Wasn't *he* going to employ him?

Then silence lasted for some time, Mr. Tucker seeming to have exhausted his resources for conversation with that one question. Presently, however, he jerked out another. "How would you like to take a little trip with me?"

"A trip!" The plane stopped now for a full half minute, while Paul took time to look amazed. He had never been twenty miles away from home in his life.

"Aye, a trip!" And the reflective, irresolute look on the face of the carpenter settled into one of determination. "I've about made up my mind to do it. I don't object to going, just for the sake of *going*. I've never had no opportunities of that kind, and I've about made up my mind to give you the chance to go along. There's others that have worked for me longer and know more about work than you do, of course, and perhaps could help more; but I always had a liking for your father, and I don't mind saying that, though I'm kind of astonished at myself about it, I've taken an unaccountable liking to you. The long and short of it is, you can go along if you want to." And the carpenter tossed down the bit of board that he had been whittling with an air of satisfaction that at least so much was settled.

"Where to?" It was all the astonished boy could say.

"Well, I ain't too sure that I know myself." The bit of board was picked up, and the whittling went on again. "Do you happen to have heard—ever—of a kind of place in the woods—or near the woods— called Chat-a-quay, or something like that? Indian kind of name, I guess."

If he had not been whittling, he would have noticed the sudden gleam of light in Paul's eyes. "Chautauqua!" He flashed the word out as if it might have been a talisman.

"Yes, I guess that *is* the way he pronounced it. You see, there is a kind of settlement there in the woods. I don't understand much about it, and it don't make no difference. Mr. Monteith, the professor you know, has got interested in it, and he wants a house built— two of 'em, in fact—and he says he wants to put the work into the hands of somebody that he knows he can trust and not have to think anything about it; and he has made me a good offer; and I'm going to do it. He put it into my head to take help along with me from here. He thinks it will pay if it *is* a long journey; and I don't mind telling you that I said to him at once I'd rather have you at my heels to do just what I told you than any other hand I had."

By this time, Mr. Tucker looked up from his

whittling and caught the gleam in the young workman's eyes. It was so bright he felt almost startled. "You like it, I guess," he said wonderingly.

"Yes," said Paul, catching his breath and trying to speak in a natural tone; "I like it."

18

THIS WAY TO THE HALL

AND so it came to pass that as the newest steamer on Chautauqua Lake, shining with paint and cleanliness, slipped softly into harbor one July afternoon, freighted with the Centerville delegation (to say nothing of several hundred other people), it was Paul Adams in his neat business suit and thoroughly business air who stood on the dock waiting to receive them. He had been at Chautauqua for four weeks and was prepared to do the honors. Various things had combined to make the Centerville representation much larger than had been anticipated. The Fentons were there, of course; they had looked forward to the treat for so long and planned so systematically that no trifling intervention could have kept them away. Young Bennett was there, not because he had at first intended, but because he discovered at a late hour that a certain professor whom he had long been anxious to see and hear was to be at Chautauqua during the Teachers' Retreat. Therefore he came.

Miss Aimie Allison was there, because there seemed no reason in the world why she should not come. Mrs.

Fenton had been so kind as to promise to take care of her, and it was such lovely weather, and they said the boating on the lake was just splendid, and the bathing ditto; why shouldn't she go? So she went. Caroline Raynor was there, because the Chesters had suddenly determined on a trip to the mountains which did not include her; therefore, her time was at her own disposal; and because Mrs. Fenton, planning day and night ways of bringing it about, had finally hit upon a plan of cooperative housekeeping with Caroline for commander-in-chief, meeting her share of the expenses by assuming the care of the household and because—oh rare and blessed experience!—Mr. Chester had (after days of hard work bestowed by Caroline to aid the family preparations for departure) placed in her hands a roll of bills and said: "Now go to Chautauqua or somewhere and enjoy yourself; you deserve to if anybody does." On examination there proved to be bills enough to give her the round trip; so, all these unexpected events combining to make her way clear, she came.

The Ward boys were there, because—well, I find, on consideration that it is very difficult to tell you why they came. They did not know themselves. No one could be more astonished than themselves over the fact that they were actually on the steamer. Certain consultations between their father and Dr. Monteith undoubtedly had much to do with it; of this, the young men were sure; only, what arguments could the doctor have brought to bear on the father to cause *him* to be the prime mover in the matter of their going? Actually suggesting it, indeed, I may say urging it, not only for one, but emphatically for both sons: entering into the details of plans, furnishing the money, and in every way pushing the enterprise. The boys did not understand it. They had not said much about it to each other, but both had lain awake of nights, revolving the matter. Possibly had they heard certain words of Dr. Monteith's one morning as he stood in Mr. Ward's store door and talked with that gentleman, they might have been wiser; and yet, so little did they understand their father that I am not sure about this being the case. "I look to Chautauqua as a means of helping your son James to a discovery of what place he was made to fill in life. That is one reason why I hope you will conclude to send him there this summer; it is a good place in which to develop to a young man his own powers and the line in which he ought to cultivate them. James has reached the point where this discovery is of the highest importance to him. I think there are grand possibilities about the young man. As for Joseph—I think you will pardon the suggestion, knowing how thoroughly interested I am in both the boys for their mother's sake. I knew their mother, you remember, when she and I were young. I should like to isolate Joseph for a time from all his old companions not only, but his old haunts, and surround him by such influences as his mother would have liked. I know of no better field than Chautauqua in which to experiment."

This, in substance, is what Mr. Monteith said about it. I think he understood Mr. Ward better than the sons did. Whether from that or from other causes, the boys were of the Chautauqua party. Of course, it is unnecessary to state that the Monteiths were of the party, also the Wheelers, and the McChesneys, and the Stuarts, to say nothing of certain men and women not so prominent in society or culture, but who were thoroughly interested by this time in Chautauqua.

It is a curious thing how impossible it is, as a rule,

to convey to people a correct impression of any place by merely telling them about it. As a matter of fact, every member—at least of the Centerville delegation—had heard of Chautauqua as a place where there were many cottages—some fine ones—boardinghouses, hotels, stores, telegraph office, post office, and other indications of civilized life; yet not one of those who were nearing the groups for the first time had realized afterwards that he had believed himself about to land in the woods and camp out in very rural style for a few weeks: a taste of pioneer life, with many discomforts and a fair chance to immortalize himself by being good-natured under difficulties. To each of this number there came a sensation of bewilderment as the boat fairly touched the broad wharf and the stream of human life began to pour off. "How do you all do?" was the characteristic American greeting of Paul Adams as he stepped briskly forward to meet them. "Claim your baggage at the other entrance, Mr. Fenton; one at a time, Mr. Parsons, the wheel won't register in couples. Mr. McChesney, the pressman, will attend to your luggage; you are booked for 279 Forrest Avenue. Mr. Bennett, I secured No. 20 for you at the Palace Hotel; here is a gentleman who will show you the way; just give your checks to him, and it will be all right. Oh, Mr. Stuart, there is a telegram awaiting you. You will find it at the office, second avenue to the right. Now, Mrs. Fenton, if your party is ready we will move on to your house; you are on Janes Avenue; just pass around the park to your left; it is a short walk."

How fast Paul Adams could talk! This was the only clear sensation some of that party had—for a few minutes at least. Where were they? Where were the woods, and the camping out, and the uncivilized surroundings, and the chance to be heroic? "Palace Hotel," and "Forrest Avenue," and "Janes Avenue," and telegrams, and the park! Were they set down in the midst of a whirling city? To be sure, there stretched the woods green and cool; but the lovely park on one side, so carefully laid out, the broad, winding avenues reaching away into the distance, the rush and bustle of business on every hand, the shout of newsboys with evening papers, the band of music in the distance, the immense piles of luggage that were being systematically disposed of by trained officials—all these things gave them a curious mixed sense of being in the woods and yet in the world that was as unique as it was interesting. Arrived at the house which the Fentons and their party had secured for the season, the effect was no less bewildering. Here, in place of the barest log cabin surroundings, they found a neat frame building, modern French windows reaching to broad piazza floors, carpets, curtains, and in short, all the needful belongings of a tasteful summer home.

"Tinted walls and lace curtains, I declare!" exclaimed Mrs. Fenton, standing in the center of one of the pretty rooms to take a general survey. "Why, Caroline, this isn't the woods!"

"Yes, it is," returned that young woman with a happy little laugh; "see that row of trees just at the side door, and those in front, and that pretty little group across the way, and hear those birds!" This was really all the time that she bestowed on the outdoor world. Her mind was intent on getting everything within the small, bright house reduced to homelike order. This, as every housekeeper knows, is no easy task, especially when you have stepped into an abode already furnished to remain only a few weeks and do not feel justified in sending to the store or the warerooms for every little article that has been overlooked. Steadily did the presiding genius of the house in the woods betake herself to her task. The others worked spasmodically, leaving off in the midst of a task to go to the dock when the afternoon boats came in, or to go to the office for a walk, or to rove through the ever-fascinating avenues, just to see where they would lead, or to follow the sound of martial music and get a glimpse of the picnic excursionists on parade. It would be impossible to give even a hint of the numerous devices which nature planned during the next few days to allure the dwellers in that cottage. Only Caroline worked on, insisting upon planning until each thing was just where she wanted it to be, set in just such a way as would contribute most to the comfort of the inhabitants.

"I believe you like it," declared Mrs. Fenton to her as she arranged and rearranged the dishes in the tiny china closet with a view to economizing space. "Here you are working away and the rest of us are just wild to get out. You haven't even seen the Auditorium yet, nor the Hall, nor anything. What do you mean?"

"I'm saving them," said Caroline, laughing. "They'll keep, but my yeast won't unless I use it tonight. I'm going to bake some bread; it will seem ever so much more like home than that which we buy."

Truth to tell she did like it, this pretty new house, small enough to be homelike, simple enough so that she might let the wings of her imagination soar into realms that would make of it her very own. What if it were, and she had entire control of its management, surrounded always by people with whom she would like to be? In that case, how would she arrange this closet, and that sitting room, and that front chamber? These were endless sources of innocent pleasure to the lonely, homeless girl. Almost from childhood, her only home had been that of a hired helper in houses of wealth and elegance. Perhaps this is the reason why such houses never meant *home* to her. "They are too large and grand and cold," she said to herself with a shiver. "I could never think of cuddling down in any corner of them and being just myself. I don't know what is the matter with them; but this little cottage is perfect. I wonder if the man who planned it has a wife and talked with her about these corner cupboards; he could never have thought them out himself without her help. How much obliged I am to her for them."

Caroline Raynor enjoyed a great deal that summer at Chautauqua. If you should ever see her and talk with her about it, she will undoubtedly have much to tell you about the lectures and the concerts and the rare and highly appreciated opportunities on every hand, but, so queer are human hearts that I doubt if she says a single word to you about those corner cupboards over which she worked with such quiet pleasure and with such a sense of making the most of a convenient little home as she had never felt before.

There came an evening when, the after-supper dishes safely stored and the room in dainty order, Caroline washed her hands, unbuttoned and hung away the trim house apron behind a convenient door that looked as though it had been hung with a special view to hiding away work aprons when work was done, and gave a satisfied little sigh as she told herself that now they might begin their meetings as soon as they pleased, she was quite ready to listen and enjoy. She knew just what she was going to have for breakfast and in just how little time it could be made ready. There was no occasion to give another thought to the house that evening. She resolved upon a walk. It was just at the fascinating hour when the soft gray mist of the departing day was hovering over all things, and yet when the sky was aglow with stars. Had she planned it all, she could not have chosen a better hour in which to get first impressions of the beauty that overhung Chautauqua. The question was, whom could she secure for a companion? The large family had scattered itself after tea as if by magic, irresistibly drawn in the ways of their various fascinations; Mrs. Fenton, having been the last to go, half provoked at Caroline, meantime, because she would not be prevailed upon to leave some household task until the morrow and come and see how lovely the lake looked in the twilight.

"Robert," she said suddenly, discovering a gray-coated figure sitting out on a bit of log under one of the tallest trees, gazing steadily up into the sky, "suppose you come and show me a little piece of Chautauqua!"

Whereupon Robert Fenton jumped up from the log with great alacrity and came toward her.

"Are you really ready?" he said eagerly. "I shall be delighted to go with you. Caroline, do you know anything about astronomy?"

"Not a thing," said Caroline, smiling over the earnestness of his tone.

"Well, I wish I did. I wonder why they don't have boys study it more! It seems strange to know almost nothing of a lot of worlds that we can look right up at. Think of Europe, for instance! I know a good deal about that part of the world though I never saw it, and perhaps I never shall—though I think I shall—but anyhow, I've not seen it yet, and I know pretty well what is going on over there; but what do I know about that star that largest one looking right straight down on us?"

"But then, people can travel through Europe, and learn the languages, and make the acquaintance of the inhabitants; and after you have learned all there is to know about that star, how much will you know of the people who live there, if there are any?"

"That's true," said Robert thoughtfully. "But that's no reason why a boy should not learn all he can about the star itself."

To this Caroline heartily assented, and Robert, with increased eagerness, began to tell her of a certain lecture that was to be delivered soon at Chautauqua by one Dr. Warren.

"All about astronomy, and just as fascinating as any storybook; Mr. Monteith says so. Not Professor Monteith, but the young man. He says he's just splendid," stopping himself in the midst of this tide of explanation as they reached a turn in the avenue, with the question:

"Now which way do you want to go?"

"Whichever way you are pleased to take me. I have not seen anything save what I couldn't help looking at when we arrived."

"Then I'm just going to take you to the Hall. The rest rush to the Auditorium first and rave over that. It is splendid, I suppose; large, you know, and makes one think of crowds and grand things. But I can't imagine people enough here to fill it—not to begin! With the Hall, now, it is different; just a nice audience would fill that, and it is so white, and so—oh, well! I can't explain, only it's nice, and you will like it. Some people don't care about it much; but I know you will."

"Thank you," said Caroline, and her heart was smiling as well as her eyes. She understood the boy;

imagined something of what he would have said if he could have expressed his feelings, and she understood and appreciated the delicately sincere compliment.

"This is a lovely avenue that leads to your favorite building," she said as she turned back to look at the straight, wide road they had traversed, lying clear-cut amid the shadows of the overhanging trees.

"Isn't it!" declared Robert, with ever-increasing enthusiasm. "This is another thing I like so much— this avenue. I tell you, Caroline, when it must be just grand, and that is in full moonlight. Ha! There it is!"

It is impossible to describe to you the delight that was in the boy's tones as the gleaming pillars of the Hall of Philosophy rose up before him; something in the purity and strength and quaintness seemed to have gotten possession of him. Whether it was a shadowy link between him and some ancient scholar or worshiper I cannot say, but certain it is that Robert Fenton, boy though he was, treading the Chautauquan avenues for the first time, felt his young heart thrill with a hope and a determination, neither of which he understood, every time he saw those gleaming pillars.

"Oh!" said Caroline.

Now what a foolishly insignificant word that appeared on paper! And yet you are no student of language if you do not to some extent realize the shades of feeling which it is capable of expressing. Let it but explode from living lips able to give it just the right intonation, and it becomes eloquent, pathetic, sarcastic—according to the mood of the speaker—but always effective. It satisfied Robert.

"There!" he said in triumph. "What did I tell you?"

They walked with quiet feet up and down the echoing floor. They walked to the outer edge and looked down on the hillside below them, over toward the lake, spanned by gleaming lights, and up at the ever-increasing stars. They walked back and stood in front of the platform and gave free play to their almost equally vivid imaginations. They were really beginning life—these two—although counting by years one was nearly a decade ahead of the other. Robert's opportunities had been by far the greater, and this bridged the difference in years and made them companionable. Robert liked her. He was not fond of most young ladies. He had arrived at the age when a certain type of free and fearless boy needs to struggle hard with the temptation to look down upon all feminine natures—except, perhaps, his mother's and grandmother's—with something very like scorn. They were, as a class, so hopelessly weak and feeble, so afraid of a fence or a stream of water to cross. They screamed at bugs and worms, and shrank from dogs, and even cows, as terrible creations; they were, in short, so lacking in those elements which a real boy cannot help at a certain time in his life putting foremost among the virtues that Robert, at least, knew few besides his mother that he cared to like, always putting Caroline first among the few. The quiet poise of her nature seemed to tone and rest his impetuous one. She was so calmly brave where many drew back and shrieked that in Robert's eyes she was a model. He stepped onto the platform at last and said: "Now I will be Professor de Profundus and deliver a lecture on the biological construction of the—well, the Gauls, say; I know as little about them as any people. Will you be audience?"

"Yes," she said, laughing; "I will, if you will have a conversazione instead of a lecture and explain to me the meaning of the words which compose your topic."

Whereupon he shrugged his shoulders and declared conversazioni in his opinion to be dangerous things. Suppose every lecturer were called upon to explain the meaning of the words he used! What would become of the lecturer? Thus they, like two happy children, gave themselves up to the pleasure of the hour. Robert, after indulging in a strain of bombastic eloquence for a few minutes, suddenly broke away to look after a passing squirrel; and Caroline moved toward one of the busts which adorned the hall, wondering much whose face it was and finally growing so interested in the dim outline of feature that she set about learning.

"Robert," she called, as she heard his step approaching.

"Eh, what? I beg your pardon, ma'am." This was the answer, in a strange voice, to her call, and turning, somewhat startled, she saw that the hall had another occupant.

19

SIMPLE ADDITION

A YOUNG man, tall, strongly built, leaning against one of the columns, roused apparently and suddenly from complete absorption in a book which in the waning light he was still trying to read.

"I beg your pardon," he said again as Caroline turned; "I heard my name and imagined myself wanted. I suppose there *are* other Roberts in the world, though just at that moment I was ignorant of it."

"How do you do again?"

This was the other Robert's voice; and, with the unceremoniousness of boyhood, he proceeded to introduce his friends after a fashion of his own:

"This is Mr. Masters, Caroline; Mr. Monteith introduced me to him this morning and said he was a friend of his. This is our friend Miss Raynor, Mr. Masters."

There was something so entirely boyish, and at the same time courteous, in this presentation that the two strangers could not help smiling at each other.

"I am not sure that your friend will like to make

acquaintances in so unceremonious a manner," the gentleman said; yet he lifted his hat.

"I am glad to meet you again." This to Robert. "I think you have a young man in your party whom I am anxious to meet; Mr. Monteith told me I would be likely to find him at your cottage: Mr. James Ward."

Robert promptly assured him that he knew of James Ward's whereabouts, and if he would join them on their homeward walk he could probably see the young man that evening.

Caroline, seeing the stranger hesitate and look inquiringly toward her, could not do other than assent to so simple a way of piloting him; nor was she sorry. Keen interest in James Ward, and intense anxiety to have Chautauqua in every sense a blessing and not a bane to him, made her alive to the importance of the companions which he chose. Who was this young man expressing such anxiety to seek him out? What would be his influence?

Almost unconsciously, while these thoughts passed rapidly through her mind, she gave him careful scrutiny. He had a frank, kind face. It seemed impossible not to trust it. Yet after all, could one really be sure of faces? What sort of a book was he so intent over? Her eyes lighted with pleasure as she recognized it. This, at least, was an old friend: *Philosophy of the Plan of Salvation.* She did not need to read the letters on the title page to make sure that the book—so like her own—bore that name.

"C.L.S.C?" she said, hardly realizing that she said it and yet feeling pleased that the Circle was widening.

Possibly this was but the beginning of her hope to come in contact with people who were interested about the same things as herself.

"Yes, indeed!" he answered with energy. "I'm a

C.L.S.C., and a C.S.L., and a C.F.M., and anything else that Chautauqua offers for people like me, who have a reasonable amount of brains and not much chance to cultivate them. I'm an enthusiast, Miss Raynor, a hobbyist—any name you like that will shadow forth something of the love and gratitude and reverence that I have for Chautauqua."

Her eyes sparkled over this. She was enough of a hobbyist about Chautauqua to admire enthusiasm in another.

"You have been here before, then?" she said.

"Indeed I have! I was here when Chautauqua was picked up out of its original woodsiness and developed step-by-step into the city that it is. To appreciate the contrast, you should have seen it as I did—an unbroken wilderness of trees and underbrush, inhabited by birds and squirrels in summer, and snow and silence in winter. I saw it in both aspects. I could not have shut my eyes and dreamed out the contrast much faster, it seems to me, than it has grown upon me. Still I'm good at dreaming. I have royal hours roving over these grounds, looking at things with prophetic eyes, as they shall be but a few years hence."

"Why?" Caroline asked with an amused yet interested face. He was so eager she could not but be interested. "What do you expect in the future?"

"Oh, I don't know; anything that can be wrought out of my brain. In one sense, I may be said to expect it all—actual marble here, perhaps, instead of this white paint imitation; statuary worthy of the spot; one figure, possibly, to the memory of the great founder of *this* Parthenon, and one, it may be, to the memory of the one who helped to lay this floor and built this platform: that's myself, you see."

His tone had changed from an eager to a merry

one. He was recognizing the folly of his rhapsody addressed to this, a perfect stranger who, perhaps, did not sympathize in the least with his love for the place. The sentence closed with a gay laugh. But young Robert did not laugh; his whole face was eager and his eyes bright. "And marble steps leading down toward the lake, and a marble roadway to the Pnyx," he said eagerly. "It is like the Pnyx, isn't it? I never thought of it before."

"Go ahead!" declared the young man with a happy-hearted laugh. "You are as good at dreaming as I am; between us we will make Chautauqua famous." They had started for home, but paused for a last look at the Hall in the twilight. It gave their new companion a chance to see Caroline's unsmiling, wistful face.

"Did you ever see such a building as that before?" he asked her suddenly.

She shook her head. "No, and have no knowledge of the names which you give to it. Why do you call it the Parthenon, for instance?"

"Well, you know about the original Parthenon?"

"Nothing at all."

"It was a wonderful marble building in Athens, on the Acropolis. Do you know what that is?"

And again her only answer was a slow shake of the head and a wistful smile.

"It was the name given to the strongholds of cities; the highest points, you know, where the great monuments were placed and where the finest public buildings were. Athens had the finest acropolis in the world; so fine that when we say *the* Acropolis nowadays, we mean Athens, though there were others. One of the most wonderful buildings on this acropolis was the Parthenon, or the Athenaeum, or the Temple of

Minerva, whichever name you please. It was built of white marble, in the Doric style of architecture."

"What is the Doric style of architecture?" his eager listener interrupted him to ask.

"Well," looking up at the many-columned Hall of Philosophy, "it is this style: an imitation on a small scale, and in wood, of one of the grandest works of art to be found in the world."

"I don't like it that it is patterned after a Temple of Minerva," she said, looking up, nevertheless, with a new interest at the gleaming columns which, in the brilliant starlight, one could readily imagine were hewn from marble.

"I do," he said promptly, intense earnestness in voice and manner. "I like it exceedingly. Let the beautiful white temple be rescued from its heathen desecration and dedicated to the service of the good and true God our Father, and his Son Jesus Christ." He lifted his hat reverently as he spoke, and Caroline felt her heart thrill with gladness as she recognized in this a fellowship beyond that of any literary and social bond, strong as these may be; even a relationship through Jesus Christ.

"You belong to *his* Circle, then?" she said inquiringly.

"Aye, I do! I was admitted into fellowship with him on these very grounds. He found me here; or rather, it was here that he opened my stupid eyes to see him. I plainly realize now that he had followed me for many a year before that day, only I did not know it. Oh, I told you I owed everything to Chautauqua!"

They had left the "Parthenon" in the distance now and were rapidly nearing the cottage. Caroline had lost her anxiety about this newcomer's seeking James Ward; rather, she was anxious that just such companionship as she already believed this would be should be thrown around him. She liked this clear-eyed, frank-spoken man, and a curious feeling that she had known him a long time and could talk with him as a friend took possession of her. Something of this took shape in the form of a question which she suddenly asked.

"Out of the immense program that is offered here, what can be selected to the best advantage by a person who has only a portion of the time at her disposal and who wants to make the most of the opportunity so offered?"

"That is an immense question," he said, laughing. "You see, it depends on so many things; whether you have already a special line of study and need help, or whether you need to start in a certain line which you desire to undertake, or whether you are after general information. The fact is, a person can get just about what he or she wants out of Chautauqua now. What do you want?"

"Everything," said Caroline with perhaps a startling amount of energy; then she laughed. "That is too literally true to be altogether a pleasant admission," she added. "I am having my second good opportunity for learning *anything;* my first was in our local C.L.S.C."

Her companion turned and regarded her with an earnest look. "Then you are a special friend of this scheme," he said with feeling. "I am glad. I like to meet those who are indebted to the movement started here. I believe there are already thousands of them, and I believe there will be millions. There are people who call the enterprise superficial," he continued with increasing energy. "I never knew anything that was less so. It begins at the roots of things; prepares the soil, drops the seed, tends and waters it, and says to it, 'Now grow: become an oak if you can, or an elm, or a fruit tree, anything that God intended you for: you are started.'"

"I have heard that argument urged against it," Caroline said, laughing and thinking of Jack Butler.

"Of course; there is nothing better for brainless people to urge against it; and there is nothing more foolish. Superficial indeed! Is an oak tree superficial, I wonder, because it started from an acorn? Chautauqua never pretended to give men and women finished educations. It only starts them or gives a vigorous push to those who are started; *brains* will do the rest. I like it, too, because it does start people; I mean, it doesn't begin too high for men and women who had to work during the period of their boyhood and girlhood. I, for instance, who had to leave school when I was a boy of less than fifteen and earn my living from day to day, found that I could come here and have my bits of knowledge gleaned from various sources—spread out for me until I could see what I really did know, and then push on. I'm a mechanic, a builder," he said, dropping suddenly into a quieter tone. "A bit of an enthusiast on that subject too, I suspect, as you will surely conclude I am about Chautauqua. Is this your house, Fenton? Why, I designed this; it is one of my pet houses." Caroline laughed again over her own thoughts; she remembered the corner cupboards. She wondered if his wife had planned them. I am not sure that I can explain to you in what a happy mood she went to her neat kitchen and looked after the sponge for her next morning's baking. The evening had been such a pleasant one to her. The change was so great and so restful: this quiet woods and lovely lake, and the gleaming, many-pillared building, and the new acquaintance who had started a conversation simply from a platform of good sense and given her so much information and inspiration. That, after all, was the key to her happy feelings. She had added to her stock of valuables; she knew just so much more than she did an hour before. Certain names which she had met in her reading and wistfully peered at as strangers were known to her now; when she heard them again, she would be sure what they meant. "Robert," she said a little later, as Robert, having found and introduced young Ward to his new acquaintance, wandered out to the kitchen in search of companionship; "what did you mean tonight by the Pnyx? Isn't that the name you called it?"

"Yes," said Robert, eager to impart information. "Why, you know the Pnyx! It wasn't more than a quarter of a mile from the Acropolis. It was a semicircle and had a platform carved out of the rocks; more than six thousand people could be seated there, and it was there they used to have the great speeches. You wait until you see the Amphitheater, and you will understand it."

"I understand now," said Caroline; "thank you"; and she added the Pnyx to her little store of wealth. She had reached the stage where each new item of information could be labeled as so much added property.

20

"Gifts Differing"

I REALLY don't know but that girl's coming to Chautauqua just counts as a waste of so many more muslin dresses and kid boots and fancy neckties! I don't believe she has secured a single idea since she has been here; and, what is worse, I'm afraid the ideas are set too high for her to reach, especially as she has no notion of trying."

This was Mrs. Fenton's grim sentence as she stood on the south piazza one morning and watched pretty Aimie Allison step daintily over the dewy grass, skillfully raising her fresh lawn to shield it from a baptism of dew. She made as pretty a picture on the exquisite landscape of the summer morning as one need care to see. Yet Mrs. Fenton's face was grim as she watched her. Truth to tell that motherly woman found it a difficult task to mother the pretty butterfly. She flitted so airily and carelessly from flower to flower in the Chautauqua bed and so sweetly refused to do anything but flit and flutter that the earnest woman knew not what to do with her. Chautauqua ought to help her; yet how could it help the hummingbirds that hovered over the vine-wreathed window? Miss Aimie seemed to have about the stability of the hummingbird.

There was another trouble, if she had owned it to her own heart: half of the gloom on the matron's face this morning as she watched the pretty girl was owing to the fact that her special protégé, James Ward, went far too often over the lawns and down the avenues by the side of this fair butterfly. At least, so Mrs. Fenton thought. Why would not James see that now was his opportunity for cultivating other society than this brainless girl's? Good, earnest girls all about him; he met them every day and had opportunities enough to form acquaintances not only, but friendships such as would help him. Why couldn't he realize and appreciate his opportunities? Instead, he seemed to like nothing so well as the taking of morning walks with this giddy, brainless girl: Such was the severe name which Mrs. Fenton gave her on this summer morning, as she watched her step carefully over the underbrush from a recently hewn tree, James Ward, meantime, carrying her parasol and her fan and her camp chair as though he had nothing else in life to think of.

"What *can* such a pretty little piece of pink-and-white flesh get out of the intellectual table spread here? I don't like her influence over James. He is just at the age to be fascinated with a pretty face without regard to brains. Caroline, why don't you help me growl?"

"You don't seem to need help in that direction," laughed Caroline as she came through the room with a regiment of fresh towels in her arms, which she was prepared to distribute. "Besides, I think you are rather hard on poor Aimie; she may secure an idea or two in spite of her pretty muslins."

"I don't believe it," was Mrs. Fenton's still grim

response. But Mrs. Fenton was mistaken. At that very moment, the pretty Aimie paused in the midst of a sentence that was interesting to James Ward and stood on tiptoe to catch a glimpse of something within a large, airy room in the Children's Temple. It was a pretty sight. The room was cheerful looking, was comfortably seated, was decorated on one side with innumerable bright-colored somethings, was filled with a pretty buzz of life—girls, like herself, many of them young and pretty, seated before tables, with here and there a young gentleman, seeming, like themselves, merrily absorbed in some work.

"What in the world are they all doing?" questioned Aimie, stretching her neck for a better view. "They have pieces of bright silks, red and blue and all colors. No, they are not silks! I declare. I believe they are paper! What *can* they be doing? How pleasant it looks in there! Do you suppose we could go in?"

"Why, certainly," her companion said with alacrity. "Our tickets admit us to whatever is taking place on these grounds." And being in the mood just then to do whatever his fair companion suggested, whether it was to climb a tree or join a Latin class, he immediately led the way to the side door which stood invitingly open, and they were promptly shown to seats among the eager workers. Straightway a watching assistant laid before them the bright-colored papers arranged in squares.

"What am I to do with these?" whispered Aimie, smiling and blushing, addressing her neighbor on the left, a serious-faced girl.

"Why, follow the motions of the leader, if you can," with a strong emphasis on the last three words. "I can't." And she looked up at the newcomer. Her face was serious, but her eyes were laughing. She held in her hand the rose-colored paper, partly folded in a curious shape.

"But what is it for? What are they trying to make?"

"I don't know," and here her whole face laughed; "this is a kindergarten, you see, and we are supposed to be taking lessons in paper folding; it looks simple enough until you undertake to do it, and then a problem in geometry is nothing to it." Still, by this time the most of the workers had succeeded in finishing something, which they held up before each other's admiring eyes. A curious little bird's nest, looking intricate enough to have required hours of care and skill in the making, yet having been made almost in a second by the deft fingers of Madame Kraus Boelte, the skilled leader.

"Isn't it pretty?" declared the admiring Aimie. "I wish I knew how to make it!" Whereupon she seized upon a square of pink paper that matched the ribbon at her throat—for the lady on the platform had taken one up and was evidently about to launch out into something new. How pretty Aimie looked now! Her lips parted slightly in her eagerness to hear and to see and to do. Her small shapely fingers moving deftly, following the innumerable twists and turns which the teacher suggested until, with a little cry of triumph, she made the last fold and produced a star-shaped treasure that delighted her eyes. "I see how to do it; I can make those. How pretty they are! They would make lovely trimming for paper baskets. Oh, can't you get it? Let me show you. See, you made the wrong turn back here. This is the way." This to her companion on the left, and in a moment more she had reconstructed the blue paper star and set it on the table in triumph.

"How quickly you learn!" said the owner admiringly. "Perhaps you understand kindergarten work?"

"No, indeed; but I wish I did. What pretty work it is! What are all these ladies learning for?"

"Well, you see, they are teachers, some of them, and others want to be. And Mrs. Kraus Boelte is considered by many the finest kindergarten teacher in this country. It is really wonderful how skillful her little scholars become. All these lovely designs hanging over the blackboard were made, she says, by little fingers."

"Is it possible?" said Aimie. "What fascinating work it must be to teach little children how to do all those things!"

"Do you think so?" laughed the other. "I'm afraid I should never be able to do it; I should have to be taught myself first, and that seems impossible. Look! What is she making now?"

"I don't know what it is going to be, but I can do what she has just done," said Aimie, seizing a fresh bit of paper and working with speed and skill. Lo! It proved to be a boat. Her own finished, she gave help to her neighbor, then to a lady in front of her, and finally right and left from all around the table they reached forward their papers in various stages of unrepair and begged assistance.

"You are so skillful," said one and another admiringly. And Aimie, bright, pleased to be of avail and to exhibit a gift that was prized, smiled and bowed and worked with a will, eager and happy.

"The young lady in buff is very skillful with her fingers; she should join the class," said in tones of admiring approval the sweet voice and foreign accent of the teacher. And Aimie blushed, and laughed, as all eyes were thus turned upon her. As for James Ward, he admired her exceedingly. He liked to see her shine; to have her discover to others how bright and quick and altogether admirable she was. As for Aimie, she had never been so pleased with anything in her life. And I will not deny to you that her pleasure was greatly increased because she was presently called upon to extricate James Ward from a maze of confusion into which he fell in attempting to manipulate the bright papers. She blushed and laughed a great deal, but worked deftly at the same time, and quickly constructed for him a little boat.

"I don't see how you do it!" exclaimed she with the serious face and laughing eyes, watching the fingers half enviously. "I can't do anything with the little wretches; I think it is a great deal worse than *Merivale.*"

"Oh, are you a C.L.S.C.?" asked Aimie, looking at her with a new interest, as one with whom she had several ideas in common.

"Oh yes; I am in my second year. Are you a member?"

Whereupon Aimie gave proud assent and held her pretty head high, and made boats, stars, and birds' nests with astonishing celerity, and felt literary and happy.

"You ought to join the class," the new friend said, watching the swift-moving fingers. "They make lovely things, ever so many of them. I don't belong to the regular class, because I am so unskillful it isn't worthwhile, but I come in occasionally to see what is going on and secure ideas that I can adapt to the Sabbath teaching of the little ones. I'm a primary teacher. That is my forte, if I have one. Are you, also?"

"Oh no," said Aimie quickly; and the flush on her face deepened. The idea of her being a *teacher* of any kind was embarrassing.

"I should think you ought to be; I am sure you are

talented in that direction. It is such fascinating work. The little things are so bright and catch real deep, solid thoughts so quickly! My children are pretty good theologians, though they never heard that word in their lives, I presume. I think they could talk about all the essential doctrines of the church in a way that would be plain to others."

"Do you try to teach such things to little children?" asked Aimie, much astonished, and wondering greatly what her new friend would say if she could know how impossible it would be for her to pass examination on theological doctrines. "I shouldn't think they would be able to comprehend such puzzling subjects."

"Oh, indeed, they have much better capabilities than is generally supposed. If they hadn't, do you suppose they could do all these puzzling things that I find so difficult to see into? Yesterday, Mrs. Boelte taught us the use of the cubes and explained to us how skillful the little people were with the different forms in which the blocks can be arranged. I thought then that at least a kindergarten teacher would find no difficulty in understanding how readily little children grasp large subjects, if they are only presented to them in a childlike way. I get ever so much help here for my Sunday work; not that I can bring the toys in the Sunday school, of course, but I am constantly saying to myself: 'Yes that idea could be worked out on the blackboard in a sort of picture, and it would illustrate such a thing.' You ought to study this subject. I can't help fancying you would make a grand primary teacher. Are you interested in little children?"

"I don't know," said Aimie thoughtfully; "I have no little brothers and sisters, and I don't often come in contact with little people. Still, when I do I enjoy them ever so much; and I'm always stopping on the street to kiss the sweet babies and cunning toddlers whom I meet. Yes, I think on the whole I must be interested in children."

"I know you are, and I'm sure you would be just fascinated with a primary class. We get such good help here in that direction! Last year Mrs. Seymour gave receptions every other day for our benefit, and we learned ever so many things. Did you come to take up any special line of study this year?"

"I came for fun," said Aimie with a sudden sparkle in her eyes. "A large party from our Circle was coming, and I could come as well as not, so I did. I have never been here before."

"Oh, then you are just the one to take up the kindergarten and primary work. I'm sure you will like to study in that line. It is a great deal more profitable to settle on a certain line of work to carry out here, and when once it is settled, you will be surprised to see how many lectures and talks and the like that are not on the subject you have chosen can still be made helpful in that direction. Look at this obstinate paper of mine! It will not bend in the right way."

"You have given it a wrong twist on that last fold," laughed Aimie, and she reached forward nimble fingers and righted it.

All this talk had not flowed on uninterruptedly, but had come in bits between the paper foldings and the words of the leader. During another pause in the sort of familiar lecture on kindergarten work in general that was being given from the platform, Aimie's new acquaintance found opportunity to say: "There is one thing that makes my work among the children fascinating and hopeful: They are so fresh and innocent, so childlike in their ways of dealing with truths; they find it so easy to trust, so natural a thing to pray! When they

are taught that they may pray to Jesus about everything, they seem able to realize that it means just
exactly *that;* their faith is beautiful. I have a great many
earnest little Christians in my class. I confidently
expect to see them strong men and women in the
church, if they live. Don't you like to work where you
can *see* results?"

Pretty little Aimie laughed, not lightly. If it were not
a strange use of language, I might almost say she
laughed gravely. To be talked to about *working* anywhere impressed her as a singular, almost an amusing,
and yet, withal, a startling thought. She glanced over
at James Ward. He was giving attention just then to
what a new acquaintance was saying, and his face was
grave, thoughtful. Aimie could see that he knew how
to be in earnest. There flashed over her an impression
that one of these days this young man would know
how to *work* in many ways; and there came to her a
wistful feeling that *she* would like to be numbered
among the workers.

"Don't you think little bits of people can be Christians?" questioned the young lady, watching the
shadow of thought grow on Aimie's face and mistaking the cause.

"Oh, I don't know! I am not a proper person to
judge. The truth is, I don't quite know what you are
talking about; you see, I am not a Christian myself."

By this time there was the little bustle of breaking
up going on all over the room. The two-hours' lesson
was concluded; there was little time for further conversation. Yet she with the serious face and eyes that
had now grown gravely tender had a last word to say.
"Oh, I am sorry to hear that! You have a very important question to settle first, then. Won't you give it
immediate thought, and then consecrate yourself to

the work of teaching little children? I cannot help thinking that you have a marvelous talent undeveloped in that direction." She smiled brightly, held out her hand, and grasped the other's cordially, then mingled with the crowd; and Aimie, feeling a strange new sensation of companionship, looked after her wistfully. Very few of the people who could have helped her had ever cultivated Aimie. She turned toward the platform now, listening with eagerness to the after-meeting chat that was being enjoyed, wherein choice bits of kindergarten knowledge were being scattered. The leader recognized the pretty face as belonging to the skillful fingers and turned toward her. "The child should be a teacher," she said kindly; "should fit herself for service. The good God has given her a talent that she ought to cultivate."

This time Aimie had much ado to keep back a rush of tears. There was something strangely sweet and tender to her in this being singled out as one who should occupy a place in the world of workers. There had been times in her life when this fair butterfly felt in her secret heart a touch of sorrow that she should be *always and only* reckoned among the butterflies.

She went home across the fields. It was well that all the morning dew had dried away, for she was reckless as to her fresh muslin and let it trail over the long grass, her hands full of bright-colored papers, her face full of pleasure, and her voice so triumphant as she told her story of acquired knowledge at the dinner table that the lady of the house at the head of the table and the housekeeper at the foot exchanged significant glances, the one saying almost as plainly as words could have done, "Is it possible that she is at last interested in something besides her ribbons and laces?" and the other a sort of half-triumphant "I told you so!" but neither of them knew—nor did Aimie, for that matter—how the serious-faced girl went home thinking about the bright new face and deft fingers and coveted that soul to shine as a jewel in her crown.

21

✦━━❦━━✦

FLATS AND SHARPS

IT was curious to see how the different elements which composed the family in the Fenton cottage gravitated toward their respective attractions. Individuality showed plainly here; perhaps in no one more plainly than in Irene Butler. I think I have neglected to herald the arrival of the Butler girls, sent thither by the *ennuied* Jack, who declared Long Branch stupid and Saratoga insufferably hot and avowed his determination to see what that camp meeting was like before he was a year older. Miss Irene was nothing loath. She had heard recently of so many things that were specialties at Chautauqua it did not seem probable that high art would be ignored. She had not found *just* what she sought, it is true, and a blessed thing it was for her that she had not; but she had found a new absorption. Not a day was she in the vicinity of the clay-modeling department before she became enamored of the work, joined the class, and was thenceforth to be seen morning, noon, and night with little vicious-looking lumps of clay in hand, patting and pinching into shape. And what shapes!

"Never mind," laughed Mrs. Fenton when her husband was maliciously displaying an unfinished dog that Miss Irene had left on the window seat. "I am rejoiced. I feel like writing her father a congratulatory letter. He will live to bless the day that Irene ever heard of Chautauqua. Bless your heart! Clay is cheap, and ducks and cats and puppies can sit around on mantels and take up much less space than one of her oil paintings. If you knew how the Butler mansion groaned under its weight of paintings, you would rejoice with them over this respite in the shape of lumps of clay."

"But what a bore it must be to the teacher," protested Mr. Fenton. "Think of his having to sit there hour after hour and watch this burlesque of his divine art! Don't you suppose Miss Irene's cats and puppies are positive trials to him?"

"No, I don't suppose any such thing. He is a man of sense. He knows as well as you and I do—a great deal better, probably—that the men and women who come here to play with clay are not geniuses; in that line, at least. The majority of them, I suppose, haven't even a *streak* of talent for modeling."

"Then what is the use in his spending his valuable time from day to day over a set of commonplace people who will never accomplish what they are trying for?" asked matter-of-fact Mr. Fenton.

They were sitting on one of the side piazzas in the cool of the day. Mr. Masters was one of the group. He was the first to answer Mr. Fenton's question.

"The grand thing about it is that here and there is one who touches the lump of clay in such a fashion that the artist's skilled eye detects genius. 'There is a power that must be cultivated,' he says to himself, and though the embryo modeler doesn't know it, the eye of the teacher is on him or her during the entire class, directing, guiding, offering just such suggestions as shall help that one; and *that one* you and I will hear from in the future, Mr. Fenton."

"Then I'd dismiss the bunglers and give my time exclusively to the genius, I believe," declared Mr. Fenton, laughing.

"And you would thereby defeat one of the pet schemes of the Chautauqua platform, that of discovering to people their own power. Once let it be understood that none but geniuses would be admitted to the modeling classes, and none would apply. Power in this line as in every other lies dormant in many a brain, and you have to popularize a study—bring it in the form of almost play—before you will discover to the individuals what nerve in them responds to touch."

"Well, then, at best, all the rest of us, when we go in there to make clay sheep and puppies, are but another sort of clay for the teacher to manipulate for the benefit of his undiscovered genius."

This was Mr. Fenton's merry reply; but a chorus of voices protested. "It isn't possible to learn ever so little a thing, about ever so obscure a study, without getting actual benefit therefrom," Mr. Masters said positively; and Caroline added that she believed she had demonstrated that in her own experience several times.

"Well now," persisted Mr. Fenton, "prove your own theory. Take me for an illustration. I've been for two days puttering in there on a piece of clay, and I'd like to have you tell me what good it has done me."

"Why, Father," exclaimed young Robert, "I should think you could prove that for yourself. Don't you know how you told the man yesterday about the sloping roof and the end window, and how pleased he was, and how you told me afterwards that you never thought of that way of planning until you were busy making your clay house?"

Amid the general laugh that followed at the father's expense, he tried to sustain his position by lamely hinting that it was the house builder, and not himself, who reaped the benefit.

Miss Effie's tastes were no less distinctly marked than her sister's. If the pretty Aimie was fond of fresh muslins and bright ribbons and morning walks, what could be said of Effie Butler? As usual, she apparently lived and moved for the purpose of displaying fresh and elaborate and altogether inappropriate toilets and wandering through the more closely peopled avenues or going boating on the lake. As yet she had made not even a pretense of being interested in anything that had to do with the distinctive features of Chautauqua.

"I know why that lake was created," declared Mrs. Fenton. "It is for the purpose of keeping Effie Butler out of other mischief while the rest of us are busy with our work."

Had she and Joseph Ward only been congenial spirits they might have lounged through the world together to their mutual comfort. As yet Joseph was as little interested in Chautauqua proper as was Miss Effie herself, the main difference between them being that he lounged through the world in most unbecoming attire and with startling disregard to the finer proprieties of life, while with Miss Effie, every separate attitude of negligence and *ennui* seemed to have its appropriate costume and grace.

During these days, James Ward was undeniably restless. Happy by spasms that were apt to leave him with a restlessness upon him that amounted at times almost to irritability. Certain questions of grave import were pressing themselves upon him for settlement, and he seemed not ready to settle them.

Paul Adams went as systematically about his work as though he had months before this determined on just what to do and mapped out not only his present, but his future. He worked hard at the new buildings which were springing up as if by magic, and he worked harder, if possible, over his book. He had bought two hours of time out of the midst of the day from Mr. Tucker; that gentleman, it must be admitted, showing an unusual willingness to grant such a favor and watching with curious eyes to see what would be done with the extra time. Others were no less astonished than he with the disposal that was made of it. Joseph Ward chuckled over it at intervals during one entire evening.

"What do you suppose he has done now?" he said, beginning to his brother the talk about Paul as though there were no other person to bestow that pronoun upon. That James understood to whom he referred was evident by the half-impatient movement with which he threw aside the book he was reading and said:

"I'm sure I don't know; how should I?"

"Well, sir, he has joined the class beginning Latin. Pitched into it exactly as he did into Rome: means to drive right through the book. I never saw such a queer fellow since I was born! What does he want with Latin? I asked him if he expected to be a college professor, like Dr. Monteith, and he stopped his everlasting saw and stared at me as if I had given him another idea, and said: 'Well, who knows? I'm sure I don't. It's a chance, you see, and it came right to me without any looking of mine. Dr. Monteith gave me a ticket, just to be kind, I guess. Jack Butler said he might better have given me a boardinghouse ticket. I didn't agree with him there,' says Paul, 'because I can earn my own board; but I made up my mind to go in and learn all the Latin I could this summer, just to show the doctor that I was grateful, you know. I can't tell what I may want to do with it; it won't do me any harm.' So at it he goes like a madman. Did you ever see a fellow act like him?"

"No," said James testily, "but I wish I could see a few." Meantime, he—James—attended lectures steadily, seeming to choose them by accident instead of design; seeming to have no settled purpose other than could be said to fill Caroline's life, that of "picking up" from every available source whatever she could. As for Robert Fenton, his mother laughingly called him the "Assistant Superintendent of Instruction," so eager was he over every branch of study or entertainment offered on the grounds. I do not know that young Robert will ever be aware of the fact that he was the first originator of the Centerville branch of the C.L.S.C., but certain it was that he steadily did what he could to bring it into prominence. His eager face and earnest eyes and keen questions were known already to many habitués of the grounds; and more than one in authority had singled him out as one of whom Chautauqua would one day be proud. As for his mother, she was already almost proud enough of him and so grateful to him for opening this wonderful avenue of culture, not only to her but to his father that she could not, day nor night, forget her joy. Yet there was at this time creeping over her heart a shadow of anxiety for this same Robert.

While they sat on the piazza during this summer evening of which I write, discussing the value of the clay modeling department, there occurred a diversion.

someone of the many neighbors who lived in tents near the Fentons was indulging in a private musical rehearsal: striking solitary notes on the organ, prolonging the sound until it faded into distance and silence.

"That is a very sweet-toned instrument for a small one," said Mr. Masters, arrested, as he always was, by the first breath of music. "I wonder whose make it is?"

"I wonder who is making the music, and is so fond of E-flat?" said young Robert. "He, or she, keeps running back to that. No! There comes F-sharp; now she has jumped to A-flat." Whereupon Mr. Masters turned toward him wondering eyes.

"How do you know?" he questioned, great astonishment in his voice.

"How do I know? Why, by my ears. Can't I hear? There she goes back to E-flat again; that is a pretty tone. She must be trying chords. There's upper C! That's too sharp, my friend, for a quiet night like this."

"Robert," said Mr. Masters, wheeling his chair in front of that young man, "do you mean to tell me that you distinguish these notes by name as they are struck at random?"

"Why, of course I do. Why shouldn't I? If you were in the other tent there yelling A at the top of your lungs, would I have any trouble in knowing that you said A instead of B or some other letter?"

"And you can tell musical notes as readily as you can letters of the alphabet?"

"Why not? They have a sound of their own, as much as the letters of the alphabet have. After I have learned them, why shouldn't I be able to tell them?"

"I can't," said Mrs. Fenton; "and I am quite familiar with the scale, or used to be when I was a girl."

"Oh, well, Mother, you have never learned. If there

was a fellow in there going through with the Chinese alphabet, I shouldn't be able to tell one sound from another, because I don't know the sounds. After you learn them of course you can tell them."

"How long have you been able to do this, Robert?" It was still Mr. Masters's voice questioning, and he was evidently very much roused and in earnest.

"Ever since I learned how, of course," laughed Robert. "I was bewitched with it for a few days; couldn't let the notes alone. Every time I passed the Children's Temple when it was vacant—and sometimes when it wasn't—I went in and practiced; shut my eyes, you know, and touched the keys, and then opened them and found out whether my thought of the sound was right. Then there is a fellow as interested in it as I am; young Brown—you know him, Father. He found out I was practicing, and we tried it together: went off in the woods and yelled ourselves hoarse. But we have got so now that we can tell with our eyes shut and our ears too, most. Why, Mr. Masters, is there anything strange about it?"

"Rather strange, I should say. How long have you been taking lessons, Robert?"

"Why, ever since we came. I began the first morning, and I haven't missed a lesson."

"Do you mean that you never took music lessons before!"

"Not a lesson; unless what I've taken of the birds in the woods can be counted in. They are rare little chaps to teach music, I think."

Mr. Masters turned toward Caroline a puzzled face. "Doesn't that strike you as extraordinary?" he asked.

"Just what are you referring to?"

"Why, this young man's ability to tell off the notes in that fashion, as they are touched?"

She shook her head, smiling. "I didn't know it was an unusual thing. I think I can do it, though perhaps not so correctly always as Robert. Isn't that F-sharp, Robert?" she asked, turning to him as the practicing in the tent continued.

"Yes'm," said Robert without an instant of hesitation. "I shouldn't wonder if someone was practicing on that very thing. Professor Seward wants us to give a good deal of attention to it. That is some of his class at work, I'll venture."

Mr. Masters's bewildered look in no sense changed. "Do you read music?" he asked of Caroline.

"Why, no, I suppose not," she answered, laughing. "That is, I am learning. Like Robert, I took my first lesson the day after we reached here. I like it; there is a perfect fascination about the system to me. I went to singing school a few times when I was a young girl, but I fell into a perfect slough of despond over what they called the transposition of the scale. It seemed as intricate and as hopeless as Latin looked to me, then, and I fell into the idea that a special gift was required to know what they were talking about; so I turned back in despair."

"Caroline," said Mrs. Fenton, "I am astonished! I didn't know you ever gave up anything."

"I don't think I am very fond of giving a thing up after I once undertake it; but, as I tell you that awful transposition of the scale was too much for my faith."

"Yes," said Robert with a burst of laughter; "I asked a fellow in the graduating music class once to tell me what it was, and you never heard anything like the bungling, bewildering lingo he got off! I haven't the least idea that he knew what he meant. But I have discovered what it means, and that Professor Seward is Professor Seward still, if he does climb a chair."

Whereupon both he and Caroline indulged in a hearty burst of laughter, and the rest looked mystified.

"What *are* you talking about?" asked his mother.

"Why, Mother, if you understood music I could explain. There is some awful jargon about steps and half steps, and chromatic tones, and oh, I don't know what!—regular Greek, you know. Just as you got a lot of notes learned—fixed in one place—off they went and changed their names and their places of residence, thirteen different times. A fellow would have to make up his mind to give a lifetime to get acquainted with them. Well, Professor Seward told us how he illustrated to the children in Boston the change of key. He said to them: 'Children, who am I? What is my name?' They piped out, of course that he was Mr. Seward; and they giggled over it ever so much, you may be sure. Then he mounted a chair, and he said: 'Well, children, who am I now?' 'Why, you're Mr. Seward!' they chuckled.

"'What! Am I Mr. Seward still? I am ever so much higher than I was before.' But they insisted on it that he was Mr. Seward anyhow, high or low. 'Very well,' he said. 'Here is *do,* but I want this tune to be sung higher than our last was. Suppose I put this note up here; what is it now?' And of course the bright little things understood that it was *do* still, and they had *transposed the scale!*"

A lightning flash of intelligence passed over Mr. Masters's face. "This is all extraordinary to me," he said earnestly. "I haven't looked into the tonic sol-fa system. In fact, I may as well admit that I rather obstinately refused to look into it. I said the old system was good enough; couldn't be improved. But I've read music at sight pretty respectably for years. I can sing rather difficult music with a little study; but I can't distinguish isolated notes when I hear them and give them their proper names."

"Professor Seward says," declared young Robert with eagerness, "that half the musical people in the country are no better off, and they always seem to him as queer as though he should ask a man what a certain word was in a sentence, and he should say: 'Excuse me, I can read the *sentence,* but I don't know the *individual words.*'"

The evening bell pealing out at the moment interrupted this conversation and suddenly dispersed the talkers.

22

❦

"IT'S IN THE ATMOSPHERE"

IN one of the pauses between the many meetings that mark a Chautauqua Sabbath, just as the twilight was falling softly on hill and grove, the pretty Aimie, in her fairest of muslin creations, went out for a restful walk along the lakeshore, James Ward at her side.

This last item marks a continued affliction to Mrs. Fenton. She had laid many plans to keep James more under her influence, and less in sympathy with Aimie. As yet these plans were failures. The Sabbath evening walk was a disappointment to Caroline. She, too, gave much thought to James Ward; she believed that he was near certain decisions that would influence all his future. The thought that disturbed her was, What attention was he giving to the most momentous of all questions? How much was Chautauqua going to help him in this matter?

"Oh Aimie, where are you going?" she had called after the girl, with a vain hope of recalling her and holding her companion from this frivolous influence. He had been grave during most of the day.

"Only for a little walk by the lake. It is so lovely

there!" Aimie had returned sweetly. She had long since given over the folly of refusing to recognize Caroline as among her friends.

"To rest her brain after the heavy strain there has been on it all day!" said Mrs. Fenton with a curling lip; she was losing all patience with Aimie. True, the child had become absorbed in kindergarten work, and was very skillful, but what did Mrs. Fenton care for this, so long as she constantly beguiled her protégé into tête-à-tête walks, and so filled his mind that he could come to no resolute position regarding anything?

Caroline did not respond with her usual happy laugh; she, too, looked grave and troubled. Mr. Masters had stopped on his way to his tent with a book for Robert. He sat down now on the lower step of the piazza where Caroline was, and said inquiringly:

"Anything going very wrong in your world, Miss Raynor? Your face looks worn with responsibility."

"I'm trying to carry responsibilities that I don't know how to manage," she said, smiling a little. "It is a special fault of mine."

"We are most of us good at that, I suspect: shouldering burdens not meant for us to carry. Is that what you mean?"

"I don't know," she said with a troubled face. "How far ought we to reach after responsibilities? I think I am a little discouraged tonight. There are certain of our party in whom I have a peculiar interest. That young man who has just passed out of sight is one, and our Robert is another. Sometimes I am afraid that they are not going to get at Chautauqua what I specially desired for them. Indeed, there are hours when I see hindrances instead of help growing out of this visit here."

"For what sort of help are you hoping?"

"Oh, the highest that can be had, of course; and, as I said, I see hindrances. The very lavishness with which other attractions are presented tends, perhaps, to ward away the mind from matters of higher importance."

He shook his head. "False idea," he said emphatically. "Proves too much, you see. If we *abuse* advantages, we may turn them into hindrances, it is true, but that is not a necessity of the advantages. There is nothing in the beauty spread around us with such a lavish hand that should lead the honest soul to forget God. What is your special anxiety concerning Robert?"

"Why," said Caroline, glancing in his mother's direction and lowering her voice, "I am afraid he is being led astray. You know what an eager, quick-brained young fellow he is—so ready to catch ideas and so anxious to learn? Well, his father and mother are not Christians, and he has not that safeguard; and just now he is deeply interested—indeed, I may say fascinated—with young Mr. Monteith. You know him?"

Mr. Masters bowed assent.

"Then you know just how fascinating he can be, if he chooses, to a boy like our Robert. He takes Robert with him out boating and fishing and rambling through these woods, and chats with him by the hour. Mr. Masters, do you know how dangerous a companion he can be to a young boy if he chooses?"

"Just in what way do you mean? Intentionally?"

"Perhaps not, so much as heedlessly, to give himself the pleasure of seeing how quick-witted a boy can be, or how well *he* can explain abstract falsehoods. He insinuates, rather than plainly speaks, false ideas, doubts, apparent absurdities of old standard theological doctrines; puts questions that are easy enough to ask, but quite difficult for a boy to answer; and, in short, without really intending to do so, unsettles the faith in which Robert was reared. And he is so fascinating in his manner you know, and so exceedingly well informed. He can tell just the thing that a boy like Robert is keenest to hear and astonish him so much with his great wisdom that I do not think it strange that Robert should speedily acquire a habit of quoting him on all occasions and grow into believing that what he thinks is true, and what he discards, false."

"An excellent argument in favor of the widest culture," her companion said, regarding her with a meaning smile. "To present solid foundation truths of science and art and theology in the most fascinating style is exactly what Chautauqua aims at."

"Oh, I know," she said in eager assent; "but Chautauqua presents foundation *truths* in an attractive manner; I am talking about one who presents *falsehoods* in an attractive manner."

"Give the boy a few years of such lectures, lessons, conversations, etc., as Chautauqua affords, and he will be proof against such a pretty glazing over of the false."

"That may be, but in the meantime? He is not proof against it today."

"In the meantime we must unite our forces and meet error with truth as wisely and as fascinatingly as we may be able and surround him with such a circle of prayer as his soul may not be able to escape from. I wish he had a praying mother. What about young Ward?"

The shadow on Caroline's face deepened rather than lifted.

"Oh, James," she said, "tries my patience greatly. It

is not that I fear for his moral or intellectual progress now. I believe him to be fairly started. I think he will, without doubt, be a scholar and an efficient worker in some branch of honorable industry; but what I fear greatly is that he will fritter away the leisure in which he might attend to the all-important question until he suddenly wakens a man in the world, with a man's burdens to bear, and with an idea that there is no time for such questions. That is what Satan seems to succeed in putting into the minds of most busy men— the impression that there is no time for the most important interest of all. I know that James is troubled. I know that Dr. Monteith is anxious for him; thinks about and prays about him a great deal. I know that he has said some earnest words that James finds it difficult to ignore; and yet here he persistently takes these quiet hours that he might have in which to settle the great matter and fritters them away on that pretty young girl, who will laugh and chat with him as aimlessly as a bird might, in bird language, and forget him as readily."

"How would it do to try to influence him through the young lady? In other words, set our whole battery of influence and effort in her direction, looking to her to attract him in the same line?"

"Oh, Aimie!" said Caroline, shrugging her shoulders in a manner worthy of Mrs. Chester herself, her tone not only hopeless, but almost scornful. "There is not enough to that poor child to influence *anybody,* much less a person of strong will such as James has."

Mr. Masters laughed. It was so evident that Caroline was strongly prejudiced in favor of James and against the pretty Aimie.

"She seems to have sufficient influence just at

present to be a source of anxiety to his friends," he said significantly.

"Anything will do to create a diversion," said Caroline wearily. "I am so disappointed in regard to that young man. I expected almost nothing for his brother, but I had great hope for him."

"You are speaking in the past tense. Do you mean that he is, in your feeling, beyond hope?"

"No, not that," still speaking wearily, as one discouraged; "but nothing works quite as I plan it."

"Ah! That is bad for planners. It is better to give over planning the side that your arm is too weak to reach, and learn to trust."

Meantime, all unconscious of this discouraged tone concerning them, young Ward and his fair companion pursued their somewhat aimless walk among the trees, winding in and out of avenues, according as the shade or the beauty lured them. They came presently upon the Amphitheater with its bewildering rows of seats stretching up and up the hillside. The path from which they reemerged was on a level with the great platform, and thither they went, stopping together in front of the desk.

"How *big* it is!" said Aimie impressively, looking back and back over the intervening space to the last line of seats away on the hilltop. "Why did they make so *immense* a place?"

"Extremely doubtful," quoth James Ward, looking ahead and around him with the eye of a prophet. "They had too large ideas, I think, when they laid this whole thing out."

"People *ought* to come," said Aimie with a touch of energy and a sort of wistful look in her blue eyes. "I wish they would! I wish all Centerville were here, and everybody whom I know or have to talk with."

Her companion laughed slightly, looking at her curiously.

"Just why do you wish that?"

"Oh, I don't know," with a little nervous movement, as of one unused to analyzing and explaining her own feelings. "It makes me feel different from any other place I was ever in. All the people seem different—seem in earnest. They act as though they had something to do and liked to do it, and it makes living seem nicer, someway—more important. I don't know how to express it."

She went on presently in the same tone of suppressed eagerness.

"The meeting here this morning made me *feel* so! I don't think I feel contented with life as it has been. I'm getting discontented with people, too. I used to enjoy walking and chatting with Ollie Chester so much! Every year when she went away to Long Branch or somewhere, I used to look forward to receiving her letters, and I thought they were *so* splendid! And when she came home she had so many things to tell me! Yesterday, I received a letter from her, and I don't know what was the matter with it. It just seemed to me too silly for anything; whole pages of it I skipped. I don't like to think of going home and hearing her talk all the nonsense that she will."

How fast little Aimie's wings were growing! Young Ward looked down at her with a fancy that in a new and altogether unexpected sense he would need soon to look up to her.

"It is in the atmosphere," he said with a short laugh that was meant to have a note of sarcasm in it. She did not detect it.

"I think it is," she said earnestly. "At least, *I* never felt in this way before; and I have been to a great many places. This morning I wished that I was a faded old woman and had been a missionary to *somewhere* for forty years."

"My!" ejaculated James Ward.

"Well, I did. It was silly, too, and I know it. But I did want to be counted in, to feel as though it was worthwhile to take up room in the world."

They went on now, walking down the long platform, out at the little gate, down the hill into the valley below, on through the winding avenues, bending their course toward the lake, but they came out presently in line with the long stretch of seats under the great trees that mark the Auditorium. This platform, too, they mounted, and looked back and back up the hill.

"You say yourself that you never thought of these things before; never realized any responsibilities until you came here where everybody one meets is so wide-awake. Why wasn't the other life the pleasanter?"

"I don't believe I can explain it," she said doubtfully. "But I think that the *work* was *there* for me, even though I didn't see it, just as that path up the hill would be there all the same if I shut my eyes ever so tight."

Now he looked upon her in undisguised admiration. She was a logician, though she didn't know it. She arose suddenly from one of the chairs on the stand and ran down the steps. "I will take a seat in the audience," she said, "and you may be the speaker. It is Sunday, so you must preach a sermon or deliver a missionary address, or something of that sort. I have a fancy that you may someday be one of the speakers here when this place is all filled up with people, perhaps; so you may as well practice on me."

"What an utterly wild idea! Worthy of Paul Adams!" he said with flushing face. Yet he liked it. He felt the blood tingling to his fingers' ends with the thought of the power that might be in him and that possibly might someday be drawn out.

"It isn't wild at all," she said with pretty obstinacy. "It is one of the most sensible ideas I have; and I really expect it."

But he would make no demonstration for his small audience that day. So presently they strolled away again, still moving toward the lake. "You know, Mr. Ward"—it was one of this girl's rare, and to James Ward, fascinating ways, this persisting in addressing him as Mr. Ward—"You know, Mr. Ward, that this life is only a little piece of the 'Circle' about which we heard this morning. A circle has no end, you see; and if it is true that we are only getting *ready* to live afterwards, don't you think it may make a great differ-ence with our work there what we do toward getting ready here?"

He gave her another of those surprised looks. "You didn't get that thought from the missionary sermon this morning?"

"Yes, I did. One of those missionary speakers this afternoon said something that I will remember: 'Death doesn't interrupt some people's work,' he said 'They have been working for the dear Lord for years; and when they get into his presence, they can go right on.' I've thought about that ever since. It is a foolish feeling, I suppose, but I cannot help thinking that the only thing I could go on with, if I were in heaven, supposing I could get there right now, would be to fold those bright-colored papers. It is really the only work I ever did in my life with a feeling behind it that perhaps sometime, if I learned how, I would like to try to use it to help little children; and while teaching them about the papers, I would try to teach them about the way to heaven. But I should have to *learn* the way, you see, before I could do it; and that I haven't learned."

Her voice was very low, very full of feeling. It would have been impossible for even Jack Butler to have sneered at the tremulous tones. James Ward felt not the slightest inclination to sneer; instead, he was strangely moved. Not all the earnest words that had been spoken to him from many sources seemed to have the power over him that lay in this low, timid voice.

They walked on and on, unmindful of the lake spreading like a sea of glass before them, unmindful of the quiet plains of the Holy Land, through which their feet were treading. They wound around Palestine Avenue, walked on toward the south, thence onward to Lake Avenue, and finally, just as many stars were gathering in the evening sky, came out in view of the gleaming pillars of the Hall of Philosophy.

All was quiet there. The sunset meeting which had been held in that white, still place was closed sometime since, and their feet, as they stepped on the floor, resounded through the vacant Hall.

"It is lovely here," said Aimie. "I like this building; I can't tell why. I came early, oh *real* early this very morning! Just as the sun was getting ready to rise. It was *so* beautiful here! Still, and grand, and solemn. I thought, what if the air all around us here were full of spirits planning for us all—for a great many more than us. Planning wonderful things—just carrying on their work, you know; doing what God has given them, having been told so much more about us than we know about ourselves that they can see ahead and know who will stand over there tomorrow, and what he will say, and what that will do for you or for me, and what we will do in consequence, and what others will do because of *us,* and then on and on? Oh, do you see, what I mean? It makes me dizzy, and I never had such feelings before."

"It is in the atmosphere," said James Ward, and his face was without a sneer.

"Still," said Aimie timidly, "I don't half like any of it. These feelings will not last. I shall go home, and Ollie will come home, and she will come to see me, and we will walk and talk and be just as silly as ever. I don't like any of it. I wish I had somebody to help me!"

Nothing had ever gone to James Ward's heart like that pitiful little cry for help. He was intended by nature to be a strong-willed, self-reliant man. It was part of his fight with himself during these days that his proud nature struggled against the sense of need of help from one stronger than himself. The war which he had waged with his fierce nature for so many days was over, and once more, all unwittingly, had Aimie Allison's shy little voice come in to break an evil spell.

"Aimie," he said. It was the first time he had ever called her by that familiar name; "I will tell you just what you and I both need. I have known it for several days and have struggled against it. We need the power of God to help us: We need to belong to his kingdom. I have been thinking about this matter ever since that evening on the boat, when Dr. Monteith asked me how many important questions I was going to settle at Chautauqua and what my conscience put first in importance. The fact is, Aimie, my mother made plain to me in my childhood before she died what was the most important question in life; but I have never felt willing to settle it until tonight. Shall we go together,

Aimie? Shall we kneel down under this roof, with the stars looking in on us, and give ourselves to God in an everlasting covenant?"

"Yes," said Aimie simply and quietly; and together they knelt on the floor of the Hall of Philosophy.

The missionary meeting held in the Amphitheater was well underway when a slight rustling near one of the side entrances proclaimed some tardy arrivals, and those who were sufficiently disturbed or sufficiently heedless to look around saw two young people slip quietly into a vacant seat.

"Two silly young things who have been out walking," said a grave-faced woman to herself. "What a pity they could not find a better way in which to spend Sabbath evening! This is one of the drawbacks of Chautauqua. It lets down the bars and gives young people a chance to do unwise things."

"I am afraid that young man is not advancing," said Dr. Monteith with a sigh; and he leaned his head on his hand and forgot to listen to the sermon, while he tried to plan ways of reaching James Ward.

"I wonder if there is really any hope of trying to influence that pretty little simpleton," murmured Caroline as, with disapproving eyes, she watched the two late ones slip into seats. "I wonder if I ought to try; it seems so hopeless!" Then she sighed.

And the missionary sermon went on, and the thoughts of a few heart-troubled ones went on, and, all unknown to them, a song went on in heaven.

"Strike all your harps in glory!" called to one another the watching angels. The ringing call went up and down and across the celestial fields. "Strike the golden harps! Two more from among the children of men redeemed."

23

"It Was a Wonderful Meeting"

ALL day long throughout the streets and avenues of Chautauqua there had been the bustle of preparation. The very air was full of something unusual. People went and came with important faces and hurried manner, as if now, indeed, the hour had arrived for which they had long been waiting.

"The Sunday School Assembly must be an important affair," Effie Butler said, laughing. "Everybody one meets today is full of it. Who has heard the Chautauqua bells? Is there anything very wonderful about them? I think I must have heard it remarked at least a dozen times today that they were going to ring tonight."

It chanced that Mr. Masters was present when this question was asked. He had come in to see Robert Fenton about some scheme dear to that young fellow's heart and now turned from him, laughing. "Yes," he said; "they are wonderful bells. There are none like them, I think, in all this country."

"What is there peculiar about them?"

"Their power. They can be heard so far. I am not

quite certain, but I think they sound now in every state in the Union, and their volume is increasing all the time."

"Oh, Mr. Masters, how can that possibly be?" And while the others could not help laughing at her puzzled face, she said with pretty indignation, "I believe you are making sport of me. You needn't think I believe such a story as that."

This was too much for Mr. Masters's gravity, and he went away laughing, leaving the puzzled Effie wondering over what he could possibly mean. And the bustle of preparation went on. Boats came and went all day, landing their burdens quietly with less parade and music than on other days because in more haste. The evening drew on; the early teas in tent and cottages were disposed of; everywhere, people were making ready to go to the opening of the Assembly. When, just as clocks and watches pointed to seven, the Chautauqua bells pealed forth on the quiet air, old Chautauquans, and indeed many new Chautauquans who had heard their echo from afar, paused for a moment in their hurried preparations and exchanged delighted glances or clasped hands in token of their joy in hearing the glad sounds. Still, there were those who, like Effie Butler, wondered what in the world people *could* mean; there was certainly nothing extraordinary about those bells.

In the Fenton cottage it was Caroline, strange to say, who was tardy. Mrs. Fenton nearly lost patience. "Do hurry, Caroline!" she called from the foot of the stairs. "We are the last ones; even Aimie has gone."

"I can't think why you are in such haste," Caroline said, appearing at last with composed face. "The first bell rang only a few minutes ago; there is nearly half an hour yet."

"Yes, but we wanted to get near the platform, you know; and the meeting is away down at the Auditorium." At this point Mr. Masters passed the door. "What, not gone yet!" he said, halting and lifting his hat. "I thought I was the last one. Then, Miss Raynor, I'll carry your camp chair."

"Shall we take *camp chairs?*" asked Mrs. Fenton, halting doubtfully while her husband folded the evening paper. "Why, there will be plenty of room! What is the use in carrying chairs such a long distance?"

"More comfortable," said Mr. Masters with a mischievous gleam in his eyes, as he shouldered the article in question and took rapid strides forward.

The avenues were nearly deserted. The night was somewhat cloudy, and a slight rain had been falling.

"What a pity it seems that the night is not clear," said Caroline as they hurried on. "A first meeting always starts off so much better with a good attendance. I suppose people will be afraid of rain tonight."

"Possibly," was her companion's brief reply. And Caroline looked at him inquiringly, wondering why his answers were so brief and his tone so peculiar tonight. On they hurried, striking at last into Simpson Avenue. Caroline came to a sudden halt and gave an exclamation of delight. Away down the avenue as far as her eye could reach, on either side, was one blaze of light: illuminated mottoes, flags, Chinese lanterns, flowers, ribbons—anything that could lend a glow of color to the bright scene had been displayed, and the whole effect was such as she will remember all her life. Her taciturn companion stopped but a moment, however, for her to enjoy the scene, then hurried her on.

They had lost sight of the Fentons, Mr. Masters having followed his own fancy in the way he was leading Caroline and Mr. Fenton having gone sturdily forward by the path he had first chosen. The result was that when they reached the point from whence the great, glowing Auditorium was visible, they were quite alone. Here they stopped again, Caroline involuntarily with an exclamation almost like dismay. Stretching before them away down the long line of seats that had always before been empty when she looked at them were heads, heads, heads! A perfect sea of heads. Chairs in the aisles, chairs at the sides, chairs even away back behind the last row of seats. People, people! Caroline had never in her life seen such a gathering. For a full minute she stood transfixed, looking down that hill on the throng; then suddenly she said: "It is full! The Auditorium is actually full!"

"Rather," said Mr. Masters; "that is a fact." Then the comical side of the whole matter rushed over him. Her composed and assured manner, her certainty that there was no need for haste, her pity bestowed on account of the weather and the supposed sparseness of the company, her amazed eyes as she gazed on the people—all were too much for one who was continually tempted toward the merry side of things. He threw back his head and indulged in a ringing laugh. It was suddenly hushed, however, for Caroline did not smile, and when he looked closely, he discovered that her eyes were full of tears.

"You are used to crowds, I suppose," she said apologetically, smiling now through her tears; "but I never saw so many people together before, and I can hardly tell you how strangely this moves me. I know it will sound like a strange mixture of thoughts to your mind, but I can only think of these words: '*After this, I beheld, and lo a great multitude which no man could number.*'"

"A great company of people *is* a wonderful sight," he said gently.

They made their way now as rapidly and silently as possible down the hill on the outskirts of the great throng.

"I am so sorry to have delayed Mrs. Fenton," Caroline said remorsefully. "I did not dream of such a scene as this. Where can we go? We might as well stand still as advance; there is no room anywhere."

"Yes, there is," he said, pushing forward. "Come around to the back of the platform; I have some choir tickets; they will admit us to the stand, and we can crowd this chair into some knothole in the trees."

The first part of this plan, at least, by dint of systematic and persistent crowding, was carried out, and at last Caroline was seated on the right wing of the great platform with leisure to look over the wonderful sea of heads stretching before her. Not long to look, either, for the moment of commencing had arrived; and directly those bells whose sweetness had stolen into her heart ceased pealing, Dr. Vincent appeared at the front of the platform and announced the formal opening of the seventh Sunday School Assembly.

"A wonderful meeting!" These were the words in which Caroline was wont to characterize it in after months. And with that sentence she stopped. Who can describe such meetings? Could she put the wonderful play of light and shadow among those grand old trees into words? Could she describe the hundreds and hundreds of eager faces shining clear in that beautiful electric light? Could she repeat the ever changing play of expression and describe the telling gestures that had so much to do in fixing the thoughts of the different speakers on her mind? Several times she essayed to describe to those who had only heard of Chautauqua some of the glories of that first meeting and realized, by the well-bred stares which they bestowed on her that her enthusiasm was unaccountable to them. After that she contented herself with the expression: "It was a wonderful meeting."

It closed in a blaze of glory. The most remarkable display of fireworks that ever delighted the eyes of thousands of children, to say nothing of the grown people who, as Mrs. Fenton said, liked them just exactly as well, only they didn't want to own it. Among the wonders was a brilliantly illumined fountain which blazed and glowed and shimmered, now with green, now with blue, and then with the loveliest blending of crimson and purple and gold!

It was when they had ascended the hill, supposing the beauties of the evening were entirely over that they turned for a last look and saw displayed in letters of fire the word *good-night!*

"Oh, good night!" repeated Caroline with a regretful little laugh. "I hate to say it. I want this evening to go on and on."

"We get according to our needs, or moods, or something, don't we?" said Mr. Masters. "Now it isn't the hymns, nor yet the presentation speeches which I take home tonight, but this sentence, and the thoughts which hover around it. Chautauqua simply means a glorification of love; so that it takes the ordinary range of life, and instead of leaving it to be busy-handed only, lifts us up into the highest thoughts and lets us walk through the world, reading all that God's pen has written. Now, what is your inspiration?"

"The real stain of the blood of Christ; the actual color by which we conquer," she answered in undertone.

"Amen," said Mr. Masters.

24

MAGNIFICENT DISTANCES

THERE never was a more excited boy than Robert Fenton as he sat in the doorway fanning his flushed cheeks with his hat and in full tide of talk with his mother, while she picked over a large dish of black-berries.

"It was perfectly splendid, Mother! Oh, *grand!* Everybody says so; and I can't tell you anything about it. I think it is just a shame that you didn't hear him."

"Well, why did they put a grand lecture at such a heathenish hour? I thought we might better miss eight o'clock in the morning than any other hour in the day."

"That is just where you make a mistake. Some of the grandest lectures there will be on these whole grounds are to come at eight o'clock in the morning. I heard ever so many say so; and they began this morning. Why, all the philosophy lectures come at eight o'clock. I'm going to them, too. Chautauqua isn't like any other place in the world."

"But people at Chautauqua eat just as they do in other places. In fact, I believe they eat a little more here than anywhere else; and somebody has got to prepare food for the body."

"Oh, well, it's mean to have you, Mother, missing things for the sake of getting folks something to eat. I just wouldn't do it. You and Caroline aren't the ones. Let the folks attend to those things who can't appreciate the lectures. Let—" he lowered his voice considerably and bent his laughing eyes closer to his mother as he completed the sentence—"let Effie Butler and Aimie Allison and that set get the dinners; only I wouldn't want to eat them. I don't believe they know how to get dinners. Do you?"

A warning shake of the head was the only answer he received to this saucy speech, and he continued in louder tone: "Well, I would buy lots of bread and milk and blackberries, and let people live on them while the meetings lasted. That's what *I* would do."

"And who would pick over the blackberries?" asked his mother significantly.

"Give each one a saucer full, and let 'em pick 'em over as fast as they eat 'em," he answered quickly, helping himself to a generous handful of the unpicked ones. "Anyway, Mother, I don't feel one bit reconciled to your losing things. I think it is just horrid."

Mrs. Fenton gave that wistful little sigh as she said: "After all, Robert, I presume I did not miss much. You see, I know almost nothing at all about astronomy, and it is not likely that I should have understood much of it. Astronomical lectures are for those who have studied the science."

"I beg your pardon, Mother, but so far as this one lecturer is concerned, you are mistaken. I don't know anything about astronomy, either; at least, I didn't before I heard this lecture; I know a little now. But I understood almost the whole of it. You see, Bishop

Warren knows so much about the science that he can afford to talk so that people can understand him; and he made everything just as plain as sunlight. Father liked it, and he says he doesn't know anything about astronomy, but he said this lecture was the grandest thing he ever heard in his life. But then Father is different from some people; he understands things. While we were walking home he explained something to me in that lecture that I didn't get at all; he made it just as clear!"

The mother looked up from her blackberries long enough to bestow a very bright and tender smile on her boy. There was nothing that her loyal heart liked better to hear from his lips than praise of his father. He was looking at her with thoughtful eyes.

"There's a great difference in folks," he broke forth suddenly. "Some of the boys in our Circle can't get their fathers and mothers to have anything to do with it. Ned Holcomb says his mother says it is just an excuse to have a good time. Just think how you and Father have taken it up and pushed it all the time! I tell you what it is, I don't believe there are any more mothers and fathers like mine."

"Foolish boy! Trying to flatter his mother," she said, but her voice trembled and her eyes shone with something besides a smile, and never was flattery more sweet to a human heart.

"It is true," he said stoutly. "If you knew the mothers that some boys have! Humph!" And the contemptuous sniff with which they were dismissed told volumes.

"It was too mean not to have heard that lecture!" he declared, returning to the subject of his thoughts. "Mother, there were some of the grandest things in it!

I will tell you what he understands besides astronomy; he understands boys!"

"Then he is a wise man," said the mother, laughing.

"Well, he talked about how boys like to manage things. They began, he said, by managing the cat and the dog. Mother, don't you remember how I used to make that old Caesar of mine go back and lie down in the stable when he wanted to follow me awfully? Think of making a Caesar mind you! He said a boy tingled with power to his fingers' ends. I know that's true. There are some things that I'm sure I can do. When I get hold of a piece of work, if it is hard there is something inside of me that sort of makes me keep at it until I conquer it. Then just as soon as I can do it I want to try something else."

"What has all that to do with astronomy?"

"Why, it is an illustration, you see, of the power that is in people, and of the fact that they were meant to be conquerors. Mother, do you know how particular they have to be with their astronomical clocks? If one of them gets out of order and goes to gaining two seconds a week, it has to be fixed; that is, each second must be made to take one three-hundred-thousandth part of a second more time. Doesn't that make you dizzy?"

"Not at all!" said Mrs. Fenton, laughing; "for I am sure I should never undertake to do it."

"Yes, but Mother, only imagine what precision there must be up in the sky. Oh! I'll tell you about one thing that you would have liked. Mother, you know we came almost a thousand miles to Chautauqua; and don't you remember how tedious the journey seemed all that hot afternoon and how tired you were?"

"I should think I did!" was the mother's hearty assent.

"Yes, and the Stanfords and Burtons and some of those people told us it was too far to come for a few weeks. I do wonder what they would have thought if they had heard the lecture this morning. He illustrated the distance of the planets by imagining a little child starting from Chautauqua to take a journey to the sun. He put him on an express train, and away he went, miles and miles and miles, leaving the world behind. Time passed, and he grew to be a big boy, then a middle-aged man, then an old man, traveling, traveling all the time. By and by he was seventy years old, and died, his journey not half done. Then he started another from that point: a child, growing up to manhood, to old age, flying along on that express train for seventy years; then another, starting from the point that that one would reach when he was seventy, and then another, and another, and three hundred and fifty years after the train first started—that flying express train that never stopped for wood or water, or to take on passengers—*three hundred and fifty years afterwards* that train has not reached the sun! And yet he says that the distance from the earth to the sun is just a unit of measure!"

"A unit of measure!" repeated the bewildered little mother.

"Why, yes; like a foot rule, you know. If I had a foot rule, I could measure and say it is so many feet from this door to that corner cupboard. Well, they use the distance between the sun and the earth like a foot rule; such a star is so many distances from the earth to the sun."

"Oh!" she said; and she looked admiringly at her handsome boy. He was capable of explaining to his mother what he knew himself.

"Yes, and he says this express train might fly along

on a smooth track for six thousand years and reach Neptune, and there the sun would be, shining away. And yet we could travel on it so far as to lose sight of the sun altogether. Mother, what a little speck of an insignificant thing this world is!"

"What a wonderful God to have made all the other worlds!"

This said Caroline, as she dropped potatoes into the bubbling water and stopped to look after her roast in the oven. She had come from the little pantry at one side, where she had been listening to this second edition of the morning lecture.

"Oh, Caroline!" said the eager boy, "you heard it, didn't you? Wasn't it glorious? Yes, I was thinking a few minutes ago about that—how wonderful God, the planner of it all, must be! I don't know what Mr. Monteith could say to that lecture; I saw him taking notes. I should think he must suppose that God was capable of doing anything, if he believed what the lecturer said."

"Perhaps he doesn't believe there are any stars," said Caroline quietly.

"Caroline!" said the astonished Robert. "What do you mean?"

"Why, there is no telling what heights of absurdity a man may reach who is as fond of saying 'I don't believe' as he is. He doubts the existence of facts which are just as clear to me as the stars, and I thought possibly he might be star-blind also."

"Is Mr. Monteith an infidel?" asked Mrs. Fenton in a voice of dismay. This inconsistent little mother, who wanted the best for her boy, who was so firm a believer in the existence and the power and the goodness of God that she shrank with horror from having her boy come in contact with one who doubted, yet did not in any way acknowledge her allegiance to him or obey his plain commands!

"Oh, I don't know what he is!" said Robert restlessly, shrinking from any condemnation of his friend and yet feeling bound to be loyal to the truth. "He has some queer ideas; I don't understand them very well, and sometimes it seemed to me as though he didn't."

"I wouldn't try to understand them, Robert," spoke his mother earnestly. "If he does not believe in God, he is not a good man, however much he may know. The God whom your grandfather followed all his life is one in whom you ought to trust."

But Robert nestled uneasily and let his mind rove over certain specious objections that Mr. Monteith had suggested, and among other things thought to himself: "If Mother believes in him, why doesn't she serve him?"

If the mother had but known that such were her boy's thoughts!

Two forces were at work during these days in connection with Robert Fenton. Whatever spirit possessed Kent Monteith, whether he was fascinated with the boy's keen intellect and wanted to see how far it would reach, or whether he was merely thoughtless, certain it is that he was doing much to undermine the faith in which the boy had unthinkingly rested hitherto.

Meantime, Robert Masters had apparently resolved on cultivating young Robert's acquaintance. He constantly sought him out, offered him books to read, discovered his favorite studies, and talked with him about them; not from away above him, as the boy recognized always that Kent Monteith stood, but more as a companion—and yet a helpful one, who had lived more years with wide-open eyes and was, therefore, in some respects ahead. Robert liked it, this meeting him on a certain equality, and Kent Monteith had a dangerous rival in his affections. The more so because he, though invariably good-natured, was also invariably selfish, giving attention to Robert when it pleased him to do so, and gracefully shaking him off when it suited his fancy to do that. On the contrary, Robert Masters studied opportunities for serving him and giving him pleasure. He loved the woods, and so did the boy. He was wise in woods lore; knowing a hundred things of which the boy knew nothing, it gave him pleasure to impart. He knew the lake, every foot of it. He was at home with the fish, and he planned certain fishing excursions, some of them by moonlight, in which they fished and talked; and the elder fisher did more than talk; he watched, aye, and prayed, for he was fishing for a soul.

25

"There's No End to It"

PERHAPS there was no one at Chautauqua who worked more industriously to resist the forces for good that were working around him than did Joseph Ward. He recognized even more forcibly than while at home the unmistakable and increasing change in his brother and in Paul Adams, and resented both almost as a personal grievance. He looked with lofty indifference on all the efforts made to interest or amuse him. He held aloof from every point where he would be likely to get help, and sneered at all suggestions hinting toward a deeper interest. Even the Jubilee Singers failed to receive any praise from him. "They were well enough," he affirmed, "but after all, they would not compare with the Negro minstrels whom we heard last winter."

This attempt at comparison so vexed Mrs. Fenton that she declared her determination to have nothing more to do with the fellow; since he was determined to be ruined, why, let him. Dr. Monteith worked away patiently in his efforts to reach the young man, utterly unconscious, meanwhile, as many a good father is,

how industriously his own son was working to undermine the faith of another. Still, so far, the doctor's
efforts had been as unavailing as any other's. So while
he by no means gave up effort, he lost heart: there
seemed to be nothing at Chautauqua to reach Joe
Ward.

"He is cast in a coarser mold," said the Professor to
himself with a sigh. "I don't believe we can reach
him."

One morning the subject of all this solicitude
strolled quite away from familiar avenues, exploring a
portion of the grounds which he had not seen before.
He came upon an energetic young fellow of about his
own age engaged in flooring a tent. Stopping, hands
in his pockets and whistling slowly, he watched the
operation for a few minutes, then asked:

"What are you about?"

As the actual work that he was about was clearly
discernible to the naked eye, the young man thus
addressed seemed to conclude that the question
struck deeper and answered accordingly:

"Speculating."

"Speculating! What with? Whose tent is that?"

"Mine, for the present. Do you want to rent it?"

"Not much."

"Know of anybody who does?"

"Not a body."

"Oh, well, there'll be people enough who do; no
trouble about that. This is the place for people. Just
lend a hand with this plank, will you? Then when you
are raising your tent, I'll do as much for you."

"*My* tent!" Joe repeated the words in an amused
tone; the pronoun seemed to strike him strangely.
"That is an article along with most other things that
I never expect to own."

"Why don't you rent one and go into business?"

"How?"

"Easy enough: rent a vacant lot, then rent a tent, put it up yourself, add all sorts of nice little fixings that will make it look tasty, then rent it for a good sum as the crowds come in, and you have quite a nice bit of money over and above expenses."

For almost the first time in his life Joe was interested in a matter of business. There seemed to be something so independent and so free and easy about this sort of work that it took his fancy. For a full half minute he held his end of the plank aloft while he considered.

"Come," said the brisk young man, "step spry! I want to get my house in order before the next boatload comes in. I expect a crowd."

"Where do you get your money to rent your tent and lot and other things?" asked Joe, fixing his end of the plank with precision.

"Well, I have an uncle here who lent me money enough to start with. It doesn't take much."

"Oh!" said Joe with emphasis. "Well, I haven't an uncle here or anywhere else who would lend me a red cent. Bring on your uncle, and I'll consider your plan."

But he considered the plan almost in spite of himself. He hovered about that tent nearly all the morning, sometimes helping, oftener standing with hands in his pockets looking on, occasionally offering some advice. "That won't fit in there," he said, as the energetic young worker brought a board that was designed by him to occupy a certain niche.

"That shall fit in there," he declared as the board, as if to prove the statement of his looker-on, ground on its edges and refused to take its place. The worker dealt it vigorous blows with his fist.

"It won't go in," said the looker-on.

"It *shall* go in," said the worker. And he took his hatchet, and, adding the strength that was in it to the strength that was in the arm and the greater strength of will which was behind the arm, the discomfited board yielded the point and slipped quietly into place.

"That's power," said the young man composedly. "I guess you didn't hear the lecture this morning, or you wouldn't have been so sure about its not going in."

"No," said Joe with a slight sneer. "I didn't hear it. Did you?"

"That I did! And a famous one it was. I wouldn't have missed it even for the sake of getting up this tent two hours earlier, and that is saying a great deal."

"Seems to me you mix things."

"'Course," said the other, dealing sturdy blows with his hatchet and making a wedge for his board. "You don't suppose I mean to stick to renting tents and putting them up all my life, do you? This is only a stepping-stone, so to speak, toward the house I mean to have to rent. That's why I went to the lectures—to learn how."

"To learn how to rent houses? Was the lecture about that?"

"That, and some other things, a good many other things, in fact. Bishop Warren, you know—he's the astronomy man; you wouldn't suppose that astronomy had anything to do with renting houses, now, would you? But you see, it was one of those lectures that made a man remember that he lived in a wonderful world, with wonderful worlds all around him and wonderful things going on, and that he had a wonderful mind and was meant to do wonderful things himself, and that he could accomplish almost anything that he set about with a determination that it *should* be done, especially if he saw that it was the right thing to do and had a reasonable belief that the one who managed all these amazing worlds would give attention to him too. At least that is what I got out of the lecture. I came home twice as determined to accomplish what I have undertaken."

"What's that?"

"What's that?" repeated the young man, and he stopped as if half puzzled for a minute, then laughed. "Hard to tell," he said briskly. "There's no end to it; there's a beginning, though—pay my way at Chautauqua for the first thing; then pay my way at school this winter, and earn a good deal of money next summer, and go to college finally, and build my house, and rent it, and build another, and do ten thousand things in the world that ought to be done with the money I earn."

"And join the C.L.S.C.," added Joe, those letters representing to him the height and depth of human ambition.

"Oh, I've been a member of the C.L.S.C. for two years. That is what started me in this line. Are you a member?"

"No!" said Joe in intensest scorn, and turned on his heel and walked away. Still the memory of the talk clung to him. The atmosphere about him was full of suppressed energy. He had been insensibly breathing it at the very time that he had been dodging it from day to day. It was a relief to him to discover it taking shape in this tangible form that he could understand.

"Suppose I had an uncle, and a tent, and should earn a dollar; what would Father think?" he asked himself, as he put his hands in his pockets and walked down Foster Avenue, kicking the pebbles from under his feet. Mrs. Fenton would have felt a trifle less discouraged with the worthless boy could she have known that the thought of giving a pleasant surprise to his father was a very agreeable one over which he lingered tenderly. On the whole, though none of those most interested knew it, an advance had been made with Joseph Ward. To get a young man to think steadily about anything not positively wrong is an advance. The result of his thinking appeared in the course of the day in an astounding request that he made to Mr. Fenton.

"Borrow twenty-five dollars!" repeated that gentleman, so lost in wonder as to fail to find further words to express himself.

"Yes, sir," said Joe, looking up with composed face and laughing eyes into Mr. Fenton's troubled ones. He had no more idea of getting the money than he had of being sent on a voyage of discovery to the moon; but it suited his idea of fun to ask for it.

Now Mr. Fenton was a man who had made the little money that he had by slow and laborious steppings. He knew no royal road to fortune; indeed, half a lifetime of hard work and patient small economies had brought him no fortune, only a very modest bank account, hardly sufficient for the "rainy day" for which most people look, and he had schemes and hopes for his one boy, Robert, sufficient to swallow the whole sum a dozen times. Twenty-five dollars was therefore no trifle to him. It represented hard work and self-denial. He was not one who spent twenty-five cents a year in mere self-indulgence. He was not one who had been able to cultivate his natural generosity to a very great extent. You are not surprised, then, that the audacious boy's petition nearly took his breath away.

"What do you want of it?" he asked at last, too much astonished and disturbed to make his question less direct.

"Want to go into business." And young Joe laughed pleasantly. The sentence had a pleasant sound. No harm in using it, though he never got any further.

"Into business!" And it was clear to the young man that he would certainly have to explain himself. Mr. Fenton's astonishment and perplexity were too real to get away from. So he briefly detailed the plan of the tent. Mr. Fenton asked a good many questions and, almost to his dismay, saw that to a person of energy and enterprise the scheme was feasible; but he by no means wanted to risk twenty-five of his hard-earned dollars in such precarious hands as Joseph Ward's. Still, it was a pity that if the young fellow really had an earnest thought it should not be cultivated. "Why don't you write to your father and ask him to lend you the money? He is better able to lose it than I am."

The last part of the sentence was on Mr. Fenton's lips, but I rejoice to tell you it remained unspoken. Troubled as he was, he resolved not to hint to the young man that he distrusted his good intentions.

"Father! He wouldn't trust me with twenty-five cents if it should save my life! He gave the passage money out here to my brother for fear I should spend it in peanuts and candy!" The boy did not speak scornfully; as a rule he was too good-natured to be scornful; but that he felt the trammels with which his own folly had bound him was evident. "Besides," he continued, "by the time I could write and get an answer, the time for making the money would be about half gone. Folks have to work fast down here."

This was true, and Mr. Fenton felt the force of it. He was exceedingly troubled. He wished that he had never seen Joseph Ward or his brother. Wasn't one boy as much as he could be expected to think of and plan for? Let Mr. Ward do for his son. He was the one to assume risks in his behalf. Still, something held him from saying an immediate no, much to the waiting young man's astonishment. He had expected it in less time than had passed.

"Well," said Mr. Fenton at last, slowly, irresolutely, "I can't answer you just now. Money isn't very plenty with me, you know; but I'll think it over today and let you know in the morning. And meantime you think it all over again, and perhaps you will change your mind and conclude it's too much of a risk."

And Joe Ward chuckled, hardly waiting until Mr. Fenton was at a respectful distance. "I won't change my mind," he said aloud, "and neither will you, old fellow. Your mind is that I won't get a cent of your money, if you know yourself, and you think you do. I agree with you: we are of the same mind for once. I don't expect it."

Mrs. Fenton was washing the tea dishes. She had banished Caroline and asserted her right to command the kitchen into order herself. Meantime she was freely expressing her mind to her husband.

"The idea! The impudent boy! That is all the thanks we get for the kindness we have shown him. He just wants to waste it and disgrace himself and us. I'm sorry he ever came with our party. There is no use in trying to do anything for him. Twenty-five dollars, indeed!"

"It seems a good deal of a pity that the first notion the boy ever had toward doing anything for himself should be crushed," Mr. Fenton said thoughtfully. "I don't suppose he would do anything with it, though; still he might. Paul Adams, if he had time for such an enterprise, would make a good thing out of it, but Joe is made of other stuff. I don't know as there would be any very great risk; I think likely his father would pay me back if I told him the whole story; still I don't know. He might say I deserved to lose it for trusting the boy. Joe told me frankly that his father wouldn't trust him with twenty-five cents. And John Ward, while he is honest, is cross-grained and might take a position that he had no call to pay for the follies of his boy. Still, it is a hard case. I can't help thinking what if it were our Robert!"

"Small danger of it ever being our Robert," the mother said, pitching the dishwater with energy into the sink. "He is made of different stuff, at least."

Still she winced under the reference. It made her mother heart go over all the arguments in favor of doing something for the Ward boys. She was disappointed in James. He still took too strong an interest in Aimie Allison to please her. She was in a chronic state of disappointment over Joe, and yet she felt unwilling, almost unable, to give him up. Her sleep that night was disturbed by troubled dreams. She rented and set up and put in order many tents. Young Joseph Ward appeared and tore them down again and swam away with them into the lake, her own boy Robert smuggled under one of them. In the middle of the night she wakened her husband with this question:

"Have you the least idea that he means anything but nonsense and waste?"

"Who? What?" asked Mr. Fenton, struggling to get awake enough to understand.

"Why that Joe Ward; have you any faith in him?"

"I don't know"—awake now and thoughtful—"I wish he meant it; if he doesn't mean something soon, he will go to ruin; and the question is, how are we ever going to be sure that if we had helped him with this notion, it might not have been the turning point?"

After that he went to sleep again, but his wife could not. She tossed and turned her pillow, and turned it back again, and thought "What if it were her Robert!" But that was nonsense. Still, he might be out in the world sometime, and his father gone, and she gone, and he in need of friends. They were by no means rich, and the boy needed all they had. Could they bestow any on other boys—worthless ones? The longer she lay awake and thought about it, the more puzzled did she grow. If only she had been a Christian and had known how to secure unerring counsel instead of wrestling blindly with the Golden Rule, not knowing it for a rule at all! The next morning Mr. Fenton had time to make the fire in the kitchen stove and attend to various other duties connected with their peculiar style of housekeeping before his usually wide-awake wife made her appearance. When she came she seemed singularly absentminded: opened dampers that ought to be shut and closed the slide that must always be left open.

"Look here!" said her husband, after she had in this way created a fierce smoke; "what are you about?"

"I don't believe I know," laughing a little. Then, while Caroline went to their bit of a cellar for milk and bread: "Robert, I've been thinking, and I don't know but we ought to do it."

"I shouldn't wonder," he said, making no pretense of not understanding her. And so the question which had been to them a momentous one was settled.

Now the fact was that by far the most bewildered

party in the whole transaction was the prime mover—young Joseph himself. As I told you, he had not the remotest expectation of receiving the money, and when he stood two hours afterwards beside Mr. Fenton with the twenty-five dollars actually in his hand, he was as one dazed, and gazed first at it and then at the giver. He had never been a trustworthy boy, you will remember, and he had never been trusted. This was actually the first time in his life that he had ever held money in his hand that he was to do with as he chose.

"I would go with the boy and buy the tent for him and make sure that he was not deceiving you. If you don't, he will be as likely to buy cakes and lemonade for all the boys in the grove as anything else."

This was Mrs. Fenton's parting advice; but her husband shook his head.

"No, if we have made up our minds to trust him, let's trust him. I'll act as though I expected as a matter of course that he was going to do just what he said, and maybe it will astonish him into doing it."

He was right about the astonishment. "About that little matter, Joe," Mr. Fenton had said, beckoning him from across the lawn where he stood leaning listlessly against a tree, his hands in his pockets. Joe came willingly, roguishly; he expected fun. Mr. Fenton had "cooked up" a way of good-naturedly saying no! This was the way the boy put it to himself, and he was curious to see how he would do it.

"About that little matter, Joe—I've decided that I ought not to let you have so much money without your father's consent. He might not like it, you know, and of course you would never pay me back, and I can't afford to lose it." Would he be likely to say it that way? Joe thought fast, but had only gotten thus far when the sentence was finished.

"I've decided to invest with you. Here's the twenty-five dollars, and here is a note for you to sign that you will pay me the whole with interest at the end of twenty days—for I suppose you will be ready to pay by the time the assembly closes. Now if you will sign the note we'll be all shipshape, and I hope you'll succeed."

Joe examined the note curiously, read it slowly, turned it over, and examined the smooth surface.

"Who's security?" he asked at last.

"Your word and your name. I'll risk it, my boy. I'm a poor man, as you know very well, and I can't afford to lose even twenty-five dollars; but I'll try it, and believe if I lose it, it won't be your fault."

A curious lump came into Joseph Ward's throat. A curious fluttering in his breath. He felt his pulses quicken. Somebody had trusted him, and that a man, a businessman; trusted him—Joe Ward, the spendthrift, the good-for-naught! And Mr. Fenton was a man not given to trusting everybody; a shrewd man, not easily deceived. Joe knew that.

"Mr. Fenton, you—you won't repent this." It was every word the poor fellow could say, and he turned and walked rapidly away. "It's something in the atmosphere of this queer place!" he muttered.

26

"I MEAN IT, AND I MEAN IT
FOREVER"

IT was a different scene that the white-pillared Hall of Philosophy viewed next. I wonder if the story of all the varying events which have transpired under that fair building will ever be written? It was the pretty Aimie who was prominent in this one. Even Mrs. Fenton admitted that she grew prettier as the days went by. Her companion was not James Ward on this particular morning, but Mrs. Fenton herself. As that lady emerged with flushed cheeks from some domestic task in the little kitchen and brushed her hair, she expressed her mind to Caroline.

"What do you suppose that little pink-and-white child wants of me this morning? She kidnapped me in the Hall last night and asked me if I wouldn't take a little bit of a walk with her, all alone, just as early as I could."

"Who, Aimie?"

"Yes, Aimie; and I'll venture that pail of blackberries that she and James have made complete idiots of themselves, and she wants to confess the fact to me and get me to negotiate with her mother. If these two simpletons have engaged themselves to each other, they ought to be drowned a little in the lake. A mere boy and girl! She away back in her teens, and he worse! A boy in his teens is twenty years younger than a girl of the same age anyway. But I just expect it. What am I to do?"

"I don't see how you can do anything," Caroline said with troubled face. "If I were her mother, I would try hard to bring her to a sense of the ridiculousness of it all; but I don't see how we are any of us to blame."

"Yes, that's the trouble. Her father and mother will blame us—blame me, at least, because she was put specially in my care. I wish I had been asleep when I said I would take care of her; but how was I to help her being a simpleton, since she was born one? I hadn't the least idea that James Ward would be guilty of any such folly. Were they intimate before they came here, Caroline?"

"He used occasionally to walk home with her from the Circle," Caroline said thoughtfully, "but I never gave the matter any thought. Her mother knew all about it, for I met them one day walking together, Aimie, and her mother, and James. They all seemed equally pleasant, so of course I didn't think of it twice; but here it is different. We feel, in a sense, responsible for one so young, and I've tried hard to have Aimie realize that she ought not to be so much in company with James while away from her father and mother. She has been doing better for a few days, I think."

"Well, she's going to do worse this morning, you may depend, and I'm sure I don't know what to say to the little dunce. I wish she were at home with her mother. I'm glad I haven't any girls to bring up. They are worse than boys, I believe, though James is quite as foolish as she. If my Robert ever gets to parading around in this fashion, I don't know what I shall do! The only young woman he cares about as yet is you, Caroline, and I feel comparatively safe about that." Saying which, half laughing, half vexed, and wholly troubled, the motherly woman set her sun hat in order, took her sun umbrella, and joined the small, fair creature in buff, who stood outside waiting.

"It is good of you," said the little Aimie, "to leave all your cares and take a walk with me this morning. I hope it hasn't inconvenienced you."

"Oh no!" said Mrs. Fenton, resolved on being as cordial and as gentle as she could, and try her powers of influence over the child to bring her back to common sense. "We have the dinner all planned, and Caroline is managing it. She is worth half a dozen of me at anytime. Caroline is a grand girl, Aimie; and she will make a grand woman. She hasn't frittered away her girlhood on follies. She is fresh for whatever life can offer her womanhood. I don't like to see little girls play at being women. It not only spoils them for ever being true women, but spoils their enjoyment afterwards." She looked keenly at the girlish face beside her and wondered, *Did Aimie understand what she meant?* There was a heightened color about the fair young face, but at the same time there was a calm in her eyes and a sweetness about her mouth that gave no sense of being consciously wrong, or even foolish. Mrs. Fenton did not know whether to be encouraged or the contrary. If Aimie were so much a child that she could not reason, what was to be said to her?

They turned down the broad and singularly pleasant avenue leading directly to the Hall. Aimie seemed instinctively to bend her steps in that direction, and

Mrs. Fenton, with curious surmisings, followed her lead. She knew that the child walked that way every morning, sometimes quite early.

The Hall was deserted now, the early lecture having been concluded and the crowds gone elsewhere. The cool lake breezes were playing through the building, and an air of summer calm rested on it.

"Have you been here before this morning?" Mrs. Fenton asked, as they helped themselves to chairs.

"No'm, I didn't come to the eight o'clock lecture. So many people say they are grand, but I don't know enough to enjoy them, so I save my strength. Oh yes'm! I was here *very* early this morning—before most people were up. I like the Hall then almost better than at any other hour of the day."

She seemed in no haste to reach the special object of this walk, if it had a special object, but talked in a desultory manner of the lectures, the concerts, and whatnot, while Mrs. Fenton, restlessly eager to go to the Auditorium for the morning meeting, heartily wished that the conference were over.

"Did you hear the lecture yesterday afternoon?" questioned Aimie, calling her companion back from inward fuming.

"Of course I did!" spoken with energy. "I would not have missed it for a great deal."

"Wasn't it just splendid? I think I liked it better than anything yet except the Children's Meetings; you don't know how nice they are! You don't attend them, do you? Well, Mrs. Fenton, you would be surprised to see how much the little things are learning; and not only the little things. I suppose I ought to have known long ago all those lessons about the Bible, but I didn't. When I went to Sabbath school I used to be very much mortified when the teacher gave me a reference to find in one of those little bits of books in the Old Testament, because I could never find the place. I've fumbled and fumbled, and grown red in the face over it many a time, but I never thought of learning them until I went to the Children's Meetings. They have such an interesting way of remembering their position that I learned it too."

Now the truth is that Mrs. Fenton herself had been annoyed more than once in that very manner. Hosea and Joel, and Amos and Obadiah, and all the list of books with few leaves were mixed in inextricable confusion in her mind. It was only at the last meeting of their Circle that someone asked her to refer to a prophecy in Micah, and she looked her Bible over before the Psalms and after the Psalms, unable to determine where Micah was located. So, while she laughed over Aimie's story, she also blushed and resolved to look in on that Children's Meeting the very next morning and see if mayhap she might learn to locate Micah.

It was wonderful how eager was Aimie's interest in Children's Meetings and, indeed, any other meeting that she could think of this morning! Mrs. Fenton looked at her watch, and declared it to be growing late. They must hasten back, or they would lose the grand opening at the Auditorium, which she wouldn't miss for anything. Thus called to order, Aimie, with deeply flushed face and downcast eyes and sweet lips that quivered a little and lower tones, said: "I have something to tell you, Mrs. Fenton."

"Have you?"

Despite her good resolves, the lady's voice was dry and unsympathetic. How could she be tender and encouraging when she felt it her duty to apply harsh measures; to unhesitatingly explain to the child that she was a simpleton and ought to be sent home to her mother by the next boat?

I think Aimie's sensitive nature felt the coldness of the tone, for her eyes drooped lower.

She went on hurriedly:

"Yes'm; I felt as though I ought to tell you, and indeed I wanted to, though I hardly knew how to do it. I need your help; I am so young and ignorant."

There was a tender pleading note in the almost baby lips, but Mrs. Fenton in spite of herself felt severe. It was so silly! Why, the child wasn't so very much older than her Robert!

I am sure but the thought of Robert helped her to feel severe.

"Young people are expected to be ignorant of a good many things, and to remain so," she said coldly. "Their time for knowledge will come fast enough. It is the height of folly to hurry one's life."

The drooping blue eyes were raised a moment to her face in grave questioning; then they fell again.

"Yes," she said simply. "I don't expect to do great things, of course; nor to be of much importance in any way; yet there are things that I ought to know, and to do, perhaps. You see, it isn't a passing fancy that I may forget tomorrow. I am not like that at all. It is a settled thing: settled for life."

I am glad she was not looking up just then. She would have seen Mrs. Fenton's lip curl: a compassionate curl it was, though, after all. As if they didn't all talk so, silly girls! But she began to feel sorry for the child by her side, who was trying before her time to be a woman. How could she best speak so as to help her feel that this was probably not "for life" at all, but a schoolgirl whim that should be laid aside at least for years.

"If I were you, Aimie," she said suddenly and with vigor, "I would bring my good sense to bear in this matter; I would resolutely resolve to think no more about it until I was twenty; then if you are of the same mind it will be time enough to think about such serious responsibilities."

She was looking full at the pretty child now, anxious more than she could tell as to the result of her words. There was an unmistakable deepening of color in Aimie's cheeks, but the voice was steady—steadier than it had been at all—and her wide-open blue eyes, full of sweet gravity, were leveled at the matron.

"I cannot," she said simply; "I have made a solemn pledge. On my knees in this very hall I promised to belong to the Lord Jesus Christ forever. Besides, Mrs. Fenton, I might not live to be twenty; then it would be all too late. And indeed—indeed—I would not take back my pledge, if I could. It is very sweet to belong to him, body and soul. I mean it, and I mean it forever."

Who shall describe to you Mrs. Fenton's state of mind? What an egregious blunder she had made! And when one came to think of it, what a *stupendous blunder* it was! Here had she actually been seeming to counsel a young girl to wait until she was twenty before she gave her heart to Christ! The blood rushed violently into her face. The first inclination to laugh passed suddenly and left an almost necessity for tears. "Aimie, child!" she cried, "I do not know what I have been talking about. Forget every word I have said! I did not understand you in the least. I mean, I thought you were talking about something else; something entirely different."

"No, ma'am," said Aimie in grave innocence. "I only mean that I belong to Christ now, and I thought

I ought to tell someone older than I who could advise me. There are things that I might do, if I knew how; and there are a great many things, I suppose that I ought not to do, but I am so young and so ignorant about it all that I shall keep making mistakes; I felt the need of help. If you would be so good as to help me, Mrs. Fenton."

Perhaps Mrs. Fenton will never feel so grieved and humiliated again as she did in that hour under that cry for help. She was womanly and motherly and tender in all her feelings and impulses, despite the irritation which she had suffered to creep over her concerning this little girl; it was but a surface irritability, after all. Had the child been sick, no mother could have watched over her with more careful tenderness than Mrs. Fenton would have brought to the emergency; skillful tenderness, too. She was a deft-handed woman. She knew both how, and what, and the best way of doing. Had Aimie wanted to know how to fit her next pretty dress, or loop her skirt, or clear-starch her laces, Mrs. Fenton could and would have given prompt and wise assistance. Had it been the question of preparing almost any article of food in a housekeeper's list, this matron would have brought skillful hands to the work; but to be called upon to direct a young Christian what to do for Christ and what not to do that would be called against her, this indeed was work from which she shrank back appalled!

There was a silence so complete and so long lasting that Aimie looked up in timid inquiry and found that her companion's eyes were full of tears.

"You have come to the wrong person, dear child," she said, and her voice was tremulous. "I don't know anything about it. I do not belong to him myself. It is a shame to me to have to admit it. I am glad for you,

Aimie; I know it is a good way. My mother was a Christian, and she used to hope that I would become one while I was young, but I never did. I wish I could help you, dear child, but I don't know how. All I know is, to be very glad that you have made so early and so good a choice. If I were your mother, I should be more glad of that than of any news that could come to me from you."

"Not one yourself!" said Aimie in wide-eyed wonder. "Why, Mrs. Fenton, I thought you were!"

Once more Mrs. Fenton felt humiliated. It was true that Aimie had sought her out as the proper person with whom to talk without giving a thought to the possibility of her not being in sympathy. She knew her as a woman who always occupied the fifth seat from the front in their church, who was nearly always in her seat, be the weather pleasant or forbidding. She knew her as one who superintended the making of delicious coffee at all the church festivals; as one who helped set tables and decorate rooms when anything for the church was being done. She knew her as one to whom the girls were always appealing in the sewing circle—"Mrs. Fenton, do you turn this up so, to hem?" "Mrs. Fenton, is this the way to put in this sleeve?" "Let's ask Mrs. Fenton, she will know!" "Mrs. Fenton, how does this little apron go together?"

"You should have chosen Caroline for a confidante," said Mrs. Fenton with a great throb of sorrow at her heart and a twinge almost like jealousy as she thought: "What if her boy Robert were looking for help in the same direction?" She could not give it, nor could his father!

The walk back to the cottage was a quiet one. About Mrs. Fenton there was a sense of embarrassment. The foolish little girl on whom she had hitherto looked down had suddenly soared above her world into realms of thought that she was unable to reach. She must actually look upon this dainty bit of flesh and blood with respect hereafter! For Mrs. Fenton respected a real Christian wherever found; and something about Aimie—a sort of sweet dignity and quiet, such as she had never noticed in her before—stamped her at once in Mrs. Fenton's eyes as one of royal adoption. The matron had suddenly forgotten her anxiety to be off to the morning meeting and walked slowly along beside the fair young girl, in great doubt as to what to say. Something ought to be said to her.

"Have you talked with anyone about this?" she asked her, hesitating over the words, as one painfully unacquainted with the dialect.

"Only Mr. Ward," Aimie said quietly. And indeed she could hardly say that she talked with him. It was rather that he talked with her. He pointed out the way for her—made it so plain that she could not but understand, and himself led the way.

"He too!" said Mrs. Fenton. She gave a little start, and there was a flush on her face. Was she glad? Yes, really and truly. Looking on, she knew enough of the power of the religion of Jesus Christ to be sure that an actually enlisted soldier, serving under his banner, was sure of victory. Then who should rejoice more heartily than she to hear that the boy whom she had "mothered" in her heart for these many months was safe? Then what about that twinge that was like pain? Oh me! The real *mother* could not but have a heart-spasm over the thought that the boy to whom she had given just a small corner of her heart, a small fraction of her care, had strided ahead and reached the Rock, leaving her Robert still among the breakers! Yet, remember, she had never in her life pointed out the

Rock to him, nor urged his feet to hasten to it! Inconsistent mother!

It was a difficult story to tell to Caroline. Remember, she did not understand the language!

"You are late," said the young woman as Mrs. Fenton and Aimie emerged from under the trees and came into sunlight—Aimie passing the two with a bow and smile and going directly to her room. "All the world has gone to meeting. I waited for you and the bread. The last loaf is out of the oven, and Miss Butler says she will look out for the meat. She is not going out this morning. Are you ready now?"

"I don't know," replied Mrs. Fenton in a slow, dazed tone, and Caroline, looking at her, was partly amused, partly troubled. Evidently the little Aimie had left her in a peculiar state of mind.

"Did you decide what to say to the child, and did all you could say do any good?"

"No; or rather, yes. Oh, I don't know!" and then Mrs. Fenton laughed a little.

"I am a simpleton, Caroline; it is all right. The little thing is just as sweet as she can be and wiser than most of us. And as for James, I don't believe I will worry about him anymore. I only wish my boy were as safe." Whereupon, to Caroline's utter dismay, the usually bright-eyed, cheery-faced woman lifted to her gaze eyes that were swimming in tears.

hands, the union of hearts, and the furtherance in every possible way of an intelligent Christian unity among all those who live under our flag, and who believe in our Lord Jesus Christ," no hands rang together more heartily or held in the cheering longer than did those of Paul Adams, albeit he had never, in the sense that the speaker meant, believed in the Lord Jesus Christ. He intended, fully, to return to his Latin as soon as Dr. Vincent sat down, but of course he waited for the Chautauqua salute with which General Fisk was greeted. He even fumbled in each pocket for a handkerchief and drew it forth, somewhat soiled, indeed, but loyal to the occasion. How could he help adding another to the white wings? He had no special knowledge of the name—General Fisk—and I think would have turned away directly the salute was over, had not a young man at his left questioned another after this fashion:

"Who *is* General Fisk, anyhow?"

Whereupon young Bennett, who stood with Jack Butler just back of Paul, commented thus: "Shouldn't you suppose that any person who laid claim to the very slightest amount of general information would know General Fisk by name?"

The half sneer which accompanied the words made Paul Adams resolve to stay and see if he could discover who General Fisk was. Not that he "laid claim" to a large amount of general information, but he had resolved sometime before this that his stock should be increased whenever opportunity afforded.

Altogether, it was a remarkable day to Paul Adams. Forces, the power of which he by no means realized, had been stirred within him and would not be likely to sleep again.

"What a thing it would be to understand all about

such a speech as that!" This was what he said as he walked away with James Ward, in whose company he again found himself.

"What do you mean?" questioned James wonderingly.

"Why, *that,* what I said. I'd like to understand all about it."

Young Ward did not know whether to feel annoyed or to be patronizing. Was it to be presumed that *he* did not understand all that had been said?

"I don't know that it took a great deal of wisdom to understand what we heard today," he said at last. "I did not find any difficulty."

"You didn't!" There was just the suspicion of a sneer in Paul's voice. He did not believe that. "Well, then," he said, "you are just the one to help a fellow. What's Lutzen? And who were the Swedes? And what did they sing? And who was Gustavus Adolphus?"

Then was James Ward embarrassed. "I don't know that I can answer such an army of questions as that," he said, flushing. "In fact, I didn't hear half of those names. It was a reference to history, I suppose."

"Exactly; I suppose so too. The question is, what history? Where? What was there about it to make folks remember? Those are the things I want to know. I say it would be fine if a fellow knew about them. Between you and me, Jim, if I'd had your chances I believe I should know more about them now."

"I believe you would," said James Ward gravely, all the sense of superiority gone out of him. "I believe you would. I abused my chances, Paul; wasted them and my whole life besides; so did you waste yours. The thing for us to rejoice over is that we are both so young we can in a sense catch up with the people who have got ahead. I mean to try it, and I have begun by taking Jesus Christ for my pattern. I believe that is the only sensible way. Will you try it?"

Paul, ready-tongued usually, had no sort of answer to make. He was utterly dumbfounded. He had been much too busy over his own plans and pursuits to notice, as others had, the change in his old associate; so this sudden raising of a new flag had all the force of a wonderful surprise about it. He did not half understand the sentence. He did not know whether James Ward actually professed to be what his mother called "converted" or not. Even if he meant that, Paul had no clear idea of what such a term conveyed; but it meant something, and something new and strange. It was the added force to this wonderful day. It gave to Paul Adams the first gleam of respect that he had ever felt for James Ward. For the first time in his life he recognized a dividing line between them, superiority being on the other's side; and speaking of forces, there came immediately another clearly defined one into his life. "He shan't get ahead of me." That was the way in which he expressed it to himself. Exactly what it might mean, the future must define.

It is a curious study of how intersecting lives, all unknown to themselves, influence each other! James, after he left his companion and walked on alone thought the interview over; paused over Paul's numerous questions; realized that the boy had caught at the strange names and yearned over them as he had not. "He was born to be a scholar!" he said emphatically. "I believe he will be one; how strange that no one ever thought of such a thing! I suppose nobody helped him. I might have helped him if I had taken the trouble to help myself. How many things

I might have done that I haven't!" He quickened his steps, as one who had wasted time to make up.

As for Paul, before he slept that night he discovered where Lutzen was and who Gustavus Adolphus was and why they sang that day.

28

COMMISSIONED TO SHINE

IF you have up to this time been even a careless reader of this volume, you have doubtless discovered that the center of Chautauqua life was the "Hall in the Grove." A beautiful grove, with trees old enough and grand enough to be worthy of their baptismal name—"St. Paul's Grove." About the Hall you have heard. White-pillared, simple, plain, yet suggestive of such a brilliant past and hinting of such a glorified future. I don't know how to describe it to you—the effect that this bit of green and white, with a glimmer of lake between, had on all the genuine Chautauquans. The simple truth is that their hearts were there. They loved every green leaf that gently waved a welcome to them as the passing breeze stirred its emotions.

On a certain August afternoon it was in gala attire. Every column was festooned with twining vines. The platform was aglow with flowers and mosses and bright berries. The treasures of the woods had emptied themselves into this favorite spot to add to its glory. The occasion was a special one. Something in the air would have told you that, almost before you caught a glimpse of the special adornings and of the speed with which the Hall was filling.

"Humph!" said James Ward to himself in a somewhat discontented tone as he surveyed the crowded building and then took his seat on the stump of a tree that had been left near the entrance for ornament. It did not improve the vines growing thereon to call on the stump so often to assist in seating the audience, but people must have seats.

James Ward continued his mental grumbling. *If this lecture was prepared expressly for the members of the C.L.S.C., according to program, I should think the crowd might wait until they are seated; especially as it is not time yet for the lecture.*

There was not much comfort, however, in grumbling to oneself, so the occupant of the stump presently sought in his pockets for something with which to beguile the waiting and drew therefrom a little book which had been given him the day before, the attraction of which was those fascinating letters— *C.L.S.C.* A letter written by William Cullen Bryant about the Chautauqua Literary and Scientific Circle. James Ward was not sufficiently posted in the literary world to have a very clear idea as to who William Cullen Bryant was, still he knew that the name was an honored one and that it was esteemed by members of the Circle a rare tribute to have a letter bearing that signature. So the young man settled himself as comfortably as possible on the stump and prepared to study it.

At this juncture appeared Robert Fenton and, leaning over the reader's shoulder, demanded to know what interested him so deeply.

"I'm reading Bryant's letter," said James. "Have you seen it?"

"Bryant's letter! Who? The poet? Oh, that letter about the Circle! I remember. No, I haven't seen it, but I want to." And he leaned forward and joined in the reading.

"Ho!" he said, after a minute's silence. "I didn't think he was one of them?"

"One of whom?"

"Why, a Christian man; that sounds like it." And he read aloud:

> The friends of religion, therefore, confident that one truth never contradicts another, are doing wisely when they seek to accustom the people at large to think, and to weigh evidence, as well as believe. By giving a portion of their time to a vigorous training of the intellect and a study of the best books, men gain the power to deal satisfactorily with questions with which the mind might otherwise become bewildered.

"I don't think that is true of all men," declared Robert. "Do you?"

"I should suppose it would be."

"Well, it isn't, or else some men that I know haven't given 'a vigorous training' to their intellects, for they have about as unsatisfactory ways of dealing with puzzling questions as they could have. Look at young Mr. Monteith! He mixes a fellow up on all sorts of questions until he doesn't know what he believes and feels a little like thinking that nobody believes anything anyhow.

"And listen to this, it is a prophecy."

> It may happen, in rare instances that a person of eminent mental endowments, which might oth-

erwise have remained uncultivated and unknown, will be stimulated in this manner to
diligence, and put forth unexpected powers, and,
passing rapidly beyond the rest, become greatly
distinguished and take a place among the lumi-
naries of the age.

"Ward, as sure as you live, I believe that applies to
Paul Adams! I'm just as sure that he is going to be a
luminary as I am that you are sitting on this stump."

Young Ward had no answer, for the reason that he
was springing from the stump and making ready to
give place to a lady who was moving toward them,
none other than little Aimie herself.

"Am I so late?" she said, breathless. "I hurried.
What! Isn't the lecture commenced? And the seats all
taken! How nice of you to save this stump for me!
What are you reading?"

"We are just finishing an important letter," explained Robert.

"I have read Bryant some," remarked little Aimie in
a dreamy tone. "Aunt Annie reads him ever so much.
Oh! We will be at home for his memorial day, won't
we? I mean to recite *Thanatopsis* in the Circle. Don't
you suppose we will have a special meeting on Memorial Day? I used to recite *Thanatopsis* when I was
in school. I thought it was doleful then, and yet I liked
it. But I knew almost nothing about the author. I
think it is so nice to know things."

Over that sentence James Ward smiled thoughtfully.
He was still listening to the ring of Robert's words
about Paul Adams: "I'm just as sure that he will be a
luminary as I am that you are sitting on that stump."
Was that the division? Must he sit on the stump and
let Paul shine? Was not there room also for his shining?

He was not satisfied with merely sitting and looking on. He would never be satisfied with it anymore.

"I am the Light of the world." He thought of the verse just then. It had been quoted by Professor Holmes in the Normal Class that morning. And he had immediately followed it with the words: *"Ye are the light of the world,"* placing a peculiar and solemn emphasis on the pronoun.

It came to James Ward at that moment like an inspiration—the thought that he had been commissioned to shine. The glorious Light had shone down into his heart; the life-giving voice had sent him the message: *"Ye are the light of the world."* Yes, he would shine from henceforth; a reflected light that should help to light the nations home.

"Hark!" said Aimie. "It is begun." And the voices around the stump were hushed.

Dr. Meredith was the speaker, and the C.L.S.C. people knew enough of him to have been on the eager watch for this lecture, which had been prepared expressly for them. The stump proved no mean sitting, after all, for the ringing voice of the speaker penetrated through the trees and reached them clear and strong.

Those golden sentences poured out so rapidly were none of them lost. "Leisure Hours" was the topic, and as the doctor proceeded to unfold to his listeners the wonderful things that could be accomplished if moments usually wasted were carefully guarded, one person at least felt his cheeks glow with something very like shame. Perhaps it would have been difficult to find a young man who had wasted more leisure hours than had James Ward. In fact, his hours might almost have been said to have been all leisure, for the reason that he had not chosen to keep them filled. Be sure, as he listened, he made some strong and stern resolves as to what should be done with time in the future.

There were many points in that lecture which seemed specially suited to his needs. Aimie turned toward him with a meaningful smile as the speaker told of having overheard a young man on those grounds say that he had "an awful memory!" and after expressing in very strong terms his opinion of the ignorance and folly evidenced by such an admission, added: "I tell you, young man, you can secure just as good a memory as you choose to have." James Ward returned the smile, laughed outright, indeed, but at the same time blushed. Not twenty-four hours before he had said in somewhat dreary tone to this same Aimie:

"You see, there is this against me: I have a very poor memory. For some things my memory is simply awful! Now Paul Adams is a real genius in that line. He has only to read a thing over once or twice that he really wants to remember, and the very language of it belongs to him."

No wonder he blushed; but he gave even more careful heed to what followed. In reality it was a guidebook of instruction on the acquisition of memory, and more people than James Ward, listening, made resolutions to acquire.

"There!" said Robert Fenton. "Listen! He is describing Ollie Chester, for all the world. The boys are always telling how she goes on. Do you know her, Ward? She is one of those girls who know all the people living in the big houses, and who they married, and when they married, and how they dressed, and what relation they are to Mr. So-and-so of Boston or that lovely Mrs. Somebody of New York, and all that sort of thing. She thinks she has a good memory because she can get off loads of trash of that kind; but she is a dead failure in history. It is just as he says, her mind is all lumbered up with that sort of thing."

An impatient nudge from young Ward reminded Robert that Dr. Meredith, and not himself, was the speaker. But the tongues outside could not be kept still. Aimie laughed outright over the description of the man who would sit of a winter evening by a glowing fire in dressing gown and slippers, and let his thoughts float off on a sea of reverie propelled by the laws of association, and when interrogated as to what he was doing, would reply that he was thinking.

"That's exactly like Uncle Ned," said Aimie. "He will sit by the hour staring into the grate, his eyes full of wisdom, and think. And I don't believe anyone has ever seen any results."

"I've done a good deal of that sort of thinking myself," said young Ward meaningly. "At least, I have never been able to discover any results."

Then did Aimie's bright cheeks flame. *What sort of thinking have you been doing?* said her conscience to her. *Don't you live in a house that is made of glass, and wouldn't it be well not to sit here on this pretty stump and throw stones at your uncle Ned?*

From that moment Aimie gave earnest and undivided attention to Dr. Meredith and learned how to think not only, but on what topics to expend much thought.

When I carefully consider all the grounds gone over at Chautauqua during that eventful summer, I find that I return again to what was before my deliberate conclusion that nothing more helpful to the Circle occurred during the six weeks than the lecture that they heard, some of them under difficulties, that summer afternoon.

"Who is Dr. Meredith?" Aimie asked as, the lecture over, they moved away.

Robert Fenton was prompt with his answer. The boy had talent for discovering who all Chautauqua celebrities were.

"He is a Boston pastor, among other things, and a Bible-class teacher. Fred Stuart says he has a perfectly wonderful Bible class. They meet weekday afternoons. There are as many as two thousand members! So Fred says, but it doesn't seem possible. It is awful large, anyway, and as interesting, Fred says, as any of these lectures that we get here. He's going to preach tomorrow evening. Not Fred Stuart, you understand, but Dr. Meredith."

"I shall go and hear him," said Aimie with emphasis.

"Don't you think this lecture will be published?"

"It ought to be. Of course it will be in the *Chautauquan*. They will not let the finest thing we have had here slip away from us. What about that *Chautauquan*, Fenton? Have you subscribed for it?"

"Father has. Oh, of course we must have it! A great many of the Circle readings will be printed in it; besides, only think of having Cook's lectures, and Professor Browne's and Dr. Meredith's, and all the wonderful sermons and lectures that will be put in it! Everybody ought to take the *Chautauquan*. A library for a dollar a year!"

The afternoon's work was over. Speaker and listeners went their ways. It may be that the speaker felt depressed. He may have fancied in the reaction that followed the excitement of effort that the effort was vain and the hour wasted! Such things have been. It may be that not one of those who lined the avenues and sped their various ways said a word to him about the help they had received from him that afternoon; not a word of the light he had thrown on hitherto bewildering subjects; not a word of the mountains in their way that he had reduced to molehills; not a word of the resolves taken, and the great draughts of courage infused through his eloquence! Such things have happened. I do not know that Dr. Meredith will ever meet, on this side, any of those whose souls he uplifted that day. But I cannot help hoping that he will, and that they will tell him, frankly, all about it. I can but feel that men, even great men, need sometimes to know, even here, something of what they have accomplished. Would it not be well for this one to know that on that summer afternoon he touched and widened circles that shall continue to widen through all time, and then in eternity just begin to grow.

29

THE BOOK

THE great Amphitheater was filled to its utmost. There is really no more attractive spot to be found than that Amphitheater when it is lighted up of an evening. At least, so all Chautauquans think. There is something very fascinating in those rows and rows of circling seats, rising high and higher, filled every one of them with people. If you love to study faces, a seat on the platform of the Chautauquan Amphitheater is the place for you. There are so many people, so many different types of character represented.

Then there is the view of the platform itself, filled—crowded with eminent men, doctors of divinity, lawyers, judges, statesmen, orators. That platform is really a grand sight when it is brilliantly lighted and every seat is taken. Back of it is the great choir platform, crowded also. Rows and rows of young, bright, interested faces. It is a charming sight enough even before they burst into song, adding their trained voices to complete the effect.

The preacher, on this particular Sabbath evening, was Dr. Meredith. All the people who had heard him the afternoon before in the C.L.S.C. wanted to hear him again. All the people having friends who had heard him wanted to be numbered among the hearers.

"I hope he will take a magnificent text," said young Monteith, as he settled himself to be a listener.

Jack Butler chanced to be his companion and at this point regarded him with surprise. "I did not know you thought there was any magnificence in his present textbook to select from," he said inquiringly.

"Certainly I do." And one well acquainted with Kent Monteith would have seen that he was annoyed. He was much too scholarly to like such a wholesale way of putting his peculiar views. "Certainly I do. I am not such a fool, I trust, as to be unable to see the matchless imagery of language, the display of rhetoric and logic and intellectual power generally, as they appear in the Bible. One need not necessarily sub-scribe to all the dogmas taught in a book in order to admire it."

"That is true," Jack said meekly, feeling himself quenched; and then both waited for the text. Simply four words: *Thy testimonies are wonderful*. Something very like a sneer marred the handsome face of Kent Monteith. His hopes of listening to successive flights of eloquence with some of the grand passages of the Bible for starting points faded, and he resigned himself to listen instead to a series of platitudes about the excellency of a book in which he did not believe. Still, sit back though he did with folded arms and indiffer-ent look, it was impossible not to give thought to what followed.

"It may be well for us," said the speaker, "to pause for a moment on the threshold and consider the mar-velous antiquity and vitality of this book." Straightway a scholar, as in some lines at least Kent Monteith certainly was, took up the thought and admitted to himself what he might not have mentioned to another that the Bible was a very old book. Then he listened.

"Begun in the Arabian desert, ages before Homer sang, and finished fifteen hundred years after, on an island in the Aegean Sea, this book has come down to us from that remote antiquity unscathed and entire, and is as fresh and as full of life today as when prophets and apostles first indited its burning words, and its power and influence were never before so great in this world as they are now. This is a wonderful fact; it is a unique thing. Let us turn aside and see this great sight. I need not remind you that many a book that once bid fair for immortality has long since gone down to oblivion. Of all the millions of books which have been written since the dawn of literature, how few, even of the very best of them, have escaped the ravages of time and the forgetfulness of men?"

Now no one in that great audience knew better than Kent Monteith that this statement and other kindred ones which followed it were true. Actually, the knowledge came home to him so forcefully at this time that he wondered curiously how it was that doubt and unbelief first crept into his mind concerning this old and wonderfully preserved book. There was something in the manner of the speaker and in the rush of his burning words which held the handsome-faced young skeptic and obliged him to listen.

When he lifted the massive Bible to the view of the audience and said: "The fact that I hold this grand old Bible in my hand tonight is one of the most stupendous miracles ever wrought by God Almighty!" There was something so convincing in the very act, and in the lightninglike train of thought which it suggested that Kent Monteith felt simply annoyed at the sarcastic smile which played over Jack Butler's face as the latter turned to him for sympathy.

He moved impatiently, almost turning his back to Jack, and all the time lost not a word of the rush of eager sentences from the stand.

"No book has ever been so persecuted and trampled upon. If I could bring to this platform tonight a man concerning whom you were certain that he had outlived the centuries; who had been flung into the sea and not drowned; who had been cast into the fire and not burned; who had been made to drink a deadly poison and was still alive and well, would you not say that the broad shield of Omnipotence had been over him, and he had lived and moved and had his being in the heart of a perpetual miracle? This Bible is that man. It has been flung into the sea, and yet not overwhelmed; it has been cast into the fire, and has refused to burn."

At this point Kent Monteith met the gaze of young Robert Fenton's astonished, searching eyes. Despite the man of the world's habitual self-control, a slight flush appeared on his face as he recognized the fact that this statement, though incapable of contradiction, had but the day before been treated by him in such a manner that Robert was left at liberty to draw an exactly contrary conclusion. The questioning in those earnest young eyes was so apparent that Mr. Monteith found cause for thankfulness in the fact that half a dozen seats divided them.

But the speaker was not done with these two. "Let me call your attention," he said, "to the unity of this book. And perhaps the first view of the Bible would lead us to the conclusion that we would be less likely to find there a true interior, positive unity, than in any other book that we know of in the world; for it is not, after all, one book. It is made up of sixty-six different tracts or pamphlets; and these are the work of forty different writers, and these separated by fifteen hundred years. They lived in different circumstances. Some of them were cultured, some were ignorant. Some were in kings' houses, some were fishermen on the lake of Galilee. And under all these varieties of circumstance and of intellectual constitution, they sat down and wrote a book in three different languages.

"And yet the very moment we begin to study it we are impressed with the positive oneness of the doctrine that runs through it from beginning to end. It is a *great* unity, as it must be to correspond with the mind of God: the unity of a cathedral, not of a hut; the unity of a great piece of mechanism, not of a walking stick. There is a grand central truth that runs through the book from beginning to end. Man *lost* may be *saved* by the blood of sacrifice. That is the Bible from one end of it to the other."

What a strange sermon it was! Kent Monteith actually lost portions of it by taking time to wonder how it happened that so much of the ground gone over between young Robert and himself should be touched upon! If it were not absurd, he might almost fancy that the boy had been detailing to the orator the doubts which had been suggested to him. It certainly was no wonder that the young artist's face burned a little. He felt so conscious that the hints which he had thrown out, viewed in the light derived from this lecture, would appear worse than shallow to the keen-brained boy.

The speaker grew more personal and practical. "Above all things," said he, "it is important for you to study the Bible as spiritual beings, because it answers questions that you can find answered nowhere else.

The profoundest questions and largest needs of humanity are spiritual. How can a man be just with God? Who will deliver my soul from going down to the pit, saying I have found a ransom? Who will bring peace to the weary, tempest-tossed heart? Leave me in darkness concerning these, and no matter what else you tell me, life is a riddle, death is a terror, and the mysterious afterwards a horror and a woe!"

Of what use to try to make of such a sermon as this nothing but food for the intellect? Kent Monteith sat back with folded arms and gave himself up to annoyance. He must not even grumble aloud, for this was Sabbath evening, and he was one of an audience gathered for the avowed purpose of worshiping God. That which he had been looking forward to as a lecture had been boldly advertised as a sermon. What man in his senses could grumble because it was exactly what had been promised. He must not even complain of that last sentence, clear-cut though it was: "May God grant you the blessings promised in his Word to them that love his truth, and ever save you from the blasting mildew of infidel folly and falsehood!"

At that moment Kent Monteith would have given much had he not spoken "folly and falsehood" to the clear-eyed boy looking over at him.

30

"All Mixed-Up"

OTHER faces besides Robert Fenton's had been objects of study on the evening of Dr. Meredith's sermon. Dr. Monteith, sitting too far away from his son to watch the effect of the argument on him, albeit he thought much of him, gave special attention to Paul Adams. The play of feeling on that young man's face was marked. To Dr. Monteith it was puzzling. There was more than keen interest, more even than astonishment, though that was evident. There seemed also to be a feeling of incredulous dismay. The doctor, studying the changes, astonished at the display of feeling, became deeply interested, and at last resolved as soon as possible to have a talk with the boy.

"There is certainly more depth of character than any of us have given him credit for," he said to himself musingly. "How his face changes! I wonder what line of thought he can be carrying out. I declare, I believe the boy is a genius in disguise."

It was an interest born of this watching that made the doctor suddenly desert his company at the close of the service and wedge his way through crowds to reach at last Paul Adams's side.

"Well," he said, after they had walked a few steps in silence, "you were interested, I saw, this evening. What do you think of such a sermon as that?"

"I don't know what I think."

The answer was prompt enough, but was, I might almost say, moody in its tone. Dr. Monteith was bewildered.

"Didn't you like it?" he asked at length, seeing that Paul, beyond that short answer, seemed bent on silence.

"Like it!" There was no mistaking the energy in the tone, and yet, strangely enough, there was not only energy, but a sort of pent-up indignation. Dr. Monteith found himself utterly at fault in trying to discover the boy's mood and so was of necessity silent in turn.

"Look here!" burst forth Paul at last: "I'm all mixed-up. Do you, and folks like you, believe all that that preacher said tonight?"

"I can speak for myself, Paul, and—well, yes, I can speak for a great company of Christian men and women that we believe with heart and soul all that he said tonight."

"Then I'm just dreadfully mixed-up that's all." And there was a curious note of dismay in Paul's voice.

The doctor's reply was full of questioning sympathy. "I don't quite understand, my friend. What has so mixed you up? Perhaps I can help you."

"Why," said Paul, speaking rapidly, eagerly, "I didn't know it. I knew about Mother, of course, how she was always reading the Bible, and thought it was a wonderful book; and I knew they took texts out of it and had the Sunday school children learn out of it, but I didn't know that great scholars thought it was grand and wonderful and all that."

"Why, certainly," said the good doctor with alacrity. "It is generally accepted as the most wonderful book that the world has ever known, or will know. How could it be otherwise, my friend, since it is the only book that we have from God?"

But Paul ignored the question and burst forth with his dismayed astonishment: "Then why in the name of common sense didn't we study it? I made up my mind back there that first night at the Circle that I would know all there was in one book, anyhow. I never had known anything about books, and I somehow decided that I wanted to; and I thought by the way you talked that that book about Rome was the most important one there was, and I went at it. It wasn't long before I found out that other books had to be studied too, and when I came down here it seemed to me from all the talk I heard that Latin was about as important as anything, and so I plunged in and gave every bit of time I could spare; and it seems, after all, that the most important book there is in the world Mother has had all the time, and I never read a page of it in my life! Now what I don't understand is why people who knew it was *the book* didn't tell us about it and set us at it as we went at *Merivale,* you know. I should know a good deal about the book by this time if I'd gone into it with all my might."

Utter dismayed astonishment kept Dr. Monteith silent for a few minutes, then he said:

"But, Paul, don't you know we studied the *Plan of Salvation?* That tells all about the Bible, and we gave as much and as careful attention to it as we did to *Merivale.*"

"Oh yes," said Paul; and the doctor wondered

afterwards whether there could have been almost a sneer in his voice. "I know we studied a book *about* the Bible, but it wasn't the *Bible,* you see. How was I to know that the book we were reading *about* in another book was the most wonderful book in the world? Fact is, I suppose it is because I am an ignorant fellow, but I thought likely that that book was ahead of the Bible, or you wouldn't have taken it up instead of that. Don't you see how it is, Professor? I never read any at all in the Bible. Nobody ever talked to me about it except Mother. It is the only book she ever reads, and I thought that was the reason she liked it; and I didn't know it was a grand book." The dismay in the tones was distinctly marked, and there was also a suggestion of feeling, as one who had somehow been defrauded of his rights.

Dr. Monteith had never been so bewildered in his life. How was he to answer this ignorant boy who jumped at such strange conclusions, utterly unwarranted by facts? At least the doctor earnestly hoped they were unwarranted. By this time they had reached the latter's cottage, but he laid a detaining hand on Paul's shoulder. He could not let the boy slip away until his questionings had been in some manner answered.

"Come in," he said earnestly. "Come up to my study; I want to talk with you! This is a new phase of the question to me, I must confess." Seated in the beautiful little study, by the green-covered table under the shaded light, the doctor looked full into the earnest, troubled face of his visitor. "Now, my friend, do I understand you to mean that the experiences which you have had with the Circle led you to think that we gave the most important place to other books and shoved the Bible out?"

"Well, I didn't put it that way. But I'll leave it to you to know what a fellow is going to think. For most a year I heard talk about all the things we've been studying, and I never heard a word about the Bible only as we would look into it once in a while when Walker copied from it a verse or two. I didn't think anything about the book, you see: forgot there was such a one. And when I came here, as I told you, I pitched into Latin because everybody talked about its being the foundation.

"I thought likely enough that the reason why I didn't know anything was because I hadn't got any foundation; so I thought I'd set to work and get one, and I've worked hard at it; but if what the man said tonight is true, seems to me I've begun at the wrong end and haven't got the foundation, after all. I'm all mixed-up, as I told you. I don't know what I think."

You would have been sorry for Dr. Monteith, could you have seen his distressed face. He arose and began to walk back and forth in the little study, pondering how he could best undo what his heart told him had been grave mischief. Actually, he had helped to start this soul from the sandy foundation of human learning without so much as a visible attempt to set his feet on the Rock!

As for Paul, he was astonished at the doctor's distress. He had not expected that more than a passing kindly thought would be given to his perplexities. He had not imagined for a moment that anything which he could say would have power to trouble Professor Monteith. He watched the grave, anxious face with a kind of awe. For fully five minutes the silence lasted, the boy meditating, meanwhile, how he could best express his apology and slip away, when the doctor drew a chair close to his side and laid a quiet hand on his shoulder.

"My friend," he said, "I have made a grave mistake. Loving the Bible as I do, making it the guide of my life and my daily study as I do, think what it is to me to have made upon you the impression that it is even *second* in importance! In my eagerness to help you upward, in my fear lest I should hurry you and so set you against the highest way, I have been almost silent about 'the Book.' Too much we have left it out of our Circle. We have, as you say, studied *about* it instead of studying at the fountainhead; but, my friend, while I have made this serious mistake, and so seemed to put aside the first interests, it has only been seeming. Paul, I have prayed for you by name on my knees every day since I first invited you to join our Circle. I have asked the Author of the Bible to lead you, through it, to himself. Now, what I ought to do next is to ask your pardon, and the pardon of every member of the Circle, for misleading you and them. The Bible is first, best, purest, highest; incomparably above any and all other books: God's own message to us. Paul, if you would give yourself to its study long enough to find in it your Savior, you would love it with all your soul. Your mother is right: Good mothers, my boy, are almost always right. She is a good mother; wiser in the true wisdom today than some of those who stand high. Do you forgive me for misleading you?"

Now was Paul Adams almost beside himself. Coldness, haughtiness, lofty superiority always amused him and made him impudent. No one had ever asked his forgiveness before.

"Dr. Monteith," he said—and his voice was low and husky—"I didn't mean—I didn't think—I wasn't finding fault with *you*. I never had anybody like you, and I—well, there's no use in trying to tell it, but I kept on with *Merivale,* often and often when it seemed all bosh to me, just because I thought I would like to please you; but this talk tonight about the Bible kind of took me by surprise, and I said right out what I thought. I didn't mean to blame you."

"I know it, my friend. I know everything you would say; there is no need for apologies on your part. You have shown me a mistake that I have certainly made. What I want to know is, do you forgive me, and will you give me a token that you do?"

"I'll do anything under the sun that you want me to," declared Paul with a sort of reckless earnestness. Very few people had influence with him, but it may have been because very few had cared to win the chance of exerting influence.

The doctor, who had studied his somewhat singular nature carefully, took prompt advantage of the seemingly reckless promise. "Then I am going to ask you to promise to study this wonderful book with the greatest daily care, looking all the time to find in it the history of your own heart and the Savior which that heart needs."

"I'll do it," said Paul with strong emphasis in his voice; "I'll do it, sir. I made up my mind tonight that it ought to be read if it is the kind of book he said; and I'd be glad to be told just how to read it."

"There's another thing, Paul. Are you willing to kneel down with me and ask God to forgive me for leading you astray?"

Can you credit the fact that in this Christian country, surrounded always by Christian people, Paul Adams knelt and, for the first time since his early childhood, heard himself prayed for?

31

◆ ►◆◄ ◆

EVADING THE POINT

THE Hall was nearly filled when Caroline came. She had been beguiled into walking there by the most circuitous route that Kent Monteith in his great familiarity with Chautauqua grounds could plan.

"We shall be late," she had said to him several times, speaking anxiously, and with that polite disregard for truth which is a habit with some people, her companion had answered: "Oh no! I think not." So the first of the conference was lost to Caroline. This was a trial. The informal meetings of the C.L.S.C. had been to her quite as helpful as any other exercise.

"We shall not lose much if we are late," Kent Monteith had said. "It is simply talk that they are having today all about things which people have known for a lifetime."

"Some people," she had answered, smiling, in no wise annoyed. She realized her own ignorance as much as, possibly more, than ever; but since she was learning, every day it had ceased to be so sad a thing to her. When they entered the Hall, the thing which annoyed her was the one that the young man had meant should give her pleasure: the walking down the length of that Hall with many eyes on her and with some, at least, knowing that she was accompanied by Kent Monteith, the young artist who, the wise ones said, was destined to be famous. Notoriety of that sort would never be pleasant to Caroline Raynor. It was only one of several mistakes which her companion made in his judgment of her character. Only second to this was her annoyance over the undertone conversation in which he persisted, though he must have seen that she wanted to listen.

"I admire Vincent for his patience with this sort of thing," was one of his comments. "It is a mark of genius, I suppose, for a scholar to be so good-natured over what must bore him immensely. Imagine a man's having to stop in the midst of a flow of thought to explain to somebody how to pronounce *moustache!*"

"Yet, if somebody doesn't know, why shouldn't Dr. Vincent tell him?" persisted Caroline. "This isn't the time for 'a flow of thought'; it is the time to ask questions and have them answered."

"Why doesn't somebody go to the dictionary and discover for himself, if he considers the pronunciation of the word an important question? It is the triviality of the interruptions with which I am quarreling. This is a time for important questions and careful answers, in my opinion."

Caroline gave her head an emphatic shake. "No," she said earnestly: "that is what has been the fault of all literary societies everywhere. They confined themselves to what a few of the cultured leaders were pleased to consider important questions and left out all talk about that which they might have known for years, it is true, but of which some of their less fortunate listeners were in utter ignorance."

"Such as the pronunciation of *moustache,* for instance," he said, stroking his own silken one in good-humored sarcasm.

"Yes, even that; if there is a right and a wrong way to pronounce it, why should I not be taught the right?"

"I insist that you could go to the dictionary and learn, without taking Dr. Vincent's valuable time to tell you."

"But the trouble is, I should not discover myself in the wrong unless in some way my attention was called to it.

"I think you like the whole Chautauqua movement very much, only you have such a habit of talking at random; of saying things that at most you only half mean, just to see what reply people will make. I wish you oftener talked just as you thought or that we were always sure what you thought."

Her tone, which had been light at first, grew serious. Something in it touched the listener, apparently more than he wished her to see.

"Why do you care?" He asked the question almost tenderly and waited with marked eagerness for her answer.

"I care on his account." There was no mistaking the earnestness in Caroline's voice now. She inclined her head as she spoke toward young Robert Fenton.

The boy sat just in front of them, ignorant of their presence, wholly absorbed in the enjoyment of the hour.

"Robert is at the age when he believes in his friends." There might have been some sarcasm in Caroline's voice now, though her manner did not indicate it. "And it is so unfortunate as to believe all you say; possibly more than you say. He draws inferences, perhaps, which you may not intend. It is injuring him; undoing much good that he might, and I believe would, otherwise get from Chautauqua. I cannot think what your object is."

He was disappointed in her reason for caring. He showed it instantly by the manner in which he settled back with a slight frown on his face, but he spoke lightly enough.

"The boy is fortunate in having such an interested friend. I half envy him."

Caroline, startled, looked up, relieved to discover that the Round Table had adjourned.

"Come!" her companion said, observing this also and rising. "I am glad this boring meeting is over. I beg your pardon. Everything bores me today outside of the actual conversation which I am anxious to carry on with you. Let us take a walk! There are some things that I want to say to you. There are too many people here."

"There are some things that I want to say to you," Caroline said, trying to smile and gathering her papers preparatory to carrying out his suggestion.

"I am glad. Occasionally you make me feel that the last thing you have any desire to do is to bestow the slightest attention on my unworthy self."

There was just enough of mock deference in the tone to enable Caroline to take this as trifling, so she answered it with a laugh, although the color in her cheeks deepened.

"I want to talk to you about Robert," she said. "Mr. Monteith, I do you the honor to believe that you have no intention of doing him harm and no idea that you are harming him; but I tell you in all earnestness that you certainly are. You are undermining the faith in which he was reared." She did him too much honor, and in the light of Dr. Meredith's sermon, he realized it; but he answered evasively.

"What is a faith worth that can be so readily undermined?"

"Not much, it is true. Robert hasn't genuine faith. If he had, I should not fear for him. He has simply his early education, not founded as yet on 'solid rock.' But what use is there in your pushing even the sand on which he stands from beneath his feet?"

"I wish you cared a little for my welfare, Miss Raynor, instead of bestowing your entire interest on Robert."

"Mr. Monteith, I do care." She spoke the words earnestly, and the color flushed deeply in her cheeks. He entirely mistook the cause. How could he know that she blushed over the thought that she had really given very little time or prayer to this young man?

"Thank you," he said; and his voice was very gentle. Then, after a moment of silence, "I don't mean any harm to the boy, Miss Caroline. He is a bright young fellow, and I like to trip him up a little and see him scramble out. Honestly, I don't believe I have injured him; he is too quick-witted. I am not half so bad a fellow as I appear to be. I am more in earnest about a good many things than you have any idea of. I am sincere in thinking that we have had a little too much mixture of religion here this summer. I enjoy purely scientific lectures, without any hint of that which does not strictly belong, and—"

But anxious as Caroline was to hold him to the subject of Robert until she had secured what she wished, she by no means intended to let him slip away with that bit of sophistry still on his lips; so she interrupted at this point.

"Please tell me, Mr. Monteith, which of the scien-

tific gentlemen here is so poorly prepared for his work
that he has introduced into his lecture that which does
not strictly belong there? Is Joseph Cook one?"

"I shall not commit the folly of criticizing Joseph
Cook, I assure you," he said, half laughing, half annoyed. "I am not of the same caliber as our friend, Jack
Butler. Let us drop that part of the discussion. I will
even admit that the hint about matter that did not
strictly belong is in bad taste when one remembers
the eminent scholars to whom I applied it. They are
Christian men, firm believers in their theories of
religion, and I am not. That makes all the difference in
the world, I presume. But, suppose the thing is not
quite to my taste; I have never, for a moment, believed
that the Chautauqua idea was originated in an attempt to please my taste. Now, will you talk of something else?"

"Will you first promise me something?"

"I could find it in my heart to promise you almost
anything."

"Thank you. It is not a very startling promise that
I ask for, nor one that will tax your generosity greatly.
I simply want to know if you will not avoid a form of
talk such as you have been indulging in with Robert,
talk calculated to set him to doubting and speculating
instead of resting."

"Why, I promise," he said, laughing again, "though
I warn you that I don't believe it will do any good.
The boy is of an investigating turn of mind, and he
will get at the root of things. He is not the sort of
fellow to be put in a corner like a good boy to learn
his Bible lesson and recite it to his teacher. He will
want to know what it means and also what it doesn't
mean: to refuse to answer the questions that he asks

me is not going to keep him from learning the truth sooner or later."

By the time this sentence was concluded, Caroline's eyes were flashing.

"I hope with all my soul that he will learn the truth," she said; "it is what I constantly pray for. Mr. Monteith, you mistake; I do not want to keep him in ignorance of anything. If, instead of answering his questions *in your way*—giving answers which I know you will admit, after thinking about them, are not worthy the name of answers—you will refer him to your father for information, it will be all that I can ask."

He winced under that. How could he help it? But Caroline did not care. If he wished to stand well in her eyes, he had lost ground wonderfully during the last few minutes. She liked frankness; she detested sophistry.

"Now to prove to you," he said with a great show of earnestness, "how little I care for this whole thing, I will promise not to speak another word beyond a civil good morning to the boy while we are at Chautauqua. I mean nothing, I assure you."

She by no means wished for this. She could readily see that a pointed neglect of Robert at this time might lead to more harm in the end than the present apparently warm friendship existing between them could do; yet it hurt her to think that he had meant so little by his kindnesses that he could throw the boy off so easily. She would have liked him better if he had at least meant friendship.

"I exact no such promise as that," she answered coldly; and to his suggestion that they should drop the boy and talk about something else, she replied that she thought it quite time to go home.

"Oh, not yet!" he said eagerly. "You are always in haste to go home if I chance to be with you. I have had no opportunity to show you the wonders of this place or to tell you anything, and I had promised myself so much pleasure in doing it."

They had wandered by one of the many crossing avenues back to the Hall by this time, and as it was being glorified by the setting sun, they stopped to admire it.

"This Hall is of itself an actual inspiration," the young man said. "Let us sit down. It would give me much pleasure to tell you about it—about the old hall after which it is modeled, or at least that suggested it. The wonders of the Parthenon, that grand old mass of marble, would have just delighted you. I can imagine how your eyes would glow over even a description of it. May I tell you about it?"

"I fancy I have a passably clear conception of the ancient model," she said, still speaking coldly. At another time it would have given her delight to learn more—to hear him talk—but she could not so soon forget that he had wounded her; had shown himself to be selfish and indifferent to the mischief that he did.

He was by no means willing to dismiss the Parthenon so soon. He had counted on it—on his description of its ancient glory—to light up her face with one of those rare, eager smiles. He began to talk in the easy, half-narrative, half-conversational way in which he was so gifted, but at every point Caroline annoyed him by merely assenting to his statements as something that she had known before, and no glow came to her face.

"Yes, I know," she said simply when he told her about the statuary that graced the ancient temple or described the view from the point on which he stood when he last visited the ruins.

"I thought you told me you knew nothing about all these wonderful things!" he said at last, a shade of annoyance plainly visible in his tones.

"People can learn, you know," she said, speaking lightly. "I have learned a great deal at Chautauqua." And then she insisted on going immediately and by the most direct route to the cottage.

32

⊷⊷⊷

"THAT IS A FACT"

DO you know anything about tent life? I wonder if you have really any idea of how pretty a spot its white wings can enclose. Had you known nothing of it and been able to step inside of young Ward's when the finishing touches had been given to it, you could hardly have failed of being charmed. Wonders had been done with it. In the first place, the floor was covered with matting of a neat pattern and pretty coloring. Joseph Ward had not aspired to any such elegance, but a motherly neighbor who had five boys, gone from her out into the world of business, had watched the young man's enterprise with almost a mother's interest; had counseled matting by all means and enforced her advice by dragging out from her capacious attic enough to cover the tent floor. Then every member of the Fenton cottage seemed to have become individually interested in "Tent No. Twenty-five," which name Joe had given it as soon as the stakes were set: Only he knew the reason therefor.

Caroline had washed and ironed and mended certain sheets, spreads, etc., rented from the Association at a low figure, because unlaundried, and then had spent parts of two days putting into completest order the cots which occupied all available space, after which she was persistent in her statements that curtains were needed to divide the roomy tent into compartments.

"Such nonsense!" declared Mrs. Fenton. "As if nobody ever set up a tent before, and as if it would ever come to anything! You are all growing wild over that boy's folly."

Then she went down into the depths of her trunk and fished therefrom certain old-fashioned chintz curtains of delicate pattern which she admitted she had "stuffed in," moved thereto by some dim notion that housekeeping in the woods might demand something of the sort; but the well-furnished cottage had not needed them. They were pronounced by a chorus of eager voices "the very thing for Joe's tent," and Mrs. Fenton, still insisting that it was "all nonsense," sewed steadily away into midnight—shortening, turning, hemming, puckering—until she had the wherewith to convert the one large room into five.

People who go to Chautauqua and watch the crowds pouring in to demand abiding places learn to economize space. Young Robert caught the spirit of the hour, and himself cut and trimmed and fashioned a lovely hat rack, composed of the natural branches of a brave young tree that had to be sacrificed to make room for a new house. This he skillfully set in one corner of the tent, near the entrance. Paul Adams looked in upon them one day while two or three of the helpers were at work, asked a few questions as to space and intentions, then after a consultation or two with Mr. Tucker and the laying aside of certain pieces of lumber, pronounced by that worthy of "no account," he left his Latin grammar unopened for the space of one evening and sawed and hammered and planed, and brought around the next morning a table that exactly fitted into a certain spot in the tent. Then, forsooth, it must have a spread! And who should become interested in that but Effie Butler herself, concocting out of a cast-off white muslin a ruffled and plaited garment that revolutionized the plain pine boards, making them into such a thing of beauty that Paul Adams stood and stared at it in amazement and wondered in his heart if his mother knew how to make such a "rig," and felt a dawning sense of respect for Miss Effie Butler, while Mrs. Fenton was elated and declared she should not regret any of the trouble now, for the enterprise had actually startled Effie Butler into doing something useful! So the tent furnishings grew.

When the separating curtains went up, Caroline, finding more than enough, confiscated one and curtained off a corner by itself for toilet purposes. But it was left for the little Aimie to add the finishing touches which, after all, glorified the whole.

What were they? Oh, I can hardly tell! A few yards of cheesecloth, a yard or two of blue cambric, and lo! the toilet stand and the openings designed for windows and doors blossomed into beauty. Even the improvised hat rack came in for its share of burnishing, and when James Ward, directed all the bright, happy afternoon by Aimie's skilled eyes and tongue, had finished his work with hammer and tacks, and stepped down from his perch, all the helpers stood back and exclaimed and admired.

"Look at it!" said Mrs. Fenton. "Here we have been at work for two days, and the child comes in with her bits of cambric and her needle, and in two hours transforms the place so that we don't recognize it!"

"I have just added the cake and sweetmeats," declared Aimie with her happy little laugh. "But what would they be worth without the more substantial dishes?"

"The beds, for instance," said Joe dryly, but he was well pleased with it all.

These days were bringing unusual experiences to Joe. It was the first time since his mother kissed him good-bye that he ever remembered receiving kindly help from others. Much of the constant help that his father had given him had been rendered in such a fashion that the boy had not recognized it as help, and here were all these people at work with him with as much energy as though they expected to reap results! Part of the time Joe did not know whether he liked the new order of things or not. He felt in a constant state of embarrassment. There was another who was embarrassed somewhat. Accidentally, Dr. Monteith had discovered something of the history of the tent; discovered, also, that the loan of twenty-five dollars had given Mr. Fenton an influence over young Ward that probably no other person possessed. The instant question became, "How can that influence be turned to account for the boy?" Seeking out Mr. Fenton during an hour of leisure, Dr. Monteith overwhelmed him by presenting the case to him.

"I'm sure I don't know how to do anything for boys," he said in a tone that was almost pitiful in its pleading. "My own boy is more than I can understand. I've never felt that I was the proper guide for him in anything. It has worried me ever since he was born. I don't want to have influence over other boys. I don't know what to do for them."

"Yes, but, my friend, you *have* influence over them, you see. There is no possible way of escaping it. This young fellow, because of your kindness to him—the world has not bestowed much of that article on him, I fancy—has concluded that you are the best friend he has, and he is almost ready to do anything you suggest. That is a heavy responsibility in connection with just such a young man as he."

"I should think it was!" said Mr. Fenton, wiping his forehead. "I tell you, I don't know what to do with it. There is no reason for it, either. I'm nothing to the boy. I only lent him a little money; a mere trifling business transaction. Nothing to think of twice."

"Look here, my friend! Did you lend the boy the money because you recognized in the matter an excellent business investment, or did you lend it because you wanted to hold out a helping hand to one who was very low down the hill and who seemed for the first time inclined to climb?"

"I suppose," said Mr. Fenton, dropping his eyes and blushing as though he had been caught in a meanness, "I suppose I was trying an experiment that I thought might help him a little. I hadn't much hopes that it would amount to anything."

"Exactly! Don't you suppose the boy understands? He knows you did not do it for an investment. He is not used to kindly deeds. You have the boy's heart somewhere in your hands."

"What can I do for him?" said Mr. Fenton, mopping his forehead again and looking actually frightened. He had felt the responsibility of his own boy so greatly, how could he have it added to?

"What does he need?"

"What he needs," said Dr. Monteith with a gravely sweet smile, "is to accept the Lord Jesus Christ and serve him forever. It is the only way of safety and honor for him, as for others."

"Yes," said Mr. Fenton, the nervous flush on his face rising to his forehead. "I knew you would say something like that. Now you see, I'm not the one; I don't know the first thing about helping a fellow in any such direction, or influencing him."

"May I ask, my friend, whose fault it is that you do not?"

It was a gently put question. The tone was tender and grave, yet it carried such weight with it that it seemed to Mr. Fenton's conscience almost like a blow.

"I suppose it is my own fault," he said slowly. "But, Professor, tell me this: How can I direct anybody on a road that I know nothing at all about?"

"I don't know." It was all the answer that this question received. Positively spoken, accompanied by the gravest of looks. There were no other *words,* but the look added nearly as plainly as words could have done, "Does that view of the case remove your responsibility?"

Meantime the white cots in the tent were not spread in vain. There were several reasons for this. In the first place, it had been made, as I have told you, most inviting. A few shillings in New York parlance, a few hours of skilled labor, a careful expenditure of space, an unusual display of taste had made fairyland out of the prosaic canvas walls. The pretty Aimie was daily adding to these effects by bringing mosses and ferns and scarlet leaves and berries, wherewith, in lieu of pictures, to decorate the canvas walls. Who is so foolish as to suppose that men—most men—care for none of these things? Many of them have not the least idea that they care for such trifles. Yet the most obtuse specimen among them is well aware that one room which contains all the necessaries connected with brief living, he hates; and another, containing not

another article that he is capable of mentioning, he
likes. Why? He doesn't know. Ten chances to one it is
the bit of blue or pink cambric, or cheap Nottingham
lace, or bright mosses and berries that he has not seen
at all and might affect to despise if he did. Certain
persons who had reared tents for renting at Chautauqua ignored this phase of human nature, and the
consequence was that young Ward's cots were all
rented before theirs. Another reason was, he had
friends: Dr. Monteith, for instance. When the boats
came in laden, and the question of importance was,
"Where shall we lodge?" as hotels and cottages, filled
with permanent guests, became out of the question, it
was easy to suggest a specially neat and well-managed
tent on Lake Avenue. Still a third and all-important
reason was the fact that crowds of people—unexpectedly immense crowds—poured into Chautauqua and
filled every available space. Of course, the five white,
carefully made cots found pleased occupants. Five
dollars a night for the privilege of occupying young
Ward's tent! At that rate, how long would it take for
the boy to secure twenty-five dollars with which to
pay his note? *What an enormous price to pay for a night's
lodging,* groan the uninitiated. Well, it is true there were
cheaper cots than that. They could be had in some of
the tents for fifty cents each. But there were some,
many, it transpired, who chose the exquisite neatness,
the careful conveniences, the constant attention to
comfort, the touches of refinement seen everywhere,
and cheerfully paid the dollar a day.

"Of course you needn't sleep in them unless you
want to," would Joe say innocently to any who hinted
that his cots were high-priced. "There's cheaper ones;
but there's been fifty cents a day spent in extra work
on these, and we calculate to keep them looking just

so all the time." And whatever the "just so" covered, it took the fancy of the people.

The sensation with which Joe Ward fingered over the first twenty-five dollars he had ever earned may possibly, by some, be imagined, but it cannot be described. What to do with it was a question that kept him awake the half of one night. To give it to Mr. Fenton was his first thought. His second was to wait for that until the second twenty-five was earned. There was almost no risk about it. The first week of the assembly was hardly over, and here were the crisp bills representing a quarter of a hundred! What did he want to do with it? Mrs. Fenton would surely have forgiven him, could she have known that he just longed to enclose it in an envelope and send it to his father. The thought of the elder Ward's utter amazement and incredulity made Joe laugh aloud in the middle of the night and caused his brother to wonder what in the world was the matter.

"Dreaming aloud," said Joe; and he laughed again.

What fun it would be! His father had told him dozens of times that there was no hope of his ever earning a cent. Joe liked to disappoint people. It was a great struggle. He argued the question for one mortal hour; told himself several times that he was a fool, and turned over, and turned his pillow, and answered his invisible opponent snappishly to the effect that, of course, he would have another twenty-five, and there wasn't the least danger of his making a slip, and, of course, he meant to take up his note: never meant anything more in his life. Then he lay still for a while, his eyes fixed on the strongly defined rafters, and at last, sure by the steady heavy breathing that James was asleep, he expressed his determination aloud:

"No sir! Joe Ward, you don't do it. He trusted you,

and you were never trusted before in your life—not even by your father. *He* couldn't help it, to be sure; there was nothing to trust; but the other one did it! And he shall be paid tomorrow; not one hour later will I wait. I'll earn the other twenty-five, and maybe a trifle more. In fact, I know I shall. I see a way to do it, and this first one shall be in Mr. Fenton's pocket before nine o'clock tomorrow morning."

Then Joe went to sleep.

It was owing to this resolution that he dressed himself with unusual care the next morning, even waiting to blacken his boots. The occasion was a peculiar one: He was to take up his first note.

"Suppose it was twenty-five hundred!" he said, counting the bills over lingeringly once more. "I'd like to pay out money; as true as I live, I would—always supposing I had it to pay. There is a kind of excitement about it. I just believe I shall pay out twenty-five hundred yet; twenty-five thousand, maybe! Folks do."

This wild flight of fancy made his eyes sparkle. A close student of human nature, watching him, would have been sure that Chautauqua had either created or awakened in this boy a spirit of enterprise. In the near future, the boy with his twenty-five dollars will develop into the man with his twenty-five hundred, and they will seem as nothing to him compared with these five crisp bills.

You understand, I suppose, that during this time our young businessman was an inmate of the Fenton cottage, his proportion of the expenses duly arranged for by his father. It was not, therefore, a rare thing to meet Mr. Fenton; yet the boy's cheeks glowed with excitement. He put on an air of as complete indifference as though this little business transaction were an everyday occurrence, and sauntered into the sitting room after Mr. Fenton.

Once there, he talked about the weather, the meetings, the crowds that constantly gathered, and even the hopeful look of the peach crop, before he reached the grand object of the interview.

"Well, sir," he said at last, laying down the book he had been opening and shutting for the last five minutes, "I've come to take up that note this morning."

"What?" said Mr. Fenton in genuine astonishment.

"My note, you know, that I gave you. I'm ready to take it up."

"Why!" said Mr. Fenton. "It is only a few days since you borrowed the money. You can't be ready to pay it so soon!"

"I am ready," repeated the young businessman, and he gravely and tenderly counted out the precious bills for the last time. Then he dived into his vest pocket and produced four shining coppers, laying the whole with an air of great satisfaction on the table in front of Mr. Fenton.

"What is all this?" said that bewildered gentleman.

When Joe gravely explained that this was, as nearly as he could calculate, the interest due on the loan, the face of the elder gentleman relaxed in a broad smile. The ludicrous side of the whole transaction presented itself to his mind, relieving the embarrassment.

"It is the most satisfactory investment I ever made in my life!" he said heartily. "I have been almost as much pleased with your success, and especially with the vim with which you went to work, as I would have been if you were my own boy."

Then, a memory of Dr. Monteith's hints coming forcibly to him, the embarrassment returned. How was he to say anything toward helping this boy to the place where, according to Professor Monteith, he ought to stand? I wonder to what extent the gracious Spirit of God hovers near to suggest and help those who never ask for his help. It would be perhaps a difficult question to answer, but it would certainly seem as though the tender Spirit, of whose very existence as a helper Mr. Fenton was lamentably ignorant, chose wise words for him to say at that moment. Nothing would have been easier than for him to have utterly disgusted the young man before him by the repetition of a few platitudes on a subject about which he himself was ignorant. To have talked with young Ward about religion from a platform which professed itself as above that on which the young man stood would either have irritated or hopelessly amused him. What Mr. Fenton did say was: "Joe, they say that you and I are both working on the wrong road."

"On the wrong road!" repeated Joe, surprised yet complacent. There was nothing offensive in being quoted as on the same road with the eminently respectable and thoroughly respected businessman. Joe recognized it as a compliment.

"Yes," said Mr. Fenton, fingering his bills in an embarrassed manner. Then, suddenly he raised his eyes and looked full into the young fellow's face. Since he had undertaken this plain speaking, he meant to carry it out, new business though it was to him. And something of the great importance of the subject served to add gravity to his words and subdue his embarrassment. "They say, my boy, that we ought to be on the road with the Lord Jesus Christ, and I don't know but it is true. Anyway, it is worth our while to think about it."

Said Joe, "That is a fact." He had not intended to answer thus. The words seemed almost forced from him by reason of his great surprise. He always answered all such appeals in a thoroughly amused, good-natured manner; but for some reason, Mr. Fenton's singular way of putting it took hold of him. "That is a fact," he repeated, still in utmost gravity; and he put on his hat and went out without saying another word. The thing had never impressed him as a fact before. He walked the length of the avenue, down toward the lake, still with the grave, preoccupied look on his face, and then he said aloud once more: "That is a fact."

33

COOPERATION

THE next thing that our Chautauqua friends did was to absorb themselves utterly in a scheme of cottage building. It is not known in whose wise brain the first thought concerning their brilliant plan had birth, though Mrs. Fenton believes that it grew out of Joe Ward's earnestly expressed wish that they had a house of their own. Caroline took hold of the thought with vigor, and Robert Fenton may have been said to dash into the center of it on first mention. The scheme was a novel one. It grew by inches; but, when fully developed, was unlike anything that had been planned before, even in that most original of places.

"People have cooperative all sorts of things nowadays," Mr. Masters had said. "I wonder why it wouldn't be a good idea to have cooperative house building?"

Somebody repeated that sentence to young Ward, who said it was exactly in a line with what he had been thinking of. So, what was at first simply talk grew in a very short space of time into actual deeds. A cottage at Chautauqua, owned and controlled by the

Centerville C.L.S.C. Such was their ambition. After diligent investigation it was discovered—and the discovery was reduced to actual figures—that one thousand dollars would not only buy a lot, but build and furnish a cottage. Notwithstanding the skepticism of some on this point, the enthusiastic young people succeeded in getting the signatures of responsible parties to the statement.

The next thing in order was to raise the money. It was Mr. Fenton who proposed that the thousand dollars should be divided into shares of fifty dollars each, and that each person who chose to join them should take one or more shares. Then young Robert took up the matter with glee; prepared a paper and circulated it that very evening at the tea table to secure the names of stockholders, his eyes shining like stars over the fact that his father not only took a share for himself and one for his wife, but coolly forged his son's name and added another fifty. Caroline surprised them all by giving her signature. Mrs. Fenton knew her as a careful economist, but even she did not understand how fifty dollars could have been saved for this purpose. The pretty Aimie unhesitatingly took a share, admitting that it would only need a little careful planning of her pin money to meet such a small amount. Of course, the president of the Circle took one, but carefully refrained from doing more than that and counseled that each one's stock should be confined to that amount in order to make an equal interest. This required some correspondence with members not present at Chautauqua and bade fair to cause delay, until the president proposed to go security for certain absentees. So, before the close of the second day, the amount named was secured.

It was a surprise to some that Joe Ward's name was

among the stockholders; but sundry long talks with the president had been held before he finally signed it, and the wise ones hinted that he had given his note for part of the payment, and that the president of the Circle had promptly discounted the note.

The new scheme met with great favor, even Effie Butler rousing to the importance of it and actually offering a suggestion or two as to the length of the front windows and the size of the parlor. A builder who could do wonders was the next requisite. Mr. Tucker was out of the question. He shook his head wistfully when the project was explained to him; admitted that the whole thing just took his fancy, and he should like no better fun, but them two houses that he had promised for the professor were larger and finer and had more work on them than any on the grounds, and would take every single inch of his time while the meetings lasted. "You see," he explained, "his lots is so near the Amphitheater there, as they call it—though I don't see no theater about it—and they won't let a fellow saw a board or drive a nail while the meetings is on—and they are on most of the time; so we make slow work, and I can't go into it nohow; but I know a man who can. His name is Scott, and a likelier kind of a builder I ain't met very often. He is just finishing of a house down on Janes Avenue; it went up like lightning. I never saw anything like it. One morning no sign of a house on that lot, and the next, there it stood! That fellow *worked!* I've seen a good deal of fast work in my day, but I'm free to confess I never saw anything in our state like the way that house went up. No sham work either; I watched it. Fact is, it kind of fascinated me, and I hung around there at all hours and watched; and neither that man nor the other—there's two of them, and they worked together; the other's name is Brooks—well, sir, neither of 'em shirked a hair; it was just downright honest hard work. You see, their *word* was at stake. They had promised the house at such a day and hour in good shape, and says Mr. Scott to me: 'When I pass my word for a thing, I calculate to do it if it is a possible thing to do. And if I have to go without my dinners and work all night this house shall be done at the time.' Well, sir, it was, and they moved in, and the owner himself told me that the house was every bit it promised to be. You might go and see it: it is right round there on Janes Avenue near the corner."

"We like men who can keep their word," said Dr. Monteith, to whom this explanation was made; and he wrote in his notebook the names of the builders in question.

The result of this conference and several others was that Mr. Scott was engaged to build the cooperative cottage. Now in addition to all their other pursuits, the excitement of watching a house of their own go swiftly up was added. What a delight it was to some who had never really expected to own a foot of land can be better imagined than described. Perhaps to none was it more of an inspiration than to Joseph Ward. He spent every moment that could be spared from his two tents on the ground watching the progress of the new building. You did not know that he had two tents? Well, it chanced that a tenter living near to him, with whom he had exchanged certain neighborly kindnesses, was unexpectedly called home. And having become interested in the young man's enterprise, placed his well-furnished tent in Joe's hands with full permission to rent at his discretion, with the understanding that when the Assembly closed, the tent and all its belongings should be safely housed in a spot named. So a stranger of but a few days' acquaintance contributed his mite toward the young man's education. For that Chautauqua was educating him into a businessman was evident. His first taste of enterprise had been so thoroughly relished that it had taken complete hold of his imagination. From that time Joseph Ward reveled in a world of his own, wherein houses and lots owned by himself abounded. Meantime he was no mean helper at the new house whose walls rose swiftly as he sawed and planed and hammered, guided by the skillful eye and cheery voice of the master builder. Almost he decided that he would be his own carpenter, building his own houses.

There was one stockholder whose name I have neglected to mention. This was no other than Paul Adams. The fact astonished nobody more than himself. He was so amazed when Mr. Fenton showed him his name on the contract, and opposite it those magic figures that beyond one short, sharp whistle he made no sound. Yet the explanation was simple. I have told you that Mr. Tucker was deeply interested; had many questions to ask.

"So you don't let anybody in unless he belongs to your A.B.C., eh?" was one of them.

"No," said Dr. Monteith, smiling. "It is connected with our own local Circle."

"Well," after a meditative pause, during which he whittled a chip as he always did when in deep thought, "I don't belong to no Circle, don't expect to—not of a book-learning kind; but I know somebody who does, and I don't see his name here. I want it put down in black and white. Never mind if the number *is* made up. Drop out one of the folks that ain't here to speak for themselves; if they'd wanted to be in, they ought to be here, and I'm bound he shall be in anyway. You are better at writing than I am—more used to it; you just write his name and the figure while I count out the fifty. It isn't any more than I meant to add to his wages; he deserves it if a boy ever did. I hired him kind of low in the first place, because I didn't more than one-quarter believe in him; and I ain't raised 'em because I was kind of afraid of setting him up more than would be good for him. Folks are uncommon afraid of that, you know, in this world, though I think myself people get set down a good deal oftener than they get set up. Here's the fifty: good, clean bills. Have you got the name ready?"

"You haven't given me the name yet," Professor Monteith said, his McKinnon pen unscrewed. His smiling mouth told the story of his satisfaction.

"Why, Paul Adams, of course," said Mr. Tucker, astonished that anyone should presume to be so dull as not to know the boy in whom he was specially interested. So it transpired that Mr. Fenton showed Paul Adams his name that evening written in beautiful characters, with the remarkable sum of fifty dollars set down opposite. After the first astonished whistle and the silence that followed came a look of intense gravity.

"I don't know about that," he said, shaking his head. "Fact is, I made up my mind to drive my own nails right straight through this world, and I kind of like to stick to it. I'm obliged to whoever did it, I'm sure, but I don't know about it, as true as you live."

"Every nail of it is your own," Dr. Monteith said with a pleased smile. He liked Paul none the worse for his strong ideas of independence. "Your employer told me that the sum put down here was not a cent more than he owed you, above what he had already paid. He has been contemplating a raise of wages for some time, and he thought you would like to invest the money in this way."

"Did Mr. Tucker put it down?" said Paul; and his voice was eager, and his eyes were bright. This made it certain that thus far in his business life he had been a success.

Oh, the pretty house! If you are the fortunate owner of several houses, or even of only one, you will hardly be able to enter with complete success into the feelings of certain of these Chautauquans who had never possessed a foot of land before, as they watched from day to day the magic process of house building, realizing that these rooms were to belong to them.

"Little pieces of home!" Caroline called the different rooms. "And I, who never expected to have even a piece of a home, should enjoy it thoroughly."

Mr. Masters looked down at her almost pityingly as she said it.

"Did you never really expect to have a home?" he asked her; and Caroline, detecting the undertone of feeling in his voice and remembering that he also had been one of the homeless ones, answered brightly:

"Oh yes! Indeed I did, and do. I would not for a moment forget it. I look for *a house not made with hands, eternal in the heavens.*"

This young man who was himself a builder, you will remember, liked to watch the progress of the new house almost as well as did the stockholders. He was at this time engaged in directing the uprearing of three new and elegant cottages on one of the main avenues. They represented thousands, where the co-operative cottage did hundreds; nevertheless, the heart of the builder was in this cottage which he was not building. He hovered about it, giving a wise suggestion now and then, keeping posted on all the improvements and giving a careful eye to all the details.

"I don't know how it is," he said, laughing; "but I feel as though I were somehow a piece of the enterprise. I wish I could have taken hold of it myself. The thing fascinates me, though I could not have done better work than is being done for you. Why, Mrs. Fenton, you have the corner cupboards!"

"Of course we have," said that lady briskly. "I do not believe Caroline would have invested in the enterprise if we had not included them in the plan. She thinks nothing in the housekeeping line is so important."

"Oh, Mrs. Fenton!" said Caroline with a deprecating laugh; but she did not stop the little woman's tongue.

"I'll tell you what she said when she first regulated them, Mr. Masters. She assured me that some woman must have planned them; that no man would ever have thought of them in the world; and she was sure the builder's wife must have insisted on them."

"I wonder where his wife is!" was Mr. Masters's rejoinder as he laughed lightly. "He planned them, carefully, expressly for her benefit, and she has never had the grace to thank him. She can take no credit to herself. I wanted to economize her time and her patience, so I studied it up. Do you really like them, Mrs. Fenton?"

"Of course I do; I wouldn't be a housekeeper if I didn't. It is quite time your wife had the benefit of them, I think, Mr. Masters."

"Sometimes I think so," he said quietly. "I wish I were sure that she approved." Caroline had moved entirely away and was studying the view from one of the western windows. She was in no mood to hear these two frolic over her little dream of home.

Perhaps the one whose absorbing interest in the building scheme astonished them the most was Effie Butler. She was not a stockholder, for the reason that she had never become a member of the C.L.S.C., for which Mrs. Fenton unhesitatingly expressed herself thankful. "She doesn't belong," would that emphatic lady say with energy. "She is off of a different strip. Don't you know that people are in strips? Whenever I see a new face I can calculate in a few minutes from which strip it came. Now Effie is a good enough little goose, but she isn't one of our strip, and I'm really glad she isn't connected with this thing."

This was early in the house building. As it progressed it became evident that if Effie's money was not in the enterprise, her heart was. She watched the progress of events with the deepest interest. She entered with zest into the discussions about furnishings, exhibiting such decided talent for originating pretty things and offering to show how to get them up at trifling cost that it became the custom to defer to her opinion. "She really hasn't gotten herself up like a wax doll all these years for nothing," Mrs. Fenton admitted. "She knows what is pretty, and how to plan it. I wonder if everything about us, rightly managed, would become a talent?"

"And a power for good?" said Caroline. "That is an idea. I suppose it is so. All the pretty little plans that Effie and Aimie and girls of their stamp seem to have, bubbling up continually, were intended to influence for good the people with whom they came in contact."

"Dear me!" said the matron, her cheeks flushing, "don't speak of Effie Butler and our little Aimie in the same breath, I beg, as if they belonged to the same strip! Why, Aimie has more sense in her little finger than Effie has all over her."

And Caroline, smiling quietly, was content to have it so, remembering, as she did that it was hardly a week since Mrs. Fenton had expressed herself in equally plain and uncomplimentary terms about the pretty Aimie. Others beside Caroline looked on with satisfaction over the fact that the sweet-faced little girl was taking such strides into the motherly woman's heart. She did not forget that Aimie had come to her first for help in the new life that had opened before her; and though she had been unable to give advice, still she looked upon the child as in some sense belonging to her, and watched over her with a new and tender care. As for Aimie, neither did she forget that Mrs. Fenton was the first to whom she had spoken of her new experience. Perhaps it was this that awakened in her heart an intense longing to bring this woman into personal acquaintance with the Lord; and perhaps, though the matron did not know it, it was the subtle, powerful influence of answered prayer that daily twined her heart so closely around Aimie's. In more ways than one was the new recruit working.

Mrs. Fenton had refused to consider the two girls as from the same strip, yet it is true that heretofore they had been quite too much alike to have the slightest interest in, or patience with, each other; but new interests had developed at Chautauqua; a powerful charm held them both: both were singers. Aimie not by any means a remarkable one, but she had a sweet, clear voice and a reasonably correct ear, while Effie was, much to her own surprise as that of any other, under the cultivation which Chautauqua offered, suddenly blossomed into a soloist of no small

power. It was Professor Case who detected the voice
that was flutelike in its sweetness and was yet not
singing loud enough for a less watchful ear to hear
distinctly. It was he who called her out, and encouraged her, and drilled her, and, in short, amazed her by
his emphatic statements as to what she could do and
ought to do.

For a time she was bewildered. Who had ever told
her that she ought to do anything, or expected her to
do anything but dress well, and keep the parlor in
order, and dance gracefully, and have as good a time as
she could? She had even grown up, so far, with a sort
of feeling that it was unladylike to be intensely interested in anything. Almost against her will, the choir
rehearsals began to interest her. The class of music
which was being studied was elevating, and without
realizing its influence, she felt its power. The walks to
and from the rehearsals were taken, nearly always, with
Aimie, as they two represented the most of the musical
talent from the Fenton cottage. It would have
astonished, and at one time it might even have offended, Effie Butler, to have hinted that the society of
little Aimie was elevating. Yet I wonder if you think
that anyone can daily walk and talk with Christ as
closely as did this new disciple of his without having
an elevating influence on those around her.

It was new companionship for Effie. New themes
were discussed, new influences set at work. Partly
unknown to herself, half shrinking from the spell, the
silent steady weaving of the new life went on around
her. She actually did not like to admit it that Chautauqua charmed her, yet it is true that she ceased to
talk about hopes as though they were the aim and end
of all existence. It is true that she retired each night at
an unprecedentedly early hour in her hitherto dissi-

pating life. It is true that she awoke each morning without the sense of weariness and ennui to which she had been a victim, and found herself listening to the birds and enjoying their song and planning with some show of mental energy for the occupations of the day; but it was not until one eventful evening when the Amphitheater was crowded away to its remotest tier of seats with eager listeners; when the platform was seated with its grand chorus of four hundred voices; when the Jubilees had alternately hushed and thrilled the audience by their weird, grand eloquence of song; and when she, Effie Butler, in floating robes of purest white, with no other ornament than a few sprays of delicate natural flowers, had come out alone before that great audience and sung a sweet, bright song and had been greeted by the delighted listeners with such deafening bursts of applause that she was obliged to appear again that her foolish young heart went over entirely to the Chautauqua side. Henceforth no more extravagant devotee could be found throughout the length of the avenues than Effie Butler.

"I wonder if everything about us, rightly managed, would become a talent!" That was the way Mrs. Fenton had expressed it, you will remember; and Caroline had finished the sentence in the way in which she was sure the elder lady meant it. She thought of it again as she watched Effie Butler's voice, God-given, lead her steadily into daily companionship with what was ennobling.

Did God design that through the channel of song she should be led up to him? What a grand thing it would be to have that voice sing only his praise! And that idea, from that time, took hold of Caroline.

34

"THE FIRES OF GENIUS"

MRS. FENTON'S face wore an air, not only of perplexity, but anxiety. She sat in the low chair by the western window of her own room; but she was not looking out at the lovely sunset. In fact, she was not looking at anything but her own troubled thoughts. A shadow passed the window, causing her to look up, and she seemed relieved to discover that the substance was Caroline.

"I'm glad you have come," she said, calling after her. "Come here, please, as soon as you can."

And Caroline, wondering, washed her hands in haste, set aside the peaches she had been preparing for tea, and obeyed the summons.

"I did not know you had returned from the Hall," said Mrs. Fenton. "Sit down! How long have you been in the kitchen?"

"I don't know; half an hour perhaps—long enough to pare the peaches. Why?"

"Have you heard anything peculiar? Any unusual sounds? Oh, I don't know that you could hear them from the kitchen! Well, Caroline, have you noticed anything strange about Irene Butler during the last few days?"

"Nothing more strange than that she seems to have deserted sculpture," said Caroline, laughing. "There is an unfinished dog standing on her toilet shelf who has stood there with half a nose and not a suggestion of a tail for three days. I remember thinking it strange that she did not take pity on the poor creature and finish him."

"That is one of the signs!" exclaimed Mrs. Fenton, by no means laughing, but in real distress. "She has not been to the class for nearly a week, and you know how completely fascinated she was with it. Caroline, I am thoroughly alarmed about her."

"For what possible reason?" asked Caroline, looking as though perhaps *she* ought to be thoroughly alarmed about the distressed little woman before her. "That a woman like Miss Butler abandons a new fancy suddenly is surely no cause for alarm. I suppose she has gone back to her first love and means to devote herself to painting."

Mrs. Fenton shook her head. "No! That is another strange symptom. Do you know only yesterday morning she brought brushes and a tube of paint, and threw the brushes into the fire and the paint into the alley, as she said to me with a strange sort of half-laugh: "I have done with all that senseless folly; henceforth my life is—listen!"

"What do you fear?" asked Caroline, changing color suddenly as there arose on the quiet air a sort of sullen murmur or mutter from the room above, rising higher and higher, until it expended itself in a half-yell, and silence followed.

"Caroline!" said Mrs. Fenton, leaning forward and speaking in a distressed whisper: "She has been going on in that fashion for half an hour. I came in here to write a letter, and I haven't been able to do a thing but listen to her; I've really become so frightened that the cold chills run over me. I never heard anything like it. I believe in my heart that she is insane!"

"Much painting has made her mad," said Caroline, hardly realizing what she said; then she rallied. "Why, Mrs. Fenton, she surely has not given you grounds for thinking that! She has seemed perfectly rational in the family."

Mrs. Fenton shook her head. "How much grounds do you need? How many brains has Irene Butler to be turned, anyway? She has appeared strange for several days. Didn't you notice her last evening stirring her tea with a knife? And when Robert passed her the butter, she tried to take it with a spoon! I tell you the poor girl's mind is giving way. Just listen!" For the strange muttering sounds had commenced again, rising as before to what resembled maniac yells, then sinking away into silence.

"She ought to be looked after," said Caroline, rising. "She may injure herself. What can we do, Mrs. Fenton? I am worth very little, for I frankly confess that the one thing of which I stand in mortal fear is insanity. Where is Mr. Fenton?"

"Gone to the five o'clock meeting: so has every other mortal in our family. We are all alone. Suppose she should take a fancy to come downstairs? Shall we lock the door and run away?"

"There is Robert!" said Caroline with a relieved air. Startled as the nerves of the two women had been, the sight of the cheery-faced boy, whistling a strain from one of the grand bursts of triumphant song which the Jubilees sang, had a reassuring effect, boy though he was.

"Robert," his mother called, "come here and listen." The muttering had commenced again with renewed vigor.

"What's up?" the boy asked wonderingly, for his mother's face was pale, and so was Caroline's. They told him briefly their fears and bade him listen to the sounds.

"I'm going up there," he said positively. "Just in the hall, Mother, near enough to hear what she is saying. That will give us an idea as to what fancy she has, and we can know better what to do with her. I shall have to hunt up Jack, and I want something definite to tell him, though I don't believe he has brains enough to comprehend the very mildest forms of insanity. Oh, Mother! Of course I am not afraid. I will only stand in the hall; she need not see me, and if she did, I can quiet insane people by looking steadily at them. I can, really, Mother. Don't you know when I went with Dr. Pierson to the asylum, how the noisy ones would stop yelling and come toward me as quiet as mice? I'm going up as far as the head of the stairs this minute."

And leaving his mother divided between her admiration for his bravery and her fears of the result, he darted away.

Then the two left behind to listen did it breathlessly. They heard the boy's nimble steps up the stairs, pausing in the upper hall, and all was still again. Suddenly the mutter arose on the air, growing louder and louder, until it culminated in that yell which was growing so fearful to the listeners below that they shuddered. Then they heard the boy coming swiftly down the hall; down the stairs—almost flying, it seemed to their excited fancy. Had the insane woman caught sight of him, and was she in hot pursuit? The instinct of motherhood sent the frightened little mother toward the door to meet and help her boy. He rushed into the room, and instantly Caroline closed and bolted the door and stood trembling to discover that Robert had thrown himself, face downward, on his mother's bed and buried his face in her pillow, where he was shaking as if it were an ague fit.

"What is it, my darling son?" entreated his mother. "What did you see? Oh, why did I let you go!"

Then Caroline, in firm, low tones: "Robert, you are not the boy I think you, if you are not able to control yourself for your mother's sake."

She knew her material and felt sure that even though he had gone momentarily insane himself, a plea for his mother would reach his brain. Instantly the curly head was lifted from the pillow and showed a face convulsed, not with fright, but with uncontrollable merriment.

"Oh, Mother!" he said. "Don't you see, I am dying to laugh? And I mustn't let her hear me. Oh, it is too funny!" And he went off into an outburst that was only controlled by a sudden retreat into the pillow.

The two women looked at each other. "Is the boy gone daft?" said the mother, going back in her haste to the tincture of Scottish blood that was in her veins and taking refuge in one of their expressive words. "Robert, sit up and stop laughing: Tell me what it all means! Remember, I have been thoroughly frightened. I don't feel in the least like laughing."

He sat up instantly, but his eyes twinkled with merriment. "It is so funny," he giggled, trying to speak so they could understand. "Why, Mother, she is not insane; it is the fires of genius that you hear roaring. She has become an elocutionist, and the way she is getting off *The Maniac* is enough to make Miss Boice's hair stand erect." Then while he retired into his pillow again, the two women looked at each other and felt foolish.

"Who is Miss Boice?" said the mother, speaking irritably. She felt that she had been sufficiently frightened to justify her in feeling cross at somebody.

"Miss Boice is the elocutionist," explained Robert, coming out of retirement. "Why, Mother, you have heard her recite that magnificent poem "The Last Hymn." She is the teacher here; a perfectly splendid teacher, and Miss Butler has been doing her class up brown for the last week. I wonder I didn't think of it before I went upstairs. I met her in the woods the other day, and she was going it tremendously. She does the effusive style in the woods.

> "How often, Oh, how often,
> In the days that had gone by,
> I had stood on that bridge at midnight,
> And gazed on that wave and sky.
> How often, Oh, how often,
> I had wished that the ebbing tide
> Would bear me away on its bosom
> O'er the ocean wild and wide."

This verse he rendered with all the italics which I have supplied, breaking down on the last line into a roar of laughter, rallying again to say:

"Oh, but that is nothing to the way she is getting off *The Maniac*. I'd have given something for a peep at her. She rolls her eyes, I know. I've seen her roll them in class. Mother, I beg your pardon for frightening you so. I didn't mean it; but if you would just go to the head of the stairs and listen a minute you would know that I couldn't help it."

There was no use in chiding him for laughter. He

was off again, rolling over and over on the bed in his paroxysm, until at last Mrs. Fenton, feeling cross and foolish and amused all at once, let the latter get the ascendancy and sat down on the foot of the bed to laugh too.

"We ought to be relieved enough to laugh," said Caroline, sitting down on a trunk at the bedside. "I thought it was serious business. I didn't know she had any taste in the direction of that study."

"Oh, she has!" burst forth Robert. "Amazing taste! You just go upstairs and listen three minutes, and you will never doubt it again."

"Robert!" said his mother severely; and then they all gave themselves up to a perfect uproar of laughter.

This was the inauguration of Miss Irene's public career. At least, she did what she could to make herself as public as possible in the line she had chosen. The daubing and puttering had all been as nothing compared with her infatuation for the study or rather the display of elocution. It was not long before she made a confidant of Mrs. Fenton, assuring her that she felt she had mistaken her vocation; that now it was plain to her she had always been designed for a public recitationist of no common order.

"It is not my place to move the masses," she said complacently, in trying to argue herself into the sphere which she had chosen. "It is like painting. You cannot move many people with paintings. The common mind is pitched on too low a key to respond; but when you do come in contact with a soul capable of understanding your idea, it is moved mightily. It is just so with elocution."

"But Miss Boice succeeds in moving the masses, I should think," dissented Mrs. Fenton. "At least, there are masses enough here who are perfectly carried away by her style, which you say is so quiet as to be unworthy the name of elocution."

"That is precisely an illustration of my meaning," said Miss Irene complacently. "Thank you for suggesting it. Miss Boice has a sort of imitation of the real—like lace. Don't you know there are plenty of common people who wear imitation lace and are perfectly satisfied with it; even think it is real? I never could endure the stuff. Now this lady who presumes to teach is capable of reaching the masses by her imitation of the real thing. She is commonplace, and they are commonplace, and she and they suit; but there is nothing of the tragic about her. I could never be satisfied with any commonplace selections such as she makes. Nothing less than Shakespeare or some other mighty genius fits my needs. Oh, I shall never trouble her! She is on too low a plane to realize even this. I can see in class how absurdly jealous she is. She actually tries occasionally to repress me. She is foolish. Our paths will probably never cross again. I consider my range of talent as so different from hers that there is no more danger of our being rivals than there is that that evening star over your head will undertake to rival that bit of a dewdrop at your foot."

It is distressing to be obliged to tell you that Miss Irene's small audience belonged so completely to the class of people described as on a lower plane that she impatiently brushed the dewdrop out of existence and rudely said, "Oh, nonsense!" and abruptly went to the kitchen where, as she stirred vigorously at a meek-looking mixture in a large yellow bowl, she said: "I wish some people didn't have to be either insane or idiots!"

The poor woman did not know that this was to be but the beginning of troubles. After that, she spent wakeful nights sighing over the thought that she ever suggested Chautauqua to Miss Irene. That poor, bewitched woman also spent wakeful nights rehearsing her poems. Indeed, the "fires of genius" seemed to roar loudest soon after midnight, and Mrs. Fenton, whose room, you will remember, was directly under that of the genius, used to have to lie and listen to the roll of words as the performer paced back and forth, interrupted only by occasional snappish appeals from the suffering Effie that she would "come to bed and behave herself."

Neither did the family succeed in keeping their trials to themselves. One evening Mr. Masters confided to them the fact that Miss Irene had persistently sought and finally obtained audience with the authorities at Chautauqua and beseiged them to let her try her new-fledged wings on the Chautauqua platform. She had assured them that they were deceived in the elocution teacher. She was utterly unskilled in the higher branches of the divine art; she was calculated only for the masses, whereupon she was good-humoredly informed that the masses were the very ones they liked to move; that anyone who spoke on a Chautauqua platform must speak for the masses, because, having been educated to expect something good, they would certainly come *en masse* to hear it. When to this was added the explanation that the committee listened with great delight to the teacher in question and believed her to be mistress of her art, Miss Irene was so good as to assure them that such a conclusion was owing to the fact that nothing better had been presented. If she could but be allowed the opportunity which she craved, she would give them a contrast that would astonish the people.

"It is so trying to be connected with the creature,"

sputtered Mrs. Fenton, fanning herself violently, when she heard of this climax. "Though I believe I am glad, after all. She will surely have sense enough to lay aside her new accomplishment, for the present at least. After having utterly failed in her attempt to gain a hearing, mortification will keep her quiet."

But Mrs. Fenton was mistaken. Miss Irene was by no means discouraged. A trifle indignant she was, it is true, and she rehearsed her trials to the boy Robert, who in great glee repeated the story to his mother. Miss Irene believed that it was simply jealousy on the part of the teacher of elocution which kept her back.

"Mother," reported Robert, "she says the committee here is making a great mistake. They would find it immensely to their future advantage if they would give her a hearing now. 'No one can tell,' she says, 'what it might do for Chautauqua for her to be able to look back and say that on these grounds she commenced her career.'"

And then Robert went off into his merriest of laughs, checking himself to ask a question: "Mother, don't you think she really must be half-witted?"

35

DECIDED

I WANT you to take a ride on Chautauqua Lake. You will never find a smoother, brighter, more fascinating lake on which to ride. Still I admit that it does not always or often present the appearance that it did on the evening in question. Simply a blaze of glory. It was the evening of the Illuminated Fleet. The *Mayville,* the *Shattuc,* the *Jamestown,* and all those other boats whose names are so familiar to Chautauquans were on the scene aglow with beauty. White lights, red lights, green lights, blue lights! How they danced and sparkled and glowed! All these wonderful lights, shimmering over the water, changed the lake into a sheet of crimson and gold, over which the boats glided silently, like fairy forms, keeping time to the most entrancing strains of music from various bands on board. The special occasion of all this magnificence was the reunion of the Chautauqua alumni. There had been an enthusiastic meeting at the Auditorium, addressed by Dr. Vincent and Professor Sherwin and the irrepressible Frank Beard. There had been music by the Jubilees and the choir with its several prominent soloists, including Effie Butler, who was really taking rank among the most prominent ones, and then as many as could get passage on the several boats marched down to the shore and went gaily on, for the purpose of enjoying the illumination and the fireworks.

The largest steamboat, having been reserved for the use of the choir, was speedily filled with what must surely have been one of the merriest companies that ever trod its decks. Two of the party, soon after reaching the upper deck, secured seats that commanded a full view of the witchery going on around them and enjoyed both the sight and their own conversation. I shall not undertake to tell you which interested them the most.

"I thought Dr. Vincent gave us one of his best efforts tonight," the gentleman said, leaning forward to draw his companion's wrap more closely around her.

"Yes," Caroline said. "Though as to that, I have never heard him when I did not think the same. Isn't it curious what an eager crowd he draws, though the people must have heard him on these grounds so often?"

"Not as often as they would like. There is much grumbling because he is so chary of his lectures here. I heard a man say last night that he would give a hundred dollars if he could hear him preach next Sabbath."

"Isn't this a perfect fairyland," said Caroline with a sudden burst of enthusiasm. Then she went back to the meeting again. "What do you suppose Dr. Vincent means about the tomorrow of Chautauqua? What can he do that has not been already done here?"

Mr. Masters laughed. "I fancy it is as he says; he hardly knows what he means. But was there ever anything more finely expressed than the touch of explanation that he gave us tonight? I have that written out. Let me read it to you by this wonderful, many-hued light. I have a fancy that the scene fits the wording.

"'We have a Chautauqua of tomorrow. It lies along the edge of a golden horizon.'" As he read these words Mr. Masters looked up and inclined his head with a meaningful smile toward the eastern sky, lighted at the moment with a glory from the uprising of many-colored balls of fire, which threw off showers of brilliant sparks as they ascended. "'I see it rising up, shining in beauty. Far away extend its possibilities, and lo! its possibilities pass into certainties. Dream climbs on dream, and the climbing dreams are transformed to granite, and on the path there, formed up the cliffs, I see pilgrims marching, their faces heavenward, holy purposes animating their hearts, and the desire to live in this world for God's glory, and in the future to bring up those to God whom they have won by faithful service.'

"I believe that is the finest passage in the address tonight, though I know by your eyes that you don't think so."

Caroline laughed. "It is grand," she said, "but I linger over certain other sentences more."

"As for instance—"

"Well, what he said about Chautauqua sanctifying science. 'It points to the sun, and says: On the face of the sun, the Chautauqua student beholds the cross of Jesus Christ.' Don't you remember that?"

"You always get the kernel," was the quiet answer.

Then they hushed their talk, for the bands were playing the most exquisite strains of "Oft in the Stilly Night."

These two people, enjoying themselves, were either entirely unconscious of, or indifferent to, one of the boat's party who was standing near and observing them closely. The truth is, Kent Monteith occupied a good deal of his time during these days in watching one of the couple. A very strange experience was this elegant young man passing through. You will remember that it was because of what he called a whim of his father's that he first made Caroline's acquaintance; that he had continued that acquaintance had been at first the result of accident and then of a sort of good-natured curiosity. He could not tell himself when, and in truth he could not understand how it happened, that his good-natured curiosity deepened into what, to say the least, was a very different feeling.

All his pride—and he had a great deal of it—rose up against this having more than a kindly passing interest in a girl without education not only, but who earned her living in a way chosen usually by only the lowest in the social and mental scale. That, you will understand, was his way of putting it, not mine.

He chafed over the folly of it all. He called himself a brainless simpleton and various other hard names as he tossed of nights on a pillow from which sleep had fled, or took long lonely tramps through the woods; yet the fact remained that he was more interested in Caroline Raynor than in any other person living.

On the evening in question, he alternately paced the steamer's deck, seeming to be one of the promenaders, yet alone with his thoughts, or leaned against the side in position to get a view of Caroline. He was going over again the problem which had troubled him during the last week. He was astonished over the conclusion at which he had *almost* arrived.

"I shall live in Florence, in any event," he half

muttered, his eyes fixed on the side face that was lighted up by the brilliant surroundings, as well as by the pleasure of the owner's thoughts; "I don't know why I should care what certain upstarts would say: I am in a position to be above them if I choose. For that matter, who is going to know unless she or I tell it that she had any other than the most respectable position? Her style of face would do credit to any society; hang me if I understand how she comes by such refinement of feature and manner! They must be her legacy from some old German aristocrat; royal blood in her veins possibly, who knows? That would account for a certain indescribable poise about her that is very marked. I don't know why I should care, really. As for that sleepy old town of Centerville, I should like to give it a sensation that would last for a twelvemonth, perhaps—until I brought her back from abroad, ablaze with jewels and all the rest of the gewgaws that make up the average woman. How exceedingly well they would become her! The style that she would affect—she will always be exquisitely simple in her tastes; and in that again she will show that curious, high-bred air. I wonder what she would say to Venice! She would be more interested, though, in Rome. Curious, how thoroughly conversant the girl is with the ancient city. I should want to blush for almost any traveled scholar who undertook to talk with her about it. How I shall like to take her to the Sistine Chapel! Then I'll have a picture taken of her just as she looks when she stands studying one of those old masterpieces."

You can see how this young man confused his tenses. What he would do if—seemed inextricably mixed in his mind with what he intended to do as soon as possible.

Perhaps it may seem a strange thing to you that the

young man who was at this moment talking so socially with Caroline had never received from Mr. Monteith a second thought. He had inquired casually one day who that Mr. Masters was who seemed to be everywhere and had been answered that he was a builder who had been associated with the improvements at Chautauqua from the first. "A mere mechanic," had this elegant aristocrat said within himself and thereafter dismissed the subject. Not that he really intended to be aristocratic in the disagreeable sense of the word, but it had been the habit of his life and the education of his foreign experience. By what curious process of reasoning he was sometimes able to think of Caroline entirely apart from her surroundings and experiences of life, I do not pretend to explain.

It cannot be said that the young man enjoyed the wonderful display of nature and art that was spread before him on lake and sky that evening; indeed, he hardly saw it at all, while Caroline and her friend constantly interrupted their conversation with such exclamations as, "Oh, see that rocket!" "Look at those wonderful colored balls of fire!" "Isn't the music exquisite?" "How gorgeous the *Jamestown* looks!" and the like. He, busy with his thoughts, saw neither lights nor colors, and heard no music save as it all mingled in a confused and rather distracting way in his perplexities, for he saw perplexities in the way of his cherished wishes. It was Kent Monteith's misfortune to have had few perplexities in his path hitherto; almost no obstacles to overcome; consequently, he chafed under these as they presented themselves. Still he grew more and more fixed in his resolution to have his own way, cost what it might.

Presently the two, one of whom was holding his attention, espied him leaning against the railing of the boat, and bowed and smiled. Then they discussed him for a moment.

"That young man looks almost out of place in this gay scene; lonely, I mean," said Mr. Masters. "Isn't he singularly without special friends? I should expect so brilliant a man to be surrounded always by followers."

"It is very hard to be friends with him," Caroline said quietly.

"Why?"

"He so constantly jars on one's sense of what is right. From a Christian standpoint, I mean."

"I know. Hasn't he rather dropped Robert Fenton?"

"Quite dropped him," Caroline said, her face taking an annoyed expression as she remembered the scene connected with the dropping. "That is an illustration of what I mean when I say it is hard to be friends with him." Then she told of the effort she had made to have Robert shielded and the indifference he had manifested toward the boy. "It tried me," she said, "to think that he cared so little for Robert. It was not friendship at all, just the following up of a passing fancy. Mr. Monteith impresses me as though most of his friendships were no stronger than that, and as though his professions of regard, if he ever makes them, might be *professions* merely. What a lovely transparency on that boat! See the motto in letters of fire! Oh, how beautiful that is!" And thus Caroline dropped Kent Monteith quite as easily as he had dropped Robert Fenton.

It was about that time that he turned from the deck and went downstairs into the saloon with resolute step, saying with firmly compressed lips and a look of decision on his handsome face: "I shall certainly do it."

36

—◆—◇◇—◆—

"The Blind Gropings of Genius"

MOST unexpectedly, at least to the sufferers, the current of Miss Irene Butler's thoughts was changed. Before the change, however, came two eventful days. I mean the grand temperance meeting inaugurated at Chautauqua on a certain Saturday evening by a lecture from that remarkable woman Mrs. Yeomans of Canada.

It may be possible that she has spoken to even larger audiences than that which greeted her in the Amphitheater that evening; but she certainly could never find a more enthusiastic one. Those who came to hear the lecture, expecting simply to be entertained, were entertained certainly; but they were also treated to clear-cut, directly put, incontrovertible logic on the liquor question, and especially on the license law.

"The fact is," said Kent Monteith, "if there was a man in the audience tonight who advocated the license law, I feel rather sorry for him on the principle that a degree of sympathy ought to be bestowed on the one who is down. They certainly were terribly scathed."

If he hardly liked the Saturday evening lecture, I don't know how he endured the day following. With one exception, and that one Joseph Cook, the platform was filled all day with lady speakers. Mrs. Lathrop of Michigan, Mrs. Woodward of Ohio, Frances Willard of everywhere. What a day it was! Whether Kent Monteith approved or not, he was present all day, an attentive, even an eager listener. How was it possible for a man of sense to be other than attentive? For certainly if ever women had silver, nay, golden tongues, and lifted their voices grandly for the cause of truth and right, it was on that day at Chautauqua. The different meetings followed each other all day in quick succession, and all day the crowds gathered, each gathering seeming larger if possible than the preceding one. Grand work for the cause was surely done that day. In some directions more was done than many dreamed of. For instance, the inhabitants of the Fenton cottage realized disastrous consequences. It was Miss Irene again, and this time she took for her confidant the pretty Aimie, thereby so astonishing and embarrassing that young lady on whom she had hitherto looked down from a lofty height that the fair-faced girl could hardly recover from her flutter enough to listen.

"I want to talk to you," Miss Irene had said; "because you appear to me less selfish than the rest of the family; they are all so absorbed in their own pursuits that it is almost impossible to hold their attention. Don't you think they are intensely selfish?"

But Aimie, flushing hotly, declared that she did not think so at all; and this little episode served to bring back her self-control. She had no fondness for listening to criticism of any sort on these friends of hers. Still Miss Irene insisted that they so impressed her; but magnanimously added that it was not strange, there were so many things going on calculated to absorb the common mind.

"I have something of importance to tell you," continued the artist and elocutionist. "I talked with Mrs. Fenton before, but she is a very difficult person to talk with; she has so many ideas of her own and, like all persons set in her mold, is very hard to move. You know what has been interesting—I may say absorbing—me for a few days? Well, I have given it up entirely! Not that I do not plainly see that I have talent in that direction of a marked order, but, after thinking the whole matter over most carefully, it has become apparent to me that it is my duty to hold the masses. You get my meaning? I explained it carefully to Mrs. Fenton, but perhaps she did not make it clear to you that elocution, like painting, is extremely limited in its reaches; that comparatively few people are touched by either of these sublime arts, while one's own ideas, clothed in glowing language and accompanied by appropriate gestures, will hold an immense audience spellbound. We had an illustration of it last Saturday evening and all day Sabbath. There are those who speak of Mrs. Yeomans and Miss Willard and the rest as rare geniuses set apart to a special work. I admit that they are rare, but after all, they are commonplace—intensely commonplace—by the side of what I feel myself capable of doing. You see, I speak plainly. I hold it to be mock modesty that restrains a person from recognizing and admitting her manifest talents. It is only an *undue* estimate of oneself that is to be deplored. I have quite determined to enter the lecture field."

Little Aimie was certainly a good listener. She sat as one spellbound under this avalanche of words. In truth, she no more knew what to say to this woman than did the pretty red-and-brown bird who just then stopped at the window and chirped a good-evening to them. At last Miss Irene seemed to observe her silence, whether or not she did her dismay.

"I tell you, my dear, when I sat there on Saturday evening and saw that immense audience listening to that woman and heard the outbursts of applause, and when I saw the throngs gather all day Sabbath, no less a crowd to hear those women in the afternoon than came to hear the giant Cook in the morning, I tingled to my fingers' ends with conscious power. I find that I crave this recognition from the public; need it, indeed, to inspire me to greater efforts. I suppose, my dear, you have no such intense aspirations after the grand heights of life. You hardly understand what I mean, do you?"

What was little Aimie to say? She had not that keen sense of the ludicrous which was at once Mrs. Fenton's amusement and torment; she had not Caroline's clear-sightedness which would have instantly labeled this whole entire flight of genius "folly," yet she dimly perceived the folly and the fun, and was at the same time distressed by the intense earnestness which the woman before her threw into all these spasms of nonsense which took hold of her. "Why cannot people be so intense in doing really *grand* things," moralized this little girl, while the woman before her waited, looking patronizingly down on the fair bit of flesh and blood.

"I don't know," said Aimie at last, feeling obliged to speak. "Yes, I can understand ambition, I think, and earnestness, such as you seem to have, but I cannot understand the object, quite. I know something that I would like to do that I *long* to do, and that if I thought

I could ever accomplish, I would be glad to give all my life to. If you had the same object I could understand your eagerness."

"And what is the object, you dear little mouse? I did not know you had one intense aspiration. The soul has gleams of immortality, it seems, no matter what body it is hiding in." This last sentence in a sort of musing aside.

Aimie took little note of it. She was thinking just how to word what she wanted to say.

"I think," she said, speaking slowly and carefully, the pink flush meanwhile deepening on her cheek, "I think if I could help to lead one person to understand and love the Lord Jesus Christ as much even as I understand him now, so that he would be that soul's eternal salvation, it would be ambition enough to fill a lifetime. If that were your motive, Miss Irene, I could understand you."

Said Miss Irene, regarding her attentively for a full minute before she spoke:

"What a queer little thing you are!" Then she stooped and kissed her.

I have thus somewhat at length described the changed character of Miss Irene's aspirations in order that you might fully understand their development. When you meet her on the Woman's Rights' platform next winter, I trust you will recognize her and accord to her genius the tribute which it merits. Viewed in the light of a private member of society, or as one of a family party, she was a failure. Mrs. Fenton lost every atom of patience with her before the season at Chautauqua was over; even declaring after having learned that she was making steady efforts to be admitted on the Chautauqua program as one of the platform speakers that it was really unendurable to be brought before the committee of instruction in this offensive manner, and that she should certainly tell Irene Butler if she couldn't act less like an idiot she must find some other boarding place. To be sure, out of pity for Effie, she never told her exactly that, though she did plainly speak her mind and received as a reward the following:

"Mrs. Fenton, I forgive you, and I shall never bear the least malice toward you. In fact, I am encouraged by the view you take of it. I suppose there never was a genius yet who had not to suffer martyrdom at the hands of some well-meaning friends."

37

ABLAZE

NOW although Kent Monteith had arrived at a momentous decision, it was some time before he acted on it. There were several reasons for this. In the first place, he was not one of those who settled questions once for all. They had to be settled many times over, and though he did not actually unsettle this one again, he went over all the pros and cons, and possibilities and annoyances, and blamed fate that it should have set him so hard a lot; yet felt that he must follow that path and no other.

Another reason for delay was that the decision involved seeing Caroline Raynor alone. This was not an easy thing to accomplish. Not that she seemed in the least to avoid him, but she was, as he expressed it to himself, "exasperatingly busy over some confounded scheme or rather, and had a train following her all the time."

In company Kent Monteith always used more elegant language than this, but when he talked to himself he seemed to feel no need for elegance. However, after watching her movements carefully all one day, he planned successfully to meet her in the avenue leading to the Hall in the Grove, just as the clock was striking four on the Saturday preceding the temperance meeting. He generally planned to waylay her on these pilgrimages to the Hall. His father's cottage was situated on an avenue which she had to cross, and he had discovered that she was more likely at this hour than any other to be alone.

"I have been watching for you this half hour," he said, speaking with an injured air, as one who was somehow defrauded, and turning to walk with her without invitation. "I suppose you are going to the Hall, of course? I believe you would arise in the night to attend a service there."

"Perhaps," she said brightly. "I like to go there."

"I wish you would like to do something else better, just for once. There is a certain charming spot on the lake that I have a great desire to show you, and this is a perfect evening for the trip. Won't you come with me for a row and a visit to a small paradise, and omit just this one meeting?"

"Thank you, but this is our C.L.S.C. anniversary. I could not miss that, you know."

"There is always an anniversary of some sort," he said impatiently. "Miss Caroline, could you *never* do what I ask? Just call to mind the number of invitations that I have given you on these grounds, always declined, and the Hall nearly always in the way. Couldn't you be induced to lay aside your plans and try mine, just for once? I presume the meeting will progress to a favorable issue if you are not present."

I think it was because he saw not the slightest sign of wavering in her face that he was irritated into making this sarcastic close. The sarcasm did not ruffle her.

"I don't doubt it," she said, still speaking gaily, "but you see, I should not be able to progress so favorably without the help of the meeting. I need all the aid I can get; besides, Dr. Vincent is to speak to us."

"Well, you have heard him before."

"Which is one of the reasons why I want to hear him again."

"Then you positively will not go with me?"

"Positively I cannot. There are special reasons why I wish to be at this anniversary."

He walked beside her in an annoyed silence. He seemed not to know and she did not enlighten him with the fact that the members of the Circle were to form a procession at the Hall and march to the Amphitheater, but when the Hall was reached and the preliminary exercises were concluded, he discovered the program and turned eagerly to her.

"At least, I suppose I can walk with you to the Auditorium, and then perhaps if the meeting proves less important than you suppose, you will be able to follow out my program?"

She shook her head. "You are not a member of the Circle; we are to walk in procession."

"Then I will follow at a very respectful distance, and you will join me at a later hour!"

This also was negatived. "There are special reasons, you remember I told you, why I want to hear all that is said today."

"Are there special reasons why you don't want to hear what I have to say?"

"Certainly not!" she said, regarding him with grave disapproval.

"I beg your pardon," he answered, vexed at his own folly. "There is just this thing that I want you to do for me, Miss Caroline; I have something very special to say to you. If you will be so kind as to appoint a time when I may see and have five minutes of uninterrupted conversation, I will not intrude myself further on this Circle."

He could no more help speaking somewhat irritably than he could help being a proud man; he was so sensible of the great honor that he meant to confer on her and the seas of trouble through which he had waded to reach a decision, and it seemed *so* annoying that she should appear utterly indifferent to it all.

She regarded him with surprise and took time to wonder what he could want with a private interview; meantime he pressed his question: "Shall it be this evening?"

"Oh! Mrs. Yeomans's lecture is this evening. We must neither of us miss that. She is said to be grand."

"I hope she is, I am sure. I am not fully in sympathy with a platform orator from the feminine ranks; but don't let us get into a controversy on that point. Madam Yeomans may lecture each hour in the day for all that I really care." This he said hastily, forestalling her evident intention to answer him, and added: "Then will you appoint an hour tomorrow and take a walk or a ride with me?"

"Tomorrow will be Sabbath, Mr. Monteith. I neither walk nor ride for pleasure on that day."

"I beg your pardon," he said, biting his lip. "I forgot your peculiar prejudices; though really it seems to me as though you never did anything for pleasure on any day. Well then, Monday. What objection is there to that?"

Almost to her annoyance as well as amusement, Caroline, giving a rapid mental survey to the program, decided that the days were unusually full, and she did not know of a single hour during Monday or Tuesday that she would call her own.

But her companion was persistent. He urged that the Tuesday evening meeting would close reasonably early, and that he would wait, if she said so, until its close, if she would promise him an uninterrupted hour then. It was with actual embarrassment that she reminded him of the C.L.S.C. campfire which was immediately to follow Tuesday evening's sermon. What mental epithets he bestowed on the C.L.S.C. Caroline never knew, but he caught eagerly at the suggestion of the campfire. Would she walk with him to and from that unique entertainment? Doubtless that would secure for him as much privacy as Chautauqua ever afforded to any person. At least, he would be satisfied with that if she would positively promise. So what could she do but promise? Though she did it reluctantly, wondering meantime if she had not almost a tacit engagement with both Robert Fenton and Robert Masters.

All the beautiful walk from the Hall to the Amphitheater, she gave to wondering why Mr. Monteith should so persistently seek to see her alone. Could it be anything about Robert Fenton? Had he seen how wounded the boy was, and did he regret his promise and seek to be released? She had never wanted him to make so absurd a promise, and of course he was released from it; but surely there was no need for so much mystery. If he were Irene Butler's brother, she told herself with a mixture of amusement and vexation, "I would think that the making of important mysteries out of nothings ran in the blood. As it is, I don't understand him."

Then she fell to wondering sadly whether this gifted young man must really go away from all the

blessed privileges of Chautauqua utterly unhelped in
any way by his three or four weeks' sojourn there. Still,
if one will not let himself be helped, who is to blame
but himself? This method of reasoning did not, however, satisfy Caroline. She had that most probing of all
questions to answer to her conscience, "Had she done
what she could to help him?" She recognized his need.
The realization and acceptance of a personal Savior
was what he above all things ought to have in order
to save him from himself, even looking at it for this
life only. Nothing was clearer than that Kent Monteith
would wreck himself on the rock of his own pride
unless his utter nothingness could be shown to him;
and since he was so cultured a man, who could show
him this save Jesus of Nazareth? It was not until the
roll of the beautiful C.L.S.C. song filled the Amphitheater that she roused from sad questionings and gave
herself to the pleasure and profit of the hour.

Yet all through the busy three days that followed,
Caroline failed to get entirely away from a feeling of
almost dismay over the engagement for Tuesday evening. But I do not know what Kent Monteith would
have thought of her, could he have known that her
heart was troubled by a sense of the responsibility
which she would have to assume in having another
talk with him. I think he would have been dismayed
as well as amazed could he have known how earnestly
she prayed during those days that the right words
might be given her to influence his future for Christ.
That at least she might be kept from putting a stumbling block in his way. He who looked upon prayer
only as an amiable weakness to be tolerated, especially
in women, because it was rather becoming than otherwise. What such a young man can think of his
praying father I do not know.

Unless you are a Chautauquan you have never seen a campfire of just the sort that the members of the Circle and their dear five hundred friends indulged in that night. In looking back upon it all afterwards, it really seemed as though the enthusiasm, which had been growing all through the weeks, reached its height that evening. Imagine a long, long line of faces, two abreast, defiling in regular order around the Amphitheater, down the hill, then up the hill, led by bands of music playing gayest marching airs, they preceded by a company of boys, each bearing high in air a huge, flaming torch, and above them all floating the Stars and Stripes carried aloft by eager hands.

It is not an easy picture to describe. To have entered into the spirit of it, you should have been one of the triumphal procession, or possibly, like Robert Fenton, one of the torchbearers. Caroline had been much relieved to find that he was numbered among those honored persons; at least he would be saved the mortification of discovering that his favorite companion could give him no attention that evening. He had never been made to feel that he was an unnecessary third person when in company with Caroline and Robert Masters. It was not so easy to avoid an embarrassing explanation with the latter. He had adopted a fashion of taking things for granted. For instance, he said to Caroline on their way from the afternoon conference, "Shall you attend the first service tonight, or would you like me to call for you in time for the campfire?"

"I shall go to the service," she had replied and then, feeling that that was but half answering his meaning, added, with flushing face: "By the way, I have made an engagement to walk with Mr. Monteith this evening;

he wishes to consult me, I think. He expressed a special wish to talk with me."

"I am selfishly sorry," he said good-humoredly. "I had a fancy for seeing the campfire in your company."

She saw nothing of him during the triumphal procession; indeed, the weird light, ever changing, ever proceeding, gave her little opportunity for recognizing friends. There was also exceedingly little chance for connected conversation. If Kent Monteith expected to hold his companion to one topic, he was disappointed. She was unaffectedly interested in, and delighted with, the whole unique affair, viewing it much as a child would have done, with inexpressible delight. Indeed, it often seemed to Caroline during these hours of freedom at Chautauqua that she was having her childhood of which the heavy cares of life had defrauded her. She chatted gaily, pointing out the grotesque shadows in the edges of the woods as the torchlights flitted by, exclaiming over the beauty of this and that cottage brightly lighted in honor of the procession, glancing from one topic to another with the excitement of one who had abandoned herself to enjoyment.

Kent Monteith had never seen her in exactly this mood, and it interested him wonderfully. He graciously accommodated himself to it, taking the lead presently in pointing out the exquisite effects of the lights and shadows in such fascinating language that despite the shade of annoyance with which she had commenced the walk, she found herself enjoying every moment of it. At last the great procession began to coil itself around the massive pyramid, built to blaze twenty feet in diameter, more than twenty-five feet high, so carefully planned and so carefully fed with oil that when the torches of six eager boys, detailed for the purpose, were applied, the whole mass burst, as if by magic, into flame.

Then burst forth the exclamations of delight, and delighted recognitions began to be exchanged as faces hitherto shrouded in the gloom of night flashed into full prominence, their features shining with the reflection of the flame. Then it was that the people began to realize how large their procession had been as they looked up and down and around the hill. Higher and higher rose the pyramid of flame, the people retreating from its glare in regular order.

"Ha!" exclaimed Kent Monteith, his artist eye flashing. "Wouldn't this be a scene for a painter's brush? I wish I could sketch it. I wonder if I can carry the picture in my mind and do justice to it? I would like to make a grand painting of it and hang it in that Hall of which you are so fond. Do you really like that place better than any other spot in Chautauqua?"

"I think I do," she said, smiling. "I saw the Hall on a wonderful evening. It was the first real view I had had of the beauty all about me, and the spell that was woven then has gone with me all the time. Then I get my special helps there. Little, almost chance words, dropped conversationally by great men that seem to lift me right up. Ah, I would like a picture of the Hall!"

"It shall be my pleasure to make you one," he said eagerly—so eagerly that for some reason which she could not readily define, she was sorry she had spoken and relapsed into sudden silence.

But someone was speaking, mounted on an extemporized platform; so they gave attention. On Caroline's part it was undivided attention from that time on until the immense company broke into song and made the night vocal with the grand old words:

Should auld acquaintance be forgot,
And never brought to mind?

Altogether it was a scene not only for the eye of an artist who transfers paintings to canvas, but for those artist souls who transfer living pictures to the canvas of their minds, and there they hang and are feasted over forever. Caroline, at least, would never forget the first C.L.S.C. campfire.

"What was all this for?" It was the first question Kent Monteith asked her as they turned to descend the hill. It was the first jar on the evening's pleasure.

"Why, it was for—delight," she answered slowly. "For—I don't know what. It cannot be put into words; if you do not see what it was for, I cannot tell you."

"Oh! I see it from an artistic standpoint," he said quickly, having no desire that even she should possess quicker perceptive faculties than himself. "It was a beautiful sight, certainly. I was only wondering what was probably the mind of the author."

"I think he is an artist and a poet in disguise," she said; "and this is a painting and a poem, both of which deserve to be immortal."

He laughed, not unpleasantly. "You are an enthusiast," he said, "and enthusiasm becomes you well." Then immediately was Caroline sorry that she had said anything of the kind.

Directly they had reached the foot of the first hill, Mr. Monteith struck off abruptly into a side avenue. "We have had enough of procession and torchlight and music and people for one night," he said authoritatively. "I claim your promise now. I told you I had something of importance to say to you."

He talked rapidly and well. I suppose you know in

substance what he said. He had fully resolved at last on bestowing the greatest honor in his power on Caroline Raynor. He realized what an honor it was. He did not even forget that he was making some sacrifice in family pride in order to do it. Still, he had reached the point where he was really glad to make it. He expected to overwhelm her with astonishment. He had so entirely believed in her honesty of manner that he knew she had not the slightest conception of the truth, therefore he was prepared for the absolute silence in which his earnest and manly explanation was made. Had Caroline been less astonished than she was, I think she would have detected the undertone of condescension. But if *she* were astonished, what can I call the man at her side when she interrupted him suddenly with an earnest protest, the opening sentence of which was:

"Mr. Monteith, I beg your pardon. I should not listen to such words." For a full minute after her eager voice had paused he was still. Could he credit his own hearing? Had she possibly misunderstood him? Could she actually be plainly and pointedly declining the honor he had bestowed upon her? You will remember I told you that Kent Monteith had been accustomed all his life to having his own way; to securing just what he wanted when he wanted it. I do not think the possibility of a failure in this direction had ever crossed his mind. Is it any wonder that at first he could not credit his senses?

I have no idea of attempting to tell what either of them said. In fact, I am sure that not even Caroline herself could tell you. The feeling uppermost in her mind was dismay. There are those, and by some they are called wise people, who say that no truehearted girl ever receives an offer of marriage which she must decline. That the attentions preceding this conclusion are so strongly marked that one who wishes can check them and save an ordeal humiliating to both. Whether or not this is a general rule, certain it is that it has its exceptions. Never was any person more amazed and bewildered than was Caroline Raynor. It is true she had been completely absorbed by other matters; but even if she had not, the fact was that the gentleman in question had been too uncertain as to what his final conclusion would be to mark his preference for her very strongly. No sooner, however, did it begin to dawn on his astonished mind that the girl to whose lowly position he had resolved to sacrifice himself, while he raised her to the very summit of human honor—for he believed firmly in himself and intended to rise to the highest, and of course take her with him—no sooner did he see the possibility of disappointment than he became, as was his nature, a hundredfold more determined; and although Caroline's words were plain, earnest, and unmistakable in their meaning, he persisted in arguing with her, in cross-questioning her as to the strange wherefore, and at last, losing his very small stock of self-control, he exclaimed irritably:

"You may as well admit at the starting point that your interest is centered on some other person. It is the only possible way of accounting for such a state of mind."

Up to this point Caroline had respected him. In this sentence it was impossible not to recognize the ring of a selfish nature. The voice with which she answered was earnest still, but cold.

"You are right, Mr. Monteith. There is another in the way. If there were no other reason for my answering you as I have, the fact that I love with all my soul

One whom you not only disregard, but of whom you speak carelessly and lightly would be an insuperable barrier between us forever."

He was so utterly unacquainted with the subject that he actually, in his heat, did not recognize the "shibboleth."

"What in the name of all that is extraordinary can you mean?" And his tones expressed genuine astonishment. "What friend of yours do I treat with disrespect?"

"The Lord Jesus Christ. The best and dearest friend I ever had or ever expect to have."

He was calmer after that. When he recovered sufficiently from his surprise to speak again, his tones had changed, and he was again the courteous gentleman, a trifle condescending, it is true, but still not offensively so. He essayed to explain. He believed now that he understood her; that her pointed refusal was because of this religious fanaticism which had entire possession of her. He was profuse in his assurances that she was mistaken. He did not think lightly of her religion or any person's religion. He respected his father too much for that. He had been careless, possibly, on some of his expressions; it was the lamentable result of too long a sojourn abroad. He looked to her to help him correct all such mars in his character.

Altogether, Caroline has reason to remember the C.L.S.C. campfire. She went home humiliated. She went over, in the silence of her own room, as many of the details of their brief acquaintance as she could recall, and tried to discover whether, in her ignorance of society and her meager experience with the world, she had done aught that could justify Kent Monteith in being so astonished, and apparently indignant, over her answer. There was another thing to think of. She had prayed for an opportunity to witness before him for Christ in some strongly defined way. Could the words which she had felt impelled to speak in haste and heat be called a true witnessing for him? Much she feared that when Kent Monteith thought of them afterwards, they would serve only to anger him.

So the eventful day closed in her doing like many another: trying to peer into the future and discover whether God could possibly use to his glory any effort of hers to honor him that evening.

38

"Paul, a Servant of God"

TO one member of the Centerville C.L.S.C., the Chautauqua meeting closed unexpectedly early. Paul Adams, who had expected that work on the new cottages would detain him some time after his friends were gone, found, a little to his dismay, that work progressed much more rapidly than he had planned and that Mr. Tucker was ready to leave on the morning after the campfire. That gentleman apologized as earnestly as though he were violating a previous contract. "I meant to see the thing through," he told Paul, "and I meant you should see it through; but there's that man at home waiting for me—been waiting ten or so odd days, and getting in a hurry. I ought to go. If it wasn't for that stop we've got to make fifty miles or so this side, and there wasn't some work to see to there that I needed your help in, you should see it out anyhow; but the fact is, I've got so kind of used to having you around to do the right thing at the right minute that I ain't no kind of courage to stop and tend to that work without you." And Paul, his face aglow over this frank acknowledgment that his employer found him

forth on every page of the book; and Paul had declared allegiance to him forever.

"Halloo!" said a familiar voice as he sat dreaming in his chair, and Paul gave a sudden start and came to his feet to discover that another than himself was taking a late walk, and his old friend Joe Ward stood before him.

"Dreaming?" asked that worthy.

"No, thinking," said Paul laconically.

"Planning how you will build a great pile on this very spot someday which will make the doctor laugh away down to his boots? All right; do it! Build of marble, Paul. We'll go shares. I'll furnish the gold, and you furnish the brains; and between us we'll make some of the *tomorrows* that Dr. Vincent talks about come to pass."

"His *tomorrows* will come before our time," said Paul gravely.

"No, they won't; not all of them. He's the kind of man who will keep on having *tomorrows* as long as he lives. By the time I get my million ready to spend, he'll be just in the mood to have a good bit of it spent here. It won't be long to wait, either. I'm going to have the funds ready before I'm gray. You be on hand, my lad, with your plans. I've a notion that you and I have got to work together. You will have the brains, I know; and we'll do something or other on this spot that will be worth thinking about. Meantime, old fellow, you are going home in the morning, I hear? Well, I came out to hunt you up. If you feel just exactly like it, and happen to meet Father, maybe you will tell him that I've made up my mind to a thing or two since I've been down here. I can't be James, and I can't be you; but I kind of feel as though I wanted Father to know that he needn't be sorry anymore that I'm Joe."

"I'll tell him."

Paul said this most heartily. And then he got down from the professor's chair and put his arm through Joe's, and after a silent last look at the Hall, he walked home with Joe, they two speaking words together that were better than marble columns or millions of money, for they represented manhood.

Counting from the *Almanac,* Paul Adams had been but nine weeks away from home. Viewed in the light of all the experiences through which he had passed and the many tears which his mother had shed for him, the time should have been counted by years. He went over it all as he shouldered his old-fashioned satchel, after bidding good-bye to Mr. Tucker, and walked up the familiar street from the depot. How entirely natural, and yet how utterly unnatural, everything looked! Can you understand the two states of feeling possessing him at the same time? The Paul Adams who looked about him on the familiar streets and homes was very different from the Paul Adams who had walked down that same street on his way to the train one June morning.

Nothing anywhere would ever be to him as it had been. There are many to whom it applies. Well for them if, like Paul Adams, they can smile joyfully when they think of it. He was so glad to have all things different! His mother had been looking out for him just as she had been during many days of his absence. The boy had many lessons to learn. One of them was that when away from home he ought to write to his mother. Beyond the first scrawl that told of his safe arrival—and even that was suggested by Mr. Tucker— she had received no word. It had not occurred to her son that he ought to write. Oh, the trials of those nine weeks to his mother, separated from her one treasure for the first time in her life! When Paul is older and wiser he will look back on those bright weeks with one sorrowful memory: through ignorance, he neglected his mother.

The widow Adams had been true to her nature and borrowed all the trouble that her fertile imagination could concoct out of the scanty crumbs of knowledge which she possessed. Chautauqua might have been a lair for wild beasts, or a settlement of Indians, for all that she knew to the contrary. Only this bright fact she had to give her what comfort it could: she had herself gone to the depot to see the delegation from the Centerville C.L.S.C. start for its distant center. She knew that that center was Chautauqua. Someway, it made her seem a little nearer to her boy to be among the eager crowd at the depot and hear mentioned again and again the place to which he had gone. Then, too, Mrs. Fenton had shaken hands with her and told her they would find Paul and take good care of him, and she had sent a clean pair of stockings and a handkerchief by the same careful hands. Dr. Monteith also had told her they should see Paul the next evening and give him news of his mother, and he had shaken her old hand warmly and left a paper in it which he told her was to do errands for her in Paul's place until he returned. The paper proved to be a ten-dollar banknote.

On the whole, Mrs. Adams had gone home comforted; but the comfort did not last. She lay awake of nights and planned her disasters by lake and by land, and wept her bitter tears, and prayed her sorrowful prayers, and looked older and more worn than Paul had ever seen her look when at last he opened the door of the dismal little kitchen and walked in. Despite her watching, he came unexpectedly—as people generally do. It was while she was stooping over the oven to take out a johnnycake that she had baked for her supper, and he bent over her and kissed her. She gave a startled little scream. She was not used to having kisses. I don't know why he kissed her, unless it was that at one of the stations on the road he had watched a grand-looking young man bid good-bye to what was evidently his old mother, and had admired with others the tender kiss which he left on the withered cheek. I do not mean that the boy Paul was copying his example for effect. I mean, rather, that for the first time in his life that had impressed him as an eminently fitting thing to do; had made him think of his mother's wrinkled cheek, and have, then and there, a strong desire to feel it pressed against his lips.

"Oh, Paul!" she said; and then she set her johnny-cake on one chair and herself on another, and looked at him. What was different? Had he grown tall? Certainly he had, and sunburned, and his hair was longer; but those were not the changes that she meant. She surveyed him slowly from head to foot. His clothes were the same; she had patched them carefully; she knew them well. The hat was the same; the boots were the very ones that he had taken to be mended but the day before he went away; yet she felt it thrilling through her—some nameless, distinctly marked change about her boy.

The feeling lasted while they were at the tea table, and they lingered over that meal as they two had never done before: and the boy praised the johnnycake and the roasted potato, and said he was glad to get home to her cooking again; and the mother almost laughed outright and was secretly glad that she had been so busy with her work that day as to get herself no dinner, therefore this royal tea. He talked with her freely, as he had never done before. Told her about that wonderful mysterious Chautauqua. Gave her bits of the life there; glimpses of the lake, and the bells, and the fireworks, and the music, which sounded exactly to her like the one fairy story she had read in her girlhood.

Then she had her bit of news to tell. She thought about it curiously afterwards. How differently she told it from what she had intended.

"Paul," she had meant to say, "don't you think a wonderful thing has happened to us? Yesterday Mr. Ward came to see me, and he said his boys were coming home in a few days and he wanted things pleasant for them, and he hired me to go and live there and be housekeeper. He says you can have the little room next to the boys, and I can fix it up for you, and he gives me good pay. Isn't that news?"

She had never once thought of consulting him, though hers was a timid, clinging nature that would have been glad to consult, had Paul ever given her a chance. She did not tell him in that way. Looking up at him with that curious, bewildered look, she said, instead:

"I have got something to tell you." Then she repeated Mr. Ward's offer, saying nothing about the little room that was to be fixed up for him, and ended with, "What do you think about it, Paul? Hadn't I better accept it?"

Then did Paul take to stirring his weak tea thoughtfully with the pitiful little silver teaspoon— sole relic of his grandmother Adams's better days— and give himself up to grave thought. This was a revelation not in keeping with his plans. He had had grand daydreams at Chautauqua. If he did not write to his mother it was not because he did not think much about her. In his dreams he saw the dingy kitchen transformed by paint and paper and white curtains and new furniture into a place of beauty. Even the transformed kitchen would not suit him long. He knew that, and although he meant to make haste slowly, he could not help taking occasional flights into a farther future, delighting his heart with the sort of house that he would one day build for her and the adornings that her own room should have. It was this thought which sweetened the somewhat bitter one that a door, not of his opening, was showing his mother the way to a less toilsome life. Perhaps it would be better in the end. He could save more and work the harder, and bring the beautiful "home of her own" into nearer view.

"Well," he said at last, his mother waiting with an entirely new feeling of deference for his opinion, "do you like the plan?"

"Why, I like it if you do," she said doubtfully. She had liked it exceedingly in the morning. "It wouldn't be hard work. They have a most convenient house, and they do live at such sixes and sevens nowadays, I'm sorry for them. You could—board there, you know." She hesitated a little over what word to use. A certain fine instinct told her, looking into the new light that had come into his handsome eyes that she must say nothing to him about the room that Mr. Ward had said could be fixed up for him. She had supported him all his life, but not with that look in his eyes.

"But then, if you don't like it," she added eagerly, "why, we won't say another word about it. Let him find a housekeeper where he can. If you would rather Mother would stay in her kitchen, I shall like it as well as ever, now that you have got home."

"I guess I do like it," he said, after another thoughtful silence. "At first it went right across my plan to take care of you; but I can't give you just now all you need, and this will help out until I get squarely on my feet, and be an easier life for you. I mean you shall have everything you want, Mother."

"Bless your heart!" she said, catching up the corner of her apron to brush away the tear. "I've got you again; and that is every blessed thing I want."

He rose up from the table—they had sat late, and his homecoming had been late. He looked at the ticking clock in the corner and saw that it almost marked the hour when his always-tired mother went to her bed, and he had another thing to tell her. He busied himself steadily about the kindlings and the fresh pail of water, though she protested that she could do it all as well as not; then he came over to her as she sat down by the little stand table for a minute.

"Your bed is all ready," she said. "I kept it ready, because I was hoping every night that you would come."

Her old worn Bible lay on the table, and he knew that she would struggle through a few verses after he was gone, and then that she would kneel down and pray for him. He reached for the Bible, and without a word turned the leaves and began to read: "Paul a servant of God, and an apostle of Jesus Christ, according to the faith of God's elect, and the acknowledging of the truth which is after godliness: in hope of eternal life, which God that cannot lie, promised before the world began." These two verses Dr. Monteith had shown him one day, smilingly calling them "Paul's confession of faith." Since which time the boy had studied them, until they had seemed to become a part of himself and were adopted as his own confession.

"Mother," he said gently to the poor bewildered

little widow, "that means me. I am a servant of God, and I shall surely have the eternal life; for God who cannot lie has promised it to me. Mother, let us pray."

A moment more and mother and son were on their knees, and the family altar was set up in the widow Adams's kitchen.

39

THE "YESTERDAYS" AND THE "TOMORROWS"

THE last day at Chautauqua! The evening on which our party reached those enchanted grounds one of their number had exclaimed: "Only think of a six weeks' vacation! We shall have time for everything."

The feeling with which some of them looked at that last day was that somehow they had been defrauded of their time. They had meant to do this and that and the other thing; to go here and there, and lo! one morning the talk was all of tickets and timetables, routes and baggage. The holiday was gone. Yet they filled that last day full to overflowing.

"I'm going to every single meeting there is today!" was Robert Fenton's ambitious declaration at the breakfast table; and some of the others, though less outspoken, seemed to be doing their best to vie with this undertaking.

One of the special features of the day was the procession; when the different organizations which have their center at Chautauqua formed unbroken line and took together a farewell walk through their beloved grove. Of course, during this trip it was the most natural thing in the world for those who loved to walk together to be found in each other's company. You may, if you choose, explain in this way the fact that the pretty Aimie in her whitest dress and bluest ribbons walked beside James Ward.

"How pretty it must all look to those standing outside and looking on," said Aimie as the leaders rounded a curve in the avenue. "I wish I could be in the procession." And she twisted her neck to get a view of the lengthening column, but it stretched away beyond her vision.

What a lovely walk it was! Past the Temple, the Amphitheater, the Hall of Philosophy, away down the hill to the Auditorium, and then back to the Amphitheater!

"Dear old Hall!" said Aimie tenderly, some unshed tears standing in her blue eyes as she looked at the white-pillared structure for the last time that season. "Oh, I wonder if I shall ever see you again! What a summer this has been! I love every board in that floor. Haven't we had just delightful times at the Round Table meetings? Oh, I do feel so sorry for those poor C.L.S.C. people who stayed at home! What do they know about Chautauqua?"

"We must tell them all about it," said James Ward cheerily. "I'm sure you can describe the Hall, and the grove in which it stands, with the lake at its feet."

"Do you know Paul Adams calls it his grove? He says he leaves the saint off and says to himself: 'Paul's grove! Paul's grove!' and then laughs all over inside to think that he ever heard of it. Isn't he a queer boy?"

"He is a genius," said James Ward. "We shall hear from him yet."

"I know it," said Aimie. "And we had to come to Chautauqua to find it out! Isn't that strange?"

But James Ward answered with a meaningful smile that they had to come to Chautauqua to find out a great many things. And Aimie, blushing much and smiling back, was suddenly silenced.

There had been several concerts held in the great Amphitheater, but by common consent that last one, led jointly by the two leading professors, Case and Seward, was pronounced the very finest of all. I think the beautiful shower that came pouring down so copiously on the thirsty earth—which the great audience securely sheltered looked out and enjoyed—but added to the pleasure of the hour.

"It was all beautiful," said Mrs. Fenton, as they picked their homeward steps carefully over the sparkling grass; "but oh, to think that it is the *very* last! I wonder that they had the heart to close with the 'Hallelujah Chorus,'" and there were tears shining in her eyes. Nobody answered her for a little; the spell of the swift-coming parting overshadowed them all. But at last young Robert remarked that he supposed they ought to sing hallelujah because there was such a place as Chautauqua, and they had all been in it all summer.

"Aye," said Mr. Masters, "and mean to be in it next summer."

Household matters received very little attention in the short space between the afternoon and evening meetings. Caroline set the bread pan away with a remark halfway between a smile and a sigh, to the effect that it made very little difference what became of that dish, nobody would ever want any more bread.

"Not mixed in that pan," said Mrs. Fenton, resolved on being cheerful. "When we get into our own house next year we must have one of the granite tins; they are ever so much better."

Very early in the evening the tide set toward the Amphitheater, where the farewell service was to be held. It had been supposed that great numbers had already left the grounds; but if this were true, they must either have returned or sent their friends, for all standing, as well as sitting, space was occupied. There were many speakers at that farewell meeting. Prominent among them, Professor Seward, the apostle of the new system of music that began that season at Chautauqua its triumphal march toward the revolutionizing of art.

"It is really a singular providence," said the professor, "that the first formal effort for the introduction of this system into this country should be here at Chautauqua, where the inspiring thought has been from the beginning to adopt great and good things for the masses."

"That is a concise and truthful way of putting it," said Mr. Masters, speaking in undertone to Caroline. "It describes both the Chautauqua idea and the tonic sol-fa system of music. I think that is destined to become universal."

And Caroline replied that for the sake of suffering thousands who had been proved incapable of understanding the bewildering contradictions of the other system, she earnestly hoped it would. These two did a good deal of undertone talking between the exercises. Constantly there seemed to occur to one or the other of them a something left unsaid that ought to be put in before the next morning's parting.

"What has become of Kent Monteith?" Mr. Masters asked during a musical interlude.

"Robert Fenton says he went to Boston yesterday morning by the early boat."

"Did he, indeed! I wonder what hastened his plans? He told me last week that he expected to remain in this region for some time."

"Robert and he had a conversation a day or two ago, during which Robert spoke very plainly as to his change of views, and the misstatements that he believes Mr. Monteith to have made to him; and he—Robert—thinks the gentleman was annoyed. He judged so by his manner. Mr. Monteith told him he was disgusted with the fanaticism of Chautauqua and would be glad to get away."

During this explanation Caroline kept her head drooped and her eyes on the copy of the *Chautauqua Carols* that she held in her lap, so, though he looked steadily at her, Mr. Masters failed to get a glimpse of her eyes.

"I wonder if he has been annoyed by other conversations held at Chautauqua?"

She had no answer for this, unless a deepening flush could be called answer, and only smiled very slightly in reply to the laugh which he could not quite control.

Of course the farewell address was by Dr. Vincent. His closing sentences were so full of the plans and purposes that go far toward making Chautauqua what it is that somebody, gifted just then with an inspiration, called for the Chautauqua salute for Dr. Vincent; and surely all the white handkerchiefs in the world responded at that moment! "Let us put it into words!" shouted a voice. And immediately the air rang with cheers.

The seventh Sunday School Assembly was over; yet the people refused to credit it; refused to leave the

Amphitheater to loneliness. They had crowded to those seats so long, had come early and stayed late for so many days that to go away now with the feeling that the bells would not call them again was an inexpressibly saddening thought. They gathered in groups, and shook hands, and laughed a little, and used their handkerchiefs for other purposes than salute, and went a few steps as if the resolution had been taken to go home, then paused in groups again and looked back to the platform where were gathered crowds engaged in handshaking.

Presently there burst before their waiting eyes a beautiful gold light, in the midst of which revolved a star. "Fireworks!" said the eager children. And those who had firmly resolved that *now* at last they were going home turned at the sight, and speedily retraced the steps, and mingled with the crowd again. It was not until the rockets and balls and red lights and golden lights and wheels and stars had all spun and whirled and hissed themselves into silence, and the beautiful, firelighted word *good-bye* had burned in silent beauty before them, and the Chautauqua bells had pealed out their final warning that at last the crowds moved off reluctantly, up and down and around the hill.

"I am glad we came to Chautauqua," said Robert Fenton with a somewhat husky voice, speaking to his mother as he trudged at her side up the avenue. "I'm awful glad we came to Chautauqua! I don't suppose I shall ever be gladder of anything; but I'll tell you what I wish. I wish we had been at home for ten months, and this was the night we were packing up to come here!"

Both father and mother, who but a moment before had had much ado to hide from each other the evidences of dreariness which possessed them, yielded to the pressure of this curious wish and burst into hearty laughter. So they went home with good cheer, after all.

"I don't know that I ever felt less like going tamely home," Mr. Masters said, as they turned into an avenue that hid the Amphitheater from view. "Suppose we pretend that you are a pilgrim and take the route that will give you one last look at your shrine?"

"The Hall in the Grove?" said Caroline, smiling. "Joseph Ward says that Paul went on a pilgrimage there the evening before he left; he found him sitting in the professor's chair, preparing for future greatness; that is Joe's rendering of it."

"I don't wonder he went there," said Mr. Masters. "What a sacred place that Hall must be to those three boys—four boys, indeed!—I think I may put Robert Fenton in for the fourth. Few can love the Hall any better and with reason than he. I don't think Robert has been troubled by a shadow since he heard Dr. Meredith's sermon."

"And but for the Saturday afternoon lecture in the Hall he would not have heard the sermon," said Caroline. "He took one of his violent fancies to Dr. Meredith."

"And with good reason. I hope the doctor will know someday that he had a hand in setting the boy's feet on the Rock. It is a pity that all these grand people cannot know what they have been doing."

By this time they had reached the Hall and taken their seats in silence. Something of the same feeling that had made Paul Adams take off his hat held Caroline quiet.

"Do you remember," her friend asked, speaking in

subdued tones, "the first evening you ever saw the Hall?"

"Do I remember?" By the glimmer of the night lamps he saw her eyes flash. "I shall always remember that; but we must not sit here"; and she rose at once. "I want to get just one last memory of it to take home with me, and then I am ready. The 'tomorrow of Chautauqua!' I wonder what it will be! I have faith in it as I never had before. It will be great because of the wheels it has this year set in motion. Why, even I, from my narrow circle, know of wheels enough to make it famous. I wonder how this place feels all deserted! Can you fancy a sense of desolation that may come creeping over it tomorrow and tomorrow and tomorrow, when it waits and watches for the sound of feet, and they do not come; and by and by the autumn leaves come and blow in here, and no feet rustle them; and by and by the snows come and drift in here, and no feet make footprints? Oh!" and she shivered.

"I'll tell you what will break the stillness," he said eagerly. "The bell up on the hill there will ring out its gay notes on each memorial day. The doctor said, you know that it would ring at noon, and that wherever we were, true Chautauquans would hear its echoes. Don't you think the Hall will hear them and understand? The bell will say to it, 'Coming, coming, coming; they are coming back! Chautauqua, priestess of the old, evangel of the new.' Oh, the old Hall will understand!"

They laughed, both of them. They were persons not given to letting their fancies run wild after this fashion. All the more because of this they enjoyed it.

"Those memorial days!" said Caroline tenderly. "I am glad there are twelve of them. I think *I* shall hear the bell echo. I am glad so many of the special days are

Sabbaths. I am glad the special object on those days is to pray for the interests of the Circle. I believe I am glad for everything."

"The yesterdays of Chautauqua," said Mr. Masters; "what of them, I wonder? Do you suppose there were weird council fires burning here on this spot where the Hall stands tonight? Do you think the red-faced chiefs planned conflicts and conquests, and looked up to the Great Spirit to invoke his aid? I fancy I can see their dusky forms hovering around us tonight; hovering over us, mayhap, the spirits of the yesterdays! Do you suppose they think their dear old camping ground is desecrated?"

"Ah! I don't know," Caroline said thoughtfully. "One cannot help wishing that the warriors could come back, and here, in their old campground, get a touch of the new life that flows in its veins; the old name spelled over again. Not Chautauqua, but Charity, which is love. Love supreme to the Great Spirit, love universal to mankind. 'Thou shalt love the Lord thy God with all thy heart and with all thy soul and with all thy mind; and thy neighbor as thyself.' Don't you wish, by the light of our modern campfire, the dark-faced ones could gather and learn to spell that word?"

"Chautauqua must reach out after their descendants and help them to spell it," he said, in a low, moved tone. And then, "But Caroline, it is possible that even among the 'yesterdays' some of them groped and learned the story. Listen!

> *"In de dark wood, no Indian nigh,*
> *Den me look heaven, and send up cry*
> *Upon my knees so low,*
> *Dat God on high, in shinee place,*

See me in night, wid teary face,
De spirit tell me so.

God send he angels, take me care;
He comes heself, he hear my prayer,
If inside heart do pray.
God see me now, he know me here;
He say: 'Poor Indian, neber fear!
Me wid you, night and day.'

So me lub God wid inside heart,
He fight for me, he take my part,
He save my life, before.
God lub poor Indian in de wood,
So me lub God, and dat be good!
Me'll praise him two times more!

When me be old, me head be gray,
Den he no lebe me, so he say:
'Me wid you till you die!'
Den take me up to shinee place—
See white man, red man, black man's face,
All happy like, on high.

Few days, den God will come to me,
He knock off chains, he set me free,
Den take me upon high.
Den Indian sign his praises blest,
And lub and praise him wid the rest,
And neber, neber die."

He repeated the words with matchless tenderness, and the tears which had been ready to fall all the evening came unchecked from Caroline's eyes.

"It is beautiful," she said with broken voice. "Oh, I wish so much that all the dark-skinned men of the woods could have felt the Lord looking down on them!"

"Ah! Now," he said, "you have let tears come; and the parting from the Hall in the Grove should be in smiles, because of its prophetic glory. Come, let me tell you a story of tomorrow:

"Lift up, lift up, thy voice with singing,
Dear land with strength, lift up thy voice;
The kingdoms of the earth are bringing,
Their treasures to thy gates, rejoice!
Arise and shine in youth immortal,
The light is come, thy King appears,
Beyond the centuries' swinging portal,
Breaks a new dawn, the thousand years.

"Caroline, if ever persons had cause to rejoice over the tomorrows, whatever they may bring to us, it is you and I. For we have learned to look forward to the 'youth immortal,' where we fully expect to arise and shine, and the Lord has given us, through the agency of this very Chautauqua, and this very grove, and this very Hall, the blessed privilege of walking through all the tomorrows of our earthly future together."

Said Caroline: "Bless the Lord, O my soul." Then in the quiet of the hushed woods, as with one mind, their voices blended: "Glory be to the Father, and to the Son, and to the Holy Ghost; as it was in the beginning, is now, and ever shall be, world without end. Amen."

Other Living Books Best-sellers

400 CREATIVE WAYS TO SAY I LOVE YOU by Alice Chapin. Perhaps the flame of love has almost died in your marriage, or you have a good marriage that just needs a little spark. Here is a book of creative, practical ideas for the woman who wants to show the man in her life that she cares. 07-0919-5

ANSWERS by Josh McDowell and Don Stewart. In a question-and-answer format, the authors tackle sixty-five of the most-asked questions about the Bible, God, Jesus Christ, miracles, other religions, and Creation. 07-0021-X

BUILDING YOUR SELF-IMAGE by Josh McDowell and Don Stewart. Here are practical answers to help you overcome your fears, anxieties, and lack of self-confidence. Learn how God's higher image of who you are can take root in your heart and mind. 07-1395-8

COME BEFORE WINTER AND SHARE MY HOPE by Charles R. Swindoll. A collection of brief vignettes offering hope and the assurance that adversity and despair are temporary setbacks we can overcome! 07-0477-0

DR. DOBSON ANSWERS YOUR QUESTIONS by Dr. James Dobson. In this convenient reference book, re-nowned author Dr. James Dobson addresses heartfelt concerns on many topics, including questions on marital relationships, infant care, child discipline, home man-agement, and others. 07-0580-7

THE EFFECTIVE FATHER by Gordon MacDonald. A practi-cal study of effective fatherhood based on biblical principles. 07-0669-2

FOR MEN ONLY edited by J. Allan Petersen. This book deals with topics of concern to every man: the business world, marriage, fathering, spiritual goals, and problems of living as a Christian in a secular world. 07-0892-X

FOR WOMEN ONLY by Evelyn R. and J. Allan Petersen. This balanced, entertaining, and diversified treatment covers all the aspects of womanhood. 07-0897-0

GIVERS, TAKERS, AND OTHER KINDS OF LOVERS by Josh McDowell and Paul Lewis. Bypassing generalities about love and sex, this book answers the basics: What-ever happened to sexual freedom? Do men respond differ-ently than women? Here are straight answers about God's plan for love and sexuality. 07-1031-2

Other Living Books Best-sellers

HINDS' FEET ON HIGH PLACES by Hannah Hurnard. A classic allegory of a journey toward faith that has sold more than a million copies! 07-1429-6 *Also on Tyndale Living Audio 15-7426-4*

HOW TO BE HAPPY THOUGH MARRIED by Tim LaHaye. A valuable resource that tells how to develop physical, mental, and spiritual harmony in marriage. 07-1499-7

JOHN, SON OF THUNDER by Ellen Gunderson Traylor. In this saga of adventure, romance, and discovery, travel with John—the disciple whom Jesus loved—down desert paths, through the courts of the Holy City, and to the foot of the cross as he leaves his luxury as a privileged son of Israel for the bitter hardship of his exile on Patmos. 07-1903-4

LET ME BE A WOMAN by Elisabeth Elliot. This best-selling author shares her observations and experiences of male-female relationships in a collection of insightful essays. 07-2162-4

LIFE IS TREMENDOUS! by Charlie "Tremendous" Jones. Believing that enthusiasm makes the difference, Jones shows how anyone can be happy, involved, relevant, productive, healthy, and secure in the midst of a high-pressure, commercialized society. 07-2184-5

MORE THAN A CARPENTER by Josh McDowell. A hard-hitting book for people who are skeptical about Jesus' deity, his resurrection, and his claim on their lives. 07-4552-3 *Also on Tyndale Living Audio 15-7427-2*

QUICK TO LISTEN, SLOW TO SPEAK by Robert E. Fisher. Families are shown how to express love to one another by developing better listening skills, finding ways to disagree without arguing, and using constructive criticism. 07-5111-6

REASONS by Josh McDowell and Don Stewart. In a convenient question-and-answer format, the authors address many of the commonly asked questions about the Bible and evolution. 07-5287-2

THE SECRET OF LOVING by Josh McDowell. McDowell explores the values and qualities that will help both the single and married reader to be the right person for someone else. He offers a fresh perspective for evaluating and improving the reader's love life. 07-5845-5

Other Living Books Best-sellers

THE STORY FROM THE BOOK. From Adam to Armageddon, this book captures the full sweep of the Bible's content in abridged, chronological form. Based on *The Book,* the best-selling, popular edition of *The Living Bible.* 07-6677-6

STRIKE THE ORIGINAL MATCH by Charles Swindoll. Swindoll draws on the best marriage survival guide–the Bible–and his 35 years of marriage to show couples how to survive, flex, grow, forgive, and keep romance alive in their marriage. 07-6445-5

THE STRONG-WILLED CHILD by Dr. James Dobson. Through these practical solutions and humorous anecdotes, parents will learn to discipline an assertive child without breaking his spirit and to overcome feelings of defeat or frustration. 07-5924-9 *Also on Tyndale Living Audio 15-7431-0*

SUCCESS! THE GLENN BLAND METHOD by Glenn Bland. The author shows how to set goals and make plans that really work. His ingredients of success include spiritual, financial, educational, and recreational balances. 07-6689-X

THROUGH GATES OF SPLENDOR by Elisabeth Elliot. This unforgettable story of five men who braved the Auca Indians has become one of the most famous missionary books of all time. 07-7151-6

TRANSFORMED TEMPERAMENTS by Tim LaHaye. An analysis of Abraham, Moses, Peter, and Paul, whose strengths and weaknesses were made effective when transformed by God. 07-7304-7

WHAT WIVES WISH THEIR HUSBANDS KNEW ABOUT WOMEN by Dr. James Dobson. A best-selling author brings us this vital book that speaks to the unique emotional needs and aspirations of today's woman. An immensely practical, interesting guide. 07-7896-0

WHAT'S IN A NAME? Linda Francis, John Hartzel, and Al Palmquist, Editors. This fascinating name dictionary features the literal meaning of hundreds of first names, character qualities implied by the names, and an applicable Scripture verse for each name. 07-7935-5

WHY YOU ACT THE WAY YOU DO by Tim LaHaye. Discover how your temperament affects your work, emotions, spiritual life, and relationships, and learn how to make improvements. 07-8212-7